WHAT PEOPLE ARE SAYING ABOUT

The Little Wagons

Here at last is a captivating novel set in the formative days of the Mafia, in nineteenth-century Sicily. Crozier Green zooms in on this volatile period of the historically embattled island: at the dawn of a unified Italy that was anything but. Green's Sicily is a brutal landscape inhabited by characters of outsized passions, despite the double-bind of poverty and exploitation, in the manner of Émile Zola. It's an alluring backdrop for the story's love triangle, one rife with betrayals and complicated by the strictures of "brotherhood."

The Little Wagons plays with the old legends of Mediterranean Secret Societies: exotic tales shrouded in decorum and notions of honour that mask the eternal struggle for power. Yet its rich narrative details—from the hell of working the sulphur mines to the trauma of surviving Palermo's prison fortress—can only come from an author's deep research. The reader is richer for Green's nimble fusion of fact and fiction.

Carl Russo, author of *The Sicilian Mafia: A True Crime Travel Guide*

The Little Wagons

The Little Wagons

Crozier Green

TOP HAT BOOKS

Winchester, UK
Washington, USA

First published by Top Hat Books, 2016
Top Hat Books is an imprint of John Hunt Publishing Ltd., Laurel House, Station Approach,
Alresford, Hants, SO24 9JH, UK
office1@jhpbooks.net
www.johnhuntpublishing.com
www.tophat-books.com

For distributor details and how to order please visit the 'Ordering' section on our website.

ISBN: 978 1 78535 528 8
978 1 78535 529 5 (ebook)
Library of Congress Control Number: 2016941203

A CIP catalogue record for this book is available from the British Library.

Design: Stuart Davies

Printed in the USA by Edwards Brothers Malloy

"Beware penury, and take no comfort in that it lies far from the protection of your fortress door. Poverty and despair are the omnipotent catalysts of vengeful change. Do nothing, and they will lay siege to your sanctuary."
CG

Part One

The Ciavallotta Mine, Sicily. 1864

Chapter 1

He crawled through the narrow tunnel on hands and knees. The yellow rocks in the wicker basket on his back scraped against the low roof. The rough fibres of the basket dug painfully into disfigured flesh, aggravating wounds inflicted by the caverns of the Ciavallotta mine: wounds that had healed to leave a ten-year map of torture on his sixteen-year-old body. In another year or so, he knew the stress would lead to permanent disability. The gruelling toil had, for the time being, produced a lean hard body of condensed muscle, and the Mediterranean warmth had bronzed his skin so the yellow scars showed through like wind-blown straw on dark sand.

Tommaso di Bova hauled the sulphur blocks up to the furnaces: the *calcaroni,* where the yellow rock was melted down to a foul liquid and cast into blocks, to be sent away to countries he knew nothing of. Sicily was the only land he knew. It was the land that inflicted punishment on the gangs of human rock-transporters: *the little wagons;* the children who worked the mine. He had carried his first lump of the yellow mineral from the Sicilian bedrock to the surface at the age of six, and he was determined to bear no more. Tomorrow would bring one chance to rise above the penury and the virtual slavery. It was a chance he would die for. It was a chance he would even kill for.

As Tommaso crawled his painful way through the narrow galleries and tunnels of the mine, he hacked and coughed on the foul air that held only the promise of a short life for the little wagons, yet there would always be those who would throw themselves at any such opportunity for scant reward. In his home town of Favara, the closest to the mine, the incentives needed to be no more than a few lire for the volunteers to be legion. Some, like Tommaso, had no choice: their parents bartered them into a usury whose only token could never be redeemed in this life, no matter the quantity of sulphur dragged from the bowels of the earth. This was a lesson Tommaso lived with and slept with: the only lesson of value ever to come out of Ciavallotta.

A flicker of yellow light showed the end of the narrow tunnel, whose black maw gave way to a larger gallery with steeply-sloping steps carved into the earth. Ancient, rough-hewn timber props sagged and cracked as they supported the weight of the mountain above the gallery's rocky staircase. Thick as a man's waist, each prop was worth more than Tommaso's daily quota of twenty baskets of sulphur. The yellow mineral was in plentiful supply, but Sicily was denuded of forest: a legacy of the rape of her natural resources, courtesy of the invaders from Rome. Such were the legends recounted by the pickmen in the deepest caverns of Ciavallotta: caverns so deep that it would take more than Tommaso's six hours rest-allocation to ascend to the bunk-house on the surface, and then make the return journey back to his pickman. Tommaso was one of the *carusi:* the boys who carried the sulphur, a little wagon. The pickmen, the *picconieri,* they were different. Yes, in the depths of the mine they were also slaves to the sulphur, but above ground they were an elite group, and every caruso wanted to be one of their number.

The sound of braying mules rolled down the stepped gallery as Tommaso approached another one of the mine's junctions between the smaller, deeper tunnels and the major shafts that ran close to the surface. To his left, steel rail-tracks climbed a shallow slope, their burnished tops converging in the shadows below a distant dot of light: the exit from the mine. Tommaso wouldn't taste the sweetness of the surface before one more trip back to the seam, but for now he was happy to dump the contents of his wicker basket into one of the wagons that would be pulled by the mules, up to the sanctity of the light.

A voice croaked from the shadows. "Tommaso, one more basket and you're done for the day."

The little wagons all knew him as 'Toto', and he cared for the mules. He also kept a tally of all the baskets dumped in his wagons, so it paid to show him respect.

"Toto," responded Tommaso, "why spend your time in the darkness? You could be up above, breathing the fresh air."

"The air above is thicker than the shit from my mules. The calcaroni, they burn non-stop and the fumes can blister paint. I'm happy where I am."

The hunched figure of Toto emerged from behind one of his animals and he slapped her hide, causing a little yellow cloud of dust to erupt into the dim glow of the oil lamps. He was small and wiry, with skin so pale he could have been albino. Like the mules he tended, his eyesight had been affected by the constant darkness. The wizened wrinkles on his brow and cheeks were testament to the scrunched-up face he presented to the searing brightness of the world above.

"Tomorrow is Sunday," replied Tommaso. "No one works. Get above, go to a taverna and take one of your animals. Drink until you fall down. The pickmen will throw you over your mule and she'll bring you back to the mine."

"I might just, but not for the pleasures of the taverna, or even one of the whores. Tomorrow is a special day; is it not?"

Tommaso found himself fixed by the glassy stare of the mule-keeper as Toto picked the stub of a pencil from behind his ear and made a mark in a curled-up notebook, pulled from the pocket of his leather britches. Toto was playing with him. There was little the old mule-herder didn't know about the secrets of the mine.

"I've heard they'll enrol another pickman tomorrow," Toto continued, as he licked the tip of the pencil and made a mark in the dishevelled notebook. "Might even be you, Tommaso."

"Don't count me amongst their number, Toto," said Tommaso in a whisper, for fear of being overheard. "A pickman shares nothing with those beneath him. He wouldn't even tell you the name of his own father if you threatened to cut his balls off."

"Ha, most of them don't even know their fathers, and there's mice in here with bigger balls," replied Toto in full voice.

"Be careful what you say, old man, in case one of them hears you. I've seen them cut out a man's tongue for less."

Toto rolled up his notebook and stuck the stub of his pencil behind his ear before shuffling closer to Tommaso and resting on the side of one of the wagons, where the light from the oil lamps was brighter. He smelled like one of his mules. Tommaso could see the dirt embedded in the lines of Toto's wrinkled skin and the milky cataract covering one of his eyes. Despite such handicaps, the old man's face still conveyed a look of resignation.

"The only time you see a pickman near my mules is when they want a ride to the surface. I can say what I like. They don't frighten me. I've seen them come and go over forty years. They think I don't know their secrets. Well, let me tell you, Tommaso – I know plenty. Do you ever hear one pickman talk to another about a toothache?"

"Yes," said Tommaso. "They all seem to have bad teeth."

"Their teeth are fine; it's just one of their secret ways. When and where the toothache started tells when and where they swore loyalty to their boss – their *capodecina.*"

Tommaso moved away and hefted the empty basket onto his shoulder for his final trip to the seam. He stopped in front of Toto, his voice a conspiratorial whisper once again – "I don't need to know these things."

"You do need to know this, Tommaso," said Toto as he fixed him with his one good eye. "They always make sure the carusi they select are moved from the deep tunnels up to the surface before the contest."

Tommaso felt a mixture of excitement and anticipation rush through his body. His pickman had gradually worked him up from the deepest shaft of the mine over the last few days.

Despite having only one good eye, Toto could obviously make out the look of shock on Tommaso's face. "It's you and Lorenzo Fratelli," Toto said with a smirk.

Tommaso's previous state of elation suddenly left him to be replaced by one of despair. Lorenzo Fratelli was also a little wagon, but one who was despised throughout the mine. Tommaso and he had numerous run-ins over the past few years and traded blows on each occasion. Fists and rocks had been their only weapons in the past, but soon it would be knives and pickaxes. Tommaso would be ready.

He tried to hide his disappointment by turning the challenge back on Toto. "They say the mines are getting rid of their mules, old man. In Caltanisetta they have steam engines to haul this shit up to the surface. They even have great big cages that can carry fifty men up from the depths in minutes. What then for an old mule-keeper?"

"Won't happen in Ciavallotta."

"The pickmen been sharing their secrets with you then?"

Toto's voice dropped the tone of benign jest to one of warning. "No, Tommaso, the mine shares its secrets with me. Every day it takes longer to fill the wagons ready for my mules. Every night more and more carusi sleep underground because the climb back to the bunk-house takes too long. The closer the sulphur gets to the devil; the less he wants to let it go. Ciavallotta is dying. In another few years, there will be nothing left here but dirt."

"There are other mines close by."

"And how many have these wonderful new steam engines and cages to carry the men underground? No, Tommaso, the devil has given up enough of his gold in this part of Sicily." Toto turned away and disappeared into the shadows with one final warning: "Find a way out whilst you still can, young man. Find a way to leach the sulphur from your blood."

* * *

Lorenzo Fratelli pushed his way through the skinny wraiths of the other little wagons like an angry bull. As the last working day of the week neared an end, more and more carusi scurried up to Toto, laden with their baskets of yellow rock. The exit from the steep shaft saw numerous heaving bodies, darting around the thick timber props and scampering up the stone stairs in the flickering light of the oil lamps. They all knew Lorenzo as 'The Horse'. He had earned his nickname by pulling two fully-laden baskets up the main tunnel from the base-seam of the mine. No little wagon had ever managed this feat before or since. As they rushed to unload their precious cargo, the carusi stepped quickly out of his path to avoid a bone-crushing swipe of the ham-sized fists.

Lorenzo's pickman preferred him to be muscular and stocky, so he provided the food that was a banquet compared to the meagre rations endured by the scrawny wretches who also carried the sulphur. When Lorenzo slept in the mine, it was away from the other little wagons. He had the dubious satisfaction of knowing he was closer to picconieri than he was to carusi.

Born in Napoli, Lorenzo Fratelli was the bastard child of a family whose descent into poverty had hit rock-bottom when the youngest of his siblings was already picking pockets in the Piazza San Cosimo. His sister had barely reached puberty when her face was disfigured by the *sfregio*, the serpentine facial-scar that the pimps bestowed on their chattels. Forever after she would be a whore. Lorenzo's own life had a value measured only in lire, and when the picconieri had made their first push east to pressgang new carusi, his mother had gladly sold him for the price of a week's food and rent. He was six years old; seven when he carried his first lump of sulphur, and the last ten years had been a fight to rise above the calling he hadn't made. Lorenzo had no doubt that this fight would regenerate itself every time he kicked and clawed his status above his peers. Tomorrow was only the first round, and one opponent stood in his way.

Feigning a need to replace a lump of rock in his basket, Lorenzo stopped momentarily on the slope. Doing so enabled him to look down the steep shaft and pick his moment. He lifted a large block of sulphur from the basket on his back. Being careful to select one that was as round as possible, he set it on one of the rough-hewn steps. Rock-falls were common and many died as a result, so suspicion was unlikely to be cast on him if the rock found its target. Not that it would have mattered. Life in the mines, as in the rest of peasant Sicily, was cheap and the rule of law weak. Whatever the circumstances, he knew there would be no repercussions. Patiently, he waited for Tommaso to appear at the bottom of the steep shaft.

* * *

Tommaso pushed through the agony of the day's final basket of rock. He thought on Toto's last words to dispel the pain that would be left in the mine until Monday's sun rose over the low hills of Caltagirone. Tommaso knew that Ciavallotta was no different to the other Sicilian mines. Ciavallotta ran on brutality and machismo. Compassion was punished with beatings, whilst any demonstration of competition, or even open aggression amongst the carusi was rewarded. This caused fractious divisions amongst the teams but was tolerated as long as it encouraged them to pull more rock from the earth. To this already dangerous mix was added the fragility of life in the yellow hell. Avalanches of rock occurred daily and Tommaso had seen too many pulverized bodies, flattened into grotesque misshapen caricatures of their once-human form.

As Tommaso hauled the week's last basket back up the steep incline of the main tunnel, his gaze was constantly on his footing. The slopes were treacherous and the rough-cut steps barely gave purchase to the carusi who carried their own bodyweight in sulphur blocks. Constant noise assailed him, as the cacophony of the mine workings echoed and reverberated off the cavern walls. Through the din of the workings a new sound reached his ears, but it took a few seconds to filter out the background noise from the peal of danger.

Shouts and yells cascaded down the tunnel as little wagons ahead of him were knocked over in a scree of moving debris. The contents of the wicker baskets on their backs added to a phalanx of rock cascading down the shaft, gathering pace with frightening speed. The hard crack of rock striking rock was replaced with the sickening thump of boulders striking yielding flesh. A full-blown avalanche was only seconds away as Tommaso's senses locked onto the warning, and he glanced up to see a wave of rock and debris barrelling down the shaft.

He could neither escape up nor to the side. Instantly dropping the wicker basket, he scampered down the tunnel. Just metres away was a small hollow to the left, where work had started on carving a new tunnel into the bedrock. If he could tuck his body into this sanctuary, he would escape with no more than cuts and bruises from the passing avalanche. Tumbling in a barely controlled fall, the roar of the rocks boomed behind Tommaso as the landslide pushed a shock-wave of air ahead of it.

Suddenly he was hit with a dead weight, pummelling the breath from his body.

He was sure it was time to die, and images of his last moments, crushed below the rocks, flooded his mind. He could see the bright-red froth from his mouth stain the yellow floor as broken ribs pierced lungs and he drowned in his own blood. He imagined the punishing weight as the pressure of the rock squeezed him like a lemon.

It was not a rock but the body of a little wagon that struck Tommaso and became wedged in the hollow with him. The young boy, little older than seven, must have tried to escape the rock-fall by riding it like a crab in a mudslide. The scrawny limbs would have snapped like dry twigs in a stampede of wild horses once the scree of gravel and pebbles had grown to stones and rocks. This broken and disjointed bag of bones and tissue had become one with the rubble pummelling into Tommaso, just ahead of the bone-crushing boulders. He watched the young boy's eyes bulge impossibly far out of their sockets, and the pale cheeks tighten to open blood-red lips for a final silent yell of pain, rendering the body a corpse. The dead weight collapsed onto Tommaso, like a sack of kindling.

Once the tumult had passed, Tommaso crawled from his sanctuary, pushing the lifeless body of his erstwhile saviour quickly to the side. Tommaso gingerly put pressure on his limbs but there was no pain, no shock of the death sentence brought by a fracture. Relieved, he shook the dust from his mop of black hair and looked up to where the avalanche had started. Oil lamps were scattered along the floor of the tunnel, and a dark corridor marked the trail of devastation from its beginning further up the shaft. Through the clouds of swirling yellow dust he could see his nemesis: Lorenzo, The Horse.

Lorenzo turned to head for the surface, whilst others around him made their way down the shaft to rescue the contents of abandoned baskets. Clearly, anyone above the fall had no such concerns, and Lorenzo was last in line of those upstream of the devastation. That The Horse had precipitated the avalanche was self-evident in Tommaso's mind, but this was not just another episode in the rivalry between them. Tommaso smiled, realising just how much of a threat he must be to his adversary. Lorenzo had blown his chance to remove Tommaso from the competition, which would start tomorrow, Sunday.

It was of little consequence that five crushed and broken bodies left shiny-red streaks in the yellow rubble. There would be more to willingly fill their places in the morning, and those who were still alive blessed themselves and carried on. Tommaso left the corpses where they lay. If he were found to be carrying dead bodies instead of rocks when the pickmen arrived, he would be soundly beaten. Within minutes the tragedy had passed, and the bloody shreds were dragged out of the mine. Tommaso retrieved his basket and wasted no time in filling it to its absolute limits with the blocks littering the tunnel. Some of these had been from the baskets of those who had perished and there was a fight to retrieve the windfall, as a lengthy trip down to the work-face could be avoided.

Tommaso quickly pulled his final basket up to Toto's mules and heaved the last load of the day into a waiting wagon.

"You want a ride to the surface, Tommaso?" said Toto as he appeared from the shadows of the small cave that housed his forge. He ambled forward in that peculiar gait, defining those who have spent their lives underground in cramped tunnels. Taking his pencil from behind his ear he made another mark in the crumpled notebook, before grunting and heading back to the glowing forge.

Being able to read and write was a gift not offered to carusi, and the others were unsure if Toto really possessed the magic of speaking on paper. Tommaso knew. The old mule-keeper had taught him how to write his name. Tommaso was no longer 'x' – the mark of the others. He was an individual whose abilities demanded respect, even from the oafish Lorenzo Fratelli.

"You know how to play the game," continued Toto as he emerged into the light of the oil lamps once again. "Just get off the back of the mule before the mouth of the tunnel and lead her out into the open. Tell the bosses I sent you because I have to replace a shoe on my Barbara here. That way you won't get beaten for breaking the rules."

Tommaso watched as Toto carried a red-hot shoe in a pair of crudely-fashioned tongs and pressed it against Barbara's hoof. The cloud of white smoke that flowed from the process had the acrid smell of burning mule and Tommaso gagged on the pungent odour.

"You shouldn't name your mule after the patron-saint of the sulphur miners, old man. God will punish you, even if the picconieri don't," said Tommaso, fighting back the bile in his throat.

"In every mine in Sicily, there's a mule named after Santa Barbara."

Tommaso thought carefully about the old man's offer. A free ride to the surface would be a fitting end to the day's toil and would set him up for the next day's adventure, but there was more to it than just the generosity of an old mule-keeper. "Are you taking sides, Toto, or will Lorenzo be offered the same ride to the top?"

"Lorenzo left here a short while ago with Stefano, his pickman. Barbara here pulled them up. That fat bastard Lorenzo is the weight of two loads of sulphur; probably why Barbara lost a shoe." Toto threw a handful of coarse nails into his mouth and dropped the crude tongs in favour of an equally crude claw-hammer. With speed borne of a skill cultivated over forty years of caring for his mules, Toto spat a nail into the claw of the hammer before tapping it precisely into a hole in the shoe. Tommaso watched, fascinated, as the old man flicked the hammer around to hit the nail squarely and drive it into Barbara's hoof. With barely a pause for breath the process was repeated, and another nail secured the cast-iron shoe.

Conversation with Toto was at an end for the day and Tommaso climbed aboard one of the mules before hitting her a slap and releasing the brake on the sulphur-laden wagon behind.

Chapter 2

The following morning was a Sunday, and the mine lay silent. Tommaso had roused a band of his companions from the bunkhouse in Ciavallotta and led them the five kilometres to Favara and the piazza in front of Chiesa del Purgatorio. The inhabitants of the town were in a mood of anticipation. Just a few weeks previously, Cesare Giuliano had tipped the bathwater over the threshold and placed his cap above the door, in the time-honoured fashion of celebrating the birth of a son to the Giuliano family. This Festival Sunday was to be the culmination of his celebration: the christening of a new son into the Giuliano dynasty, and families from all over the valley would descend on Favara. Cesare was more than just an overseer in the Ciavallotta mines: he was the *rappresentante*, the leader of a group of families who controlled every aspect of life in this part of Sicily. No one was more powerful. This was Cesare's first boy. It was assured the number of families gathering to join the celebrations would be many, and each one, from the humblest to the greatest, would be using the occasion in the time-honoured Sicilian way, to exchange favours for influence and influence for favours.

The festivities would start early – just after morning mass, and Tommaso had reason to be there on time. As his team approached the piazza from one corner, Lorenzo's approached from the opposite side. The two groups eyed one another but resisted any attempt at open aggression. They knew this would be put down and they could be banished from the activities. Beyond this, however, there was a ritual each of them would be eager to participate in, and one giving the winner more credibility than being victor in a bloody brawl.

The squeals of wild pigs announced the beginning of the festivities, and carusi from both teams took their places in the shade as they watched the wild Sicilian Black Swine being penned in Piazza don Giustiani. Trestle tables from the mine had been provided by the overseers and were laid out in rows, awaiting their burden of food and wine. Such wooden bench-seating as could be spared from Chiesa del Purgatorio would be carried carefully into the square after the baptism and then the celebrations would begin. The roasting spits had been prepared and the block-wood fires encouraged to life with dry kindling, scenting the air with the incense of sun-bleached timber as the blazes crackled and sparked. Tommaso watched intently as the ritual began and the smallest of the pigs was led from the pen to be made ready for slaughter in the square. It was a tradition that the first pig would be offered as a victim to Father Russo, the Priest of Chiesa del Purgatorio. It was also tradition that he refuse, selecting a high-ranking man of honour from the village for the first kill. Thereafter, the pigs were butchered at the hands of those of lower rank, but the size of the pig increased as the status of the butcher fell.

Each carcass was hung upside down to drain, often still kicking, before the belly was sliced from throat to tail and the glistening innards slithered onto the terracotta stone of the piazza. As soon as the still-warm offal splashed on the ground, it was carefully sorted into hearts, kidneys and liver by women with metal buckets, who hovered on the edges of the piazza. This was a prize to feed their families for a week or more and was fought over by young and old. The men, all pickmen and overseers, took no part in this mad scramble for pigs' innards. They stood back and mocked the women, occasionally aiming a swift kick at any who strayed too close.

The remaining pigs smelt the blood and went into frenzies of squealing, as if aware of their fate. The noise increased the tension Tommaso felt as the final kill approached: the one reserved for a little wagon. With four pigs remaining, simple slaughter was no longer the order of the day. The Sicilian Black Swine were more wild boar than domesticated pig and the killing took on a primitive combat between man and beast, as each butcher took to the pen with only a knife to face an ever more large and vicious prey. The crowds flowing into the piazza beside Tommaso grew, and their blood-lust increased as the final four kills began. The little wagons jostled with one another for a better view and Tommaso delivered a few contemptuous kicks to his companions, none of whom would dare challenge him.

Eventually, eight pigs hung eviscerated in the square and two unfortunate individuals snorted in the pen awaiting their fate. Tommaso risked a glance across the piazza to where Lorenzo stood. That same rigid anticipation was evident on his rival's face, and their stares locked across the heads of the baying crowd. Tommaso hawked a contemptuous spit into the dust as he tore his gaze back to the ritual they had all followed so eagerly. The penultimate slaughter was reserved for a pickman and it was Lorenzo's pickman, Stefano, who was given the honour by Cesare Giuliano. Tommaso looked back across the piazza to Lorenzo, who tried to avoid his stare. This time, there was an unmistakable glint of a victory in Tommaso's eyes. He was certain Lorenzo wouldn't miss it.

The final slaughter was reserved for a little wagon and this was the prize: the last turnstile on the narrow lane away from the life of the carusi. This was one of the rituals on the road to becoming a pickman. The honour-code forbade Stefano from awarding the final slaughter to one of his own group, so Lorenzo was excluded and Tommaso's companions chattered with excitement as Stefano vaulted into the pen and wrestled one of the animals to the ground. Once he had succeeded in choosing his prey, it was his task to manhandle the pig to a scissor gate at the head of the pen, where two wooden poles crossed to form an 'X'. The lower section comprised the scissor into which the pig would be trapped about the shoulders when the tops of the poles were pulled apart by other pickmen who sat on the fencing.

Tommaso watched in eager anticipation of being chosen next.

Once the animal was secured, he noted how Stefano straddled its shoulders as it squealed and bucked to escape the scissor-gate. Froth flew from the pig's mouth as it swung its head madly from side to side in a pitiful attempt to break free. Its squeals echoed loudly around the piazza as Stefano leaned forward with his free hand and firmly grasped the pig's snout, yanking it back to expose yellow teeth in a bared snarl. Stefano wrenched harder on the snout until the pig's throat was exposed and the squeals took on a desperate crescendo. He pulled a straight-bladed knife and held it high in a blatant act of showmanship, then he hauled back on the snout with such force the pig's upper lip ripped from its jaw. Blood gushed and frothed from the wound. The squeamish turned away but Tommaso's gaze was still riveted to the bloody spectacle. Stefano's knife hand swung downwards in a flash and cut a deep crescent across the pig's throat.

For a second nothing happened.

The animal stopped squealing as the assembled crowd started to cheer, then the vibrant, red cataract pumped from the open wound, and the dying animal slumped to the ground. The first pulse of blood carried the strength of the rapidly beating heart as it gushed from the cut, but within seconds the subsequent pulses diminished the flow of blood to a trickle as the valiant heart struggled to pump blood through an ever-weakening body. The animal was quickly hog-tied, to be hoisted up by the back legs onto a crossbeam. Gravity would succeed where the dying animal's heart had failed, and drain the blood from the now lifeless carcass.

Stefano held the bloodied knife in his hand and looked across the square at Tommaso. Slowly, the pickman ambled across the piazza towards him in a measured and lazy pace that deliberately heightened the anticipation of the small crowd awaiting his every move. On reaching Tommaso's group, he marched up and down, tapping the blade of the bloody knife in his palm, and sending little red spatters into the dust at their feet. The tension built and

Tommaso could feel every fibre of his being urging Stefano to select *him*. With a final brazen act of showmanship, Stefano turned his back on the boys and walked ten paces away from them in the slow, ambling swagger that was almost his trademark. Suddenly, he twisted from the waist and raised his hand to eye-height before flinging his knife at Tommaso.

The movement was so swift and so fluid, Tommaso had little understanding of what had happened before he heard the swish of the knife past his ear and the thunk of the blade, as it buried itself deeply in the wooden door behind him. The boys sat stunned for what seemed like an age until the shout came from across the piazza:

"Tommaso, bring the blade. Your sacrifice awaits."

His small group of companions cheered and rushed to congratulate him, whilst smirking across to Lorenzo's group, who sat sullenly and glowered back at the victors. Tommaso attempted to yank the blade from the door behind him. It was important to show his strength and remove the knife in a clean pull, but the force of the throw had buried it deep in the wood. He had to lever the blade up and down before he could pull it free.

With the knife held high, and with a pronounced swagger of his own, Tommaso made his way to the pen where the last of the pigs snorted and paced angrily about the enclosure. He looked at the beast and it glowered back at him. Was it just his imagination, he wondered, or had the largest and most brutal of the pigs been deliberately left to the end? Had the courageous men before him picked the easiest of prey, whilst making the challenge look difficult and dramatic? Tommaso was in no doubt bravery had been the victim of showmanship. This encouraged him, as he knew his bravery was greater than any of those who preceded him in the slaughter. Only a little wagon endured the daily waltz with the dark shepherd in the mines.

With growing confidence, he leapt the temporary fence into

the pen, but the X-gate was unmanned. The last kill was always one-on-one. Tommaso smiled at the crowd around him before turning to focus on his prey: a large boar that was in no mood to meet its maker without a fight.

The animal charged him with such frightening speed Tommaso had no time to react. Head down, it bolted forwards, its snout so low it almost scraped the ground. The arch of its neck curved upwards to the powerful shoulders, which connected directly with Tommaso's legs, tossing him high into the air like a wind-blown twig. He landed heavily behind the animal with the breath completely knocked out of him. The pig had no such liability and turned on him with the agility of a cat. This time, when it charged, the yellow tusks in the lower jaw were bared as the low-slung head tracked an arrow-straight path towards the prostrate Tommaso.

He barely registered the shouts from the crowds jostling ever closer to the pen. Pure instinct, and his ability to move quickly on all fours, ensured the wicked charge dissipated in the makeshift fencing behind him, which barely contained the energy of the attack. Wooden poles, thick as a man's arm, shattered from the force of the pig's onslaught. The animal turned to find Tommaso, but he had moved rapidly to its flanks and ran at the enraged beast with a broadside attack. He launched himself feet first at its exposed ribcage. His hardened feet hit the target with the force of a Ciavallotta pick axe, and the satisfactory crack announced a side of broken ribs, confirmed by the pig's squeals of pain. In a flash it pivoted its head and shoulders in the direction of the attack and turned on Tommaso, whose flying-kick strategy had a fatal flaw because he had landed on his backside and was momentarily caught on the defensive. The pig's tusks couldn't align on Tommaso's upper body as the turn was too sharp, but the snout and the huge forehead connected hard with his pelvis and knocked him skidding forward into the centre of the pen.

The pig made to go round again for another charge, but the

pain of broken ribs halted the animal in mid-turn and it squealed in agony. Tommaso was bruised from the last charge, leaving him incapacitated for a few seconds, as he struggled to get up on all fours and look straight into the eyes of his enemy. The knife lay in the sand between him and fifty kilos of angry muscle, sinew and teeth. The pig shook its large head from side to side, all the while fixing Tommaso with a beady gaze. Together they locked stares and together they pivoted around the edge of the pen, with the knife at the centre of a circle traced in the bloodied sand.

Tommaso watched his adversary slowly suffocating, as punctured lungs failed to deliver the breath it needed. It made one last, desperate charge at him, in a burst of speed forged from pain and a deep instinct for survival. Tommaso was ready and vaulted cleanly over the animal's shoulders to land behind it, in the exact spot where the knife had fallen. He wasted no time in gaining the advantage. With the knife in his teeth, he leapt on the pig's haunches and pummelled at the injured ribs with his fists, whilst gripping the animal between his legs. More fractured bone ripped into the animal's lungs and it grunted a bright, pink spray from its bloodied snout. Tommaso decided he had displayed enough showmanship and swiftly despatched the beast with a thrusting downward plunge of the knife to the back of the pig's head. The wound was instantly fatal and the animal simply stopped in its tracks and fell dead in the bloody dust of the piazza.

The cheers, when they came, were rapturous. Those who had gathered to watch the combat relished the spectacle as a good appetiser for the upcoming festivities. It took two men, one of whom was Alberto, Tommaso's pickman, to drag the carcass from the pen and string it up to be bled and eviscerated. From the heap of glistening, steaming offal, Alberto reached down and cut the heart from the pile. He lifted it high and vaulted back into the pen where Tommaso stood, still dazed, acknowledging the cheers from the small crowd. Holding out the bloodied heart to Tommaso, Alberto made two cuts into the gelatinous tissue of reddish-purple flesh. The two pieces he had cut from the heart slithered in his hand, as if still possessed of the life once driving the noble animal in its final seconds. Passing a piece to Tommaso, he lifted the other to his mouth and proceeded to eat. Tommaso understood. This was his true rite of passage, his pilgrimage from slave to master. He must not only kill his prey, he must utterly dominate it, and be seen to do so by others, so they may understand. He was now a man: a man of strength; a man who controlled the weak; a man to be held in high esteem and honoured. Tommaso forced the raw flesh to his mouth and wolfed it down.

The crowd momentarily stopped shouting, some of the young women screamed and some turned away retching. The men and the boys stood open-mouthed in awe before breaking out into more rapturous cheering. They quickly invaded the pen and Tommaso was carried aloft into the piazza, to the shadiest spot available. A bucket of water was brought from the fountain and he gladly emptied the contents over his head and body to wash away the debris of the combat. From then, until the bells calling for afternoon mass, the group of boys listened intently to Tommaso's version of the fight to the death and provided just the right amount of their own embellishment. By the time they filed into the chapel, the account of the combat had already taken on the aura of a minor legend.

Chapter 3

Later in the evening, when the duties of religious devotion had been discharged, the festivities began. Since midday the carcasses of the pigs had been slowly spit-roasted over the open wood-fires and the crackling of the cooked meat spiked the air with pungent aromas. The carving began and the choicest cuts of meat were distributed to the assembled crowds, strictly in accordance with status. Normally this would have demoted Tommaso to the end of the queue, but his was pride of place at the head of the line, along with the others who had earned their supper by killing it themselves. The choicest cuts were laid on his tin plate, accompanied by a large chunk of bread and a pitcher of wine. He had never known such treatment. He knew it was only for the evening, but for the first time in his life he understood what it meant to be respected by those he looked up to, as well as those who looked up to him. Retiring to a quiet spot in the now darkened piazza, he found a secluded corner and sat down to enjoy the feast before him.

The sun had set and the fires died down to smouldering embers, whilst still retaining enough heat to cast a warm radiance over the festivities. Tommaso was alone. He felt weary, but at the same time elated: like a warrior after a victorious battle. He had faced death and beaten it. He had made the transition from a mere boy to a man of power and prestige, yet tomorrow he would be just a little wagon again. His only value would be the amount of yellow rock he could pull from the bowels of hell where it was found, but those were things for the following day. As the evening grew older he sat and felt the kiss of the wine seduce his tight grasp on reality, and he daydreamed of what might be. His father had always told him if he was to dream, he must dream with intent.

* * *

"I thought you preferred your meat raw, Tommaso." She laughed as she watched him flinch at the unexpected sound of her voice. "Oh, I've frightened you. I'm just a girl, and I've terrified the slayer of beasts." Maria Giuliano saw an early advantage to tease him and took the opportunity. She gazed down at him and watched the look of surprise in his eyes give way to the pleasure of seeing her again. This only accelerated his embarrassment and she took delight in watching him stumble over his words whilst still chewing on cooked pork. Had it been anyone else, she would have found the spectacle repugnant, but she could no more be repelled by Tommaso di Bova than the moths fluttering around the tallow candles could be repelled by the flame.

Today was the celebration of the birth of Maria's baby brother. Her family were being honoured, but the respect was more to do with fear of Cesare Giuliano than reverence. She held the same dread of the man who was her own father, and fraternising with carusi would be seen as a deliberate insult to him and the family dynasty he controlled. That's what made it exciting.

The rebellious hormones of puberty had hit Maria early, and they could find no escape in the sensuous avenues opened to her elder relatives. Her cousins and sisters would talk about their illicit associations with pickmen and overseers, but anything below these ranks was seen as out of bounds, especially to one as young as Maria. When she finally began to understand the physical pleasures her enforced shame was shielding from her, she focussed her confused frustration in trying to break with the traditions thrashed into her by her parents. It mattered not that they threatened to evict her from the family home for her behaviour. Even the beatings her father administered with his leather belt, on the raw flesh of her exposed buttocks, couldn't douse the fire of rebellion. The stinging swipe of the leather was never more than enough to raise the faintest of wheals on the firm flesh of her arse. Perhaps the punishment was because she was a girl. Her father had repeatedly told her: *"I wish you had been born a boy"*. Maria couldn't understand how this could be her fault or why she should be punished for it. She started to suspect that her father took a perverse pleasure from those punishment sessions in the privacy of the basement of the family home. On more than one occasion she thought to test her theory and ask for a few additional strokes of the leather, whilst exposing more of her intimate nakedness. She never had the courage to go there, but when the beatings were finished she would lie alone in that basement for a long time.

To her parents, this was a period for remorse and reflection on her wrongdoing. To Maria, it was a time of pure pleasure that was both vile in its guilt and sweet in its climax.

It didn't help that she had always been the most beautiful of Giuliano's daughters. This wasn't an accolade she created, but one that had been foisted upon her since she was a baby. It wasn't that her sisters were unattractive. They were feted by the most eligible suitors in the town, although no one had yet passed the rigours of her father's scrutiny. Maria's problem, or perhaps her blessing, was that throughout her childhood, all her relatives, her father included, had sought to make comparisons between the three siblings. Cristina, the eldest, was the most artistic and had learned to be an accomplished piano player before her tenth birthday. Carla, the second daughter, was more adventurous and only really in her element outdoors. She had been more than a match for her male counterparts when it came to horse-riding, shooting and hunting, and that when she was barely into her teens. In Maria's case, she was just the beautiful one, as if they had no other meaningful category they could put her in.

Beautiful, but without the accomplishments of her other sisters. Impetuous then, and prone to acts of wilful disobedience, often motivated by her firebrand passion that could erupt as swiftly as Etna, whose sulphurous plumes could be seen on the horizon: those were descriptions Maria felt comfortable with. Of course, those traits were only to her detriment because she was a girl. Had she been born male, then the same wilful characteristics and quick temper would have ensured her father's love; not his contempt. Maybe now that Cesare had a son, he would cease his constant torment.

In her teenage years, some deep-seated sense of self-preservation had surfaced and focussed her pubescent energies on one object of desire. That he was carusi made the poisoned chalice all the sweeter. Her guilt would swagger through her emotions, only to be knocked flat by the rampant power of physical desire. Yet, she was no whore and had no wish to be branded with the *sfregio*. The serpentine facial scar might have been a trademark of the pimps in Napoli, but there were others of her father's stature in Favara who had disfigured their daughters for dishonouring the family.

"Maria, I looked for you in the crowds today but I couldn't see you," said Tommaso.

So, he *was* watching for her. Her pulse quickened a little and she hoped he wouldn't see the red blush spreading up from beneath the bodice of her dress. "Well, I could see *you*, but then you were the centre of attention, Tommaso. Maybe you just didn't look hard enough for me?" She flounced and turned away from him as she delivered her riposte, then turned to look over her shoulder, pouting.

"I was…well, I was busy, Maria. You must have seen what happened?"

"Oh, you mean killing that poor, defenceless animal? The one that's probably on your plate at this minute?" She flounced back to face him, the accusing stare giving no quarter. "That didn't take up all of your day, now did it, Tommaso?"

His deep brown eyes stared up at her and she thought he looked like a scolded puppy. Her pretence at anger suddenly dissolved. She wanted to rush into his arms and hug him before allowing her mouth to tease his probing tongue, but she held back, determined to deliver only a promise. Sitting down close to him, she ripped a piece of pork from his plate and took a swig of wine, lifting the pitcher from between his knees and allowing her hand to brush, ever so gently, against the inside of his thigh. She giggled as she drank and let some wine dribble down the side of her cheek. Her pink tongue flicked out to catch the drops and Tommaso stared intently at her mouth. Maria could almost sense the arousal rising in him. Again, the hot blush spread around her throat. There was no hiding it, but she was past caring. The promise was growing close to warm fulfilment, but not just yet.

She contented herself with the pleasure of simply being near him: sitting beside him and feeling the warmth of his skin against her bare arm when she deliberately angled her body against his, encouraging another sliver of physical contact. His touch raised a warm, liquid feeling of pure pleasure, which momentarily chased away all thoughts of preserving her honour before she reined in her rapidly accelerating arousal. She sensed he felt nervous and maybe a little clumsy, so she moved away from the close proximity of his body. "What will people say, Tommaso? Here we are in a secluded spot in the piazza, with no one to watch over us, in case we misbehave."

"Everyone misbehaves on nights like this. We both know the rules are relaxed for just a few hours."

"Tommaso, you're not suggesting we do anything to be ashamed of?" She watched as looks of confusion, desire and disappointment criss-crossed his face to leave him looking alone and vulnerable. The desire welled up in her again, and she knew her teasing was as much to assuage her conscience, as it was to provoke a response from Tommaso.

"I'm happy just to be here with you, Maria."

Throughout the encounter she had lost track of time as it stole away precious minutes. It was only when the noise from the crowds still gathered in the piazza started to take on the raucous quality of wine-fuelled carousing, did she realise the festivities must soon close. They were all slaves to the yellow rock and the rapidly approaching morning would bleach away any false colour, having had the temerity to etch itself on their perpetual drabness. Maria knew she must decide if she could exercise enough control over both their passions, to risk more intimate physical contact.

"Tommaso, take my hand."

He obeyed instantly and she felt the calloused roughness against the soft skin of her palm stoke her arousal once more. She stood up and gently pulled Tommaso to his feet, all the while maintaining the delicacy and intimacy, accompanying the overpowering excitement promised by that primary physical contact, which can never be repeated with the same person.

The times Maria had spent in the cramped basement, when the sting of the leather sparked her arousal, had been supplemented by her early experiences with some of the hired-help who tended the Giuliano estate. The young men, usually in their teens, were often from outside the valley; although it mattered little. If they had been caught with Maria, sporting her underwear around her ankles, they would have suffered a frenzied beating at her father's hands. Yes, she would also have tasted the fiery pleasure of his punishment but the risk was well worth the reward; indeed, in many ways the risk was the reward. More than once, the thought had crossed her mind to deliberately play out this scene and allow herself to be caught naked and breathless with pleasure, beneath an olive tree on the slopes above the house. Would she be able to plead with her father to spare her lover a beating by confessing to seducing him? Perhaps not. Then the whispers would spread around the valley that whilst Maria was always susceptible to sexual encounters, the risk wasn't worth it. Of course this would have reduced the number of those succumbing to her advances, but then the ones who deliberately chose to ignore the danger would provide even more climactic excitement. Had she been Giuliano's son and caught in similar circumstances with one of the maids, then her father would probably have broken out the best brandy and a box of cigars. Somehow, she knew that her rampant sexual desires could be tamed in the future and used to her benefit. That was a skill she had yet to completely master. For now, teenage lust would suffice.

"Let's move away from here," said Maria. "The noise of the crowds tells me they're all getting very drunk and I would like to be somewhere alone – with you, of course."

Quietly they stole from the piazza, leaving the increasingly noisy celebrations behind and walked to the rear of a small taverna, some short distance from the festivities. In the narrow recess of a darkened doorway they found a place to stop. The warmth of the evening had dissipated and they had left the glow of the embers behind, but they now possessed their own fire. Swiftly, Maria pressed her body hard against Tommaso and just as swiftly her mouth found his.

* * *

Tommaso was stunned at the lack of inhibition Maria had shown in washing that first wet kiss onto his lips. The tip of his tongue found her mouth both sweet and soft. His arousal grew in anticipation of her allowing his hands to roam freely over her body, which he thought to test by lowering his fingers from her back to the firmness of her buttocks and pulling her towards him, but she deftly resisted him. He decided he would try a more subtle approach, allowing passion time to overcome propriety, and led her by the hand further into the shadows.

Those notions were shattered by a loud crash from the rear of the taverna. Two bodies shot through the doorway in a violent action that was obviously part of an ongoing fight, having started inside, just seconds before. Tommaso cursed his misfortune and pulled Maria gently by the arm to guide them both to a place of relative peace, where they could continue with what he hoped would be the vanguard of his first sexual conquest, but to do so they would have to pass the brawl in the narrow alley.

This was no ordinary spat but a full-on battle between two men who looked like they wouldn't stop until one was left for dead. Maria panicked and broke free from Tommaso's grip to run through the open door of the taverna, and to safety. Tommaso made to follow, but his route was blocked as the two combatants broke from their combined grappling and sought to assert a commanding position. In the light streaming from the doorway, the shadowy details of the fighters became clear: they were Alberto and Stefano. One had shared the bloody heart with him just hours previously, and one had selected him for the ritual slaughter. Shocked as he was, Tommaso's concerns were to avoid taking sides. His plan was to get as far away as possible, so he would not witness anything to draw him into an inevitable and bloody vendetta. Within a split second events moved to render this impossible. No sooner had thoughts of self-preservation flashed through Tommaso's head, than he became aware Stefano had seen him.

Stefano had only to turn his head slightly to register Tommaso's startled expression. Alberto, who was carefully watching Stefano's every movement, then turned to look in the direction of Stefano's stare. In the fraction of a second it took Alberto to turn, Tommaso watched as Stefano pulled a knife and flung himself across the narrow gap to Alberto. The attack was swift but Alberto sidestepped the thrust and Stefano overshot. Alberto had not yet reached for his own knife so he made for a chopping downward punch to the rear of Stefano's neck, but this fell short of its target and merely thudded into his upper back. Tommaso heard the thud of the blow but it barely fazed Stefano. He pushed rearward with his feet and jumped into his victim who, not expecting the move, toppled back under the thrust. Stefano rolled over him in a backward somersault and landed on his feet in front of the prostrate Alberto. Tommaso sensed all was lost for Alberto, as Stefano took one step forward to retain his balance, but Alberto grabbed his foot and pushed it upwards, throwing his attacker backwards.

In the few tenths of a second this gave Alberto, he got to his feet and charged his off-balance victim with his own knife thrust forward. A vicious jab to the heart was parried by Stefano's knife hand whilst his other smashed into Alberto's jaw, spinning his head through a rotation so violent that Tommaso was sure it would render him unconscious. Alberto's knees buckled and Stefano was on him in a flash. Only pure instinct could have made Alberto grab his attacker tightly around the arms in a bear-hug, preventing a fatal slash with the blade. Alberto hung on, waiting for his head to clear and trying to deny his opponent the freedom to move his arms. Tommaso saw a chance to escape but he could not force himself to flee. It was a fight to the death and he just couldn't tear himself away.

Alberto succeeded in hanging on until the power returned to his legs. He pushed violently upwards, at the same time jerking his forehead towards Stefano in a short but vicious head-butt to the face. Stefano saw it coming but was too late to do more than turn his head slightly. The blow dissipated high on his right cheekbone, which shattered with a sickening crack Tommaso could hear clear across the alley. Stefano now had a weakness Alberto could exploit, and this seemed to give him renewed strength, but as Tommaso anticipated a quick end to the fight it became obvious Stefano was immune to the pain the smashed cheekbone was causing. Stefano kicked downwards and found a target: the top of Alberto's right foot. There was a crunch and Tommaso knew the blow had broken at least one of the small bones there. Alberto staggered back, trying to cover up the disadvantage, but it was obvious he must continue with restricted movement.

The rising bruise visible on Stefano's cheek and the flow of blood from the eye-socket meant he soon would be unable to see from the damaged eye. As Alberto staggered to find how he could best balance on the damaged foot, Tommaso watched as Stefano suddenly flicked his knife in the air to change to a throwing grip and launched the blade across the short distance to his enemy. The move was so quick it was almost invisible and the strength behind the throw was astonishing. Tommaso had seen it all before. Alberto had barely time to register the action before the knife plunged into his right eye socket and, such was the force of the throw, buried itself up to the handle in his skull.

Tommaso watched as Alberto reached up to his face and felt the knife protruding from his eye socket. Amazingly he was conscious and seemed to feel no pain from the blow, but his body was showing signs of going into shock. Stefano watched and waited for his victim to fall to the ground dying, so he could retrieve the knife and get away. Alberto had not given up, however. With the extraordinary lucidity that could only come with the knowledge of certain death, he stood and faced his nemesis with the handle of the knife protruding from his eye. He stared at both Stefano and Tommaso, giving them a look each would take to their graves in their allocated time.

Stefano was first to break himself free from the mesmeric gaze. He calmly walked over to Alberto and delivered a straight-fingered punch to his victim's throat, shattering the epiglottis and instantly starving him of breath. Alberto fell to his knees clutching a shattered windpipe. Stefano put one foot on the dying man's right shoulder and gripped the handle of the knife. Alberto fell to the ground and Tommaso heard the sickening squelch and scraping bone, as the serrated blade was wrenched from the dying man's skull.

"Tommaso, stay right where you are!"

The sudden command from Stefano stopped Tommaso in his

tracks and made him realise the danger had not passed.

"Stefano, it would be better I leave before anyone else sees what happened here. Tonight's events will go no further."

"And how can I be certain you will not betray what you have witnessed here, Tommaso?"

"There is no code of honour between carusi and pickmen; make me a pickman and then you can be sure. We will both be bound by the reasons for my selection and my oath," replied Tommaso. This seemed to convey a certain sense of logic to Stefano, as he thought for a moment before answering.

"That decision wouldn't be mine alone, Tommaso. If I couldn't convince the Brotherhood, then there would be no bond between us and so there would be no trust."

Tommaso thought quickly. There was a flaw in his plan and Stefano had been quick to latch onto it. "But until then you can be sure I will mention nothing of this," he countered. "If I'm not accepted, you'll know before I do. Then it'll be just between the two of us."

Stefano laughed out loud and walked towards Tommaso. He held the point of his knife just below Tommaso's chin and forced his head upwards to look him in the eyes. With their stares locked, Stefano examined him like a cat examining its prey. He dropped the point of the knife and changed from a stabbing grip to convince Tommaso he had made the decision, reprieving him for the time being. "Very well, little wagon; I will make a recommendation to the Brotherhood. They're all aware of you now after your performance in the piazza today. By tomorrow you'll know – one way or the other." The menace in Stefano's voice was unmistakeable.

Turning, he sauntered away with the same rolling swagger Tommaso had seen earlier in the day when he walked the ten paces from him in the piazza. Suddenly an alarm went off in Tommaso's head: the same swagger, the sudden turn, the fluid movement as the knife flew straight and true. He had witnessed it twice now. He knew the tremendous power and accuracy Stefano could put behind a flying blade. Tommaso flung himself to the side as Stefano's knife whistled past his ear for the second time that day. The 'thunk' of the blade in the doorframe behind him announced the arrival of the weapon, and the warning he was now in a fight to the death. Tommaso turned to pull the knife from the doorframe but the burly pickman was only a few paces away and would impact with sickening force, whilst Tommaso struggled to remove the blade.

Once again Tommaso's speed saved him and he ducked under a bone-breaking charge to hear a satisfying 'oomph' as his attacker crashed into the heavy door. Stefano recovered quickly and took the knife in a clean pull before turning to rejoin the fight. Tommaso did not waste the intervening seconds. He knew where Alberto's knife lay and quickly retrieved it before turning to face the pickman.

Tommaso brought Alberto's blade into the fight and Stefano laughed aloud at the challenge before bellowing his rage across the narrow alley. "This isn't a pig pen, boy. There will be no victory for you in this contest. I'll string your lifeless body up from that doorway and empty your guts on the cobbles for pulling a knife on me. You've even done me a favour, you little shit. I can blame you for the murder of your own pickman, and who will argue against me?"

"I will, you foul bastard."

The voice surprised them both – it was Maria. She stood at the door of the taverna and Tommaso could see she was fighting against those who tried to drag her back inside. Before they could succeed, she threw a large stone pitcher directly at Stefano's head. Her aim was almost perfect but he turned at the last second to avoid a smashed skull, and the heavy stone pitcher crashed into his broken cheekbone. He howled in pain and Tommaso seized the advantage. He held the knife in his hand in such a way the weapon was tight against the outside of his forearm, with the sharp edge of the blade facing outwards and the handle gripped firmly in his fist. He could land a hefty punch as well as a fatal cut with the knife, using the same hand and without changing grip, but he had to be in close where the danger was greatest. Of this he had no fear.

He went for a slashing cut to Stefano's throat, but his victim moved down and right to protect the smashed cheekbone. Tommaso missed his target but managed a deep cut to the forehead, above Stefano's left eye, and with this he swiftly calculated his advantage. His enemy's right eye had closed up as a result of the smashed cheekbone; now the cut to the forehead would rain a curtain of blood into the other eye.

Stefano tried to regain his composure. To protect his blind, right flank he was forced to always move to the right and deny his aggressor a position on his weakened side. With his right hand he was forced to use thrusts and cuts across his line of vision and across his body in an attempt to inflict fatal damage on Tommaso, who knew a throw was out of the question. Stefano's left hand was permanently occupied with the task of keeping his one good eye clear of the blood raining from his forehead.

Tommaso was uninjured and matched Stefano's every cut and thrust as they circled in the narrow alley. He could move faster than the injured pickman and knew not to allow himself to be backed into a doorway. He had time to think. Stefano would realise he was losing and flight from danger was his only defence, but Tommaso had no intention of letting his prey escape. Giving a pickman an advantage, and recourse to the Brotherhood, was as good as Tommaso falling on his own knife.

Only one of them could leave the alley alive.

As they circled, Stefano came between Tommaso and Maria. In an instant Tommaso realised his mistake; his quarry had ducked in the turn and grabbed Maria. Swiftly he forced her body in front of his, placing her between himself and Tommaso, who cursed inwardly at his stupidity. The point of Stefano's knife stuck into the flesh of Maria's neck and a small trickle of blood flowed down the blade.

"Now, boy," spat Stefano, "place your knife on the ground and walk away. I don't need to tell you what will happen if you don't."

Tommaso knew the truth behind the statement, but he was also pretty sure it was the only truth Stefano would speak before he tried to kill them both. Maria presented a greater complication than just being a hostage. She was now part of the fight, increasing the stakes, and Tommaso could see the inevitability of the only outcome. All three were locked in a game having real players and bloody moves yet, to Tommaso, it looked as if Stefano couldn't lose.

Up until this time the good Sicilians of Favara had been doing what good Sicilians always did: they stayed out of the way and pretended not to notice, but some in the taverna were starting to take an interest in the goings-on. One apparently inebriated shepherd broke from the curious band of onlookers and staggered, rather more rapidly than he would have if sober, towards the alleyway. His estimation of where this actually found itself seemed somewhat obscured by excessive consumption of wine, and he staggered straight into the back of Stefano.

The timing of the drunk's action could not have been better for Tommaso. The impact caught Stefano on the left upper arm and forced his forearm across the side of his face, at the same time swinging him around to the right. Tommaso watched as the pickman rolled right with the blow whilst still maintaining his grip on Maria.

For a fraction of a second Stefano faced away from Tommaso – he only needed a fraction of a second. Turning the blade flat in his hand, Tommaso thrust the knife hard into Stefano's back.

The tip of the blade burst through the flank of muscle, straight into his victim's spine. Power to Stefano's lower body was cut as surely as the strings of a marionette and he collapsed to the ground in an uncoordinated heap. He had failed to hold on to Maria in the fall, and she made good her escape, taking the drunken oaf of a shepherd with her.

Stefano now lay vanquished at Tommaso's feet. They both knew the inevitable outcome. There was a moment's hesitation in Tommaso's final blow, but only a moment. Stefano offered no resistance as Tommaso fell on him, leading with the point of his knife to intrude into his quarry's body for the third time. The tip of the blade speared through the diaphragm below the sternum, and thrust upwards into the prostrate body of the pickman, bursting into his heart.

Tommaso stood and stared at his victim. A sudden cold fear rushed through him: he had taken the life of a pickman and a bloody vendetta must follow. In sheer panic he dropped the knife but he pulled a rational thought from the swirling maelstrom of his fear – he had to find Maria. Without thinking he rushed into the taverna, where he was instantly grabbed and thrown into a chair. Winded, he looked up to find the faces of six pickmen glaring down at him.

"You are a brave man," said the burliest of the pickmen, who was so stocky he appeared to have had the misfortune of being born without a neck. He looked down at Tommaso with a mixture of amusement and bewilderment. Tommaso read his face, but fear allowed him no time to dwell on the lack of anger he found there.

"Very brave and very resourceful," responded another pickman, who was built like a reed and had the face of a well-groomed rat. "I told you we were right to consider him," he continued, addressing the rest of the crowd.

Tommaso sat still and frightened. Maria rushed to his side and they huddled together like puppies in a lion's den.

"Pity then, Stefano hadn't agreed with Alberto, and the rest of us," said Rat to No-neck.

"Yes, shame really, as the outcome is the same – it's just that both of those who had the disagreement are now dead. I must remember this lesson in future," replied No-neck with a hint of comic timing. This had all of them laughing loudly, including a confused Tommaso.

A glass of brandy appeared and was placed in Tommaso's trembling hand.

"You see," continued No-neck, "the decision we were involved with here, was about making you a pickman, after your performance in the piazza today. All were in agreement except Stefano, and the argument broke into the fight you eventually became part of. Rather strange, don't you think?"

Tommaso's fortunes were changing faster than Rat-features could twitch his nose, which he did every time he sucked on the evil smelling cheroot clamped between his yellow teeth. Tommaso was closer than he had ever been to his dream, and his next words would make or break this turn of fate. He gulped the brandy and spluttered against its fiery descent. Another was instantly placed in front of him. "Really just proves you were all right and he was wrong, is what I think." There was a pregnant pause after Tommaso's words and he thought he had blown it, but then the laughter started again and another glass of brandy found its way to the table in front of him.

"Tommaso," said No-neck. "I am Cosimo Mutolo. Tomorrow will be your last day as a little wagon. You still must honour your quota, but return here tomorrow night and you'll be given the oath of the Brotherhood, separating those who will be subservient from those who are men of honour. Be under no illusion, Tommaso, this is just a beginning for you. It's not a ticket to riches or power but it is the first step on the ladder taking you there. Just remember, you're not the only one on the ladder, and it's hard to get past the guy in front." This elicited a few sniggers from the remaining drinkers and Rat-features seemed to find the description particularly amusing.

The old shepherd, who had been pivotal in the evening's events, stood up to leave and the laughter stopped. Indeed, all conversation stopped. He looked down and fixed Tommaso with a stare that couldn't hide a knowing glint. The eyes were old but not rheumy, the face thin but not emaciated, the smile full but not generous. "Tommaso," said the shepherd. "I look forward to seeing you again tomorrow."

With that he left to a chorus of *'va bene'* from everyone in the taverna. As the door closed behind the old shepherd, the noise and banter of the taverna commenced once more, as if on cue.

"Of course," began Cosimo again, "we have a need for *two* members of our brotherhood to replace those who have fallen. Tommaso, make yourself known to our other new apprentice."

From out of the crowd, milling about in the shadows, a young bull of a figure emerged. Dark eyes glinted from a swarthy face, nestling below a crop of tousled brown hair. A mean-spirited grin traversed a humourless mouth, as The Horse stood, arms folded over his barrel chest, and stared across the smoky room at Tommaso.

The two little wagons sized one another up but something unsaid made them both shrink back from open aggression. For just a moment Tommaso registered something other than triumph on Lorenzo's face. It almost looked like gratitude. Tommaso put this down to his consumption of brandy. He tipped a small wave in Lorenzo's direction, which was acknowledged with a barely perceptible nod of his huge head.

Chapter 4

The following day disappeared in a frenzy of making his quota and being cheered throughout the caverns of the mine, as Tommaso tried to prepare himself for the move away from the world of wicker baskets. He realised he had no real idea of how a pickman earned his wealth. Yes, he would still have to work the sulphur but the wielding of a pickaxe in caverns big enough to stand up in was nothing compared to the physical torture of the carusi. And besides, there seemed more to the picconieri and their wealth than just the yellow rock. Those things were never revealed to the lesser mortals but this only added spice to the heady mix of excitement and nervous anticipation that grew as the day wore to an end.

His companions applauded him, which he acknowledged without too much vigour. They could be his own crew the next day, and he would be whipping and kicking them to ensure their quotas were met. When he finished his own quota he left quickly, taking the wicker basket with him as a reminder of the life he would leave behind.

As the sun set on the day of his inauguration, he made his way through the still-warm streets to the taverna. Traces of blood remained on the cobbles outside the door, but of the victims of the previous night's fighting, there was no other sign; not even a mention of their passing.

Tommaso entered the taverna, to be met by Cosimo, and was taken to a small room at the rear. There, gathered in the flickering revelation of the oil lamps, were seven other pickmen and Lorenzo. Placed on a battered wooden table in front of him were a number of objects. Tommaso assumed them to be associated with the ritual he was about to undergo. His zeal was heightened as he saw the two fine hooded cloaks, folded carefully and laid on the tables. The cloaks were the visible insignia of the pickman cadre and each group sported a different identifying colour in the lining – his cadre wore green.

Thanks to Toto, Tommaso knew a few of the secrets of the order he was about to join. Each cadre comprised ten pickmen: *the decina,* and all ten were under the control of one commander, the *capodecina*. He had no idea who this would be but his identity would be revealed soon, as the *capo* must receive the oath of fealty from each new pickman.

A stocky figure shuffled in beside Tommaso and bumped against him to make room beside the table. He looked over his shoulder and picked up Lorenzo's wolfish grin. Now he was close to his nemesis, Tommaso could study him in detail. The powerful body was muscular and hard although the short stature would never be a vehicle for lithe movement or speed. There was something oafish about the large head, but the eyes were intelligent and worked a double-act with the thin-lipped mouth to deliver mocking derision when called for. Tommaso suspected there was neither compassion nor humour in their inventory.

"There's a way out for us here, Tommaso – away from the slavery and poverty."

Lorenzo had just communicated with him for the first time using something more than grunts and Tommaso was shocked at the intelligence and sensitivity parcelled up in the soft voice. The accent was not from the Girgenti hills – it was precise and, dare he think it, educated, like that of a priest.

Tommaso gave his measured response. "Lorenzo, we don't know what lies beyond that door, once we take the oath."

"I know exactly what lies beyond the door, Tommaso." Lorenzo had the last word.

Their hushed conversation was interrupted as Cosimo began speaking. The ceremony had begun. "Tommaso di Bova and Lorenzo Fratelli, you are here to take the blood oath of the brotherhood, *la fratellanza*. It is an oath binding you to this brotherhood until death. It is a condition of your binding oath that you talk to no one of the business of the fratellanza until you are spoken to first. You will be given the signals of recognition after you complete the oath. This oath is the *omertá,* it is a covenant binding you to the fratellanza until death, and it is with death you will be expelled and expunged from the fratellanza if you break the conditions of omertá." Cesare paused for effect and looked around the room, then directly at Tommaso and Lorenzo.

"First," he continued, "you will never betray the identity of your capodecina, whom you will be introduced to before you swear the oath. After meeting him you will either leave here as fratellanza, or as a corpse. Second, you will never betray the business of this group of ten, this *decina,* to other *decine* unless requested to do so by your commander. Third, you will never commit an act of violence against your capo or his family, or any of his associates, or any other members of this decina, or any of their families, unless instructed to do so by your capodecina. Fourth, you will obey all instructions of your capo without question and without concern for your personal safety. Fifth, you will treat the fratellanza as your first family. All other relationships take second place to the fratellanza. If any of your family learns of any of the business of the fratellanza, they will be put to death and you will be assumed to have broken omertá, for which you know the consequences. Tommaso, Lorenzo, do you understand the conditions of the oath? Answer yes or no." Cosimo looked at them both in turn.

"Yes," replied Tommaso, all the while wondering how Stefano had killed Alberto, if they were both part of the same decina. Perhaps some of these sacred oaths were more sacred than others. Equally, he pondered, both were dead anyhow, so there could be no retribution on the living. How convenient was that? The soft voice of Lorenzo confirmed his acceptance and the door to the small room opened to admit the commander.

They had both seen him, but fleetingly, the night before. The question in Tommaso's mind about the fight between Stefano and Alberto had just been answered, and he stood open-mouthed, fighting off every urge to speak. There facing him was the old shepherd: the one who had distracted Stefano, allowing the stalemate in the knife fight to be broken. The shepherd garb had been cast away in favour of the finest of attire from the best tailor in Palermo, and the man before him now looked younger and fitter than on the previous night.

"Gentlemen, our capodecina, Leopoldo Notarbartolo." Cosimo made the introduction and all in the room rose.

Notarbartolo spoke. "Tommaso, Lorenzo, you are now past the point of no return. The next part of the initiation is to confirm your membership of this *decina*. All who know you and understand omertá will, from this day forward, know you as part of your new family that is fratellanza." Leopoldo did not wait for an answer; such an action would have been pointless. "Tommaso, you will take the oath first."

Leopoldo Notarbartolo's voice was quiet but somehow it was also menacing. It carried an air of confidence, which comes with the knowledge that whenever he spoke, people obeyed; therefore it wasn't necessary to speak loudly. Those who knew to listen, did so intently.

Tommaso watched as Cosimo stepped forward to the table to lift two pieces of cloth, revealing two small woodcarvings of what looked like saints, or some other religious icons. A pair of small-bladed knives and two candles made up the last objects on the table. Cosimo lit one of the candles and wrapped a small carving in one of the cloths, to place it in Tommaso's left hand. His right was forced open and the small knife drew a cut along the palm, from which the blood was made to dribble over the statue and the cloth. Cosimo took the lit candle and touched the flame to the cloth-wrapped saint, which started to burn in Tommaso's hand.

Notarbartolo then spoke again. "Tommaso, repeat this after

me: I swear on my honour to be faithful to the fratellanza, as the fratellanza is faithful to me."

Tommaso repeated the first line and then continued in turn as Notarbartolo called out the oath:

"As this saint and these drops of my blood burn, so I will willingly spill all my blood for the fratellanza. As this ash and this blood can never be as before, so I can never be as I was before I became one with the fratellanza."

Tommaso continued, feverishly moving the burning relic from hand to hand. It all seemed so simple, so easy and with just a few sentences Notarbartolo stopped and turned to Lorenzo to complete his ritual.

Tommaso felt deflated. The journey seemed to have promised more than the ritual delivered, but he knew little of what lay beyond. Notarbartolo completed the ritual by placing the hooded cloaks over their shoulders. Before preparing to leave, he also presented each of them with a tightly-rolled bundle of lire. Tommaso didn't know exactly how much the bundle contained but it was more money then he had seen in his entire life. It wasn't a gift, it was his stake money. He had to hire his crew of carusi and pay them. Whatever was left over was his, and next week the cycle would begin again.

Notarbartolo turned his back on them, indicating the ceremony was over and made for the door.

"Commendatore," said Tommaso and almost immediately wished he hadn't. Every eye in the room shot daggers in his direction. Lorenzo coughed beside him as if trying to hide Tommaso's outburst. It was too late. Notarbartolo stopped, one hand on the door handle. He seemed to stand there for an age, as if deciding on his next course of action.

Tommaso's mind raced. His life as a pickman could be over within seconds of it beginning and he swore under his breath at his own crass stupidity. Eventually, Notarbartolo turned around and stared at Tommaso, a quizzical look on his face. "Yes, my young soldier," said the capo. "You have a question?"

Tommaso had been holding his breath since he first uttered his ill-timed exclamation and exhaled noisily, which only compounded his predicament. "Yes, commendatore. Forgive me; there is much I have to learn. In my hand is more money than I have seen in my entire life. I know only poverty. How is it possible that such wealth exists in a town so poor?"

Notarbartolo looked Tommaso in the eye as if searching for some insincerity. He found none and turned smiling to the others in the room before levelling his gaze back on a trembling Tommaso. The room relaxed and the atmosphere of tension dissipated.

"I like this young man," said the capodecina to the others, who nodded and grovelled in agreement. "He will not forget his humble beginnings, and this is vital for a man of honour. Years from now, if he is loyal and progresses through the ranks of the fratellanza, he will be able to return to this town – his home, and be welcomed by all, regardless of rank or wealth."

Tommaso relaxed a little.

Notarbartolo continued. "Tommaso, there is indeed much you have to learn. If we tried to explain it all to you today, you would leave this room in disbelief. For now, I can only answer you thus: we extract gold from fleas."

Chapter 5

The tightly-rolled bundle of lire had grown in size over the last year as Tommaso learned how to ply his trade as a pickman. He wasn't released from the deadly embrace of the sulphur, as he still had to hack the lumps of yellow rock from the seams, but compared to the slavery of the carusi, this was nothing. He hired his own crews of little wagons and was paid for each basket of sulphur they carried to the surface. He made his tithe to the decina and gave small amounts to those like Toto, who could keep him supplied with information that might be of use. Any scandal on Lorenzo Fratelli was well-rewarded.

His killing of Stefano had an added bonus: Tommaso inherited his crews of little wagons and the income they produced. In this he had a head start over The Horse's fortunes, but there was more to Stefano's bloody inheritance than just sulphur. The dead pickman's legacy extended to a minor empire of small criminal rackets, chief amongst which were payments from every taverna owner in Favara to ensure they received their supplies of alcohol. Of course, the alcohol sellers also had to pay for the privilege of being able to supply the tavernas. Gold from fleas, gold from fleas.

Every transaction, legitimate or otherwise, was carefully accounted for to Tommaso's capo and one tenth of all earnings paid without question. That still left an ever-growing bundle of cash and the comfort of his own cabin in the sprawling complex of Ciavallotta. Tommaso had little idea of just how all-pervasive the mine was until he broke free from the shackles of slavery that bound the carusi. The mine provided everything for those who could pay, or for those who owed their every living breath to its enterprise. There were chapels, general stores, clinics, doctors and even schools nestled in the pervasive yellow fog of the calcaroni. For now, Tommaso could content himself with the accommodation but escaping the poisonous atmosphere of the mine was something his thoughts turned to on a daily basis. He could return to his childhood home, but the comforts of the Ciavallotta cabin were like a palace by comparison. Nonetheless, this journey to the stone hovel where he was born was one he could put off no longer.

The lane seemed to narrow ahead of him as Tommaso walked through the tightly-packed dwellings sprouting from the crumbling limestone escarpment at the edge of Favara. With each step, the broken stone underfoot thinned until there was little more than the unwanted tailings of sharp rubble from the mine, defining the path. The inhabitants of the tumble-down piles of stones that served as homes sat outside in the gloom. Those who were fortunate enough to own livestock shared the space with mangy goats and snorting pigs. A few chickens pecked amongst the debris and the ubiquitous dogs wandered amongst the assorted menagerie, barking at his presence.

For the next few weeks, until the beginning of winter, this assorted mixture of animals and humans would spend every waking hour outside the cramped hovels. When the evenings grew too cold they would be forced to retire to the inner confines of a windowless pile of sharp stones. Then, the smoke from the fires that provided heating and cooking would mix with the smell of the animals penned inside. This malodorous stink would clearly define those trapped in the penury of Favara, yet still these wretches had a value: they provided human livestock for the mines – gold from fleas. For now, outdoors was preferable, even though the evenings grew chilly.

Many eyes turned towards Tommaso as he retraced footsteps from years past. The hooded cloak with the green lining sent a clear signal to all who could understand, and barking dogs were hushed as he made his way to the last of the piles of stones. One lonely figure sat outside, huddled in a tattered shawl that covered her body like a dirty shroud. Tethered to a small wooden post, jutting from a rotten door frame, was a goat whose ribs poked through its flesh. It made a small braying sound as Tommaso approached and fixed him with those protruding eyes and rectangular pupils that had struck fear into Tommaso since childhood.

The woman turned on hearing the noise, but Tommaso pulled the hood from his cloak over his head, to hide his face.

"There's nothing left here, pickman," she said. "The mine has taken my son, and my daughter sells what is left of her body in the tavernas of Favara. You can have my goat, but you will have to feed him."

"Where is Lucio, your husband?" Tommaso hadn't seen his father in five years and his sister Cora had been a child of six when he descended the mine for the first time.

"In the fields far from here," replied his mother, curiosity replacing despair in her voice. "He tends sheep in the high pastures above Cammarata. He will not return until the winter has left and the shearing is finished."

Tommaso pulled the hood from his head and crouched down facing his mother. He looked into her eyes and let his invasive stare ask all the questions of his lost childhood.

"Tommaso?" The voice croaked more than spoke, as it carried the burden of guilt borne from the wilful neglect of a life sold to slavery.

At least she recognised him; but then what mother wouldn't? She reached out to touch his face but he pushed her hand gently away. "How much?" he asked. "How much did they pay you for me?"

"Tommaso, don't condemn me. Dear Mother of God, don't condemn me for what I had to do," said his mother, fear and despair quenching the small flame of happiness sparked by seeing him again. "If you wear the cloak then you know what happens. They increased the rent and we fell behind. They said we would get you back once the debt was cleared."

"You know carusi never live long enough for the debt to be discharged. Everyone in the valley knows this." Tommaso's emotions staggered, fell, got up again, ran through his mind and tumbled over a choice of hate or compassion, as he struggled with a reconciliation he was ill-prepared for.

"Yes, my son," replied his mother, as if sensitive to the turmoil haunting his entire being. "Everyone in the valley knows this. But is the mine empty? No, Tommaso, there are carusi a plenty and every one of them has been bought from a mother and father facing eviction. Do the tavernas lack whores? No, but our daughters sell for less because they are consumed by the pox in a few years. They are allowed to return home when even the mule-herders won't touch them. Then we have to care for them. You left here as caruso. Yes, and we cried because we loved you. You return here as picconieri and expect the same compassion? No, Tommaso, there is guilt in the devil's trades and you can find no absolution here."

Tommaso's emotional turmoil was rocked even more by his mother's last statement. If he didn't have a family he had nothing. But then the fratellanza was his new family. He could leave everyone else behind; couldn't he?

"The debt is clear, mother." He looked at her and smiled to make sure she understood. From the pocket of his cloak he pulled a handful of lire and pressed the notes into the thin, waxy skin of her hand. She took the gift without looking down and he could feel the bony grasp of her fingers. The look she returned was a mixture of confusion and compassion, swimming in a sea of tears.

"And Cora? Can you redeem her?"

"Yes, yes of course," replied Tommaso, without knowing how. The fratellanza had many interests but he knew that pimping was something they shied away from. Women, it was explained to him in the days following his initiation, were to be revered. They were, of course, always subservient to their husbands and that honour cascaded down through the ranks, from capos to soldiers. Infidelity was punished by the death of all parties. These were inviolate rules of the fratellanza. Those who chose to ply their trade in sexual exploitation were animals; they could be slaughtered at will.

"Wait here," said his mother. "I have something for you." She released the weak grip on his fingers and stood, before slowly and painfully shuffling in through the doorway of the pile of stones she called home. When she returned, Tommaso could see she held a letter close to her chest as if it was a precious gift from the Good Lord himself.

"This was pushed under the door a few weeks ago. I can't read, I can barely see, but I know enough to know my own son's name on the cover." She held the envelope out to him. "I didn't open it," she said as if she could predict the first of the two questions forming in Tommaso's mind. "I don't know who it's from," she continued, accurately predicting the second.

Tommaso opened the wax seal on the envelope and extracted two thin sheets of paper from within.

"When did you learn to read?" asked his mother, a note of pride rising in her voice.

"I know a few words," he replied. "All courtesy of an old mule-herder." The writing was in a sinuous long-hand and he could decipher little of it, yet the flimsy leaves of paper still spoke to him. There was a faint perfume to the paper, and everything about the letter seemed to say it belonged to a world that Tommaso wasn't part of. He flicked to the end, nodding his head thoughtfully as he did so, hoping not to disappoint his mother. There was one last word that he could read without difficulty: the name. It was in the neat and precise signature. The letter was from Maria: the only Maria he knew and whom he hadn't seen, hadn't touched, and hadn't been aroused by since the night that had changed his life. Putting the letter in the pocket of his cloak, he said good-bye to his mother with a promise to return regularly. For sure he would be back before his father came home from the winter pastures.

As Tommaso walked back along the stony path, his emotions were in turmoil. He had made peace with his mother, so he should have experienced some elation, but clutched tightly in his hand was the mysterious letter. Its contents could spell an invitation to further precious moments with Maria, or it could be an instruction never to see her again. He had no way of knowing, at least not until Toto read the contents. That could be embarrassing, dangerous even, but the message in the letter wouldn't wait, not even until morning.

Chapter 6

Lorenzo Fratelli sat below a large cactus: one of a number of the prickly plants that, along with a decrepit dry-stone wall, marked the boundary of a sprawling lemon plantation, just to the east of Favara. It was the dead of night and only the light of a full moon illuminated the faces of those who had made the one-hour journey from the bunkhouse of the mine. They were all pickmen of the Notarbartolo cadre. Their presence on a deserted farm track, near the residence of one Gaspare Galati, wasn't the result of getting lost whilst on an evening stroll. Lorenzo had no idea of why they were there, but he was told his presence was required. He was also told to bring his pick and be prepared to use it. That instruction was from Cosimo Mutolo, the leader of this group, and the pickman present at Lorenzo's inauguration into the fratellanza.

Cosimo had continued to resist all attempts to grow a neck and still looked like he was born with a stubble-covered lower jaw that protruded directly from the confluence of his collar bones. If he wanted to turn his head, it seemed as if his entire upper body had to be press-ganged into the manoeuvre, but this didn't prevent him from being alert to the slightest danger. He had heard something and Lorenzo caught the movement of the stocky shoulders as Cosimo twisted slightly, so his hearing could tune in on the direction of the sound. Cosimo held his hand up for silence just as the noise of the soft footsteps reached the ears of the others. Cosimo made a low whistle that exactly mimicked the call of the Sicilian Rock Partridge. He received similar in return and relaxed.

Within seconds a figure appeared in the soft moonlight and ducked down into the hollow beneath the cacti. All eyes were on Cosimo.

"My brothers," he began. "This is Benedetto Carollo; he is the warden here at the Galati plantation. He is a friend of ours and of our patron, Leopoldo Notarbartolo."

Lorenzo had been a man of honour for over twelve months and was still struggling to come to terms with the arcane intricacies of the sect, but he knew enough to know that Carollo had just been introduced as fratellanza.

"Benedetto, our patron sends his fraternal greetings," continued Cosimo.

"I return his greetings and ask that my allegiance is still accepted," replied Benedetto.

"It is so," said Cosimo. "Now, our brothers here, they are of the sulphur and not of the lemons. Please explain our problem."

Benedetto looked like he had just been dragged from a comfortable bed. He was dressed in a pair of linen pants and a rough shirt, covered in stains of various sorts that Lorenzo would not wish to question. Unlike Lorenzo's group, whose pallor was pasty and pale from being entombed in the caverns of Ciavallotta, Benedetto looked the picture of health with bronzed skin and bright eyes that flickered in the moonlight. The Ciavallotta Pickmen looked like grey, old men, compared to the warden of the Galati plantation.

Benedetto looked around nervously and cleared his throat before he began. "The sulphur grew a long time ago," he said, looking at each of them in turn, as if beginning a tale of legend. "The lemons, they are just as important to the fratellanza, but they need time to produce a return. The land has to be cleared and terraced, walls erected and drainage channels dug, then the sluices for the water have to be installed before the trees are even planted. After that it can take another eight years before a single fruit is grown." Again, Benedetto paused and looked at each of them to ensure his narrative was getting through.

Lorenzo tried to look as if he understood and nodded, but it was doubtful if the acknowledgement was picked up by the warden in the pale wash of the moonlight.

Benedetto continued, unperturbed. "When the crop finally grows, the demand is so great that the owner sells the harvest before it is ripe. The fratellanza takes their share whilst the lemons are still on the trees. It is, after all, only fair payment for all our assistance over the years. The owner doesn't suffer, only the merchants who buy the harvest. It's the way it has always been."

Cosimo interrupted, as if wanting to retrieve control of the narrative. "Gaspare Galati is not from Sicily; he is from Rome and he inherited this plantation. He is popular in the town and very influential amongst the judiciary and police. Normally the fratellanza would welcome this, but Galati is not one of us. He uses this influence to expose our business dealings and our secrets. We have tried to help him understand how we take our share, but he has accused Benedetto of theft and reported him to the local police."

Lorenzo shuffled uncomfortably on the pile of sharp stones that had made up his seat for the last few hours and caused a small landslide of rubble to slip noisily onto the path. A dozen eyes pierced the gloom and shot daggers in his direction. "Forgive me," whispered Lorenzo, barely stifling a yawn.

Cosimo continued. "Of course, this mischievous complaint will never reach the ears of the magistrate, but Galati has hired a new warden who is also not of our number. Benedetto here must leave by the end of the week."

"I have nowhere to go, and what I take, I take for the fratellanza, not for myself," replied Benedetto, suddenly defensive.

"Your loyalty is not in question." replied Cosimo. "We take care of our own. Both Galati and his new warden have been warned of the consequences of their actions. They have had time to make amends and change their decision. They haven't done so. Galati has also sought to undermine our influence with the other plantation owners throughout the region, encouraging them to remove any brothers from their workers. We will protect our members, all of them, starting with my good friend here."

Despite the gloom, Lorenzo could see the flicker of relief and gratitude in Benedetto's eyes as he continued. "At sunrise, in just a short while, the new warden will walk along this path. Galati has installed a steam engine to irrigate the groves. The job of the warden is to fire it up in time for the first shift."

Benedetto fell silent and Lorenzo could feel the tension rising amongst the small group huddled quietly below the large cactus. He now knew enough to realise why his team was there. At a minimum, they would destroy the steam engine, possibly extending their destruction up to the grand house on the hill above the groves.

"Lorenzo, stay with me. The rest of you go with Benedetto," said Cosimo as if it was a military operation. When the others had moved quietly away, Cosimo shuffled closer to Lorenzo and continued. "Lorenzo, there are a number of ways you can progress through the fratellanza. They all come down to the same thing: the more risk you take for your capo, the greater the reward. The others, they've left to destroy the irrigation to the groves. There's a small risk in this. The greater risk falls on the one who will take the life of the new warden as he walks along the path. He is to be found with a Ciavallotta pick in the back of his head."

"That message will be clear, to all who understand it," replied Lorenzo as he began to comprehend his role in the night's operation. "But surely a pickaxe will lead the polizia right to us?"

"And what will they find? Twenty picconieri who will all testify that no one left the bunk house and two overseers who'll swear no one left the mine – all fratellanza. As you say, Lorenzo, the message will be clear to those who understand it."

Lorenzo sat quietly and thought through what he had just been told. Another dead labourer, killed in one of the many vendettas flourishing around this small corner of Sicily. It was nothing compared to the institutional blood-letting on the streets of Palermo, but Lorenzo had a keen sense of self-preservation. He could tell where the next few minutes would take him. He wasn't an assassin, but that didn't mean he couldn't bury the point of his pickaxe into another man's skull; he just needed to be sure of getting away with it. The fratellanza owned most of the *polizia*, the regional police force, but if Galati had friends in Rome then it may be the *arma dei carabinieri* who would investigate. The fratellanza had no influence there. The carabinieri were a military police force with civilian jurisdiction. They were as hard as nails and never recruited from the regions where they served, making them immune to local threats and bribery.

"If Galati is from Rome then he may have influence there," said Lorenzo, looking Cosimo straight in the eye. It wasn't a look of defiance and the tone of his statement wasn't a challenge, more the considered response of a master tactician.

"Your capo has asked that you be given first refusal on the kill," replied Cosimo, dismissive of Lorenzo's concerns. "He must like you, Lorenzo. This is a great honour. We understand if it's too much to ask of you so soon. You can refuse and I'll ask one of the others. There's no shame in refusing. Of course, if you do accept, you will never speak of this again. It will be buried as deep as the omertá. Those who know, will know enough to understand that you are special: chosen by our capo for greatness."

The pale, grey light cast by the moon was slowly being invaded by the colour of the new morning and Lorenzo realised he had little time left to make his decision. Something had changed. But why was he being favoured over the others? Now was not the time to ask, but it was time for brave decisions. Beyond the ranks of the picconieri, there were other strata where men of honour existed. It had never entered Lorenzo's head that he could aspire to being a capo, and one killing alone wouldn't take him there, but it might just put him on the road. There was no danger for Lorenzo. Cosimo had just about convinced him of that, and it wasn't as if his victim didn't know of the risk. The fratellanza didn't make idle threats, and anyone ignoring them did so at their peril. Lorenzo looked Cosimo in the eyes before reaching down and lifting up his pick. He spat on the head and rubbed the sharp spike with the sleeve of his shirt. He had one last question. "The next man who walks down that path will be the new warden?"

"That is so, Lorenzo. You will hear the latch of the gate as he leaves the house. He'll walk right past you. Take him from behind. Do not even give him time to make peace with God in case he escapes and identifies you."

"Tell my capo I serve him well," said Lorenzo. "And make sure I have a new pick waiting for me at the mine."

Cosimo smiled but said nothing, as he left and hurried along the path to the others, leaving Lorenzo alone with his thoughts. It wasn't the first time he had killed, but it would be the first time in cold blood. His attempt to take out Tommaso in the rock fall might have qualified if it had succeeded, but this was different: he didn't know his victim. Maybe 'assassin' was the wrong word – 'executioner' was more fitting, and like any executioner he was only obeying the law. It may not have been a law his victim would have agreed with, but that was his mistake. The warnings had been given and there was no appeal.

The soft click of a latch closing made Lorenzo sit bolt upright. His errant thoughts were blown asunder like smoke. He could almost feel the chilling breeze of his fate waft across him. He shivered and his pickaxe shook in his hands. Excitement, fear, honour and anticipation vied for their position at the vanguard of his emotions. As the soft footsteps padded towards Lorenzo's hiding place, he took a deep, quiet breath and reined in his wayward feelings. Suddenly calm, and with a clarity of thought he had never before experienced, Lorenzo changed his grip on the pick so the sharp point faced away from him. The first glint of the morning sun's rays reflected from the tip.

The quiet scrunch of his victim's footsteps passed by.

Lorenzo leapt out into the path, raising the pick above his head. He was scarcely aware of the figure in front of him before the sharp point came scything down in a vicious arc. As it connected with the base of his victim's skull, Lorenzo loosened his grip so the pick would remain buried where it had delivered its fatal blow.

The body dropped with barely a sound. Twitching limbs danced in macabre testimony to a departing soul. For what seemed like an age, Lorenzo watched stupefied as his victim died, writhing and squirming on the path, blood spilling on the dust and flowing over the dry stones like quicksilver.

Then all was quiet.

Lorenzo remained rooted to the spot, studying his victim. The clothes were what first struck him. They weren't the crumpled linen and stained cotton types that Benedetto had worn; these were tailored and of the finest cloth. The blood-soaked hair was grey, evidence of an older man but maybe the new warden was also from Rome, and Galati had picked a man of wealth and experience to take control of the plantation.

The soft whistle of a Sicilian Rock Partridge reached Lorenzo's ears and seemed to shatter the stillness. He looked up and the whistle was repeated.

It was his cue to escape.

Within seconds Lorenzo was ten metres away from the corpse on the path, running with a speed he never thought he was capable of. His heart pounded in his chest as exertion combined with exhilaration to drive away the fear of being apprehended.

When Lorenzo reached the bunkhouse of the mine, his pulse had slowed to normal and the pains in his chest were replaced by those in his cheeks: evidence of the fixed grin he sported as he ran through the empty streets of Favara.

Chapter 7

Favara had moods. Lorenzo Fratelli didn't understand more than a few but if his early life in Palermo had taught him anything, it had given him a sensitivity to things that could either threaten him, or be turned to his advantage. He had left when he was only six, but even then the city had pulled him into its cankerous heart and taught him how to use senses others never realised existed. Of course he had returned many times in the last year. He was a trusted courier for Cesare Giuliano: the head of all the fratellanza families in Girgenti. Money went out to Palermo and messages came back. Lorenzo never counted the money and never read the messages, not that he could, but the trust in him as a courier was based on more than his illiteracy. The links between the families of Girgenti and Palermo were in their infancy, but he could sense them growing stronger with each exchange visit he made, and it wasn't for him to question why. Lorenzo used each pilgrimage to his advantage and fell gratefully into the stinking morass of the city's underworld. He understood Palermo's moods: they were easy to detect for those who had the gift. There was nothing subtle or complex. Palermo lived on fear, or at least its heart seemed untouched by compassion or charity. Whatever mood the city was in, it was a variation of either anxiety or terror.

With Favara, it was different. The town responded to the seasons in a way that a bustling city never could. The spring warmth would bring back the shepherds from the winter pastures, causing the streets and tavernas to ring with a new energy. The summer heat was debilitating, so life's pace slowed. The inhabitants set out to accomplish very little, and were generally not disappointed in their achievements. The short autumnal weeks were frantic as lemons and olives ripened. Casual labour flooded the town, bringing fights and commerce in equal measure. The first cool dampness of winter would see the smoke rise from the hovels on the outskirts, as their inhabitants retreated indoors with their livestock. That cast a mood over the town that seemed to permeate it like the fumes from the animal-dung fires, only to be lifted when the promise of spring returned again.

Lorenzo had learned to read the imprints of the seasons but the effect of births, marriages and deaths still confused him. Palermo's streets and alleys had stunk of death. Bloated corpses had greeted him most mornings, and some lay for days in the summer heat before they were carted away. Of all the recollections he had of the city of his birth, the images that were indelibly seared into his young memory were those of the morning's anonymous harvest of violent death. Yet in Favara, the dead were never nameless. Of course, the townsfolk were immune to the constant attrition of the carusi, but others above the status of human livestock were venerated for days and even weeks following their passing.

Marriages seemed to be where Favara and Palermo shared a common disposition. Marriages were an occasion for colour, music, and feasting. New alliances would bring an end to vendettas, freeing up families to pursue new wealth and fortune. Of course, new kinships fanned quietly smouldering conflicts that would have simply turned to smoke if left alone.

The many differences that defined the respective cities' divergent and convergent moods were never more apparent than in how they each treated the arrival of a new one of their number. Lorenzo could not and would not attempt to understand why another mouth to feed was such a blessing, bringing so much joy. Yes, the paupers on the edge of town would have more currency to trade with the picconieri or the pimps, but many of those who were not paupers were still poor, and poverty provided a meagre harvest. Lorenzo couldn't understand why the news of an impending birth would seem to permeate the chatter and devotions of mothers and grandmothers, adding lightness and even an air of happiness to a sulphur town that had such a huge investment in sorrow.

Even the days of the week affected the mood of the town. Sundays were usually little silos of contentment, when the mines stopped and those who could enjoy the meagre benefits of the yellow rock would crowd the narrow streets and piazzas from early morning. As soon as he arrived on the outskirts of the town, Lorenzo could tell that this Sunday had Favara in a mood he had never before witnessed. The streets were quiet: devoid of scampering children and scolding mothers. Instead, sombre men talked in whispers on street corners, suddenly finding the ground at their feet of consuming interest as he walked past.

One old woman sat alone under the shade of a tree at the edge of the Piazza don Giustiani. Her rheumy eyes looked up as Lorenzo passed. He guessed she would have seen him as no more than a blur; certainly not enough to recognise him.

"The town seems sad today, old woman. I hope Father Russo has come to no harm. He was ill last time I saw him, and Chiesa del Purgatorio would suffer a great loss if he was no longer amongst us."

Lorenzo waited as she stopped sobbing for long enough to compose an answer. "No, no, Father Russo is well. I spoke to him only a few minutes ago. He gave me the terrible news. Gaspare Galati was murdered last night. They found him with a Ciavallotta pickaxe buried in his head. The picconieri have murdered a wonderful man. Pray to God, Galati will be made a saint."

The sobbing and outpouring of grief continued as Lorenzo turned his back and walked away. It was pure reflex that he did so. His conscious thoughts were occupied with recalling every second of the previous evening. He had killed Gaspare Galati, there was nothing surer, and just as inevitable would be the following investigation, led by the dreaded *arma dei carabinieri*. By the time he reached his customary pew in Chiesa del

Purgatorio, Lorenzo had gone over every syllable of his last conversation with Cosimo Mutolo. *'The next man who walks down that path will be the new warden?'*

'That is so, Lorenzo. You'll hear the latch of the gate as he leaves the house. He will walk right past you. Take him from behind. Do not even give him time to make peace with God in case he escapes and identifies you.'

There was no new warden at the Galati plantation. The only living soul to have opened the gate that morning and made his way to the steam engine would have been Galati himself. Why else did his victim's clothes look too well tailored for a labourer? And no labourer worth his toil could have endured the workload to an age where his hair had turned grey. As he stared at the altar, Lorenzo's understanding of how he was duped into killing Galati bubbled and hissed as it transformed into anger. Did the fratellanza think he was stupid just because he was built like a horse and didn't welcome meaningless conversation? Those who made that mistake did so at their peril. He lowered his head in pretence at prayer, but piety was replaced by emotions having more to do with revenge and self preservation.

He thought the quiet voice that came from behind him was that of Father Russo.

"Lorenzo, I can sense your anger. Do not let it destroy you, or what you have achieved."

He turned to where the voice came from and stared into the eyes of Leopoldo Notarbartolo – his capo. "Please, Lorenzo, save all you have to say for outside. The Church is sacred to all of us and her walls should only hear what is meant for the Lord. Please, walk with me."

Outside the chapel, in Piazza don Giustiani, were four horses and two mounted men. Notarbartolo was by Lorenzo's side and guided him gently to his mount. The other two men he didn't recognise, but they sported bandoleers and carried the latest in Beaumont-Vitali bolt-action rifles. Even the carabinieri didn't have these as standard issue.

On the ride, Notarbartolo stayed in front with Lorenzo following. The two riflemen brought up the rear and never spoke. Lorenzo had no doubt they could shoot the eye from a low-flying rock partridge at fifty metres. If he was going to make an escape he should have attempted it in the crowded alleys of Favara. He might have made it. But then what? He swallowed his anger and cursed his inability to fight his way out of a losing gambit.

They were a kilometre away from the town when he sensed one of the shooters had lagged behind the group, stopping about fifty metres to the rear. Lorenzo looked around just as the second shooter rode past and took up position, an equal distance in front. Notarbartolo cantered his mount towards Lorenzo and stopped beside him.

"Someone wishes to meet you," said the capo.

Many states of panic welled up in Lorenzo's gut. There were numerous times in his life he had felt fear but it was always of the unknown. That fear had the smooth edge of probability: there was a chance he could overcome the threat through strength and good fortune, as he had done frequently. This fear had the contours of shattered obsidian. He knew the protocol only too well.

"I suggest you dismount," continued Notarbartolo.

Lorenzo did so and willed his legs to support his weight. Facing him, angled away from the path, was a narrow lane in a copse of untended lemon groves. The gap was barely big enough for a man to squeeze through. Lorenzo looked up at his capo, who acknowledged the silent request and nodded towards the gap. As Lorenzo took the first few steps towards whatever fate lay behind the gnarled and twisted trees, Notarbartolo trotted off with the spare horse and took up station with one of the shooters.

It was the smell that hit Lorenzo's heightened senses first and subdued his racing fear. Wood smoke and the unmistakable aroma of roast goat meant they weren't alone. He pushed through the narrow gap, his arrival heralded by snapping branches and rustling foliage. What greeted him was as unbelievable as it was welcoming. A small meadow extended from the boundary of tangled lemon groves. Two bench tables, adorned with bread and wine, were laid out with three chairs, overlooking a smouldering fire whose embers had been coaxed to a glowing red. Straddling the fire was a spit supporting the carcass of a goat, rotating slowly over the heat and reaching the point where had it a voice, it would have demanded to be eaten. Turning the spit was the most beautiful woman in Favara: Maria Giuliano. He had seen her many times in the town and like most males, tried not to gawp, not because she was beautiful, but because she was one of Cesare Giuliano's daughters. Outside of Palermo, there was no one more powerful than Cesare, and the few who knew him closely, walked on eggshells when they were in his presence. It was said that the deepest mine shaft in Ciavallotta was floored with the bodies of those who had crossed him. It was also said that Maria was damaged goods. She had been seen with carusi. Even the whores in the tavernas didn't stoop so low. Of course, anyone who voiced such an opinion would join those who had made their last rapid descent to the instant graveyard at the bottom of the mine.

"I'm Maria," she said, in response to the obvious appearance of confusion on Lorenzo's face. Her voice was as divine as her looks. "Please rest," she continued, pointing to an empty chair, "and take your fill of some wine."

These were commands Lorenzo could happily obey, as his fear evaporated…almost. Imminent death seemed unlikely now, but this assignation was put together for a reason, and the extra chair wasn't for the recently departed goat. Before taking up the offer of the wine, he thought it best to reply to the introduction with one of his own. "My name is Lorenzo Fratelli, and I thank you for your hospitality."

"We will eat shortly, Lorenzo. My father will arrive soon."

"I will wait for him before taking my seat." Lorenzo felt that would be the right thing to do, despite the puzzled look from Maria.

Across the small meadow, the two riflemen took up position as the sun's glow turned from midday white to evening orange and glinted off the gunmetal barrels of their Beaumont-Vitali rifles. Another rustle of the foliage in the small gap from the path announced the arrival of Cesare with Leopoldo in tow. He stayed in the shade of the lemon trees whilst the rappresentante strode forward. Cesare was in his early fifties and the picture of health. He had probably never known the debilitating toil of hard labour but his physique was more than a match for any of his younger soldiers, who had served time to the sulphur. A broad smile beamed out from a handsome face where Lorenzo could clearly see the resemblance to Maria.

"My dearest Lorenzo," said Cesare. "I trust Maria has taken care of you. Please excuse the reception so far from my home, but I get to spend so little time away from the attentions of others." With that, he embraced Lorenzo like a long-lost brother and plunked him in a chair.

Sitting beside the most powerful man in Girgenti, eating roast goat served by a hauntingly beautiful woman and washing it down with the finest Ragusa, whilst being scrutinised by two trained killers in a summer meadow was surreal. It went on this way for another hour as Cesare thanked Lorenzo for his messenger runs to Palermo and enquired of the health and well-being of some of the capital city's honoured brothers. All this was interspersed with timely observations about how his beautiful daughter Maria was finding it difficult to meet a future husband amongst the limited supply of honourable men in Favara. Lorenzo said little, other than filling in details where he was asked direct questions.

Maria had said nothing during this time, but her silence communicated more than the words she was forbidden to speak. The chairs had been carefully positioned and Lorenzo noted how he had been guided to the middle one, ensuring Maria had to sit beside him. It was like sitting beside a ghost: her presence was there but all he could feel was coldness. When her father spoke for the third time of her inability to find a husband, Maria's seething embarrassment breeched the chill and transmitted clearly to Lorenzo. She flounced out of the chair and busied herself with clearing the remains of the meal.

Cesare fell silent, as if insulted by his daughter's actions, and then he harrumphed in acknowledgement that this was a cross he knew he had to bear. He produced a box of cigars, and Lorenzo gladly accepted the offer of a smoke. As he bowed his head to kindle the hand-rolled tobacco, Lorenzo caught the dismissive gesture that Cesare made to the shooters on the other side of the meadow, and they quietly retreated from their positions.

"Wildflowers fascinate me," said Cesare, looking across at the meadow as he lit his own smoke. "They are so fragile and so beautiful, but they have to survive in the wild so they have to be tough. You don't find them in tight little bunches, but scattered wherever they can blossom and pollinate."

For Lorenzo, the evening was continuing its surreal progress. Sitting beside him was a man who ruthlessly overcame problems by snuffing out the lives of those who caused them. Yet, here he was talking like an old shepherd who had spent way too much time with his herd.

"Walk with me a little, Lorenzo."

It wasn't a request. When they were far enough away from Maria clattering dishes, Cesare continued.

"My Maria, she is a wildflower: beautiful, tough and very resilient. Of all my daughters, she has caused me the most trouble. I need to find her a husband. She hankers after Tommaso di Bova, but I have forbidden this liaison. He can bring nothing to the fratellanza." There was a pause that clearly invited Lorenzo's response.

"Like me, Tommaso was carusi. He got to rise above that by being lucky with the blade of a knife. There are many of the same low breeding who will never rise above picconieri, especially those of Favara who have no idea of the power that lies in Palermo."

Cesare looked up, cocked his head to one side and then smiled knowingly. Lorenzo felt as if he had passed some sort of test.

"I will visit the capital soon, Lorenzo, and I'll extend an invitation to you to accompany me. There is much I have to learn."

That hit Lorenzo like a Judas kiss. Giuliano had put together a plan to have Gaspare murdered, with all the consequences that would follow, and here he was, offering the token of respect to a condemned man.

"Benedetto Carollo was weak and used the power of the fratellanza for revenge in a personal matter." These words were a bolt from the blue but welcome nonetheless, as Lorenzo had no idea how he would have touched on the subject of Galati's murder and how he felt tricked into committing it. "He lied to you, Lorenzo, and to Cosimo Mutolo when he said the new warden would be next to take the path leading to his death, at your hands."

"Forgive me," interrupted Lorenzo, "you said Benedetto *was* a weak man. Has he now become stronger because his employer has been murdered?"

Cesare smiled, but it wasn't laced with humour. For the first time Lorenzo could see the real menace that was embodied in the man beside him. That smile would have struck fear into Lucifer himself. "No, Lorenzo. Benedetto is not stronger because of this. He is dead, and his body will never be found. He has been eradicated from the memory of the fratellanza. I ordered it so this morning after hearing of Gaspare's death. Much as we hated the lemon grower from Rome, we had nothing to gain from his passing, and everything to lose. Benedetto used us for petty revenge and he was weak. I have no tolerance for such weakness. It can betray us, and we are only strong if we are one in the oath we have taken. If the omertá were broken by even the least of our number, it would betray us all. We are strong again and we will protect you, Lorenzo. No one will speak of Benedetto or Gaspare, because all who know the truth are men of honour, bound by the oath and their allegiance to me. Betray either and forfeit the pleasure of another sunrise." They had reached the edge of the small meadow and Cesare stopped, knelt down and gently stroked the petals of an orange calendula. He looked up at Lorenzo and the smile had morphed to one the Archangel Gabriel would have worn to an audience with the Good Lord himself. "Beautiful, isn't it? You know, they say the honey from around here tastes of the calendula: like sunshine."

Lorenzo's thoughts were performing a dizzying dance in his head. He hadn't been set up to kill Galati after all, but the lemon grower was dead and the carabinieri were no less a threat. He had the protection of the most powerful man in Girgenti, but that same man had been responsible for the clumsy execution of a plan that the fratellanza could still walk away from with only minor difficulties. And what then for Lorenzo Fratelli? "I've never eaten honey," he said, without thinking.

"Ah, but you will when you marry my daughter, and you will never taste anything so sweet."

Part Two

Vicaria Prison, Palermo, Sicily. 1865-1868

Chapter 8

The four-day sailing around the coast of Sicily, from Girgenti to Palermo, gave Tommaso di Bova a further taste of what prison life held in store for him after his short remand. Manacled in the hold of a small merchant-ship to twenty other prisoners, resplendent in their own filth and excrement, was a hell even more daunting than his days as caruso in the caverns of Ciavallotta. He took some comfort in the knowledge that he wouldn't have to endure prison for too long. The fratellanza had assured him of that. Yes, he was guilty of many petty crimes, as were all the lower ranks of the fratellanza. Prison was something of a rite of passage and this journey was Tommaso's own beginning.

Cosimo Mutolo's words echoed uncontrollably through his mind: *"There are a number of ways you can progress through the fratellanza. They all come down to the same thing: the more risk you take for your capo, the greater the reward."* In some ways, those words were a comfort; in other ways they now looked like the text of an empty promise.

The rail-yard boss at Girgenti had been reduced to a mental imbecile by the beating delivered by Cesare Giuliano. It was a punishment from which he would never recover. His only crime was one of failing to ensure Giuliano's rail wagons got first priority on the overnight freight to Marsala. It wasn't just the inconvenience of late deliveries that irked Giuliano into merciless violence – it was the humiliation of being openly faced down by someone he couldn't bribe or coerce by other means. He had to put down the insult and do it personally. Killing the rail-yard boss wasn't the plan; reducing him to a vegetable was. The fratellanza victim would be seen every day on the streets of Girgenti, as he shuffled with the gait of a cripple and drooled onto his waistcoat. "There goes the man who dared defy Giuliano," they would say.

And no one would make the same mistake again.

It didn't work out that way. An imbecile the mutilated rail-yard boss might have been, but he could still identify his attacker in a line up. Giuliano's legal team had devalued that significantly before the trial, but there was always a doubt the jury would side with the cripple. It was too close to call, and even the sniff of Giuliano trying to bribe any of the jurors would have sealed his fate. It was time for someone else to take the fall and Tommaso was nominated. Of course he could have refused, but no one had ever risen through the fratellanza's ranks without a stint in their university: Vicaria Prison. The deal was simple: Tommaso would be identified as the attacker by a turncoat, a *pentito* who would agree to testify against the fratellanza in return for immunity from prosecution. It was all a convenient set-up and the pentito would eventually retract his statement and Tommaso would be released. That would take about a year, maybe two, but a lot less than the ten-year sentence on which Tommaso was now embarking.

Tommaso just hadn't expected it all to progress so quickly. Within a few days of agreeing to the deal, he found himself facing the local magistrate with Antonio Ruddini, the pentito, giving sworn testimony about the fate of the rail-yard boss and Tommaso's sole part in it. Tommaso pleaded guilty and was sentenced to ten years without so much as a second's hesitation. He never even had time to say a final good-bye to Maria. Her father had forbidden her to visit him in jail whilst awaiting his hearing, but he might as well have forbidden the Sirocco to blow in spring.

For now, Tommaso could only cling to the promises he had been made by his capo and by Maria. One was resolute in assuring him of his freedom, the other was equally steadfast in claiming she would love him forever and wait two, ten or twenty years for his return. Tommaso hoped both promises could be relied on.

The journey across the interior of Sicily was only slightly more dangerous than the two hundred and sixty kilometre circuit of the north-western waters of the island, but only because of the fear of the prisoners' convoy being attacked on the treacherous roads of the Sicilian interior. The convenience and security of an unbroken rail-link from Girgenti to Palermo was still a year or more away, so the Prison Authorities had continued to transport their charges to Vicaria Prison in Palermo, by ship. The three-masted Xebec, on which Tommaso sailed, would have gone to the bottom with only the slightest encouragement from a major storm, of which there were plenty in these waters. Still, the ship was light and fast. It wallowed like a bloated turd when the wind kicked up and smelt not dissimilar, but it made the journey relatively quickly.

Finally, after rounding the headland at Addaura, Palermo hove into view some eight kilometres south and the dishevelled gang, to which Tommaso was joined at the ankle by heavy chain, was manhandled out onto the deck. The air was sharp with stinging salt, made worse by the sudden exposure to the bright glare of the sun, and Tommaso squinted as he watched the lead prisoner released from the chain and cuffed in individual leg irons. This prisoner was then stripped of his rags and these were thrown overboard, where even the squawking gulls avoided the stinking jetsam. The prison guards then set about their victim with buckets of cold water and soap-charged deck scrubbers until the poor wretch was cleaned of the dirt and excrement caked on his body. Any sores and pustules were vigorously worked at until they burst, whereupon a dousing in sea water was followed by a liberal dose of carbolic acid to cauterise the wound.

The ritual continued with its associated howls of pain until Tommaso had his own baptism of sea water and stinging disinfectant. He uttered not a sound but fixed all his pain in a menacing stare, focussed on his tormentors. They were singularly unimpressed and Tommaso knew something fundamental had changed. He was just another wretch, powerless to do anything. Whatever fear he struck into others during his days of freedom, would remain impotent during his incarceration.

The Xebec was little more than a raft of rotted timbers sailing in close formation, but it had borne another collection of prisoners on its fortnightly run to Palermo. Tommaso could feel that the entire procedure was made perfect by rote, and the scrubbing down they had all endured was just another part of the conveyance of wretches, doomed to incarceration in Sicily's toughest prison. What surprised him was the return of some of his belongings, confiscated when he was imprisoned after sentencing. This even extended to include his purse and the thick bundle of lire contained in it, although Tommaso reckoned it was lighter by a small sum. He would check this later but there was little he could do if some money had been liberated along the way.

"You'll need every lira of that in Vicaria," said the prisoner seated beside him on the deck. Tommaso turned to see he was a barrel-chested brawler who wouldn't be out of place in a bare-knuckle fight. Gaps in his teeth, cauliflower ears and a broken nose that seemed to point sideways, all supported this idea. Until now everyone Tommaso had been manacled to, had been just an anonymous wretch with no identity and no dignity. The latter was still in short supply, but following the tortuous cleaning and issue of new prison uniforms, at least his companions started to resemble men again.

"They call me Giotto," said the brawler.

"I'm Tommaso. Why will I need so much money in a prison?"

"You can buy anything you want in Vicaria, except your freedom," replied Giotto. "But that means everything has a price. If you can't pay for your bed, you sleep in a puddle of shit with the rats. If you can't pay for your food then the rats are your supper."

"How long will this last?" asked Tommaso, holding up the thick bundle of lire.

"Not as long as your sentence, so you'll need funds sent in. But that should be easy for one of the brotherhood."

"Sounds like the prison authorities have learned some lessons from the fratellanza," responded Tommaso with a smile.

Giotto looked at him and laughed. It wasn't mirth. It was derision. "You know of nothing outside Favara; do you, caruso? Palermo is home to powerful families who could snuff out the life of every one of the fratellanza's blood line. They are the greatest of all Sicily's men of honour. They control Vicaria and every single lira flowing through Palermo and the northern coast."

"They cannot be men of honour," replied Tommaso with a sniff, "or I would know of them. They must be different."

"They are different but they are the same."

"When men talk in riddles, it's usually because they don't have answers." Tommaso looked at Giotto and returned the malevolent stare he received.

"Do not insult a man of honour from Palermo. I have been imprisoned in Vicaria before," replied Giotto, and Tommaso couldn't fail to notice the threatening tone. "You have much to learn, caruso, if you live long enough. Where you're going you've no protection, other than your own cunning. Survive, and you will understand the real strength of the oath you took back in that small taverna."

A hundred questions rushed to seek their answers, but before Tommaso could ask any, Giotto had shuffled off to sit close to the guard. The conversation was over, for now.

The Xebec cleared the harbour wall amidst a flutter of furling sails and glided slowly towards a small jetty, atop of which sat a steam engine and a few carriages. Tommaso was fascinated by the wheezing thump and occasional hiss of the machinery he could hear as they drew closer. Mixed with the fresh Mediterranean sea-breeze, the pungent whiff of burning coal and hot oil brought a sense of excitement that momentarily eradicated his despair. It was a brutal irony that his first journey on a steam railway would be one that led him to prison. His daydreaming was interrupted by the appearance of the commander of the guards who had been in charge of the prisoners since their departure from Girgenti. He had proven to be a vicious and sadistic bastard throughout the journey, and his appearance now in a pristine dress-uniform did nothing to mitigate the feelings of hatred, expressed in quiet mutterings, amongst Tommaso's new-found companions.

They started to listen whilst the commander explained what would happen next. Suddenly, the realisation of their fate became paramount. Within minutes the group of freshly-scrubbed prisoners would be behind bars in Vicaria Prison. This was the last they would feel of the stinging salt-air on their faces and the final time they could watch the squawking gulls descend on a tasty morsel floating in the clear Mediterranean waters of the harbour. To a man, they blocked out the commander's ranting and harvested the memories that would become a store of comfort for the duration of their respective sentences. In Tommaso's case, the memories might have to last ten years. For the first time he started to doubt the ability of the fratellanza to make good on their promise. How could they organise his liberation from this prison citadel? It was a massive stone fortress that had served as a jail for the last sixty years. He forced the horrors of such a failure from his mind and zoned in on the commander's detailed instructions on disembarkation and the subsequent transfer to La Vicaria.

The Xebec gently nudged against the wall of the jetty and a rope ladder was flung onto the deck, along with fore and aft moorings. When these were secured, and the battered wooden hull abraded more of its rotten timbers against the granite of the jetty, a guard climbed the rope ladder and stood above Tommaso, pointing his rifle downwards. Tommaso was told to follow. The climb to the top would have been easy without the encumbrance of a set of leg irons that seemed determined to drag him off the ladder and send him to his death, crushed between the hull of the Xebec and the side of the jetty. Eventually he made it, along with his other ramshackle companions. They were immediately herded onto the last of the passenger carriages attached to the small steam-train that provided regular service on the *Ferrovia di Circonvallazione*: the narrow-gauge railway that ran around the periphery of Palermo.

Once aboard, and with the hoot of a pathetic whistle, the small train shuffled along its track for no more than the length of the pier before stopping at *Stazione Molo*, where fifty or so dock workers boarded. Tommaso wondered if the brisk scrubbing and issue of fresh clothing on board the Xebec would have been made, were it not for the prisoners' exposure to the travelling public. He looked at the stevedores and longshoremen, and they seemed to read the despair in his face. No one spoke, but Tommaso could see it in their eyes: *"Life is hard, but we are not the men furthest down. We go home to eat our pasta, and tonight we will enjoy the taverna. You will have a stale crust and a tin mug to rattle against the bars of your cage."*

Another feeble hoot of the whistle interrupted Tommaso's daydreaming, as the train clattered into the blackness of a tunnel before emerging back into the sharp Sicilian sunlight and shuddering to a halt in the open of Piazza Ucciardone. There was no platform, just the expanse of the piazza and a line of prison guards, all armed, forming a corridor to the fortress door of Tommaso's next home.

The butter-coloured turrets and walls of La Vicaria stood like sentinels above Piazza Ucciardone, their strength a testament to the security they provided to the city. The clear killing ground across the open piazza to the sea was a legacy of one hundred years of preparation for siege and invasion; some of it in vain. Now, the protection of the thick walls was directed inwards:

keeping those on the outside safe from those on the inside. The irony of the switch in roles was almost enough to raise a smile on Tommaso's lips as he looked down the line of blue uniforms to the battlements, topped with yet more prison guards, all armed and all pointing weapons in his direction.

The dock workers hung their heads and avoided eye contact as Tommaso jumped from the carriage to join the rest of his doomed companions. The walk through the cordon of guards was probably more to do with instilling confidence in the good citizens of Palermo than striking fear into the newly-arrived prisoners, but the effect was devastating nonetheless. Behind him, the train departed with another asthmatic hoot from its whistle. It was a sound he knew he would hear every day of his incarceration: a constant reminder of those stevedores and longshoremen who, whatever the hardship of their employment, could still enjoy the pleasures of a family and the sun on their faces when it suited them.

When the prison gate clanged shut behind him, Tommaso knew his world had changed. His mind retreated in search of a sanctuary and found it in the memories of Ciavallotta. He was back in the hell-hole of the mine, but this time the air was sweet and he didn't have to carry his own weight of sulphur in a wicker basket on his back. Those blessings must be a bonus?

The group of prisoners found themselves in an open courtyard, just beyond the gate. Tommaso watched as some sort of handover took place between the prison guards and those who had commanded him on the Xebec. Some papers were exchanged; the leg irons were then removed and handed back to the Xebec contingent, who seemed eager to leave without further delay.

Under command of their new masters, Tommaso and his group were escorted through another clanging door that shouted its presence as an insurmountable barrier to their freedom. Tommaso had never seen a structure of such size and complexity as Vicaria, and his next view of the prison was a long, outdoor piazza, bordered by high walls in that same butter-coloured stone, topped with armed guards. The open space was featureless and could have been a parade ground, an exercise yard or even a killing ground for those who tried to escape. After walking about one hundred metres, the contingent was ordered to stop facing yet another heavily-armoured door that slid open with a creak of protest to reveal a different courtyard and the front of a circular building. Yet more doors and corridors, bordered with green-painted steel mesh, led though the building to exit into a circular piazza whose cobbled surface was segmented in arcs: like pieces of a pie. The circumference of each arc led to the inner wall of the circular building, terminating at a metal door.

Tommaso had walked less than two hundred metres, from the world outside to the inner reaches of the prison, and had already traversed five bulwarks between the freedom he knew and already coveted, to a reality he now feared. There could be no reprieve from this hell-hole, fratellanza or no fratellanza.

The commander of the prison guards barked a series of orders and Tommaso's group was divided into two, each herded onto one of the arcs. At the bark of a further command, the doors in the boundary wall at the end of each arc opened. Tommaso's group marched in and the door clanged shut behind them. Tommaso looked back, and to his surprise the guards were left outside, on the other side of the door. His group of prisoners stood alone in a wide corridor with buttressed walls covered in glazed tiles of green and cream. The tiled floor was similarly covered but this time in white, and every tiny centimetre looked as if it had been scrubbed to a Godly cleanliness just minutes before their arrival. A faint smell of carbolic acid hung in the air and brought back memories of their last experience with the stinging disinfectant, on board the Xebec; some even flinched involuntarily at the recollection.

A voice broke the silence as it echoed off the tiled floors and walls.

"Men of honour, and those not so privileged, welcome to A wing."

From behind one of the buttresses, the owner of the voice appeared and Tommaso almost laughed out loud at what he saw. This was not a prison guard, at least not according to his dress. Rather, this looked like one of the pimps he had seen on the streets of Girgenti. The stranger sported the finest attire, which comprised striped, blue trousers whose flared bottoms splayed over black and white leather spats. A cream waistcoat, with assorted gold chains hanging from its many pockets, was perfectly tailored to lie below a navy-blue tail coat with brass buttons. The ensemble was topped off with a frilled, open-neck shirt, partially concealing a patterned silk cravat, pinned with a gold brooch.

The stranger walked slowly towards the incredulous group, swinging his silver-topped walking stick and sucking on a cheroot. He paused to look the prisoners up and down, blowing small clouds of pungent smoke in their direction and clicking the tip of his walking stick on the tiled floor as he moved forward. When he walked past Tommaso, there was a waft of tobacco mixed with the sickly perfume of bay rum that seemed to emanate from the perfectly cropped mane of black hair. This was obviously coiffed to a particular style: one that Tommaso could only describe as a butterfly cut and this only increased the mirth he felt on seeing this strange figure of a man.

Something told him not to laugh out loud.

That misfortune fell to one of the other prisoners, standing just beside Giotto, who was part of Tommaso's group.

The stranger addressed the laughing prisoner, who singularly failed to understand why no one else could see the joke.

"I wish I could be so happy," said the stranger. "But I am troubled with this toothache. It started in Naples five years ago and has bothered me ever since."

Tommaso was stunned. The toothache routine was one of the secret ways the fratellanza had of recognising another man of honour, and here it was being used by this buffoon who could only be the spawn of a pimp and a whore.

The grinning prisoner to whom the remark was addressed could only respond with more mockery, not recognising the clandestine greeting. The stranger seemed unperturbed and moved on to stop in front of Giotto.

"My dear Giotto, I have mixed feelings on seeing you here again. I trust you understand my discomfort with this toothache?"

"Indeed I do," replied Giotto. "I am similarly afflicted. Mine started six years ago, also in Naples."

"And where exactly in Naples was this, and who was present at the time?"

Giotto reeled off a list of names along with that of a piazza; none of them meant anything to Tommaso.

"My honoured friend," said the stranger to Giotto, "I trust you will perform the same duties for me on this occasion as you provided on your last visit here?"

"It would be a privilege to do so," said Giotto.

"Very well, you may start with laughing-boy here."

Tommaso watched as Giotto stepped out of line and faced his victim, who still wore a smirk on his face. That smirk became the last staging post for a charging fist that hit it with the force of a stampede of horses. Blood and tissue erupted from the clash of fist and face to spatter against the green and cream walls, punctuated by the sound of bits of broken teeth pinging off the glazed tiles of the floor. The only other sound was that of 'laughing-boy' collapsing, pole-axed.

"My name is Silvio," said the well-dressed stranger. "I trust I have your attention."

Tommaso stood stock still, like the rest of his companions, as fear replaced mirth in their ranks.

"I am A Block's Commander," continued Silvio. "I am not one of the prison staff, but I make sure the block is peaceful, clean and ordered. For these services, we are all rewarded with privileges not granted to other prisoners. We have our own taverna, a grocery store with the best victuals Palermo has to offer, and for those who can afford it, the opportunity to relieve your sexual frustrations on some of the finest whores in the city."

Tommaso looked at Giotto, who stood like a colossus beside his master. He remembered what the barrel-chested brawler had said about the men of honour being the same, yet different.

"Shortly, you will proceed to the prison stores where you'll be kitted out with bedding, clothing and other conveniences," continued Silvio. "As it is on the outside, so it is here. The more you pay, the more you receive." Silvio pulled two fresh cheroots from one of the many pockets in his waistcoat. He handed them both to Giotto, along with a Lundstrom match and received a lit smoke in return. His henchman waited for Silvio to take the first puff and then savoured his own cheroot as if it were a returning lover. "Giotto here will take payment for the protection I provide in A block, starting now. He will seek each of you out on a weekly basis to continue with this arrangement." Silvio walked over to the toothless and bleeding victim of Giotto's devastating punch, just as the poor wretch was coming to. "Of course, if you no longer wish for my protection, then you can refuse to pay." With that he kicked the prostrate prisoner with a force sufficient to defer his return to consciousness for another few hours.

By the time Tommaso made it through to the prison stores his bundle of lire was lighter by a considerable amount. The number in his group also diminished, as those who had no stock of cash seemed to have left the scene. Tommaso stood with his toes against a yellow line, a few metres from a long bench where blankets, straw-filled palliasses, tin mugs and other prison items were being handed out by trustees. On either side he was hemmed in by steel mesh panels, painted in the same green and cream that seemed to define the drabness that was Vicaria. After more lire was liberated from his stash, he was ushered forward from the confines of the mesh corridor to his pile of prison-issue clothing and other accoutrements piled high on a line of benches. He lifted these and made to leave the confines of the prison stores for A Wing, but a shout from a trustee stopped him.

"Wait, you forgot these."

Tommaso stopped. As he turned and reached out across the last bench for a pair of heavy socks, he looked straight into the one good eye of Toto. That fixed stare and an almost imperceptible shake of the head from the old Ciavallotta mule-herder put paid to any exclamations of recognition from Tommaso. As he took the socks he could feel the unmistakable crinkle of a piece of paper inside one of them.

Chapter 9

The wooden sign hanging outside the storeroom was crudely fashioned and hung by a piece of twine on a bent hook. Tommaso could see it had no sense of permanence, and this was something that seemed to distinguish the structures of the men of honour from those of the authorities. Vicaria as a prison was an immovable edifice that overwhelmed its inmates by the solidity of its stonework, but its rules and strictures, which seemed just as resolute as its masonry, were nonetheless permeable.

He looked again at the sign: "Taverna Ucciardone" it proclaimed, as if in a taunt to those who wouldn't see the piazza just outside until they were finally released from their miserable incarceration. Below this legend lay the intricate carving of a snake, which meant nothing to Tommaso. He pulled the sign to the side, as instructed on the scribbled note given to him by Toto, and shoved the required number of lire through the exposed hole in the brickwork. The door opened after a few seconds and he was quickly ushered inside.

The small room into which he stumbled was thick with the smoke of cheroots and crammed with a heaving mass of bodies, who seemed to co-exist with a discipline that was lacking in the rest of the prison. Their carousing was loud but not threatening, and tankards of wine were passed from table to table with barely a drop spilt. The crowd was so great that it seemed impossible for the room to permit another occupant unless some of the walls were removed. Tommaso was barely able to walk more than a few steps without having to negotiate an impossibly narrow path between tables, constructed from upturned barrels, and crude wooden stools occupied by noisy and drunken inmates, who nonetheless conducted themselves with the utmost civility.

Silvio spotted him from behind one of the arched pillars that supported the low, vaulted ceiling. He tapped his silver-topped cane three times on the tiled floor and the chattering cascaded into silence.

"Gentlemen," said the elegantly dressed commander. "May I introduce you to Tommaso di Bova? He is a friend of ours. His family are of the fratellanza, from the Girgenti region. Make him feel welcome in your own time." The noisy chatter erupted anew as Silvio navigated the crowded space with the elegance of a dancer, to arrive at Tommaso's side.

"May I show you to a seat?" asked Silvio.

"You can find one?" queried Tommaso, looking around and seeing nowhere free.

"Would you like to buy a place for tonight, the week, or for the duration of your stay?"

When Giotto told him everything had a price, Tommaso didn't understand that 'everything' meant anything of value, and those values belonged to a different world on the inside of Vicaria's walls. Silvio, or whatever controlling group he belonged to, had spent an age mastering a strategy to take money from the inmates. It was just another version of gold from fleas. Tommaso agreed the purchase of a seat for a week, on the condition he could pick his own. Within seconds of handing over the payment he found himself sitting beside Toto in a dark and unfashionable corner of Taverna Ucciardone.

The old mule-herder seemed to find shadows were a natural home and he all but disappeared in the dark recess of the crowded room. There could be no privacy in such a confined space, but Toto seemed to draw Tommaso into the gloom when he beckoned with a barely perceptible nod.

"Are we free to talk?" asked Tommaso.

"Nothing leaves the taverna," replied Toto. "It's why I asked you here. We will talk uninterrupted if you lay down some lire for a few tankards of Marsala."

Tommaso peeled off some more notes from his rapidly

depleting pile of cash and pushed them across the table.

"You do have your own tankard; don't you?" asked Toto.

Tommaso sighed and pushed another few lire in the old mule-herder's direction.

After a few whistles and shouts, two tankards arrived, filled with the sweet wine that seemed to be the taverna's staple beverage.

Toto quaffed a good half of his drink before turning to Tommaso. "You would do well to respect Silvio. As long as you are here, your life stops at the walls of A Block, and he controls everything inside. How you live and how you die is down to him."

"He looks like a pimp," replied Tommaso. "He wouldn't last ten minutes in Favara."

"He is of Mastrosso."

"Never heard of them," said Tommaso.

"Osso, Mastrosso and Carcagnosso," replied Toto as he looked at Tommaso with his one good eye. "You must've heard of the legend."

"I haven't."

"Then listen carefully. To admit you know nothing of the founders of the honoured societies is enough to ensure your tongue is cut out and shoved up your arse. First, lay some more money down."

Tommaso did as he was bid and the story began on full tankards.

"Long before even the Kingdom of the Two Sicilies, three Spanish Knights landed on the small island of Favignana. You would've passed it on your journey here."

"It was very remiss of our captain not to mention it," replied Tommaso.

The cynicism was lost on Toto and he continued. "The knights were banished from Spain after wreaking vengeful retribution on a nobleman who had raped one of their sisters. As fugitives, the knights hid on Favignana for almost thirty years. In that time they created what they believed would be a new order: one where honour and brotherhood would replace privilege and inherited wealth. The knights were Osso, Mastrosso and Carcagnosso. The order they created would become the basis of our honoured societies. After they decided their thirty-year exile was over, Osso travelled the short distance to Sicily and established the brotherhood to which the fratellanza now belong: *cosa nostra*. Carcagnosso journeyed through Sicily and crossed the straits of Medina to Calabria, where he founded *'ndranghetta*. Mastrosso sailed to Naples and established the *camorra*."

"All different, yet all the same," said Tommaso, recalling what Giotto had told him as they sailed into Palermo harbour.

"Yes, Tommaso, Silvio is of Mastrosso but is as true to the brotherhood as you are. To a *camorrista*, style and visible wealth are signs of success. They happily embrace prostitution as part of their business. These are things you will learn to respect, even though they are somehow wrong to those whose values were inherited from Osso."

"And Carcagnosso; what of the order he founded?"

"The *'ndrine* have a saying: 'what doesn't kill me makes me stronger.' Many have tried to wipe them out, all have failed. They are the most secretive of all the brotherhoods; they even have their own language."

"Grecanico," responded Tommaso.

Toto looked at him open-mouthed. "Yes, it's mainly Greek. How'd you know that?"

"My father is from Calabria," said Tommaso. "When I was young he used to sing me the songs of his childhood in Aspromonte and recite the legends of the region, all in Grecanico. I leaned to understand some of it."

"Don't think that will find you any favours in here, Tommaso. Beware those of Carcagnosso: the cattle rustlers of Calabria, the 'ndrine. Everyone in Vicaria fears them."

"Even Silvio?"

"Yes, even Silvio, but the Calabrians know the rules. Each block is controlled by one of the honoured societies. B Block is Osso: our Sicilian Cosa Nostra and C Block is Carcagnosso: the 'ndranghetta."

"Then why am I in A Block with the camorrista?"

"Because those who run Vicaria aren't stupid, Tommaso. Each block has a controlled population, drawn from all three regions. This mix ensures no single brotherhood becomes dominant. Even the block commanders get swapped around regularly, if they live long enough."

As interesting as the old mule-herder's story was, Tommaso was more concerned with how he was going to get out of Vicaria, rather than spend time learning its idiosyncrasies. He pulled his rickety chair further into the dark recess. "How did you get to be locked up in here?" he asked of Toto.

"I was brought here because of what I knew about the death of Gaspare Galati," he said, in an answer to Tommaso's last question. "I had nothing to do with his murder but I knew who did. The Notarbartolo pickmen could have killed me to keep me quiet, but they needed someone to blame for another crime. I was given a choice: confess to something I didn't do, or measure my length at the bottom of Ciavallotta's main shaft. I was in the cells in Favara, within the hour."

"No one spoke of this," said Tommaso, shaking his head in disbelief. "You just disappeared."

"They told me my mules would be cared for if I confessed." Toto looked hard at Tommaso, and for the first time ever he could see sadness and concern in the old mule-herder's eyes.

"Rest easy, my friend. When they installed the steam engines at Caltanisetta, they brought the mule-herder from there, and his mules. Barbara was fine last time I saw her."

Toto reached across and put a leathery hand on top of Tommaso's. "Thank you," he said, his voice an emotional croak.

Another slug of Marsala seemed to compose him, and he continued: "Tommaso, you're here because of Maria, and so am I."

"You're drunk, old man, and you miss your mules. I'm here because I admitted to beating a rail-yard boss near to death and taking bribes to ensure rail wagons were loaded with Cesare Giuliano's goods before any others. Giuliano himself committed those crimes but I admitted to them and took the sentence for my family boss."

"You thought you could undertake the *fuitina* with the daughter of the *rappresentante*: the head of all fratellanza in Girgenti? You were a fool to believe Cesare Giuliano would let this go unpunished."

"I saved Giuliano from arrest," protested Tommaso. "That's why I'm here. He had no animosity towards me after the fuitina. It's just an old custom: for the amusement of chattering grandmothers. Kidnap a woman who is promised to another, and then bring her back the following day; fuitina over and the woman is yours. It's a game, and the woman is always a willing player."

"I warned you when I read Maria's letter, and you didn't listen. You've learnt nothing from the oath you took, Tommaso. Blood ties are second only to the blood oath for a man of honour. The kidnap is not the shame of the fuitina. It's the lingering doubt that forever hangs over the woman's honour, even if you did nothing."

The accusation was left unsaid but it hung in the fetid air between them, waiting to stain its victim with a mark that only death could remove. Try as he might to hide it, Tommaso was sure the glint of pleasure in his eyes would betray the lie he now attempted to foist on Toto. "I didn't need to do anything, old man, just bring her back alive." Even as he spoke and averted his gaze to a neutral corner, the memories of making love to Maria rushed back at him, all the more poignant because of their separation.

He had prepared the old shepherd's croft as best he could for their one-night stay: the flimsy wooden bed that collapsed in a heap under the first onslaught of their passion, the small fire and the tallow candle that illuminated her simple beauty, the supper of wine, bread and cheese that had never tasted so good, and the soft warmth of a woollen blanket to swaddle the heat of their entwined bodies. The vibrant memories controlled his body as surely as a puppeteer controls a marionette and betrayed him to Toto.

"You dumb bastard, Tommaso," said the old mule-herder. "Maria was promised to Lorenzo Fratelli. Giuliano had his reasons for marrying his daughter to one of Palermo's own, and you fucked him over as surely as you fucked his daughter. Fratelli begged to be allowed to kill you."

"I would have welcomed the challenge if he'd tried, and Maria would never have married him; he's an ignorant oaf."

"Maria would've done as she was bid, and Giuliano would've let Fratelli kill you the instant you returned to Favara with his daughter, were it not for the shame she would have to bear. There was one other solution and Giuliano took it: have you locked up in here for the rest of your days."

Tommaso sat in stunned silence, his mind assembling a foggy jigsaw whose pieces locked together all too easily, forming an increasingly distinct picture of the next ten years of his life. "How do you know this?" he asked.

"You've a gift for asking the wrong questions, Tommaso. You made the same mistake when they suggested you go to prison for a crime you didn't commit. Oh yes, they promised you a rapid rise through the ranks of the fratellanza; didn't they?"

"Yes," replied Tommaso, barely able to raise his voice above a croak, as he considered the depth of his despair. "They would have the best legal representatives appeal my case. The pentito who squealed on me would later admit he was mistaken. It would take about a year."

"Hah, this place is filled with those who were promised the same deal."

The numbers in the makeshift taverna had dwindled since Tommaso first entered, and the carousing was settling down into quiet chatter. Silvio was still at his post, fidgeting slightly as if in anticipation of something. Tommaso sat in stunned silence, like a man who has just been given a death sentence.

"It will be lock-up in just a few minutes," continued Toto. "It's better you leave before Giotto throws you out. He sometimes forgets to open the door."

Tommaso was prepared to take his chances with Silvio's henchman and the door, for as long as it took to get an answer to the question foremost on his mind.

"I'm here for ten years. They won't free me?"

"You won't last ten years, Tommaso. Giuliano will give it a few months for Favara to forget about you and then he'll have you killed, probably for the price of the bar stool you just paid to sit on."

"Maria won't forget about me," said Tommaso, as if this was the one talisman that could ward off the evil that Toto was predicting.

"What Maria remembers or forgets doesn't matter. After the fuitina, marriage wasn't the only option that would preserve her honour. You were arrested by the hated carabinieri and imprisoned. All Favara knew of your sacrifice, and they will remember you in toasts in the tavernas, but only for a while. Soon there'll be another arrest and another local hero. Then they'll forget you. Giuliano will know when your name ceases to be spoken in the piazzas and the Blessed Virgin no longer hears pleas for her intervention. Then you're a dead man."

Tommaso sat stunned, staring at the floor and feeling the beginnings of a pounding headache, which he feared would last for the next ten years. It had all seemed to start so well in the back of that little taverna. The oath, the wealth, the influence: all played their part in seeming to set him on a road where even the spoils of a pickman would be measly pickings. Maria's letter changed all that. The fuitina was her idea and Toto had known of it. "Toto, you could get a message to Giuliano. You could explain the fuitina was his daughter's idea. She couldn't have married Lorenzo and she was trying to offer her father a way out."

Toto sighed and stared at the depleted contents of his tankard before wiping some of the sweet, sticky Marsala from his chin with the back of his hand and turning to face Tommaso. "Listen to yourself. You sound like a whimpering dog."

There was a glint that shone from Toto's one good eye like a beacon. Even in the dark recess of the taverna, Tommaso didn't miss it; he just failed to understand it.

"You have two choices, Tommaso: curl up and cry yourself to a pitiful sleep every night in some dank corner of Vicaria, or learn how to take control of the little dignity you have left and become a prison legend. Either way, you'll probably die without seeing the outside of these walls again. How you go, is up to you: with your mangy tail between your legs, or defending your turf in a fight to the death." With that, Toto lifted his tankard and left.

Chapter 10

The hardened wax from the tallow candle seemed trapped in time, like an insect imprisoned in amber. Its creamy trail spilt down the leg of the rickety wooden bed that had collapsed under their combined rhythm and pooled on the floor of the deserted shepherd's croft. The empty wine bottle lay where they had discarded it. They were ever grateful for the release of their last inhibitions, provided by its content. To her family and many of those in Favara, the fuitina was an uncomfortable memory made increasingly distant by the three seasons that had passed. To Maria Giuliano it was as poignant and bright as the sunrise that chased scurrying shadows westwards down the valley below.

She sat on the remains of the bed and looked out on the view, towards Favara and on to San Leone and the sea in the distance. It was less than five kilometres from her home, yet all of her father's cohorts couldn't find them that night. Had they done so, Tommaso would not have lived, yet there was eventual punishment for his sins: imprisonment in Vicaria, made all the more painful by his willing complicity in her father's plan. At the time it seemed the right thing to do, and she had never before questioned the ways of the fratellanza. The constant conflict with her father was one thing, but Maria was able to maintain the clear distinction between his rules and those of the dynasty he controlled, right up until he exiled her lover. In the months since Tommaso's imprisonment, it had become clear that the fratellanza's determination to free him had all but vanished, like the pockets of morning mist evicted from their night-time hollows around the distant San Leone.

The town of Favara talked to Maria with a voice that was the chatter of its inhabitants. In the piazzas and streets, gossip was a living, breathing entity that accompanied coy whispers and guttural laughs, depending on the content. The more reserved comments tended to focus on illicit liaisons, whilst the overt and noisy reporting of life dwelt on the ridicule of itinerant labour and ribald comments about shepherds and sheep. Somewhere in between was the serious stuff: the gossip that was news – news of births, marriages and deaths, and here in the heartland of the fratellanza, those who had been captured by the forces of the law. There was no sympathy for the polizia and the carabinieri; they were the instruments a dictatorial government in Naples used to suppress the poor.

When Tommaso was first arrested, there was violence in the streets as the people turned on the forces of the law, attacking the barracks of the local polizia and even the arma dei carabinieri. Those were brave moves and Maria could remember the fratellanza soldiers coming to the house for orders from her father, as to the next phases of the campaign to protest Tommaso's innocence.

She was so proud of them all back then.

Within a few days the violence was turned off like a tap but Tommaso's name continued to be revered and was a toast to every tankard of ale raised in the tavernas of the town. His pickaxe was hoisted above the entrance to the mine, and all who passed it, from carusi to overseers, stopped and blessed themselves, whilst whispering a prayer to the Blessed Virgin on his behalf. Masses were held, collections raised and candles lit. Even the shadow of the fuitina was lifted as Maria's status was raised to that of a minor deity.

That was three seasons ago, and in that time there was no news of Tommaso. Her father made lame excuses about the difficulty in getting news from inside Vicaria. She didn't even know if Tommaso was alive or dead. The pickaxe had been taken down from the entrance to the mine, and toasts in the tavernas were to another one of the fratellanza who had fallen foul of the dictators in Naples and the law enforced by their tyrants. The gossip hadn't ceased, and Maria's name was still to the forefront, only now the talk was of her relationship with Lorenzo Fratelli. He was a thug and an ugly brute. Maria wanted nothing to do with him, but her father's not so subtle manipulation of her life was insidious and unstoppable, or it would be if she didn't do something about it, again. The first attempt at that ill-fated match making had been thwarted by the fuitina, but Cesare Giuliano didn't give up easily. How convenient then that Tommaso was out of the picture and unable to honour the marriage mandated by his actions.

Maria picked at the tallow wax and threw the little, hard globules at the wine bottle, waiting to hear a ping for every successful hit. There were three problems she had to resolve: Tommaso, Lorenzo and her father. The chain of events started with Tommaso's incarceration. Without that, neither of the other two problems would exist. Someone was guilty of the crime of beating the rail-yard boss to a pulp and had to pay with the loss of their liberty. It was either her father, or Tommaso. That seemed intractable, so she sought another solution. Lorenzo had killed Gaspare Galati, and it had been at her father's command. Cesare might have been the head of all fratellanza in the Girgenti region, but being cautious about the affairs of the dynasty stopped at the door of the family home. Inside its walls, her father talked freely to those he trusted and didn't give a damn if his wife and children overheard.

The hours passed as she considered how best to tackle the poisoned chalice she had inherited. No one else would free Tommaso and no one else could annul the relationship her father and a willing Lorenzo Fratelli were building into her future. There was no talk yet of marriage to the ugly oaf from Palermo, but as long as those two problems remained in lockstep, she was doomed. Her goal must be to break the vicious circle and get rid of Fratelli.

It was late in the afternoon and hunger seemed to sharpen her concentration. Maria left the croft and kicked her horse in the direction of Favara, with a small glimmer of an idea of where to start on her quest.

* * *

She had no right to be there, and the encroaching darkness robbed Maria of the little courage she had summed up to make the journey in the first place. She had sneaked into the servants' storage-lockers and took some of the dirtiest clothing she could find in the hope that she could pass for a local. That diversion had taken time and now the only lights to guide her were the colourless wash of the full moon and the flickering candles outside the hovels on the edge of town. The menagerie of half-starved animals wandered from dwelling to dwelling. Dogs yelped at the slightest provocation and chickens scratched and scraped forlornly amongst the sharp tailings, making up the uneven path that threatened to see her tumble at every hesitant step. Her attire didn't help to hide her from the accusing stares of those who clustered in the shadows. They said nothing, as if waiting for the bravest of their number to make the first challenge and block Maria's way. It would only take one, and the rest would act like the vicious pack of animals they were.

She had made the journey before, but it was on horseback, during the previous winter when the wretches who occupied the meagre dwellings had sought shelter from the cold and rain. It was a simple task back then: deliver the letter and get away before anyone could see her, or apprehend her. Now she had to spend some time here, time to understand where she might look for a way to free her lover and remove the spectre of Lorenzo Fratelli from her life. There could only be one ally in her quest.

Tommaso's mother sat with her single goat at the end of a long lane of misery: the last of the stone hovels.

"You might try and hide your pale and delicate skin behind those rags, my dear, but the smell of your perfume gives you away."

His mother was a formidable old bitch. Somehow, Maria had to earn her respect and her trust. She was the only route Maria could take to finding out more about the secrets of the underworld of which she was part but understood so little about.

"Then you know, old woman, that it's the same perfume I used on the letter I pushed under your door three seasons ago. The same letter that brought your son back to you."

"Aye; and where is he now? Palermo Jail, thanks to you and your kin. You've no place here; daughter of the rappresentante or not. You're but a whore to the fratellanza. Get out whilst those rags still cling to your soft skin. There are plenty here who would take great pleasure in unmasking you and sampling the delights of your pampered flesh. Cesare Giuliano is not the only one who can make bodies disappear."

Fear and panic fought to be first in the queue to assail what little courage Maria had left. She had to turn this around and quickly. "The fuitina was my idea. It was in the letter I brought to you. There was no other way of getting the message to Tommaso. My father wanted me to marry Lorenzo Fratelli. He still does, and I'm still trying to stop him. The only way I know how, is to free Tommaso. The stain of the fuitina remains on both of us. If he is free and Lorenzo is in jail then I can and will marry your son."

"So march up to the front door of Palermo Jail in all your finery and demand his release. You are fratellanza after all. They will listen to you; just tell them your father sent you."

The old hag wasn't going to give ground. She probably trusted Maria as far as she could throw the stone hovel that sat behind her like a crumbling ruin. How hard could it be to make her believe they were both on the same side? "And what of Lorenzo?" asked Maria. "How do I make him pay for killing Gaspare Galati?"

"You know of this?" The old woman's demeanour changed in an instant. It was in every syllable of the short response.

"Yes. Lorenzo Fratelli killed Gaspare Galati. I know every detail of it, but my story is worth nothing on its own. I need to find someone who can tell the carabinieri the truth."

"You know so much, yet so little. There's no one who will turn pentito for you. The minute you open your mouth to ask, will be the start of a conversation that will be recounted to your father before the next sunrise."

"You detest the fratellanza, old woman, and there are many in the valley who share the same feelings. They would turn on us in an instant if they thought they could get away with it. Someone will tell what they know of Galati's murder and I will protect them. I can leave the fratellanza behind because no woman can inherit their power, money or influence. Tommaso has been banished by my father, and if he is ever freed, I will rush to his side and suffer the same exile. Until then, I can do more from inside that house of evil than anyone can do from outside. Someone knows enough to convict Fratelli and they will have their reasons to tell. I just need to find them. Where do I start?"

"You are a foolish young woman to abandon your family for the love of one man."

A wrinkled hand reached out and Maria took it, feeling the waxy skin and the bony grasp.

"But then my mother said the same of me when I gave my heart to a shepherd from Aspromonte." Tommaso's mother smiled a toothless grin and looked up at Maria. "When Lucio di Bova first came down from the high pastures into Favara, he was like an angry angel. I had to fight off many suitors to win his affections." Her voice was lilting now and her gaze seemed fixated on a spot in the distance. Suddenly she changed. "Tell me, have you heard anything of my son? I have no one who can let me know how he is."

"I know you think the fratellanza are all-powerful," said Maria, "but there are limits. I've heard nothing of Tommaso because my father wants me to forget about him. I don't even know if he's still alive."

"Your father is responsible for many deaths. We must both hope that Tommaso is not amongst them. This binds us together."

Maria looked into the sad and rheumy old eyes and found only compassion; no hatred. "Gaspare Galati, what do you know?" she asked.

"Galati was not the only victim. Benedetto Carollo, the warden at Galati Plantation, was also killed by your father. His soldiers threw him from the top of the deepest shaft in Ciavallotta: the one they call Cesare's Shaft, in honour of your father."

"I knew nothing of Carollo," replied Maria. "There are deaths that touch me, and there are deaths that are fratellanza business. I will only act on what is personal." Maria had evolved mechanisms to shut herself and her emotions off from the litany of fratellanza horrors she was exposed to on a daily basis. Someday soon, she knew this veil would be torn asunder, but for now her sincerity was intact. This seemed to satisfy the old woman, and she continued.

"Benedetto and his wife lived happily on the Galati plantation, and yes he was one of your father's soldiers, and yes he also planned Galati's murder but deceived everyone into thinking the victim was just another warden. Benedetto's young son, Roberto, was nine years old when all this happened. He understood nothing of the fratellanza but he did know about steam engines, and he used to follow Gaspare Galati, every morning, to the dam on the plantation and fire up the steam engine that irrigated the groves. Starting up that engine was his passion, and he never missed a day. On the morning of Galati's death, Benedetto told his son not to go and stationed himself on the path from the house to enforce his instruction."

The waxy hand still held Maria's, and its grip grew tighter as the revelation continued.

"Roberto would have none of this. He skirted round the rear of the Galati house to hide beside the lane leading to the dam: the lane on which Gaspare met his end. Roberto saw it all. He speaks little of that morning. He just says that the man with the pickaxe was a huge man: big and strong like a horse."

To Maria this was a revelation that was better than she could ever have hoped for. A witness to the murder: one who could identify Lorenzo Fratelli as the killer, and someone whom the fratellanza couldn't corrupt. It was the answer to her prayers. She gripped the old woman's hand so tightly; she saw her wince in pain. "This cannot free your son but it will remove Fratelli from my life. Thank you. Now tell me where to find Carollo's widow and the young Roberto."

"You do not think like the daughter of a rappresentante, and this is why I believe in you, Maria. You forget that you are fratellanza and responsible for the death of Benedetto Carollo. You cast his family adrift without as much as a single lira. His widow and son would tear you to pieces with their bare hands if they found you, and they are not far from here. You aren't safe amongst the hovels. It is best you leave now. Don't go back the way you came. Cross the field and cut back west to the town. There's an old sheep trail just over the next crest. Keep the escarpment at your back."

"But I must meet with them. It's my only chance. I can help them and they can help me."

"They can't help you if you're dead. For now, I will do what is needed. It will take money."

Maria had been prepared for this and thrust a bundle of lire into the bony hand.

"I will help, and you will stay alive," said Tommaso's mother as she weighed the bundle of notes carefully. "Alive, to free my son and bring him back to Favara. I don't know how you can do that, but I do know this: Tommaso cannot escape prison whilst your father is free. Ahead of you lies a choice that will determine the rest of your life: Tommaso di Bova or Cesare Giuliano. You cannot hold both in your heart."

Chapter 11

Lorenzo Fratelli had pleaded with Cesare Giuliano to be allowed to tackle the problem of Benedetto Carollo's widow and son in his own way: pay them off and find her a lonely shepherd out near Palermo who would welcome a wife and a monthly stipend from the fratellanza. Cesare refused. Fear and intimidation were his weapons of choice, and in the case of Lorenzo Fratelli's murder trial, he had nothing to lose. As the rickety freight-car bounced and rattled below him, Lorenzo had thought of little else for the last eight hours.

Chained to another six future Vicaria inmates, all men of honour from around Girgenti, Lorenzo had played cards with prisoners and guards alike as the train wheezed, clacked and shuddered its way to Palermo. Only in the last few weeks had the final rail link from Girgenti to Lercara Friddi been completed, making the journey by rail to the island's capital an unbroken one. This seemed to invoke great happiness from the guards who talked animatedly of the previous four-day journey by boat and all of its horrors. To Lorenzo, the comparison was meaningless. The constant reminders that he should consider himself lucky for the dubious comforts of an empty box-car were more fuel to fire his anger and frustration at the circumstances that had led to his conviction for the murder of Gaspare Galati.

Cesare hadn't listened to Lorenzo's reasoning because the Giulianos weren't a family that wielded their mighty powers by paying off the peasants and the poor. Bribery was endemic to their function, but money only flowed one way: upwards from poor to rich; never the other way. It was just more 'gold from fleas', and the fratellanza clung to this value as if their very existence depended on it. Others may have chosen to play fast and loose with that principle, but for the rappresentante it was inviolate. It was also a strategy that had failed to protect Lorenzo.

The fear and intimidation might have worked if the carabinieri and the judiciary hadn't always been one step ahead of Cesare Giuliano. They seemed to know, or at least anticipate in advance what the fratellanza would do to try and thwart the testimony of the Carollos. The authorities moved them from place to place, often just ahead of a fratellanza raiding party who would have had no compunction about killing the young Roberto.

Gossip never respected prison bars and Favara Jail was no exception. Lorenzo followed the stalemate from his cell and often sent word to Cesare that he must consider if there was a pentito in their midst. Even the very nature of the way Roberto Carollo was unearthed as a witness indicated a traitor to the fratellanza, and one perilously close to Cesare Giuliano himself. Such entreaties were met with silence, but when it became obvious Lorenzo was going to be convicted, the messages started to flow. Vicaria Jail was hell for those who were incarcerated there, but even hell could be made comfortable with enough lire and a pact with the devil. Cesare would make sure Lorenzo's imprisonment was well financed and accommodating. There was even a plan to ensure his freedom. All things were possible, but there was a price.

For Lorenzo Fratelli it was a pittance: kill Tommaso di Bova.

Perhaps that's why Cesare did little else to prevent the inevitable trial verdict. The Horse was the rappresentante's executioner. The sentence for murder would be just a way to deliver the killer to his victim, and that sentence was indeed a guilty one. Again, Lorenzo was told he was lucky. The death penalty had not been used for the past three years because of a general pardon to all who were convicted of capital crimes. Tell that to Tommaso di Bova, he thought, as he was led down.

Lucky not to be executed, lucky to have a patron like Cesare Giuliano who would ensure his welfare in Vicaria Prison, lucky not to have to endure the prison transport to Palermo by sea – how much good fortune could one man have? wondered

Lorenzo as he pulled at the weight of the shackles on his leg.

The air had changed. Lorenzo could see nothing from the inside of the box-car unless he peered through one of the many cracks in the dried-up wooden panels, but the smell of salt had replaced dust, and the occasional squawk of a gull announced they were on the last leg of the journey. The train seemed to bounce along with a new vigour on meeting the coast at Tonnarella. They had set off from Girgenti at midnight as a freight-train, allowing a virtually non-stop passage across the Sicilian interior, but as they hit the coast, so the train had to take its turn with the others along the main route into Palermo. The guards threw open the side door when the train was still on the move and dangled their legs over the edge of the car whilst taking in the view of the sea. They were like children on a day out, and if there had been enough slack on the chains coupling Lorenzo to his companions, he would have pushed the three guards out onto the tracks and worried about the consequences when they reached Palermo. He was a murderer after all. They couldn't hang him and he was down for thirty years, so what was the worst that could happen? He measured the amount of slack chain carefully. There wasn't enough to allow an attack. The guards were safe for now, thought Lorenzo.

Palermo was not just the last stop for the train; it was also the terminus for his future liberty. The chance of him enduring thirty years without adding to his sentence was slight. He attracted trouble like a corn-field attracted crows, and there wasn't a scarecrow in existence that could make him take flight from something he wanted. He brooded on these thoughts as the train slowed for the final time.

Stazione Centrale was a monumental building the people of Palermo were determined to be proud of. The defiance against mainland supremacy was typical of Lorenzo's home city and he couldn't help the feelings of pride as he stepped off the dusty box-cart onto the pristine marble platform. He still found it hard to believe it was a railway station. To him, it was more like a palace or a basilica. Parts were still under construction. Huge gantries extended up to the richly-decorated vaulted ceilings, and the smell of paint on plaster permeated the air. Platform signs were incomplete and confused travellers hurried about the ground floor, searching for trains and venting their frustration on anyone with a uniform. The only uniformed individuals to be seen were the guards accompanying Lorenzo and the other prisoners. They instantly became the focus of a small but noisy scrum of travellers looking for the *Ferrovia Circonvallazione*. His guards shrugged their shoulders. The crowd dispersed quickly on realising that railway guards didn't normally arm themselves with carbines and their passengers were not usually manacled at the wrist and ankles. But they weren't the only travellers looking for the small, narrow-gauge railway that delivered Palermo commuters around the periphery of the city. As Lorenzo listened to the guards' animated chatter, it transpired they were as confused as all the other passengers. Finding where and when the Ferrovia Circonvallazione departed was a major problem. Papers were hastily pulled from folders and consulted with much finger pointing and raised voices. Oh yes, they knew exactly how to transfer the prisoners from the boat to the local train but the boat was no more, and Stazione Centrale was at the other end of the line from Piazza Ucciardone, where they needed to be to transfer to Vicaria Prison. The fact they had arrived two hours early meant that no one from the prison was there to meet them.

Confusion gave way to panic.

Lorenzo realised these guards had not made the rail journey before. They hadn't a clue what to do, so they argued, and took their eyes off his group of prisoners. One guard rested his Vetterli bolt-action rifle, stock down, on the ornate marble floor of the main concourse and pulled yet another piece of paper from a leather satchel he carried.

Lorenzo huddled his compatriots around him and whispered a few commands in quick succession. The group shuffled as quietly as they could to cover the few metres between themselves and the guards.

Lorenzo reckoned he had enough slack in the chains.

He stepped forward, and in one swift movement, despite the limitations of the shackles, had grabbed the Vetterli, pulled back the bolt, and stuck the barrel under the guard's chin. The rest of the prisoners closed around the group to hide what was going on. What little of a plan Lorenzo had, involved keeping things as quiet and unobtrusive as possible. He could only hope that the murderous look in his eyes and the obvious threat of a gun barrel under the chin would ensure none of the three guards tried to be a hero. One twitched and tried to pull a side-arm but was restrained by the close crush of the prisoners around him.

"You know who I am," said Lorenzo. "And you know I've nothing to lose by blowing the top of this man's head off. My only regret would be the damage done to the painted ceiling above." This seemed to bring the guards into a temporary submission. "The keys: slowly remove them from your belt and unlock the manacles of the man nearest you, then give the keys to him." Lorenzo nodded in the direction of one of the guards, who obeyed instantly. Within seconds all the prisoners were freed and all the guards manacled.

Workmen continued with their trade and passengers hurried back and forwards looking for trains and platforms. None paid any attention to a group of men in identical blue prison serge, who stood huddled in a quiet corner of the main hall. Lorenzo carefully unloaded all but one of the weapons, retaining a sidearm. He gave the unloaded rifles to one of the prisoners, who stacked them out of sight behind a large pillar, covering them with some canvas sheeting that lay nearby. He then distributed the ammunition amongst his compatriots, with a simple warning: "Throw the bullets away as soon as you are outside. If they even suspect you have a weapon, they will shoot you on sight. Now, there are seven of us. You will leave two at a time, a few seconds apart. I will be the last to go. Just get lost in the streets of Palermo. Everyone goes a different direction on leaving the station. Try to get back to your towns and villages any way you can." The last instruction was a piece of misdirection for the ears of the guards. Escaping from Palermo would require planning and resources, and Lorenzo knew he could rely on the local men of honour to assist. In the few moments he had to pull together his plan of attack, Lorenzo had given each of the convicts the name of a taverna in a small piazza, in the old part of the city. They were to meet there that night, no sooner, as Lorenzo knew he would need time to organise their route back to Girgenti.

The first two convicts walked quietly away. Lorenzo pressed the sidearm into the spine of each of the shackled guards in turn, ensuring they understood the consequences of raising the alarm. By the time the last two prisoners walked off, Lorenzo's hand was sweating so profusely that he thought he might drop the gun. He had to give the others the best chance of escaping but each second gave his captives new courage and attracted more and more curious looks from the passersby.

Lorenzo could wait no longer. He pushed the guards to the floor where they landed in an untidy heap. He sprinted away, dropping the weapon after a few metres and scooping up a painter's smock and some buckets that were left lying around by the workmen. The shouting started almost immediately as the guards yelled out. Lorenzo tugged hard on a painter's scaffold as he ran past it, causing the entire structure to crash noisily to the floor, scattering debris and paint amongst the crowds. More shouting and screaming ensued, to the point of total confusion and panic on the station concourse. The yells of the guards were lost in the din of the injured, trapped below the collapsed scaffolding.

Lorenzo stepped calmly into an alcove and donned the

painter's smock. As he clutched the empty paint tins in his hand and stepped out into the bright sunlight, he could already smell the goat that would be roasted in his honour when he returned triumphantly to the fratellanza heartland. Of course, he wouldn't be safe there until he unmasked the traitor who had precipitated his conviction and thwarted every effort the fratellanza had made to kill the one witness to Galati's murder. Lorenzo was sure it was someone close to Cesare Giuliano. He would find them and kill them, before dealing with Roberto Carollo.

* * *

Taverna Vittime was easy to find – it was in Piazetta delle Vittime, just two hundred and fifty metres south of the imposing Duomo di Palermo, the city's largest building. For that reason alone, Lorenzo was sure all of the other escapees would have no trouble making their way to it. If they were caught, there was a chance they would reveal it as the rendezvous for the next phase of their escape, but that was a risk Lorenzo would have to take. The taverna was the local base of the di Paolo family: one of Palermo's most powerful dynasties. If the taverna were to figure in any police reports that day, then word would quickly reach the ears of Salvatore di Paolo. Lorenzo's hope was that Salvatore would provide help for them all to get back to Favara.

The taverna was on the ground floor of a ramshackle, three-storey building that stood alone on the piazetta. The first and second floors appeared deserted, their faded wooden shutters pulled tightly against windows that rarely permitted the intrusion of any sunlight. Alleyways around the building's flanks separated it from others and all four corners and exterior walls had large gas mantles attached, ensuring no one could approach unseen in the dark.

The heavy wooden door wouldn't have been out of place on a fortress, but thankfully it gave with a creak of wearisome hinges when Lorenzo tried the handle. He stepped inside to the candle-lit gloom, which gradually revealed a small number of occupants, eating noisily from various bowls. As the door closed behind Lorenzo, spoons stopped mid-way to open mouths and tankards of Marsala were set down on the heavy wooden tables. The sudden silence was as oppressive as it was menacing. Lorenzo walked to the bar, acutely aware of every noisy footstep on the sawdust-covered stone floor.

The barman was so large they must have had to turn him on his side to get him through the door, but when he spoke, he sounded like a ten-year-old girl. "What can I get for you?"

Any sort of comic reaction to the effeminate squeak from man-mountain would have been a fatal mistake. Lorenzo kept his face straight and his voice confident as he commenced the one routine that he hoped would change the mood from hostile to friendly. "Something strong for this toothache. It's been bothering me for a long time." The predictable question and answer routine settled into a comfortable dialogue that was conducted at a level loud enough for all to hear, despite the squeaky responses. By the time the introduction was complete, the occupants had returned to their meals and Lorenzo was just another customer, albeit a recognised man of honour.

Man-mountain disappeared behind a beaded curtain for a few minutes. When he returned the effeminate voice was still there, as he beckoned for Lorenzo to follow. A narrow stairway gave access to the upper floors and Lorenzo wondered how the gargantuan barman managed to negotiate it without having his sides lubricated with pig fat. Nonetheless, he made it and ushered Lorenzo into an upper room that was fitted out with furnishings fit for King Umberto himself.

"Please wait here," squeaked the barman. "I've sent for Salvatore di Paolo. He will arrive within the hour. Whilst you wait, I'll bring some hot food and a pitcher of wine."

After the meal and a generous amount of Marsala, Lorenzo

felt that finally things were going his way. For the last three months he had been locked up and chained, forced to eat slops and denied the luxuries of good wine and accommodating women. All but one of those comforts had been restored; the final one would be his to savour when he returned to claim Maria as his bride. That was Cesare's promise, and Lorenzo's new found status as fugitive should not alter that.

It may have been within the hour, it may have been later but Salvatore di Paolo arrived with his usual entourage. They had all met before. Salvatore di Paolo was one of Cesare's trusted men of honour in Palermo. He didn't look like he controlled all of the city's criminal industries. His domain started south of Via Vittoria Emmanuele and went as far west as the many citrus plantations of the *Conca D'Oro*: the 'shell of gold' encircling Palermo's hinterland, providing the city's agricultural wealth and that of the local men of honour. He certainly didn't look like a cold-blooded killer, whose victims were remembered with small shrines dotted around the citrus groves. He appeared more like a stage-performer and wouldn't have looked out of place in Teatro san Ferdinando, playing the role of noble hero. If anything, he seemed to take that very image to himself and every move and utterance appeared rehearsed to perfection. He relished the soubriquet by which he was known – The Artist. Lorenzo stood as he entered the room, but the flourish of a hand with a silk handkerchief bade him to be seated.

Salvatore di Paolo sat cross-legged and tugged at his waistcoat to straighten the seams. He then carefully aligned each of the embroidered sleeves of his shirt to perfection before clasping his hands over his knee and looking directly at Lorenzo. The grand entrance of the lead player was over. The cue for the supporting actor had been given and the lines were to be delivered.

"I would normally bring you greetings from Cesare Giuliano," said Lorenzo on cue, "but I regret, I'm not here at his request." This produced no response from Salvatore di Paolo, other than a slight pursing of his lips and a barely perceptible tilt of his head. "This morning, with six others, I escaped from a prison transfer. We are all in need of help to flee Palermo and return to Girgenti." Again, nothing but silence came back. Lorenzo was forced to continue. "We escaped from Stazione Centrale. There may have been a few minor casualties but we didn't harm our guards. I have taken the liberty of asking the others to meet here tonight."

Salvatore di Paolo held up his hand, fingers outstretched and palm facing Lorenzo. "You are welcome on my domain, Lorenzo Fratelli. We are aware of your circumstances and those of your friends. Some have already made themselves known to us. They don't understand Palermo as you do. It's fortunate they were not picked up by the other families or the authorities. You say there were six?"

The tone was icy and almost accusing but the delivery was crisp and theatrical. Lorenzo shouldn't have told them all to meet at the taverna. His escape plan had suddenly taken a downturn. "Yes, there were six others. I acted hastily when I suggested we meet here. I apologise for taking your help for granted."

Again the response was a raised hand, but this time di Paolo rose from the chair and paced back and forwards across the room as if it was a stage. His long legs moved with the grace of a dancer and each turn he made was accompanied by alternate chin scratching and hand wringing. Twice, he stopped and looked in Lorenzo's direction as if to say something, only to continue pacing again with his gaze cast downwards to the floor. Finally he stopped and spoke, his intonation rising and falling as the words flowed like it was a poetry reading. "Things are delicate here in Palermo. Five years ago we rejoiced in the liberation from Bourbon rule brought about by Garibaldi and his rebellion. This gave us a new Kingdom of Italy and the honourable societies here in Sicily embraced it. Now we are riven by discontent and divided in our allegiance to Naples. Your fratellanza, young Fratelli; they are divorced from these troubles and we are unsure of their loyalties. The other families in Palermo, they are thus unsure of my intentions. I manage this because of the distance between us, but now we have the new rail links and, all of a sudden, men of honour from Girgenti are causing problems on our streets."

The pacing continued anew. Lorenzo could feel the tension in the room increase and beads of sweat formed on his brow.

"Before I can help you, I must let Cesare know of your predicament. I will let him decide the course of action. You are his cadre after all."

Lorenzo had to respond. "But that will take days. The longer we stay in Palermo, the greater the risk."

"Not days, my young friend – it will take just a few minutes. The rail link brings the telegraph and the telegraph means I can have a message sent to Cesare and receive one back as if we were in adjoining rooms. They call it a telegram. I don't know how it works, but I do know that men of honour control every element of it."

* * *

His uniform marked him out as carabinieri: the red stripes down the sides of the dark navy britches, the gold buttons on the single-breasted tunic and the black leather riding boots up to his knees. All should have been a warning signal to Maria Giuliano to get as far away from him as possible, but this was an assignation, not a confrontation. In many ways, she was looking forward to it.

He reined the black stallion in and she tethered it beside her own horse, watching him dismount in one fluid movement to stand beside her. When they first met, her initial reaction to the pomp and ceremony of the uniform was one of repugnance. The carabinieri were the sworn enemies of the fratellanza, not only because her father's empire was constantly harassed by them, but also because their ranks proved incorruptible. Nonetheless, she needed someone she could trust on the other side of the fence and Captain Bruno Fabroni fulfilled that role. He was charming, well-educated, and had the looks of a god. Yes, older than her but not yet thirty, for sure. The tailored tunic flattered his torso but Maria had felt the solid muscle when she had brushed against him on their previous meetings. He wasn't from Favara and maybe not even from Sicily, but try as she might, Maria could not elicit one word of Captain Fabroni's birthplace or ancestry. This all added to the mystery and mystery was one element of a compound that stoked her arousal with each meeting.

He was her secret liaison throughout Fratelli's arrest and trial and the subsequent attempts made by her father to eliminate the Carollos. With each betrayal of the fratellanza she could feel herself growing closer to this forbidden suitor, and she knew he would fulfil the role of suitor if it wasn't for the almost insurmountable gulf that separated them.

"Signorina Giuliano," began Fabroni, once he had brushed the dust from his uniform. "All of Sicily will one day thank you for your bravery."

"I hope not, Captain Fabroni. No one must ever know of this. If they do, I will join the ghosts who haunt the deepest tunnels of the Ciavallotta mine." The meeting was the result of a routine she had followed during Fratelli's murder trial. Fabroni had kept it alive, even though she said she would never use it again. Whenever there was something she needed to communicate to the carabinieri, it would be by a hand-written note slipped into a leather purse, weighted down with a heavy iron ring. At full gallop past their barracks, Maria would throw this into their compound and then ride to a deserted ruin outside the town: the same one they now stood before.

"The telegraph message; when did you receive it?" asked Fabroni. There was an unusual urgency in his voice.

"A short time ago," replied Maria. "Less than an hour. I've

never seen one of these messages before and asked of the man who delivered it, what it was."

"Did this man wear a uniform?"

"Yes, it looked like that of the railroad company."

Fabroni seemed to relax a little when he heard this. "You know then it's a telegram and must be delivered to your father as soon as possible. The person who sent it needs an urgent reply."

"Cesare is hunting around Monte Caltafaraci. I can find him quickly."

"Then you must go, Signorina. But first tell me why you took this risk? Why was it so important you brought me this message?"

"You've read it. *'Horse and six colts arrived artist's farm. Escaped from rustlers. They bear your brand. Do you wish their return?'* Fratelli is the horse; the six colts are the prisoners he travelled with. He has escaped."

Captain Fabroni looked at her and seemed to struggle with a desire to reveal more about the message he held in his hand. "I am telling you more than I should, but yes, Fratelli has escaped. We have our own telegraph system, and we knew of this."

"Then I have risked my life for nothing, Captain." It wasn't for nothing, even the guilty pleasure of meeting him again was reason enough.

"Not for nothing, no. *'Artist's farm'* tells us exactly where to look, but you *have* risked your life. I have the chance to act on this information and put Fratelli and his friends back in jail, but everyone will know they've been betrayed. There will be a ruthless investigation by the families here and in Palermo. Everyone who has seen this piece of paper will be a suspect."

Fabroni took off his glove and reached out to take Maria's hand. His touch was at once comforting and stimulating. Maria almost hated herself for the sense of arousal it brought; almost, but not quite.

"Signorina Giuliano, I cannot protect you in your home. You

have done enough and taken many risks. Leave the fratellanza, leave them now. Come with me and I will create a new life for you, with the help of l'arma dei carabinieri, of course."

The last phrase almost seemed an afterthought, and Maria slowly withdrew her hand from his. The offer seemed strangely tempting, but the life she had was incomplete. Yet, if all her plans came to nothing then she would need a way out, and keeping Fabroni as one of her admirers could provide it. Despite all of what he claimed to know, Fabroni wasn't able to tell her if Tommaso was alive or not. Maria had heard nothing of him in almost a year and the lack of news made her increasingly desperate.

"Captain, there is much you have to learn about my life and the pain of abandoning all that I know and hold dear. Danger alone is not enough to make me leave. It will take more than that; much more."

"I'm sure you would be rewarded financially if you chose to tell all you know of the fratellanza."

Maria flounced away from him and looked back over her shoulder, anger burning in her eyes. "Do you think this is about money? I am not pentito, Captain. I do what I do because I will not be forced further into a life I detest. If I must leave everything I have behind, it will be for something more valuable than a handful of lire."

"I meant no insult, Signorina," replied Fabroni. "I deal with pentiti every day. Please understand that you are different, so very different."

He mounted his stallion with that same lithe grace she had seen before.

"Wait, Captain. There was no insult, and yes, I know just how different this must be for you. Please understand it is likewise for me." Maria deliberately adopted a more subdued tone and when her eyes locked on his once more, she made sure the emotion they conveyed was the opposite of anger. "I don't know who to trust anymore. If I need to get a message to you, and only you, is there another way?" She held the leather purse with the iron-ring out to him, suspended on the end of a stiff and extended index finger.

"There is, Signorina Giuliano, but it will only increase the risk for both of us."

For the first time since that night with Tommaso in Piazza don Giustiani, Maria blushed at the prospect of danger and arousal, twisted together in a new package of guilt and pleasure. The intimate heat that began with the same warm, liquid feeling, raced upwards through her body to burn her cheeks. Fabroni couldn't have failed to notice it, but he responded simply by telling her how she could contact him and only him, if she felt the need.

Minutes later, when Fabroni had galloped off and Maria had the rigid leather of her own saddle beneath her, she was catapulted back to that cramped basement room, where vile guilt and sweet pleasure climaxed in a bittersweet concoction.

* * *

Palermo was waking.

The sharp sunlight played with the shutters and cast alternate stripes of light and dark in a crisp pattern that covered Lorenzo's bed. A strip of light forced his sleepy eyes to scrunch tightly shut before opening and seeking refuge from the morning's reveille. He grunted, moved away from the glare and looked across at the others. They were still sound asleep and snoring loudly. Outside, a horse whinnied and the sound of wagon wheels clattered across the cobbles. By the next sunrise, Lorenzo hoped he would be far away from Taverna Vittime.

The noise of clattering wheels stopped to be replaced by running feet and splintering wood. Lorenzo was instantly awake and rousing the others. Shouts echoed up from the floors below as the wooden staircase reverberated to the sound of military commands.

Lorenzo ran to the shutters and kicked them open to access the small balcony outside. Three rounds fired off in quick succession from below, and masonry exploded in ballistic showers above his head. He retreated back into the room just as the door caved in, and the carabinieri arrived in a scrum of sabres and carbines, all pointed in his direction.

The journey through Palermo's streets passed all too quickly. Lorenzo had little time to think as he sat in the back of the prison wagon. The clatter of its wheels and the clip clop of the horses' hooves were the only sounds to be heard, other than the occasional rattle of the manacles that bound them all by their wrists and ankles. Flanking the enclosed wagon were at least twenty carabinieri but the confined space inside was reserved for future inmates of Vicaria.

"We were betrayed," said Lorenzo above the relentless clatter. All eyes looked in his direction and he examined each for signs of fear, but he found only anger and frustration. He doubted any of their number had turned pentito, but all would be watched closely in prison for any signs of preferential treatment or early release. Lorenzo was sure the traitor hid far away from Palermo. He knew they lay in the shadows of Favara, close to Cesare Giuliano. As the wagon and its phalanx of carabinieri arrived at the gates of Vicaria, he made a silent promise to himself. He would escape this prison and Palermo without any help, to arrive unannounced in Favara and hunt down the Judas who had condemned him.

Every gate that slammed shut behind him, as they led his manacled group deeper into the bowels of the jail, only increased the fervour with which he would now dedicate his life. Finally, when his anger and frustration abated, Lorenzo started to take stock of Vicaria Jail: the major obstacle that would stand in the way of his plans. He stood in a circular courtyard whose cobbled surface was segmented in arcs: like pieces of a pie. Facing him was a boundary wall, with doors at the circumference of each arc. One door opened and his group was marched through. The door clanged shut behind them. Lorenzo looked back, and to his surprise the guards were left outside. His group found themselves alone in a wide corridor with buttressed walls covered in glazed tiles of green and white. A faint smell of carbolic acid hung in the air.

A voice broke the silence as it echoed off the tiled floors and walls.

From behind one of the buttresses, the owner of the voice appeared and Lorenzo was dumbstruck at what he saw. There before him, dressed like an Aspromonte shepherd, was Tommaso di Bova.

Chapter 12

Toto was wrong when he told Tommaso his knowledge of Grecanico wouldn't help him. Even the very name 'di Bova' indicated a stronger tie to the 'ndrangheta of Calabria than just a few shepherds' songs and children's poems. The hilltop town of Bova was the ancient capital of Calabria, but it might as well have been on the moon as far as the rest of the new kingdom of Italy was concerned. Tommaso's father and three generations before him were all from Bova, and they were as isolated and fiercely independent as the fortress town from which they took their name. They were *'ndranghetista,* but the ritual of acceptance into Calabria's honoured brotherhood didn't wait for an indeterminate time in the future: it began minutes after the arrival of each firstborn son into the world.

The squealing newborn would be brought to a room, where an assembly of members gathered to witness the first process of acceptance into the ancient order that could trace its origins back to Carcagnosso. The infant would be laid between a key and a knife, and all would wait to see which his flailing arms touched first. It had to be the knife; touching the key would have condemned the infant to being a slave of the law. Having selected the knife, usually with the helpful nudge of a nearby adult finger, the child's father would then hoist this new member aloft, part his buttocks and spit noisily in his arsehole.

Tommaso had been baptised into 'ndrangheta, at birth, by his father. That had been witnessed by two of his prison companions. He was as much 'ndranghetista as any of the other Calabrian brothers in Vicaria, he just hadn't known it for the first three months of his incarceration. Tommaso grew up in the hell of the Sicilian sulphur mines but his ancestry was firmly with the cattle rustlers of Aspromonte, and the di Bova family was as powerful in the southernmost tip of Italy as the Giuliano family was in the Girgenti region of Sicily. The 'ndrangheta did not give up their blood members easily, and Vicaria's isolation conferred a high value on honoured brothers that accelerated their progress through the echelons of the ancient 'ndrine structures.

It began with a knife fight. Out of nowhere, Tommaso was challenged in an unprovoked attack that bizarrely only inflicted a small cut on his forearm with its first strike. Also from nowhere came the blade that was thrust into his hand along with the words – "Cut, don't kill."

Instantly, he was catapulted back to the shadows behind that small taverna in Favara. The lessons he had learned then, he used with every thrust, twist and parry, all the while refraining from a killing blow, as did his adversary.

Finally, he broke through his opponent's guard.

As before, Tommaso held the blade tight against the outside edge of his forearm, the handle closed in his fist. For three slashing cuts from his attacker's knife, Tommaso had ducked under vicious swipes and attempted to slice into his ribcage. On the fourth slash, he stepped boldly inside the lethal arc of the blade and ran a single cut across his assailant's bushy eyebrows. The wound was instantly debilitating as a curtain of blood blinded his attacker. The fight was over and Tommaso was spirited away. The crowd parted for an instant to allow his escape with his new-found companion: an elderly Calabrian who introduced himself simply as 'Master Joe'.

"I was there when your father spat in your arsehole," said Master Joe, and then went on to explain exactly what that meant and why it was so important. "Be prepared for a move to C Wing, Tommaso. We never forget our true brethren, and we won't leave them to be persecuted by those of Osso and Mastrosso."

"You can do that?" asked Tommaso.

"We can do whatever honour demands," replied Master Joe. "You have earned your first flower."

Flowers were ranks of status to 'ndranghetista and just being imprisoned in Vicaria elevated a member to the highest rank of what was the Minor Society. From there to the lowest rank of the Major Society required victory in a knife fight. Tommaso had just made the grade. "He won't even have a scar," Master Joe had chuckled. "I watched you pick the knife at your birth, Tommaso di Bova, and you have made it your servant."

Master Joe was a gangly sixty-year-old with a thick shock of silver hair and a twinkle in his eye. Like all of the Calabrian honoured society imprisoned in Vicaria, he sported the fine, white cotton shirt with brown corduroy britches that were the sartorial standards of the parochial society he had been forced to leave behind in the hills of Aspromonte. Tied at his throat was a silk handkerchief: another symbol of the 'ndrangheta. His was white. Of all the 'ndranghetista in Vicaria, only two could wear the white silk: the highest level of the Major Society.

Beyond the trappings of rank and status, Tommaso had found something else, and it was of the utmost importance. He had found he had a soul: a soul resurrected from the desiccated and bitter walnut nurtured in the caverns of Ciavallotta. The little wagons had no music and no songs. They had nothing to lift them beyond the oppression of the life they endured for the benefit of others. Even as a pickman, Tommaso had not discovered anything of a culture beyond killing and extortion. Despite their obvious leaning towards extreme violence, the 'ndrangheta nurtured a rich and varied culture of music, poetry and storytelling. Tommaso had embraced this like a drowning man clinging to a rope. For the first time in his life he understood what it meant to belong: to be part of a group bound together by history, a group for whom violence was just a defence of everything they held dear.

Courtesy of Master Joe, Tommaso had even learnt to play the *zampogna,* a hideously ugly and unwieldy instrument made from the skin of a goat and penetrated by wooden pipes, two of which sported chanters, drilled with a series of holes. The zampogna could never be described as delicate or elegant, but the sounds Tommaso could produce by inflating the oversize bladder that was the goatskin, and then rendering notes through the chanters, was enough to bring a tear to the eye of even the most hardened of Calabrian cattle rustlers. The mournful wail of the zampogna haunted the cells and glazed-tile corridors of Vicaria on many an evening. There were those who would seek Tommaso out on the following day and thank him for bringing back memories of Aspromonte; there were others who threatened to shove the zampogna up his arse.

The knife fight, Tommaso's affinity for a dead language, his birthright and the realisation of his true identity accelerated his progression through the ranks of the 'ndrangheta within Vicaria. Lorenzo Fratelli had arrived in C Wing when Tommaso was at the height of his power and influence. As Tommaso walked down the line of new prisoners, thoughts of lording it over The Horse had him salivating. Fratelli only had one future and it was bounded by the walls of C Wing. Within that small world, his life belonged to Tommaso di Bova.

"Men of honour, and those not so privileged, welcome to C Wing," said Tommaso as he walked down the line of inmates. Some lowered their heads, others nodded respectfully and a few grinned. Fratelli was at the end of the line and Tommaso shot a quick glance in his direction. The Horse just glowered.

At Tommaso's side was Filippo, a lithe twenty-year-old from Africo, in the heart of the Aspromonte. He was a native Calabrian and the 'ndranghetista's knife-fighting instructor in Vicaria. He had been the one whom Tommaso had beaten in that first fight of acceptance into the Major Society and his first flower. From that time onwards, Filippo had looked up to Tommaso the same way a faithful sheep-dog looks up to his shepherd. When Tommaso reached the stage of needing an enforcer, Filippo was the first choice: the one to collect the stipends and the one to enforce the rule of law in C Wing. He was the opposite of the menacing giant,

Giotto, who still acted as enforcer for Silvio on A Wing. Filippo traded muscle and bulk for speed and precision. A blade was always in his reach, from the weighty hunting-knife carried openly on his hip to the fine steel razors wedged below two elongated fingernails and held in place with thin wire. His victims were many, and those who bore the disfiguring sfregio counted their blessings and moved on, acknowledging they had received a warning. For others, the open wounds of pierced femoral or carotid arteries never had the chance to form scars. The condemned could only watch as their life blood pumped and splashed its final journey to the sewers below Vicaria. No matter how powerful, no matter how important, every victim of Filippo's fatal cuts went the same way. His was the lingering execution that was legend, and all who suffered it pissed their pants with as much flowing energy as the blood that pumped from their otherwise insignificant wounds. It could take an hour, maybe less. There was only one guarantee: dying alone. No one came to the aid of a Filippo cut, or they would suffer the same fate. There were many ways to die in Vicaria. An execution by Filippo was the most feared. Fratelli wouldn't know that and he wouldn't know of life in the prison and the primacy of the block commander. Tommaso could let him learn slowly and painfully, or he could have Filippo administer a quick and painful lesson. He decided on a combination of the two.

As block commander, Tommaso had detailed knowledge of each intake of prisoners. Sometimes this was from court records passed on by men of honour, but more often it was intimate knowledge of each inmate provided by a brother who could have either benevolent or sinister intent. Those inmates who were protected as senior men of honour were identified, and no harm would befall them. They usually had a guaranteed income, provided by their benefactor. Lorenzo fell into that category so he was safe, for now. But accidents were common in Vicaria, and even the guards could be bribed to shoot a prisoner who was trying to escape.

Others who suffered incarceration in Vicaria, played into the hands of their enemies from without and from within. Every influx of new prisoners bore one or two who carried a death sentence: not from the legal system of the new Italy, but from the descendents of Osso, Mastrosso or Carcagnosso. Like a cuckold husband, the victims were the last to know. The word came down from the prison guards who took a cut of every paid-for assassination. Next in line were the block commanders, who had first refusal on a kill. They would usually pass on personal involvement and delegate the kill to their enforcer, for a percentage of the bounty.

Filippo was on a mission as Tommaso had confirmed the kill only minutes earlier. It helped that the only one with a smirk in the line-up that included Lorenzo Fratelli, was the victim. He was Giovanni Noto: a fat and greasy trader from Palermo. Despite his oath, Noto had betrayed his capo, skimming too many lire from the olive groves on the Conca D'Oro. Before his enforcer could make a move on Noto, Tommaso pulled Filippo to the side and whispered in his ear. They were to kill a Sicilian brother but the assassination had been sanctioned weeks ago. Master Joe, and the others who formed the Vicaria Prison Council, would have had a message as soon as the target was sentenced. On their weekly meetings with the prison authorities, the council would have updated the condemned list and received confirmation of each victim's arrival and wing allocation. Only when the condemned was incarcerated on the wing, would the word go down. There was usually no rush for the execution to be carried out. Nobody was imprisoned in Vicaria for less than five years. On this occasion, however, an additional bounty would be paid if Noto was taken down in the first week.

The greasy Palermitan sniffed noisily and spat on the floor as Tommaso approached him with Filippo in tow. "You are Giovanni Noto?" asked Tommaso.

"And you are an Aspromonte prick," came the belligerent reply, which initiated a short burst of laughter from the assembled inmates.

Tommaso could sense Filippo's smouldering anger and held up his hand to stay the inevitable killing arc of sharpened steel. "Go to the end of the line." Tommaso nodded down towards where Lorenzo Fratelli stood, indicating Noto should follow the instruction.

"Get your fucking sheepdog to lead me," was the irreverent reply that became a catalyst for more mirth. Even The Horse joined in, playing right into Tommaso's hands.

"Filippo, when this castrated old ram lost his balls, he also lost his sense of direction and his respect for his shepherd. Send him to the back of the line," said Tommaso, encouraging further laughter.

Filippo grabbed Noto and propelled him stumbling and falling to stand beside Fratelli, all the while listening to threats and invocations of revenge from the Sicilian brotherhood. Tommaso turned his back to continue his welcoming address, but not before noting how Fratelli and Noto had struck up a sudden friendship based on joint ridicule of their block commander. He let them chatter and snigger at the back of the line whilst he continued. "I am C Block's Commander. I am not one of the prison staff but I make sure the block is peaceful, clean and ordered. For these services, we are all rewarded with privileges befitting our honoured status. We have our own taverna, a grocery store, and for those who can afford it, a brothel where you can relieve your sexual frustrations on some of the finest whores in the city."

"Hey you Aspromonte sister-fucker; does that brothel have some pretty sheep for you and your mountain-men cousins?" It could only be Noto.

Tommaso turned to look down the line. The laughter was convulsive with Fratelli taking on the role of leading the audience.

Filippo was given a quick and almost imperceptible nod.

The C Wing enforcer ambled slowly down the line of prisoners, grinning as he went, seeming to acknowledge the comic hilarity of the fat Palermitan. He stopped in front of him and the grin disappeared. Filippo hit him twice with the speed of a cat before stepping back, away from the inevitable counter attack. Noto went for him like an enraged animal, only to be brought to the ground courtesy of the slippery patch of blood at his feet. He looked down at the rip in his pants, just to the left of his crotch. A violent red cataract pumped from his femoral artery, its pulsating rhythm in joint condemnation with another fountain, spurting from its twin carotid in Noto's neck. He tried to get up, but his feet and hands were awash with his own blood, and the pool it made on the floor grew bigger by the second. Tommaso watched as the rivulets drained away and formed bright-red rectangular patterns in the gaps between the glazed white tiles on the floor of the block. He waited, along with Filippo, for that moment when the victim realised they were bleeding to death. It was in Noto's eyes in seconds. Then he yelled for help, but Filippo was there to counter any noble ideas the others might have. Noto tried desperately to plug the wounds with his own fingers. The cuts were too big and two punctured arteries would hasten the end. Tommaso had told Filippo he didn't want to wait around for the usual half-hour performance, and his enforcer had obliged with the skill of a practiced assassin. Still the fat Palermitan cried for help and looked forlornly up at the others as the colour started to drain from his face, and oblivion beckoned.

"It was a joke, only a joke." The dying man's voice quivered and shook with hopeless terror. "The Calabrians and the Sicilians: they mock each other all the time. There was no harm meant. You know this. Must you condemn me for a few words? Please get me to the infirmary."

He looked straight at Tommaso as he said this. There could only be one reply: "Make peace with God, Giovanni Noto. You have but a few minutes. Do not waste them making peace with Tommaso di Bova."

Filippo was watching on, silent and hungry for the final stroke of his signature execution. Tommaso could see it in his eyes, and only now understood why the knife-fighter was so feared in Vicaria. It was because he remained to watch his victims die: listening to their pleas, returning their haunted stares, smelling the fear mixed with the coppery scent of their escaping lifeblood. They died with virtually no physical pain but with the full realisation of their coming demise. This made the terror and futility of every last action even more focussed. They would have traded untold screaming agony for just the chance of a quick death.

Filippo grinned with satisfaction as Noto pissed his pants. The grin was still there as he walked back down the line of prisoners to take his place at Tommaso's side. The only sound to be heard in the echoing corridor was the death rattle of another victim.

"Shortly, you will proceed to the prison stores where you will be kitted out with bedding, clothing and other conveniences," said Tommaso. He no longer needed to wait for their undivided attention. "As it is on the outside, so it is in Vicaria. The more you pay, the more you receive. Filippo here will collect your weekly stipend for all the services and protection we provide." Tommaso turned swiftly and walked back down the line to stand beside the dying Noto. "Of course, if you no longer wish to be a part of that arrangement, then you can simply refuse to pay." No one smiled. No one even dared to make a noise, and Lorenzo Fratelli just glared back like a caged animal. Maybe the message hadn't yet got through to The Horse, thought Tommaso. Maybe a further lesson was required. This would wait for another day. For now he had to process the prisoners and arrange for the guards to dispose of the desiccated corpse of the fat trader from Palermo. How unfortunate he had become entangled with the metal-stamping press in the prison machine-shop, on only his first day too. Still, he wasn't used to manual labour so it was just an unfortunate accident, or so the official report would say. Of course, there were some witnesses who could tell a different story, but then Tommaso doubted few would have the courage to face Filippo. He just wasn't sure if Fratelli was one of them.

* * *

Lorenzo Fratelli watched the killer that Tommaso had introduced as Filippo walk slowly back down the line of now-silent inmates. He studied him carefully so he would know every facet of the deadly art he practiced. The killing slashes inflicted on Noto were accomplished without the aid of the hunting knife on Filippo's hip, so there must have been hidden blades in his hands or underneath his fingernails. Sooner or later Lorenzo knew he would have to find a way past Filippo to kill Tommaso. At least he understood what he was up against and how his adversaries would react. The 'Aspromonte sister-fucker' had played his hand too soon and surprise was no longer on the side of di Bova. It might take a month, it might take a year, but Lorenzo would complete the task he was given by Cesare Giuliano. Tommaso was a dead man.

For now Lorenzo had to obey, and stomach the feelings of revulsion he felt. He fell into line, following his group through to the prison stores after handing over a hefty amount of lire for the privilege. Tin mug, uniform, palliasse, blanket, and so it went on through the inventory of despair. Lorenzo took each reminder of his imprisonment and walked down the queue to receive the next, before arriving at the final yellow line and the entrance to C Wing. He could see it before him. A wide, cold corridor seemed to disappear into the distance. On either side of the stone floor, outstretched arms poked through the metal bars of crowded cells. He had never seen a room so big. Even the vaulted splendour of Palermo's Stazione Centrale seemed dwarfed by comparison, but this was no celebration of art and design. It was a cold, soulless chasm that smelt of decay and echoed with the noisy din of desperation, as inmates hurled abuse and excrement in equal measure at the new arrivals. The scale was even more confusing when he looked up and saw the same spectacle repeated on the floor above. The exposed gantries, walkways and cells were laid bare by the open void over the stone floor, now spattered with rubbish and shit from the collection of caged animals he would soon be a member of. Shafts of sharp sunlight cascaded from high windows and sliced through the gloom of the lower level, creating pools of brightness that teased the murky depths of the cells with unfulfilled promises.

Once across the yellow line, each new prisoner was forced to walk through this corridor of misery and abuse, with prison guards grinning triumphantly and pushing new arrivals towards the outstretched arms. Those who resisted were beaten with short cudgels until they fell towards the predatory scavengers who plucked and pulled at newly-issued prison kit, stripping the owner bare of his possessions. Lorenzo stood behind the line and glowered across at the guards nearest to him. The mocking confidence in their smiles waned as they took in his bulk and the ham-sized fists. He could break the spine of a little wagon in two with one swipe; a prison guard wouldn't be too much of a challenge. As the metal doorway framed Lorenzo's huge bulk, the word seemed to spread through the serried ranks of caged prisoners. It started as a shout and then died to a whisper as the background yelling abated.

"It's The Horse," carried on one wave of chatter.

"He was picconieri in Ciavallotta," echoed another.

"He's Cesare Giuliano's enforcer," carried across the now silent block.

Flailing arms were pulled back into cells to be replaced with hundreds of faces squeezed tightly against bars, as each and every inmate tried to get a glimpse of the legend from Girgenti. Lorenzo smiled at the guards who seemed to have lost their strutting arrogance. Cesare had told him he would make Lorenzo's time in prison bearable, and he had already lived up to this promise with just one master stroke. The entire population of C Wing was primed for Lorenzo's arrival. It was the work of a genius. What now for Tommaso di Bova's power and that of his tame killer?

"Wait there!"

The shout came from behind. Lorenzo stopped, just before stepping across the yellow line and glanced back over his shoulder, towards the last of the benches in the prison stores. "You forgot these," said a trustee, holding up a pair of woollen socks.

Lorenzo turned and walked back to the last bench where he looked straight into the one good eye of Toto. That fixed stare, along with an almost imperceptible shake of the head from the old Ciavallotta mule-herder ensured Lorenzo showed no signs of recognition. He took the socks and could feel the unmistakable crinkle of a piece of paper inside one of them.

Chapter 13

The lemons could be harvested from July, but the peak time for the olives was October, and from then until the end of November it was the *Invaiatura,* when the olives turned from green to black. Itinerant labour from all over the valley flooded into Favara. Monday morning at sunrise marked the first day of the olive harvest, and an impatient crowd gathered in Piazza don Giustiani, waiting for the horse-drawn carts to arrive from the surrounding plantations. Maria Giuliano waited amongst them. No one would have recognised her. Her short hair was tangled and tucked below a tattered fedora. Patched corduroy britches were held up with a worn leather belt, poking out from below the bottom of a black waistcoat. A white cotton shirt, that had seen better days, spilled open at the neck to accommodate a stained scarf tied loosely around her throat. As the trundle of the first wagon made itself heard, the crowd stirred from their early morning lethargy and started to move forwards, jostling for a better position. Maria dug the heels of her heavy leather boots into the soft earth and onto the toes of anyone trying to push past her.

"Hey, young lad," came the shout from beside her as a grizzled old shepherd protested at her stomping on his feet. "You'd better learn to give ground to your elders."

"Hasn't done you much good," she replied in as husky a voice as she could manage. The old shepherd made to take a swipe at her and missed. He wouldn't have dared if he believed she was a woman. The disguise must have been working.

The crowd pushed and heaved as more wagons could be heard in the distance, and the first clip-clop of hooves arrived in the piazza.

"Experienced olive pickers and grinders, fifty lire a basket." The shout came down from the lead wagon, which was instantly mobbed.

Maria looked up at the man who stood with reins in one hand and a horse whip in the other. He beat and whipped at the old and anyone else he didn't like the look of, until he had a full complement of fit and capable workers aboard. He wasn't the man Maria was interested in.

More wagons clattered across the rutted cobbles and more shouts offered pittances for hard labour. Gradually the crowds started to thin and still the man Maria wanted to see hadn't appeared. There was no guarantee he would on the first day, but she had learned patience. She had waited for Tommaso for over two years so another few days wouldn't hurt, and yet it would. Something inside her ached for him: a flaming passion that wouldn't be satisfied with the virtue of patience. It chewed and gnawed at her like a starving animal with a dry bone.

The press of the crowd and the emptying of scores of labourers into assorted wagons had moved her to the front of the throng when she saw him pull up in a dilapidated tip-cart with a single tired mule between its shafts. "Ditch diggers for lemon groves – twenty-five lire a metre." He was the man she was waiting for. His gold teeth marked him out. They were unique in the valley and were his pride and joy.

Maria ran forward but there wasn't a rush. Digging irrigation ditches through the lemon groves was tough and unproductive, with progress frequently impeded by large rocks and gnarled tree roots. Four metres in a day would be good going and that would take a lot more effort than combing two baskets of olives off the trees, or grinding the same number down to a paste for the oil processing. He shouted the same offer again and eventually filled the tip-cart with another four labourers. Maria sat amongst them as the cart headed off. She kept her head down, avoiding eye contact and conversation. Thankfully, due to the early start and the jolting of the cart, both forms of interaction were suppressed. Everyone kept their own counsel as the protesting mule hauled them up a steep track, a mercifully short distance from the town. They stopped beside a lemon grove where picks and shovels lay in an untidy heap beside a small culvert, dammed with a wooden gate.

"Everyone out," shouted the driver from the seat of the cart. "Start with a ditch going downhill from that culvert and beside the track. I'm going back to Favara for more workers. Have at least two metres dug by the time I get back." Everyone filed out and grabbed a pick or shovel, everyone except for Maria. "You too, young lad."

"I would," said Maria in her huskiest voice, praying the 'young lad' disguise would hold up. "But I have this toothache. It's been bothering me for the last month. I first noticed it in the back room of Taverna Girandola, in Favara town. Only last week I told my friend, Cesare Giuliano, about it." There was a stunned silence from the driver. Maria knew him as Antonio Ruddini, the eye-witness who had agreed to frame Tommaso for the assault on the rail-yard boss.

Ruddini whipped the reins, and the mule jumped forwards as if hit by a bolt of lightning. Maria fell back in the cart and was still struggling to get up when Ruddini tugged hard on the reins and stopped the cart in its tracks, out of earshot of the others. He leapt down from the seat and faced her, doubt and fear in his eyes.

"I too have suffered a nagging toothache, but for many years now. It first started in the store room of this very plantation. My good friends Cosimo Mutolo and Leopoldo Notarbartolo were with me and shared in my pain."

Maria knew Ruddini would have to respond in this way. She had witnessed the secret routine many times. "My honoured friend, Cesare Giuliano, sends his fraternal greetings." Her words seemed to wash over him, lost in the confusion that was still written on his face.

"Forgive me," he said. "We have not been introduced. This is most strange. I thought I knew all of those who were to be enrolled in our noble society."

The suspicion was evident in his voice, and Maria hadn't even begun the most difficult part of her subterfuge. "You would only know of those from the valley," she replied. If she couldn't convince him of her credentials, then her entire plan would be in danger. Over a period of weeks she had managed to purloin the clothes from those who worked on her father's estate. The previous day had seen her take off to a remote hillside and yell until she was hoarse and her throat felt like it had been scrubbed with lye. For the next four days her father and his closest cohorts would be in Palermo and out of touch with Favara. It had to be now, and she was prepared: prepared to convince Ruddini that Cesare Giuliano wanted him to retract his statement identifying Tommaso di Bova as the attacker who had beaten the rail yard boss near to death. Ruddini continued to stare at her. The doubt and concern etched on his face had not diminished one iota. "I am from Palermo, from an honoured family," continued Maria. "Even now, Cesare Giuliano sits down with my father and brothers to discuss stronger links between Girgenti and Palermo. My selection for the omertá and the place in which I held the burning saint are part of that."

"I hear great wisdom from someone whose balls have little more hair than an unripe peach and whose voice has barely broken," said Ruddini.

"You've never been to Palermo?"

He shook his head.

Thank God, thought Maria, she couldn't disguise her accent and she knew nothing of the capital city. "We die young, so we start young. My name is Pasquale Villabate."

He seemed to accept this but the suspicion still drove him to seek answers. "I welcome you as a man of honour, Pasquale Villabate, and ask you to return my most heartfelt greetings to our rappresentante. But why go to all this trouble just to meet with me?"

Maria prayed her husky voice would hold up. "I will pass on your greetings. The reasons why we must meet in secret will become obvious. I will explain them to you on the journey back to Favara. Now tell me, has Mutolo grown a neck yet?" she said with a broad smile. Ruddini smiled back and relaxed a little. With that, she hopped up onto the seat of the wagon and waited.

The ride back to Favara was still just as uncomfortable but the time seemed shorter, truncated as it was by earnest conversation. Maria started by telling what she knew of Ruddini's testimony. He relaxed even further and the suspicion was all but gone from his voice. No one could have known these things, as the details she gave were never made public. Only her father, Ruddini and the investigating magistrate knew the full story, and of course Captain Bruno Fabroni. Maria had pleaded with Fabroni to follow through on her plan but he steadfastly refused. She knew he would, but managed to get a transcript of Ruddini's confession long before the carabinieri captain knew of her real intentions. He was angry and threatened all sorts of dire consequences, but she had forged ahead regardless. Once Ruddini delivered his rebuttal then Fabroni would have no choice but to return to the magistrate and have the testimony annulled. Her next problem would be getting word to Tommaso. He had to withdraw his confession. That would be difficult on two counts. Firstly, she had no means of communication with Palermo and Vicaria, and secondly Tommaso would never withdraw his confession if he had to return to Favara and face Cesare Giuliano. The first problem would succumb to a degree of seduction but the second seemed insoluble, as it had the last time she conjured with it. Then she remembered what Tommaso's mother had told her: '*Ahead of you lies a choice that will determine the rest of your life: Tommaso di Bova or Cesare Giuliano. You cannot hold both in your heart.*' The solution was obvious. Maria's father had to be convicted of the crime for which he was truly responsible: the assault on the rail yard boss. There was also a simple elegance to the solution. Captain Fabroni would get to remove Cesare Giuliano and set the fratellanza back months or even years. Faced with that bonus, he could not fail to go along with her plan when Ruddini arrived at the barracks of l'arma dei carabinieri. Of course there was a hidden agenda: she would use every ruse and means of persuasion to leave the door open for Tommaso to assume the role of rappresentante. There were many men of honour in Girgenti who had luxuriated in the sexual favours of Maria's sisters. That taboo was as good as a gun to the head of any who fell foul of one of the fratellanza's most stringent rules: don't fuck with another man's woman, let alone the rappresentante's daughters. Maria had maintained her fidelity to Tommaso, despite the strength of her passions, but she wasn't beyond using seduction. An intimate touch here, an unfulfilled promise there and the same in return. It was a dangerous game and would catch her out sooner or later. For now it was a storehouse of unexploded blasting powder.

* * *

They had tied his brother to a wooden bridge on the main railway line from Siderno to Reggio Calabria, just south of San Nicola, where it crossed the Bonamico River. Then they strapped five kilos of dynamite close to his body and lit the fuse. Giuseppe Fabroni was already so badly beaten that he wouldn't have known what was about to happen. Had he done so, it would probably have been a welcome relief from the pain. The timing was perfect. The explosion blew down the bridge in front of a southbound freight train, which managed to stop in time. Giuseppe was the only casualty. The local polizia found barely enough of him to make a positive identification, but quickly decided that he had planted the explosives, failing to get out of the way before the blast, which killed him.

Captain Bruno Fabroni knew the truth about his brother: he knew that Giuseppe had no access to industrial explosives and his only crime was failing to sell their land, their farm, their home, and all for a pittance.

The farm was blessed with its location on the small flood-plain of the Bonamico that meandered its way to the Ionian Sea on the east coast of Calabria. Lemons, olives, corn, even vines grew in the fertile silt washed down from Lago Constantino in the foothills of Aspromonte. On rare occasions the wandering river would morph into a violent cataract and devastate the surrounding fields, as a torrent of rain gushed down from the hills to meet a rising tide and a westerly storm. In the space of a few hours they could lose a harvest, or a season's planting. But that was how the fertile soils were replenished. Generations of Fabronis had benefited from the times of placid benevolence and had to pay back a percentage when faced with the inevitable violence of nature's mercurial temperament. His father had always explained it this way, the same way he explained the *pizzo*: the payment made to the local men of honour. It was just nature's way, he would say, as it was just the way of Calabria. The violence was always there and it took a small share of your wealth, but in return for that payment, the bulk of your income was secure. It had been unchanged for generations.

Then came the railway.

Suddenly, land on the coastal stretch doubled, tripled and quadrupled in value as new businesses fought to be close to the economic lifeline that would ultimately link Calabria's east coast to the bustling port of Reggio: gateway to Sicily and beyond. The value of the pizzo grew to become a crippling burden, and the violence escalated as Bruno's father found it impossible to meet the demands of the local men of honour: the 'ndrangheta. They made no attempt to hide their identity or their extortion, because they feared no one, not even the local polizia, whom they effectively owned, along with most of the prefecture and the judiciary. The first attacks happened when Bruno was studying at Padua University in Palermo. By the time he made it home, they had killed his father and beaten his mother to the point where she would never again leave her sick-bed. Giuseppe stood fast and Bruno supported him, eventually finding a strand of decency and honesty in the ranks of the local l'arma dei carabinieri. They did what they could to torment the criminal families who controlled the region, but as quickly as they could arrest suspects, the crooked ranks of the resident magistrates released them again, often with glowing character references from upstanding businessmen, who were of course hand-in-glove with the local 'ndrangheta.

Yet the Fabronis were no pushover. They were strong, fearless and tough because they had to work hard to extract the maximum value from the land they farmed. Cousins, uncles and assorted in-laws stood together and took the violence back to their enemies. Bruno had used the little time he had between university terms to build strong relationships with the local carabinieri and the one magistrate they could still trust. The men of honour found themselves in a pincer movement between the law and eye-for-an-eye violence. The stand-off had lasted for a month and Giuseppe persuaded Bruno to return to Padua.

Then the 'ndrangheta changed tack. They had no real interest in the pizzo; it was the land they coveted. If they couldn't succeed by violence, then they had other more insidious methods.

A line of railway workers presented themselves to the local polizia, all claiming to have been attacked by the Fabronis. Charges were raised and Giuseppe had watched the ranks of his relatives decimated, as they were arrested and jailed. Bruno could only keep his counsel from a distance as Giuseppe assured him he had things under control. That was far from the case. Giuseppe was arrested for threatening the local railway franchise: *Società per le Strade Ferrate del Mediterraneo*. A forged letter was produced as evidence, and sections of track were found to have been damaged in an attempt to derail a train. It wasn't enough to secure a conviction against Giuseppe, but that wasn't the plan. The headline news in the local newspaper branded the Fabronis as villains, determined to wreck the commercial windfall everyone was set to benefit from. Suddenly, no one wanted the produce of the Fabroni farms, and the railway refused to accept their freight. It was October – the harvests went ahead but only delivered Fabroni lemons, olives and corn to rot in storehouses and freight-yards.

Then they killed Giuseppe. Almost immediately, the farm and all Fabroni lands were seized by the courts as collateral against the damages pursued by the railways. It was over. 'Ndrangheta had won. The Fabronis were evicted.

For Bruno, there was only one future upon graduating from Padua: l'arma dei carabinieri. Every town and village throughout the new Italy had a carabinieri presence. No one could serve in their home region, which suited him. After the death of his mother, he had no reason to return to Calabria. All of which partly explained why he sat in the barracks in Favara, facing a repentant Antonio Ruddini, whose Damascene conversion would have made that of Saul of Tarsus pale by comparison. It was down to Maria Giuliano, of this he was certain and all the more astounded because he hadn't a clue about how she managed it. He had told her not to pursue this because there were things she didn't understand that could easily wreck her plans, but now the door was open to put her father in jail. Ever since Bruno's family had been raped of their land, he had but one mission – to cause the most hurt to any and all of the honoured societies throughout the new Italy. All his training and the very ethos of the carabinieri would not allow any form of personal vendetta. That didn't prevent him from salivating at the thought of running Ruddini through with his sabre. However, there were better ways to quench his thirst for revenge and most of those ways were linked to the pursuit of justice for all who opposed criminality. Ruddini was just a pawn. Cesare Giuliano was the king on this chess board.

Still Bruno's thoughts came back to Maria. She would be a greater prize than her father because she had all the makings of a pentito. Yes, she was clever enough to manipulate events so as not to expose her identity and thus face a court, but her actions were just as destructive to the fratellanza. If he could only sanctify what she saw as treachery and make her realise it was in fact loyalty, then he could contemplate another step in a relationship with this woman who captivated him. For now, he had to put those thoughts behind him, and in a way this was a relief. Those disparate passions couldn't easily be reconciled. There was his love for this woman and his fiery contempt for the criminal society to which she belonged. That society, or one just like it, had robbed Bruno of everything and killed his family. The only way he could weave a strand of forgiveness strong enough to support the love he had for Maria, was if she would betray the family that controlled the lives of so many in Favara and beyond.

He looked across the bare wooden table at Ruddini and had to make a conscious effort not to lay his hand on the sabre at his side. "I should arrest you for wasting the time of the carabinieri and the courts."

"I made a mistake, Captain Fabroni. I'm an honourable man, so I had to confess to my error. I'll take whatever punishment is due."

"Who told you? Who told you to do this?"

"Only God and my conscience, Captain."

"So you could identify the person you really saw that night?"

"Alas no. I can only be sure it wasn't Tommaso di Bova."

"You're lying. Di Bova confessed. His confession supports your original testimony."

"Captain Fabroni, I recall the words of the magistrate who thanked me personally. Di Bova confessed because of my testimony. He had no defence and no alibi for that night. His sentence was inevitable, but reduced because of his guilty plea. Many men have suffered the same fate. I cannot, in all conscience, let this continue. You have my retraction. You must act upon it."

"Why did you come to me? Why not go straight to the magistrate?"

Ruddini paused, confusion and hesitancy replacing the eloquence of his previous answers.

"Captain, there is no trust in this land. We've all witnessed corruption, but the ordinary citizen cannot know its true extent. Only the carabinieri have clean hands."

"You suspect the magistrate of being complicit in crimes involving the fratellanza?"

"I know nothing of this 'fratellanza', and I accuse no one of criminality. My honesty is simply drawn to your integrity."

Fawning bastard, thought Bruno but said nothing. He collected up the hand-written statement dictated by Ruddini and swept it across the table to rest beside the ink-stand on the desk. Ruddini lifted the wood and pewter dip pen, placed its nib carefully in the ink-pot and then signed the statement with a flourish. There was no going back for him after that. Equally, there was no going back for Maria, her father and the new investigation into the assault on the rail-yard boss. Tommaso di Bova was suddenly more than just a pawn. That Maria had started a process to engineer her lover's return was self-evident. Bruno had to break that relationship by forcing a bitter division between them. Di Bova would return, only to shun Maria because she had become a traitor to the head of the family and thus to the fratellanza. That truth would be easy to disseminate, but only when it suited Captain Bruno Fabroni. There were some selfish things he had to reserve for his personal stock of vengeance.

Chapter 14

"It isn't prison, it's school." Lorenzo Fratelli looked across the upturned half-barrel at Toto and took a grateful swig of Marsala before replying. "Ciavallotta didn't allow time off for reading and writing."

"Which is why the piece of paper I slipped you was nothing more than a crude map of where to find this little taverna."

"It's a Calabrian drinking hole and I'll be damned if I give any more of my lire to di Bova and his skinny little butcher."

"Block commanders come and go, as do their enforcers. You're here for twenty years."

Lorenzo stared across the crowded cellar at Filippo who returned the look of defiance with one of his own. In less than a day, Lorenzo's ideas of what Vicaria would mean were turned upside down. Did Cesare Giuliano really understand what was going on here? It wasn't just the drinking den and the other services offered, from food to whores; it was the way sworn enemies behaved like brothers. The Sicilian way was pure and without corruption from prostitution. The fratellanza didn't dress like pimps and flaunt their wealth on trinkets and stupid hairstyles, as was the way with so many of his fellow drinkers. Yet, all around him was one big, happy family of miscreants who seemed to have forgotten the strict rules of their respective honourable societies. He looked back at Toto, who was examining him closely with his one-eyed stare.

"Why are you here, old man, and why do you seek my friendship?"

"I'm in Vicaria because of a trade: my life for a favour, my time in prison a token. The rappresentante makes demands of many."

"You are not of the brotherhood."

"Are those who pay the pizzo honourable members? Some, maybe, but all who are asked contribute, if they know what's good for them. I do not seek your friendship. I was asked to smooth the way for you: to get you settled in quickly. Who do you think arranged that little welcoming ceremony this morning on C Wing?"

"And di Bova?"

"I don't look out for him, but he likes my company, so he had me transferred here. Don't underestimate him, or the 'ndrangheta."

Lorenzo continued to listen to Toto talking about block commanders and how the various descendants of Osso, Mastrosso and Carcagnosso were segregated in ways that ensured they mixed with one another and shared their respective secrets. Nothing interested him, as nothing was relevant to his task of killing Tommaso di Bova. "Who decided the fate of Giovanni Noto?" asked Lorenzo, hoping to learn how killings were sanctioned in the prison.

"Maybe his lack of respect decided his fate," replied the old mule-herder as he swilled the last of his Marsala round the bottom of his tankard in an obvious attempt to earn another drink.

"And maybe your mules used to shit lemons," replied Lorenzo as he dropped another handful of lire into Toto's tankard.

"As it is on the outside, so it is in here. Noto was marked long before the prison doors shut behind him. A bounty was arranged and the task was given."

"So Filippo was appointed executioner?"

"The block commanders have first option, but they usually pass."

"What happens if a block commander is marked?"

Toto made to respond and then stopped, his one good eye fixed on the top of the wooden barrel they were using as a table.

"It has never happened," replied Toto, continuing his unseeing stare.

Lorenzo joined him, but his gaze was not without purpose. The weight of the barrel wasn't an issue; he could have lifted it with one hand. Gripping it was the problem, but close inspection revealed two rough-cut holes, obviously not put there by the cooper but by someone who needed to manhandle the heavy cask in its role as a table. Lorenzo measured his distance to Tommaso and also to Filippo. Each was about ten paces away, or six at a good run. There were many obstacles in the way of each target but Lorenzo's weight and that of the barrel would sweep them away like wind-blown twigs. His victim had to be di Bova. Cesare Giuliano had marked him and appointed The Horse as the executioner. There was no such sanction for Filippo, but Lorenzo would have to disable him first. Two broken legs would probably suffice.

Lorenzo stood with his back to Filippo and looked down at Toto as if to make his excuses and leave. He didn't dare look back at Tommaso's enforcer or the element of surprise would have been lost. With one fluid action, Lorenzo grabbed the half-barrel, then turned and ran to where he had last seen Filippo. He held the half-barrel in front of him, like the engine of a steam train, and covered the six paces to his first target with a colossal momentum that would brook no intervention. Bodies, tables, chairs and tankards of Marsala were flung left and right amid yells and a few futile attempts to stop Lorenzo's thundering charge. Filippo eyed him for a fraction of a second and then darted to his left. Lorenzo tracked him like a swooping hawk. The top of the half-barrel was centimetres from the knife man's head when the aim lowered to his legs. In the same instant the skinny little butcher ducked under the bone-crushing charge.

Lorenzo had missed.

From beneath the wooden staves, two attacking hands shot upwards, their long nails armoured with sharp steel to slice into Lorenzo's femoral artery. Lorenzo swivelled his hip just as the first blade ripped into him. The rim of the barrel was now turned away from Filippo's legs. Lorenzo didn't hesitate: he brought the steel-hooped edge down on his attacker's head with devastating force and was rewarded with the popping crunch of a busted skull. Swiftly he turned to where he had last seen Tommaso di Bova and made another charge, only to be brought crashing to the ground, courtesy of a slippery patch of blood at his feet.

* * *

The Ciavallotta mine hid many bodies, and not all of them were dead. The five who accompanied Captain Bruno Fabroni were very much alive. They were also the best that l'arma dei carabinieri had to offer. Silent as mice, they hid in a tunnel, listening to the yells of Antonio Ruddini, as Cesare Giuliano and his cohorts beat him mercilessly. From his concealment, Fabroni could clearly see the dimly-lit cavern where six of the fratellanza acted as judges, jury and executioners for their hapless victim. Wide-eyed terror was writ large on Ruddini's face, visible even through the livid purple wheals and bruises and through the warm glow of the miners' oil lamps that illuminated the patch of sulphur, directly above the deepest ventilation shaft in the mine. Bruno was close enough to witness the blood fly from Ruddini's nose with every strike and hear the squelch and crunch of pulverised bone and cartilage. He knew why Ruddini was being tortured – he had signed the retraction identifying Tommaso di Bova. The fact that he was deceived into it by Maria Giuliano was astounding, especially since Bruno now knew how she had managed it. Had Ruddini known, he would undoubtedly have had a different opinion and an answer to the whereabouts of the mysterious Pasquale Villabate. That very question was being fired at him by Cesare Giuliano himself, delivered with sickening thumps from a pick-axe handle, audible above the now-whimpering cries of pain.

The leather purse with the metal ring had landed in the

courtyard over three hours ago. Maria was at her work and taking a great risk, but she knew little of what was about to happen. For his own part Bruno knew much more, including where the next stage in the torture and execution of Ruddini would likely play out. They even called it Cesare's Shaft, as so many of the rappresentante's victims had been tipped down it. The shaft was narrow and dropped one hundred metres to one of the deepest levels of the mine: a level that had been deserted years ago, after a rock fall blocked the access and took twenty carusi with it.

Ruddini was minutes away from his final descent.

Captain Bruno Fabroni had an important decision to make: intervene now and spare the victim, or wait until he could prosecute a murder charge. Of his team of six, he was the only one afforded a view of the proceedings. The others could guess what was happening but they sat in obedient silence.

Ruddini's life, or the extinction of it, would not be on Bruno's conscience. His would not be the hand that hastened the tortured wretch's demise. Even if they all rushed Giuliano's group, it would only take one small shove to make another sacrificial offering to Cesare's Shaft. Two other factors weighed heavily on Bruno, influencing a decision he knew would fundamentally change the lives of many in Favara.

Bruno's mother was last to die, and then it had taken two years of pain and withering degradation, following her beating by the 'ndrangheta and the Fabronis' eviction. No one in San Nicola would help, lest they also drew the attention of the local men of honour. There were a few Fabronis left near Reggio, and she had been taken to a hillside farm where she died alone, save for a few distant cousins. He had made a decision to finish his training for the carabinieri, and it was the toughest decision he had ever made. The doctors had assured him there was nothing they could do for his mother, and a broken heart would only hasten her demise. She was simply too old and too feeble to be driven by any emotions other than sadness and fear, and they were no weapons to fight off the rigours of a twisted and brittle skeleton brought on by a plethora of broken bones. Bruno also shared those feelings, but he had retribution in his armoury, and that was powerful ordnance. He couldn't help his mother, although their separation in her dying days was an unfathomable torture for her and a fiery sadness for him. The legacy of her passing from this world to the next had to begin whilst she lay in a lonely farmhouse clinging on to a ruined life, and waiting for him to appear at her bedside. That legacy was now the catalyst for every quest for justice that drove Captain Bruno Fabroni. He had to uphold the values of the carabinieri, but occasionally he would be presented with a set of circumstances that tested such principles to their limits. This was one of those times.

As he listened to the ever-weakening cries of Antonio Ruddini, Bruno weighed the values associated with saving his life and did nothing. There was a redeeming logic in that judgement: the second factor in his decision. Cesare would deliver the final blow: he would tip his helpless victim down the shaft, there was nothing surer. Bruno would have him for murder. This wasn't part of the bargain with Maria but he would deal with it in his own way. She had been told her plans could have consequences way beyond her original intentions, and the message in the leather purse had been written in fear and panic, as she began to understand her actions would lead to Ruddini's death. Obviously, Bruno was supposed to prevent this and be rewarded with the bonus of arresting Cesare. The feelings he had for Maria were as potent as ever, but passion would always come off second best to vengeance.

By now Ruddini was kneeling before his attackers. They had untied his hands because they knew he was powerless to defend himself against the blows. There was also his corpse to consider. If it was ever found, his demise would have to look like an accident. He was seconds away from death. Bruno held his hand up as a signal to his men. He could feel them tensing behind him but they never made a sound.

Cesare walked over to the sagging and broken pile of flesh and bone that was Antonio Ruddini. "The brotherhood has no room for fools or liars," said the rappresentante, clear enough to be heard across the underground cavern. "You have betrayed me, you have betrayed your oath, and you have betrayed those who brought you wealth and status. There is but one retribution." With that he placed his foot on Ruddini's shoulder and kicked him over the edge. The only sounds to be heard were those of the condemned man's body thumping against the sides of the shaft, as it hurried down to the brimstone graveyard below.

Bruno dropped his hand.

His men rushed forwards.

Immediately Giuliano's team responded and a round cracked off from a Beaumont Vitali, claiming one of the carabinieri as a target. Bruno's men weren't without firepower and two rounds were quickly returned, claiming the first shooter. Bruno left the ballistics to the others under his command and ran forwards, sabre at the ready and shouting commands to the rappresentante and his cohorts, which were ignored as hot metal whizzed and pinged around Bruno's head.

Suddenly they were all plunged into darkness as the oil lamps were kicked and snuffed out.

And the darkness was complete: an utter blackness where vision was useless.

As if on command, all the combatants fell silent. The slightest noise might invite another rifle shot and there were at least two more shooters amongst the enemy ranks.

The first to be hit had been one of Bruno's team and the injured man groaned and rolled over on the dirt. An enormous flash lit up the cavern as a shooter zeroed in on the sound, and with frightening accuracy found his target. The injured man groaned again as another round thwacked into him. Immediately, fire was returned. Bruno's men were well-trained and sported the latest Carcano M91 rifles. The flash from the enemy Vitali had illuminated the darkness like a lightning bolt and three Carcanos opened up in return. There was no time to issue commands and no time to identify targets. The darkened cavern burst into staccato life with eruptions of light and sound as fratellanza and carabinieri were momentarily illuminated in successive flashes. Twelve rounds were expended in just a few seconds. Hot metal whizzed around like the devil's own fireflies. Bodies fell and victims groaned, but Bruno had no way of knowing victor from vanquished.

The Carcanos carried six rounds apiece and the Vitalis four. Bruno took the risk of shouting another command, instructing his men to open fire again – one round each. The lightning flashed once more and the thunder roared. In the fractions of seconds he had to perceive what was happening, Bruno could only detect supine bodies on the opposite side of the cavern. He stumbled on a miner's lamp and pulled a pack of Lundstrom matches from a pocket in his tunic. The warm light from the lamp revealed the outcome of the battle: five bodies. Discounting his comrade, this meant that one of Giuliano's team was missing. Fabroni just knew it would be the old bastard himself. He grabbed a Carcano from one of his men and handed him the oil lamp in return. They both set off towards the exit from the cavern.

"Check for Giuliano," Bruno shouted as he set off in pursuit.

"He's here," came the reply from back in the cavern.

Bruno stopped and returned to where one of his men cradled the lifeless head of Cesare Giuliano. It had been perforated by a round that left a pencil-sized hole in his forehead and a fist-sized exit wound behind his ear.

"Shit," said Bruno aloud. This wasn't part of his plan, not by any means.

"It's fine, sir," said one of his men. "It was a fire-fight and they started it. You've nothing to worry about, and we're all well rid of that bastard. We all behaved with honour and defended ourselves." He paused and looked over to his fallen comrade. "And we've lost one of our own."

"Dead?" asked Bruno, hoping he had misheard his comrade.

"First shot hit him in the shoulder, not fatal. Second shot hit him square in the throat, sir. Cesare Giuliano murdered one of ours whilst he lay wounded. We're soldiers, not police. We've the right to shoot to kill if we're attacked. You shouted a warning, sir. You shouted 'carabinieri'. Giuliano could've surrendered. He chose to fight on."

"Yes," said another. "Just tip him down the shaft; and who's to know? That's true justice after all. Let his soul forever be tormented by all his victims."

Bruno made to speak and condemn them for betraying the values of the carabinieri, then he thought about it and clammed up. There was but one exit from the cavern and the only other tunnel was the one they had been hiding in. "Gather up all the bodies and stack them at the exit to the cavern," said Bruno in a loud and commanding voice, then added almost inaudibly – "As soon as you stack the first body at the exit, rush the tunnel, all of you. Kill anyone you discover there, and shout back what you find. Then stay on guard in case anyone comes back."

They looked in his eyes and understood immediately: there could be no witnesses.

Within minutes the action was completed. The shouted response echoed down the exit tunnel like the voice of a distant ghost: "All clear, sir."

Captain Bruno Fabroni was alone with the corpse of Cesare Giuliano. He dragged the lifeless body across to the ventilation shaft and tipped it over the edge. It bounced off the walls of the shaft four times before delivering a distant thump, as it joined the dead below. The cemetery was now full.

"For Giuseppe," said Bruno, as he walked away to join his men.

* * *

Lorenzo Fratelli hung in the cell like he was crucified. Both outstretched arms were manacled above his head and secured with chains anchored to the walls. A rope was wrapped around his groin and hung from the ceiling, supporting his weight. He had managed to force one eye open. The other was swollen to the point where he feared it would never function again. With what limited vision he had, he looked down to see his toes just touching the cell floor where a sticky puddle of blood was slowly being replenished, drip by drip. A rough bandage had been wrapped around his thigh but wasn't able to fully staunch the wound inflicted on him by Filippo. At least he hadn't bled to death. The thick muscles in his leg must have prevented the stab-wounds going deep enough to rupture his femoral artery.

As more sensation returned to his body, he could sense the swelling protrusions on his head and the bruising on his upper torso. They must have beaten him senseless after he went down: slipping on his own blood and the extruded contents of Filippo's skull. That meant di Bova was still alive, but he would be missing an enforcer.

Lorenzo tugged hard at the chains but they were padlocked to eyelets anchored deeply in the walls and wouldn't budge. Each pull only succeeded in delivering a wave of pain across his body that threatened to send him back to the deep pit of unconsciousness. A raging thirst now nagged at him, made all the more potent by the small bucket of water, placed on the cell floor, just out of his reach. In desperation he tried to swing his good leg over and hook his foot through the handle, but the pain beat him back, along with the realisation that the positioning of the bucket was no accident.

The cell was windowless. The only light was the glow of an oil lamp from beyond the locked steel bars of the door. Lorenzo had no idea how long he had been hanging there like a side of meat. From the puddle of blood at his feet, the thirst and the bruising, it must have been at least a day. They didn't hang him there to recuperate. The rope around his groin now made sense: they needed to support his weight over a long period of time; otherwise he would have succumbed to asphyxiation.

Confused memories surfaced as consciousness ebbed and flowed. He remembered a priest telling him that crucifixion was cruelly and exquisitely designed to be a slow and painful way to die, but only after the centurions broke your legs. With only his outstretched arms to support his weight, Christ suffocated.

Consciousness slipped away and Lorenzo's circle of vision closed. His other senses transformed what they perceived. He could smell the honey: the honey from the calendula. It blossomed in the sunshine in a meadow on the outskirts of Favara. Maria Giuliano picked the flower for him and her father stood beside him as he listened to the buzz of the bees.

Lorenzo shook his head, trying unsuccessfully to force himself above the rim of oblivion.

They weren't bees. They were flies – great big egg-laden monsters that hummed around his bandaged leg.

The smell wasn't honey. It was the putrefaction of a wound that had succumbed to infection and welcomed the invasion of a thousand maggots to burrow into his flesh.

He kicked and flailed at the buzzing hordes, but the more he lashed out, the greater their number became until he was enveloped by a thick, swirling mass of winged corruption. They were in his mouth, his ears, his eyes, and they swooped gleefully onto his festering tissue, depositing their hungry offspring to feed on his septic wounds. He could feel them gorging their flaccid, creamy, wrinkled bodies on his living tissue until they reached the hard white of his bone. Then the wrinkled bodies grew so fat, they burst into a putrefied mass of blood and tissue that spawned yet more winged blackness to start the process once again.

He screamed in fear. For the first time in his life he faced a terror that came with the knowledge it couldn't be defeated by aggression or force.

He shook his head again and the winged hordes retreated to a single horse-fly, attracted by the blood at his feet. The smell of honey instantly changed to that of the carbolic acid they had used as a screaming disinfectant on his wound.

He heard the clank of the prison door open. It may have been this very sound that brought him back to sweet reality.

Tommaso di Bova entered and looked up at him. He paced around Lorenzo's suspended body before going to the wall of the cell and lowering the rope by a small amount. Lorenzo's feet now descended to a point where his toes supported part of his weight and the rope around his groin did the rest. Each breath was now a little bit more difficult as his diaphragm had to lift more of his body weight to fill his lungs, unless he supported himself on his one good and one damaged leg.

"Who told you to kill Filippo?" asked di Bova.

"No one."

"So, you took it on yourself to kill an honourable member without any approval? Even on the outside, you know this is against the omertá."

"It was a fight. He tried to slice me, like he did with Noto. It was him or me."

"If he'd wanted you dead then the last thing to have run down your leg wouldn't have been blood."

"It was a fight. Happens all the time. Nothing personal."

"Who told you kill Filippo?" asked di Bova again.

"No one."

Lorenzo watched as Tommaso picked up the water bucket and helped himself to a ladle full of its contents before replacing the bucket carefully where he had found it.

"Lorenzo, we'll continue this conversation tomorrow. You should last until then, at least. After that, I'm not so sure. One thing is for certain: you're already a condemned man. I can kill you now, without any sanctions, but I prefer to wait."

The cell door clanged and Lorenzo hung his head to let his arms take the strain. Within minutes he had to put his weight on the tips of his toes and push up to assist his breathing. His wounded leg protested painfully. And then there was the thirst. This had been demoted to just a minor demon whilst the horror of his semi-conscious ravings took hold; now it consumed his entire body like a fever.

It was going to be a long and painful night.

Chapter 15

"Is my father still alive?"

Bruno Fabroni looked into Maria Giuliano's eyes, and for the first time he understood the pure and simple beauty that could be revealed once all of the fratellanza clutter was stripped from her life. The question came from her heart. Its only agenda was that of a daughter being concerned about her missing father. The new-found innocence extended beyond her eyes, and Bruno found himself further captivated by this new seam of loveliness that made Maria all the more desirable. Their meeting, just ahead of the funerals for the other fratellanza dead, was unexpected, but Bruno had forgotten about the simple instruction he had given her some months past.

If she wanted a clandestine meeting, she only had to ask the postman.

Postal mail was the domain of the state, the church and commerce, but just a few of the wealthier citizens also enjoyed this luxury. The Giuliano family counted themselves in that category. As it was so difficult to ensure the honesty and integrity of the staff who made up this vital service, they were usually recruited from the ranks of the carabinieri, either retired or invalided out. The Favara postman was recently invalided out of active service and was totally trustworthy. Maria only had to give him a personal letter and it would be delivered within the hour.

The meeting place was the same as before but the mood was different, and Bruno had to think carefully about the answer to her first question. "His body wasn't one of those brought from the mine," he replied, desperate not to openly lie to her.

"So he escaped?"

"Have you ever been in the mine?"

"No, and it doesn't concern me. Did my father escape?"

"It was dark: I mean totally black. No one could see anything in the cavern once the oil lamps were snuffed out. There was gunfire, and when it was over there were the dead and the missing. The living brought the corpses to the surface; the missing rest elsewhere. I can only tell you that your father is not held by any of the forces of law and order. He isn't under arrest and the same is true for one other member of his party, who was nowhere to be found after the shooting. Antonio Ruddini rests at the bottom of Cesare's Shaft. I saw him go over the edge before the lamps were extinguished."

This seemed to satisfy Maria, or at least truncate the persistent questioning whilst she mulled over the events he had described.

"There is sadness and fear in our house," continued Maria, her voice as distant as the look in her eyes. "There is shock and confusion amongst the fratellanza. Cesare should've been in touch. The men of honour are powerless without either the rappresentante or his corpse. That's their problem; mine is one of a loving daughter."

Bruno felt the 'loving daughter' role was at risk of becoming overplayed. Maria was now the calculating consort who was happy to have her father arrested, albeit for a crime he did commit, so that she could have Tommaso back. Nonetheless, sowing the seeds of despair and confusion amongst the fratellanza was exactly what Bruno had wanted from the plan formulated in his mind, minutes before he had consigned the corpse of Maria's father to the depths of Ciavallotta. As long as Cesare was missing and not confirmed dead, then the honourable members were in a state of limbo, and without powerful leadership they would bicker and squabble. Sooner or later there would be bloodshed as long-forgotten vendettas were resurrected, and then there would be informers. For as long as he could ensure the truth about Cesare remained hidden, he held the upper hand. Concealing the truth was a matter for his conscience, reaping the benefits of his subterfuge strengthened the forces of law and order. It was a simple and powerful formula, and it troubled him not one iota.

"You told me something like this could happen. You warned me. I didn't listen," said Maria, still distant and troubled. "I thought I could control something by getting involved. I was wrong."

Bruno could see where this was going. "The crimes of the fratellanza touch nearly everybody in Girgenti," he said with all of the comfort and sincerity he could muster. "You're not alone and you have the might of the carabinieri to fall back on."

Maria looked up, and suddenly the look of despair had been evicted from her face. Her green eyes glinted, but not with tears. "Now, more than ever, is when my family need me. I brought this on by giving you the information, Captain Fabroni, but I didn't ask you to kill anyone. I will live forever with that guilt and shame, but for you – it's just a day's work." Maria turned and quickly mounted her horse. "There will be no more contact between us, Captain."

She made to kick her mount and ride away. Bruno had one last card to play or he would lose her forever. "I have news of Tommaso di Bova," he said, whilst looking up at Maria. Instantly her mood changed. She reined in her horse and dismounted.

"Is he alive?" she said with the same innocence and concern that had been evident when she asked that very question of her father.

"Yes, he is alive and healthy. He's still a prisoner in Vicaria, but he is alive."

"How do you know this?"

"Ruddini's retraction is still valid. Pursuit of the law is my duty, and Tommaso appears to be innocent of the crime for which he is imprisoned. I have much to do to ensure his release. In fact, I need to go to Palermo and discuss his confession with him. It is my case and I have insisted in seeing it through." With that, Bruno mounted his own stallion and made to leave. He had played a winning card, of that there was no doubt. Maria could choose to play or fold. The next few seconds would set them both on a course that would change their lives forever, of this he was certain.

"Wait, please don't go," said Maria. "Please understand this is a difficult and emotional time for me. I've said things in haste."

"I understand," said Bruno, barely able to keep the smile from his face. "Your father always forbade any contact with di Bova. If Cesare turns up in the next few days then he may still do so, but would you like me to arrange a visit to Vicaria where you can spend some time alone with Tommaso?"

* * *

It might have been a day, it might have been longer. The raging thirst was still there and the pain in his legs grew more intense. It seemed to Lorenzo that he had to support his body weight every few minutes now. He could feel the strength draining from his muscles. Thankfully, the delirium hadn't bothered him recently. Maybe it was a fever from the initial cut and it was now settled. Still, the demons seemed to lurk in every dark corner of the cell, waiting to pounce when he was at his weakest. Let them wait. He had held something in reserve: something that could defeat demons as well as his own tormentor.

As if on cue, the cell door clanked open and Tommaso entered. He walked around and Lorenzo pretended not to be conscious. Maybe his torturer would make a mistake and throw the contents of that water bucket over him. Lorenzo could catch a few precious drips before the vital fluid was wasted in the drains of Vicaria. Sure enough, he could sense Tommaso moving towards the bucket. Lorenzo opened his good eye just a tiny crack and witnessed him lifting the wooden ladle out, but he did not put it to his own lips; he put it to Lorenzo's.

And what a cruel torture he was practicing.

For sure, as soon as Lorenzo made to drink, the ladle would be pulled away.

Lorenzo remained motionless.

Tommaso pressed the ladle against Lorenzo's lips and reached up to pinch his nose. Lorenzo gasped and drank, careful to conserve every drop. Tommaso refilled the ladle and offered it back to Lorenzo's eager lips.

"More?" asked Tommaso, after the second ladle.

"Please," replied Lorenzo, grateful for what was less than a fraction of the hydration he knew he needed.

"Who told you to kill Filippo?"

The little bastard was clever, thought Lorenzo. "No one," he replied.

Tommaso walked behind him and cut the rope securing the last of Lorenzo's weight. The pain was excruciating, both from his upper body and from his damaged leg. He started wheezing almost immediately.

"You seek my crucifixion, Tommaso? And where will that lead you? You want my corpse but you also want something else, or I would already be dead."

"A healthy man of good strength won't suffocate if crucified," said Tommaso. "That's not how it works. Crucifixion needs other injuries and weaknesses to debilitate the body. Blood poisoning from an open wound works well, as does dehydration and starvation. Our Good Lord suffered these and died. There's no such goodness in you, Lorenzo, and there'll be no resurrection." He paced slowly around Lorenzo's suspended body as he said this. There was no triumph in his voice – no gloating, just a certainty that he had permission to kill Lorenzo, and he could torture him for as long as needed to get an answer.

"I told you before, di Bova. Filippo just got in the way. It was him or me in a fight. I only intended to break his legs. Things got out of control."

"Your attack was unprovoked, Lorenzo."

"He was in the way: in the way of my true mark."

"Who was the mark?"

"Cut me down and you will know."

"Who gave you the mark?"

"Cut me down and you'll know," repeated Lorenzo. "It's not as if I can just walk free, is it? You will still have me here, di Bova, and if I don't keep my word, you can chain me back up. Be assured, the greater the punishment, the less I'll reveal." Lorenzo needed to end it. He had suffered the rigours of being a little wagon and survived, but he couldn't tolerate much more of this. He had watched many of death's flock waiver between oblivion and salvation, as they were herded towards the pen. To escape the dark shepherd he would need cunning as well as strength, and both these qualities were rapidly draining from him. There was one last reserve of mental and physical strength, which he clung to. It was more important than life itself. Once exhausted, if he were able to use it successfully, Lorenzo would happily pass to the next world knowing he had completed his task.

"I've asked you two questions, Lorenzo. You've answered neither and yet you expect absolution from your punishment, with no sign of penitence. One answer and I will cut you down. The second answer, if you give it, brings you to the infirmary."

"I have your word, di Bova, that you will cut me down and place me in the care of the nurses if I answer both your questions?"

"We are still men of honour, Lorenzo. You have my word."

"Cesare Giuliano gave me the mark before the doors of Vicaria slammed shut behind me," said Lorenzo.

Tommaso stood looking up at him, confusion dancing across his face. He might have been from Aspromonte stock but he wasn't stupid. Lorenzo could almost read the realisation in his eyes as the answer to the second question became almost self-evident. Lorenzo didn't trust his captor to deliver on freeing him from this torture but one simple answer would now become like a rope to a drowning man. Tommaso di Bova would have to know the truth. From the shadows, a rusted iron ladder was dragged screeching along the floor of the cell. Tommaso climbed to each shackle and released the locks. At the first, Lorenzo's body swung violently and he pirouetted in agony before his second arm was released and he fell on the cold stone, the chains, still attached to his wrists, clanking on the floor of the cell. The deep pit beckoned, and Lorenzo could sense the demons salivating at the thought of his return. They wouldn't have him. He had strength left, strength he had conserved for a single purpose. "Water," was the only word he wanted to utter. His request was delivered, not by the ladle but by the bucket. The cold drenching gave a little more strength to be added to the small but powerful inventory he would soon call on.

"Who was the mark?"

Tommaso was hunkered down in front of Lorenzo, who rose up onto his hands and knees and looked deep into di Bova's eyes. "You are the mark, Tommaso. Cesare never forgave you for the crime of the fuitina. Maria was promised to me, Tommaso." It hit home, and even though he must have known it, the shock was enough to stupefy Tommaso for a second.

Lorenzo only needed a second.

He flicked his right arm and the chain whipped up and wrapped around Tommaso's neck. Lorenzo caught the free end and yanked it hard to pull his victim onto the floor and fall on top of him. Lorenzo might have been weak but he was still heavy. He wrapped his arms tightly in the suffocating chains and listened to the sound of strangled wheezing drown out the beat of drumming feet and flailing arms. Lorenzo's head began to spin with the sheer exertion of killing di Bova. He had no idea how long it would take to strangle his victim, but he was sure he had conserved enough strength to do it.

* * *

The trouble had started even before the funerals. Leopoldo Notarbartolo was first to arrive at the Giuliano residence and he was no more welcome because of that. Maria detested him and had done for years. She could see things in him her father couldn't: his overarching ambition, his vanity, and moreover his undisguised lust for Maria and her sisters. She didn't understand it back when she was barely ten and was confused about being instructed never to be anywhere alone with him. Her sisters wouldn't talk about why they protected the young Maria, but as she grew older she began to understand. It was a taboo subject in the Giuliano household, but with the absence of her father there was no longer a need to disguise her contempt for this particular capodecina. His early arrival was more to do with the fact he was wanted by the carabinieri than for any reasons of personal vanity, although Maria suspected his strutting arrogance was still a factor.

Notarbartolo was the only one to survive the killings in the mine. He had been the one who escaped: the one who ran and left the others to the fusillade of carabinieri bullets. As such, he must know the truth about her father, but try as she might, Maria could elicit no information from him. He had arrived with the local labour, early in the morning and commandeered a room in the house where he called the other capos, who were loyal to Cesare, and had private meetings with each. They left sombre-faced. It was obvious each had been told not to discuss anything with the Giuliano family.

Notarbartolo remained in the house whilst the funerals took place, as did Maria, her sisters, her three-year-old brother and her mother. He appeared only once during that time to mutter a few inconsequential words to her mother and to give instructions about how the refreshments were to be served once the mourners returned.

Those instructions were followed to the letter, and some hours later Maria stood with her sisters and her mother whilst the capos made themselves comfortable around a large dining table in the room Notarbartolo had commandeered. When the food had all been served, he cleared his throat noisily whilst looking at the Giuliano women. It was their cue to leave. Maria moved to the door, locked it and dropped the key down her bodice. She stood facing her dumbstruck audience.

"The fratellanza are the extended family," she said. "I trust you are all still loyal to your oath and to the Giulianos, as head of all the families represented here?"

The other capos looked around as if hoping the ground would swallow them up. Whatever Notarbartolo had briefed them on in his secret meetings, it wasn't this. Maria's mother looked aghast and made to break the stalemate.

"I know you are concerned about your father," she said. "But this is not the way to express it. Please give me the key and let us leave."

"The people gathered in this room know the truth about Cesare," responded Maria, clearly for all to hear. "That truth is vital to the fratellanza, and the Giuliano women are the representatives of that dynasty. We will be a party to your discussions, Leopoldo Notarbartolo, and we will act on behalf of Cesare whilst he's unable to attend personally. We may not have undertaken the omertá but we are his blood and we will not delegate his legacy to others."

Notarbartolo's face grew contorted with rage and his colour almost matched the red silk cravat tied at his throat. He was speechless and looked around the table hoping someone would rescue him from his plight. There was no such redemption. They all still feared Cesare, and no one would willingly go up against his daughters.

Eventually Cosimo Mutolo broke the silence as he angled his shoulders towards Notarbartolo. "Our oath is to the rappresentante first and foremost, but also to his family. If Cesare cannot be here then we can adjourn and await his arrival, or we can talk freely amongst his family. I have been in the Giuliano household on many occasions and the business of our brotherhood was openly discussed." Overcoming his lack of a neck, he then twisted in his chair to face Maria. "I welcome the inclusion of the Giuliano women."

Maria's mother retreated from the door and stood shoulder to shoulder with Maria and her sisters. The divisions were there, thought Maria. Mutolo was the first to voice them; others might follow. It was vital that the women stood their ground.

"All honourable families in the region are part of the fratellanza and Cesare is rappresentante," replied Notarbartolo. "But only for as long as he is fit for the role. This isn't something that can be passed down like a legacy. Cesare was chosen: chosen by the very members who sit around this table. If he cannot rule, we must choose a successor."

Heads nodded in agreement and Maria realised where this was going. She had to stop it.

"You were the last person to see him, Leopoldo, when you fled and left him to the carabinieri," said Maria. "They don't have him so you must know where he is, or else you must know his true fate. Share this with the honourable members." Her sisters and her mother shuffled uncomfortably beside Maria, but this was nothing to the discomfort Notarbartolo felt following her last remark. The inference was clear: he fled to save his own skin.

"Your tone is accusing, young lady. You weren't there, so you don't know what happened." A few heads nodded in response to this latest riposte from Notarbartolo, but not as many as last time.

"So enlighten us all. We have a right to know," replied Maria.

Notarbartolo began a long and rambling narrative describing the events in the mine. A few details chimed with the account of Captain Fabroni. Other facts were new, but most of what Notarbartolo had to say was typical boasting and vanity. Maria learned that there were only two tunnels accessing the cavern where the incident took place. One tunnel led further into the mine and concealed the carabinieri; the other was the exit to the surface and was guarded by Notarbartolo. He had no weapon. When the oil lamps were extinguished during the gunfire, he decided to make his way up the exit tunnel in search of a small locker where he knew emergency oil lamps and Lundstrom matches were stored. He had groped his way along the tunnel in total darkness by keeping his hand against the wall as he stumbled forwards. When the carabinieri made to come up the exit tunnel, he fled as quickly as he could.

"So, my father could have been behind you?"

"It's possible," replied Notarbartolo, whilst avoiding any further elaboration.

"So, you waited at the exit to the tunnel?"

"No, as far as I was concerned the carabinieri were the only ones behind me. I had to leave. I had to get away from the scene. Now, we've had enough of this, young lady..."

"We have not had enough," shouted Maria, to the astonishment of the others. "Not nearly enough. You were the last of the brotherhood to see my father. By your own admission, you ran away when he could have been behind you, needing your help. You could have hidden in the darkness outside the tunnel to see if he came out, but you didn't." The tension was getting to Maria and emotion threatened to overcome her fortitude. She could feel the tears welling up and her voice catching in her throat. If she broke down now, all was lost.

Cosimo Mutolo stood and held his hands up to try and impose some calm on the tempestuous proceedings. "Maria, the mine continues working, and we have ensured that every tunnel, every seam, every bunker and every outbuilding has been searched. If your father was in Ciavallotta, we would have found him."

"Then he escaped," said Maria, as if it was a matter of fact. All of the capos looked at one another and then at Notarbartolo. The tears welled up again but she blinked them away. Her words had to struggle past the lump in her throat. Calmly, she walked to the table and sat on it, swinging her long legs casually as she reached for a decanter of water and poured herself a glass. "I've been a party to many of my father's decisions in the past. I know of the people he punished and those he made disappear." She looked around the room as she spoke. All eyes were on her. "I know of Ruddini and the statement he retracted. My father was furious and wanted answers. Ruddini was here that very night and could only mutter lame excuses about how some mysterious brother called Pasquale Villabate had been sent to deliver the instruction to recant. No one believed this. I think even Ruddini began to doubt his own experience." Composed now, and without grief diluting her fortitude, Maria continued. "I know where he took Ruddini. I know of Cesare's Shaft." She paused and gracefully slid off the table. The soft rustle of her skirt was the loudest sound in the room. She looked straight at Mutolo. "Cosimo, you said you searched the entire mine. Did you search the bottom of Cesare's Shaft?"

The collective gasp was quickly followed by stunned silence. The capos looked round and across the table at one another, searching for a volunteer to come up with an explanation of why this was impossible. Mutolo didn't waste his energies trying to look from side to side; instead he just sighed and accepted the burden. "Maria, if you know of Cesare's Shaft, you will know why it was chosen for the gruesome task of making our enemies disappear without trace. It's a ventilation shaft for one of the deepest tunnels of the mine. That tunnel has been closed for five years because of a rock fall. There's no way in, other than down the shaft itself. That's one hundred metres down and the same back up again. No one will risk going down there."

"It was dug out of the ground by mineworkers. They must have climbed down it then and back out again," replied Maria. "Find some volunteers to do it once more. The Giuliano family requests it, and they will pay handsomely to anyone who will accept the challenge." She fixed her gaze on Notarbartolo. He was on for it. If her father was dead then his mortal remains could only be in the one place where no one had searched. Mutolo also looked to Notarbartolo who was quick to respond.

"The fratellanza consists of a brotherhood of families headed by the Giulianos and ruled by Cesare as rappresentante. If he is dead, and I beg the indulgence of the Giuliano women when I say this," said Notarbartolo as he addressed the gathering in sombre tones, "then an examination of the tunnel at the bottom of the shaft will help us confirm or refute this. I will assist in making the necessary preparations."

Chapter 16

"Palermo is not safe for someone who wears the uniform of the carabinieri, Captain Fabroni. Rebellion against the new Italy is in the air and Salvatore di Paolo is recruiting in the Conca D'Oro. The ranks of the rebels are swollen by the local men of honour. Maybe we need Garibaldi to come back and knock some heads together? His victory here, five years ago, made Palermo peaceful and prosperous, until now. But then, I suppose Salvatore di Paolo is a carabinieri problem."

Bruno Fabroni looked around the office of Vicaria's Prison Governor and noted that the spartan theme of the green and white glazed tiles was repeated without favour. The office was cold and clinical: a bit like the governor himself. "We are aware of Salvatore di Paolo and his rag-tag band of soldiers and brigands," replied Fabroni. "Any attempt at rebellion will be put down with force."

"I only offer advice for your safety, Captain. I seek no role in shaping history. That's for others of greater importance than a prison governor. Now, you wish to interview one of our inmates: Tommaso di Bova?"

"Yes. The evidence that put him here is tainted. His confession is unsound and a judicial review of his sentence is under way in Favara." It was the barest of information necessary to answer the question. Bruno only placed his trust in those who had earned it. The governor didn't qualify, nor was he likely to.

"I fear you may have had a wasted journey, Captain. Di Bova is in the infirmary. He is barely able to breathe, let alone speak. We bestowed the last rites on him a few days ago. His survival is still uncertain."

Di Bova's death would be a major blow to Bruno's plans for tidying up the fratellanza mess in Favara. Without Tommaso, he had no hold over Maria, and her role in this ever-more complex state of affairs was far from finished. As consumed as Bruno was about this fateful news, he couldn't allow the emotion he felt to display itself in his response, and there was something all too convenient and insincere about how this news was presented. "Governor, I believe Vicaria has the most dangerous stairs in all of Italy. There is barely a week that goes by without another inmate tumbling to his death. I take it di Bova has joined the ranks of those who cannot master the basic walking skills of a toddler?"

The governor paused, looked down and flicked at an imaginary piece of detritus on an otherwise sterile desk, before taking a deep breath and raising his gaze up to meet Bruno's. "Captain Fabroni, in the world you police, you must ensure that villainy cannot attain control of society. That is your job, and I congratulate on your success. In my world, behind these bars, the inmates police themselves; the prison guards are just along for the ride. We have but two sanctions: keys and carbines. Everything else is at the discretion of the men of honour who truly control Vicaria. I accept and understand the difficulties the forces of law have in bringing these reprobates to the gates of my less than perfect establishment. Nonetheless, once here, these villains are my charges. I manage them with the tools of my job. It's best that no one inquires too deeply how that is done."

Bruno couldn't decide if this was a confession designed to elicit sympathy, or a snide remark furnished with a request to stop wasting the governor's time. Neither was important. The odious man was just as much imprisoned in this hell-hole as the inmates, and he was just as much a part of Vicaria's vices as those in its cells. The governor would serve his twenty-five years in an ill-fitting uniform and measure his success by the stash of lire he had skimmed from the black market that flourished behind the prison's locked gates. "I'm not interested in the trials of your job, governor, only in my own. Di Bova fell down the stairs and is close to death, so I cannot interview him. Is that what you are telling me?"

The governor rose from his desk and turned his back on Bruno to walk over to the small window overlooking the prison exercise yard. He paused, as if checking for any irregularity in the tedious world of inmate and prison-staff alike. When he started speaking, he did so with his back still turned. The insult was gross and poorly executed.

"Occasionally, Captain Fabroni, we are faced with circumstances where even the inmates cannot escape the evidence in front of their eyes." The governor spun on his heel and levelled his gaze at the seated Bruno. "My men were brought to an incident where one of our recent arrivals had tried to strangle di Bova. Both were found unconscious on a cell floor. The victim, because of the chains wrapped tightly around his neck, and the attacker, because of a prolonged period of torture at the hands of the victim. The precipitous stairs of this establishment had nothing to do with it. Di Bova will make a recovery. His ability to undergo interrogation by the carabinieri will be determined by the skilled medical staff who currently care for him. When he is well enough for questioning, we will let you know..."

Bruno held his hand up to indicate his impatience, much to the annoyance of the governor. "I will return here tomorrow, at the same time, with documents authorising di Bova's release into the custody of l'arma dei carabinieri. We will ensure he receives the best medical treatment Palermo has to offer. We will guarantee his safety and security until such times as he is fit to return here, or is released under acquittal. Please ensure he is prepared for my return." Di Bova was an important asset in Bruno's future plans for the fratellanza. He couldn't be allowed to die a hero. If he lived and remained in Vicaria, he would continue to be a legend. Neither of those options would fit with a plan that would see him publicly reject Maria because of her treachery. Di Bova had to be back in Favara for that to carry any weight, and his fratellanza star had to be in the ascendancy. Bruno had the tools to control di Bova's life, but only if he was beyond the gates of Vicaria. "Good day to you, governor. Give my regards to Garibaldi, if he calls." With that Bruno stormed out of the office, his leather riding boots stomping on the tiled floor, and the swish of his sabre's scabbard trailing in his wake.

The ride back to Carabinieri Provincial Command on Piazza Giuseppe Verdi was about two kilometres, and Bruno didn't think twice about mounting his stallion and trotting back in the full splendour of his uniform. He was one of the elite of Italy's armed forces, and it didn't matter if that Italy included Sicily. He would be loyal to the will of the majority, as long as that will was expressed freely and without corrupt influence. Of course, this was Palermo: the heartland of the Sicilian Brotherhoods so nothing was clerical white; in fact it was more pagan grey. Salvatore di Paolo was a bigger threat than he had acknowledged to the governor, and even now the men of honour were quickly aligning themselves with the separatist cause. Moreover, they were throwing their iniquitous influence behind it. Palermo could fall to the rebels, tipping Sicily into a bloody war of independence. That could present a problem: Captain Fabroni was sworn to uphold the will of the people expressed through an elected government; Bruno Fabroni was sworn to fight the evil of the Italian Brotherhoods at every turn. However the rebel campaign turned out, l'arma dei carabinieri would remain resolute and honourable. They would continue to project strength and face down injustice. It might be difficult to distinguish where the injustice lay, but that was a problem for another day.

There was a story that Piazza Giuseppe Verdi was to be the home of a new Opera House: the biggest in Italy, maybe even in the entire world, and it was to be built facing the Carabinieri Provincial Command. This was typical of Palermo. For all the corruption and evil in her streets, Bruno still saw the city as magnificently irrepressible, but Palermitans had no concept of the destitution prevalent in towns like Favara and the slavery of her sulphur mines. The men of honour took their pizzo and it mattered not if the gold was from fleas or the Conca D'Oro. Those that benefitted blessed their good fortune, or what remained of it, and carried on. The arrival of the railway in Bruno's home town had done for the citizens of San Nicola what it would undoubtedly do to Palermo. The men of honour would become less insular and the pizzo would morph from minor irritant to economic dominance. Salvatore di Paolo as an individual held no fear for him. The confederation of numerous Sicilian brotherhoods into one coherent criminal structure, with its hooks in every aspect of Italian life, was what chilled Captain Bruno Fabroni to the very core of his being.

As he passed along the splendour of Via Macqueda, Bruno listened to the soft clop of hooves and sought to bring order to his errant thinking. He could do little to alter the direction of an entire country or even a city. What he could do was focus on one small town and its criminal fraternity: the fratellanza. He would have rejoiced if that town was Saint Nicola and he could seek honourable revenge on the 'ndranghetta, but Favara was his lot, and his focus would be no less dimmed because of it. The tools he had to hand were his uniform, his control of Tommaso di Bova's immediate future and the power of his love for Maria. With the might of this ordnance he could and would foment a change that would sweep from Favara to Palermo and beyond. He had to start small, and nothing could be allowed to suppress the first kindling of the blaze. His demons nagged at him for his pretentions. Did he really think he could make a difference and subdue the power of the brotherhoods? And what if he was faced with the choice of pursuing his principles at the expense of securing his love for Maria? What then, asked the demons? Bruno chose to ignore them and their questions: they were exorcisms for another day.

* * *

Maria Giuliano had to admit to herself that the problem of getting someone to scale down Cesare's Shaft was inconsequential, compared to getting an agreement that she could be there when they climbed out. All the capos came up with all sorts of reasons why she could never make the descent into the mine: *'It's bad luck. The carusi would never go back into the tunnels.'*

The carusi would do what they were told or face a beating.

'All the men work naked, or with just a tiny loincloth around their waist.'

We go on a Sunday when the mine is empty of workers.

'It's bad for a woman of child-bearing years to be exposed to the fumes from the sulphur.'

She had no intention of bearing children any time soon, and the fumes inside the caverns were less corrosive than those emanating from the calcaroni above ground and poisoning the entire town.

'Women simply have no place in the mines. It has been this way for centuries and we cannot break this tradition; in fact we are bound by it.'

The patron saint of all miners was Santa Barbara. The last time Maria checked, this saint was a woman.

Eventually they were forced to give in. There was no way Maria would trust them to deliver the truth of what they might find.

Despite her determination, Maria was unprepared for the caverns of Ciavallotta. Yes, she had donned boots, britches and other clothes fitting the task of making the journey into the cavern. God help her if they found Ruddini alive at the bottom of the shaft. He would immediately see through the disguise of the mysterious Pasquale Villabate. That was unlikely in the extreme but other fears assailed her. The heat as they descended and the rapid disappearance of daylight were just a few of the oppressive forces that tried to still her stumbling footsteps. This was a journey into Satan's own basement, where ominous shadows played on the bumps and hollows of the rocks created by the flickering oil-lamp glow. Thankfully, the dim light would have shown little of the terror written on her face.

All of the capos were there, along with two picconieri who had agreed to make the climb into Cesare's Shaft. That none of the group was comfortable with her presence was self-evident, so the hobbling walk down the main tunnel was punctuated with scant conversation. Occasionally a warning would be given about steps carved into the rock or a low overhang, and Maria tried her best to progress with confidence. "Leopoldo, is this what it was like the last time you descended with my father?" she asked of Notarbartolo who, typically, had cast himself as leader of this expedition.

"Almost the same," he replied. "We were fewer in number and we used less oil lamps, but this is what it was like."

"And was the mine empty?" Maria's questioning was made with a slight edge to her voice, revealing her discomfort, but this was intentional.

"We were here for a sinister purpose, as you now know, Signorina. The mine is large and many were bunked-down in its depths, but no one witnessed our visit," replied Notarbartolo, his arrogance edging into his responses, courtesy of Maria's trepidation.

"No one, except the carabinieri," replied Maria. The edginess had suddenly disappeared from her voice and her riposte was delivered with all the authority of a thunderbolt.

Notarbartolo hesitated before giving his reply: "That is a truth we all still wonder about, Signorina Giuliano. It bothers us, and you must be aware of it. Someone betrayed us all, your father included. The carabinieri came here for a reason, and they came in strength because they knew: they knew where we would be and when we would arrive." Notarbartolo stopped, and the party he led stopped with him. He turned to look back at Maria whilst holding his oil lamp high so it caught the malevolent glint in his eye. "They too descended this tunnel, but they did so many minutes ahead of us because they were told: told when our little group was still at your home, otherwise the bastards would have been behind us." He left the statement hanging in the warm dry air of the cavern. It was as poisonous as the fumes from the sulphur.

"When I last saw Ruddini," replied Maria, her voice still resolute, "he had been beaten. He didn't arrive at our home voluntarily, so I assume you dragged him away from the town, violently. Someone must have seen you and run to the barracks. The retraction of Ruddini's statement identifying Tommaso di Bova put my father in danger and the carabinieri would have worked out how he might have reacted. You all played into their hands, Leopoldo."

Notarbartolo brought the lamp down and grunted something unintelligible as he resumed the lead, and they descended further into the cavern.

Maria turned her attention to Cosimo Mutolo, who walked beside her. "Is this tunnel exactly as it was when they all came down here?" She nodded her head forwards to Notarbartolo's team as they progressed, fuming under their own little thundercloud. "I'm just trying to get an understanding: a feel for what was going through my father's head at the time. Please forgive the questions. I hope you understand."

Mutolo made a comical figure as he tried to angle his shoulders towards her and walk down the increasingly steep and uneven cavern. He somehow managed it and replied: "Things in the mine change slowly, Maria. We're fortunate to have an oil lamp each. That is never the case with carusi. They're like the rats who can find their way in the dark. It's important therefore that the main corridors into the mine stay as constant as the seasons."

"There are rats in here?" exclaimed Maria, suddenly

concerned.

"The rats only gather where there is food," replied Mutolo. "There is nothing for them here. You are safe."

From the lead of their pack, the muffled voice of one of the picconieri replied, almost as an aside: "There is plenty of food at the bottom of Cesare's Shaft."

Maria shuddered as the words struck home. She immediately overcame her revulsion by assuming this was another attempt to frighten her away. "The carusi work in the dark, then?" she asked, undeterred.

"No, not totally in the dark: there are oil-lamps hung from the cavern walls. You can see them, but they are only lit when the mine is working. They often run out of oil, leaving dark sections."

"But there are places along the caverns where fresh oil is stored?"

Mutolo sighed a little as he continued. It was as if Maria's constant questioning was more than a minor irritant, but she had good reason to expand her knowledge of Ciavallotta.

"This isn't a working seam, Maria, just a main corridor into the mine. Lamp oil is very expensive and easily stolen, so it is only stored in lockers where sulphur is being cut from the rocks deep below ground. The lamps in this tunnel are refilled by the mule-herder, twice a day, using a barrel of oil strapped to the back of one of his mules. If we were to store lamp oil in this tunnel, we would be providing heat and light to every hovel on the edge of the town."

Eventually the party reached the cavern housing Cesare's Shaft. To Maria, their arrival was uneventful. She had expected something dramatic but the cavern gave no hint of the death and torture it had witnessed over the years. The oil lamps threw their pitiful light in all directions but detail diminished with distance and she could barely make out the far boundaries of the cavern walls. Above, the high ceiling was lost in a flickering confusion of shadows with only the echoing sound betraying the vast scale their eyes could not perceive. A simple circle of rocks bordered a pitch-black maw set into the yellow stone floor like a puddle of ink. No ropes or fences prevented a sudden trip over the edge for anyone foolhardy enough to venture off the path between the two main tunnels. The group made their way as close to the rim as they dared and off-loaded the bundles of climbing equipment. The picconieri, who were to make the descent, rummaged amongst the bundles and moved the items they needed closer to the edge. Soon, the deafening cacophony of metal spikes being bashed into hard rock reverberated throughout the cavern, and little pieces of stone dislodged themselves from the invisible ceiling to rain down on Maria. She was terrified and listened intently for any warning sound of a sudden collapse of the rock above her head. Those around her busied themselves with their allocated tasks, seemingly unmoved by the imminent danger of sudden rock falls. Maria relaxed and brushed the flecks of sulphur rain from her hair as she ventured closer to the rim of the inky pool, whose depths were to be explored for the first time in years. One of the picconieri approached her. He held some sort of lamp that seemed different to the oil lamps they were all carrying. It was like a brass cylinder with a flame behind a thin wire screen, and it illuminated with less of a flicker but not much more in the way of brilliance. He held it towards her as he approached.

"We use these where there is a danger of gas," he said, and then, as if not to frighten her: "These lamps cannot ignite the gas. It's why we have them. You are safe, Signorina."

"Thank you for the explanation," replied Maria, "and thank you for volunteering."

"You've offered a sizeable fee for this, Signorina, and it's not without risk. If we don't return, what happens?"

"Half will be paid and go to your next of kin. Tell Notarbartolo who they are and he will take care of it."

The pickman shuffled his feet nervously and looked around

as if aware the slightest sound could carry across the echoing cavern. "I would rather you take care of it, Signorina Giuliano. I know your intentions are honourable." He pressed a piece of paper into her hand.

"I understand," she whispered in return.

"If we discover fresh corpses at the bottom of the shaft, then we will need some way of identifying the remains."

"Can you not pull them up to the cavern?" Maria hadn't considered that this expedition would return to the surface without an answer to her father's disappearance. If the examination of the bottom of the shaft produced the worst possible result then, at least, the family must have the remains for a proper burial. The mine could not be her father's last resting place.

"My name is Umberto Galli. Your father has helped my family many times over the years. I am loyal to him, the fratellanza and the Giuliano family, but I must also be loyal to my capo: Leopoldo Notarbartolo. No remains are to be brought to the surface. Those are his orders."

All of this, the entire performance of bringing her to this hell-hole was still under the influence of Notarbartolo. He could, and would, manipulate things to suit himself. Maria's father could be lying injured in the hills somewhere, or he could be in hiding. Neither outcome would suit the odious capo, and he could declare Cesare dead with only two pickmen as witnesses: two of his own pickmen, his own cadre. She was having none of it.

Maria looked over at the two climbing ropes that disappeared over the edge of the shaft like they were dipped in black ink. Looped hand-holds and foot-holds were just visible in the glow of two of the strange cylindrical lamps that sat unprotected near the lip of the shaft. She pushed Galli out of the way and marched straight to the edge, swinging herself over on one of the ropes after grabbing a lamp. Before anyone could raise the alarm she had started to lower herself into the blackness. Her heart was pounding and fear weakened her grip but she found the first foothold on the rope. Suddenly there were shouts, and the sound of running feet reverberated throughout the cavern. Maria lowered herself further until just her head was above the rim. She could see Notarbartolo advancing towards her with all the authority of a coward, afraid to step too close to the edge. One of the pickmen lay flat at the edge of the rim and reached over, trying to grab her arm. Maria swung violently to the side and almost toppled both of them into the deadly abyss. "I am making the descent with you," she shouted. Notarbartolo's face was as incandescent as the oil lamps. His rage and frustration consumed him. He was speechless, and the task of persuading Maria to abandon her suicidal actions was left to Mutolo.

"Maria, you cannot do this," he said. "You'll die down there, either falling to your death or succumbing to the gasses that permeate the lower levels. Please don't add to the total of those who have perished here. Your father, wherever he is, would never forgive us if we let you do this."

"I am quite capable of holding on to a rope, Cosimo, whilst you lower me into the depths and then pull me back out again. Umberto Galli will accompany me on the other rope. There's no climbing, there never was. The plan was to lower two people into the shaft and pull them back out. The ropes have hand-holds and foot-holds. I'm instructing you to make this happen. I take full responsibility for my own actions. My father isn't here to make these decisions. We've already established that I have the authority of the Giuliano family in these matters." Maria hung over a pit of death, suspended by a slender rope, which may or may not have been fully secured. Her feet were in unfamiliar boots that struggled to gain a toe-hold and her hands grew weaker by the second as fear stole her fortitude. Her voice, however, was as steady as the rocks on the wall of the shaft. She would tolerate no argument and Mutolo turned and looked at Notarbartolo in desperation.

Umberto Galli crouched on the lip of the shaft and looked directly at her as he spoke. "I can see the terror in your eyes, Signorina. There's terror in my eyes also, but not from the fear of falling to my doom. I see death every week in Ciavallotta, and the sight of a corpse burns into your mind like a branding iron. Perhaps you've seen a dead body, Maria, neatly laid out on its final resting place: peaceful and serene. The corpses lying beneath you now have no recognisable human form. They are bloated and broken bits of bodies. They've been chewed by rats until their guts burst out from decaying skin like over-ripe fruit, but the smell is not of peach and lemon. The stench of decay doesn't reach up here because this shaft still does what it was supposed to do and brings air downwards into the depths. Closer to the bottom, the putrefying smell of the dead will cling to you like oil. You will never be able to wash it away because it will haunt you for the rest of your life, however long or short that may be. If you go down there, you will leave Maria Giuliano up here on the rim. The person who climbs back out, if they make it, will forever be different."

Chapter 17

Tommaso di Bova opened one eye and then risked the other, afraid he had died and gone to heaven. Yet there was pain, and his coarse breath caught in his throat. There could be no hurt in heaven, and no infirmity. Perhaps the Good Lord had chosen not to accept the punishment for Tommaso's sins and had condemned him to hell. Slowly, his five limited senses marshalled themselves on the parade ground of mortal reality and stood to attention. He lay on a soft bed, and the feel of crisp cotton sheets convinced him this wasn't his cell. A medicinal smell, so strong he could taste it, wafted through the air reminding him of the stinging carbolic from the Xebec (how many years ago was that?). He could see the expanse of white glazed tiles and hear the sound of clinking glass. He was sure this was an infirmary or hospital. He just couldn't be sure on which side of Vicaria's walls this temporary refuge found itself.

Just looking around seemed to tire him, and his mind demanded a return to the sleep from which he had just surfaced. He fought off slipping back into the warm black void, fearing it might not be possible to escape for a second time. She appeared from the corner of his vision and stood over him, seemingly without making a sound. The face was that of an angel, made all the more poignant by the black and white of the nun's wimple.

"Signor di Bova, it is good to have you back with us."

The voice was as divine as the looks and Tommaso made to reply but only a rattling croak emanated from his mouth. The chains: the chains Lorenzo Fratelli had strangled him with; had they rendered him incapable of ever speaking again? Panic took hold and Tommaso tried to sit up in bed, encouraging his voice to come back from the dead and join the rest of his body.

"Please do not attempt to get up," said the angel. "You are still in Vicaria and are thus restrained. The wounds to your throat will recover and your voice will return, but for now you must rest." She examined the dressings around his neck and, seemingly satisfied, left as silently as she had arrived.

Tommaso checked his arms and legs by attempting to lift them from the bed. He could not do so. Turning his head was painful and tore at his throat as if being attacked with a rusty knife, but he could see the leather strap binding his right arm to the metal frame of the bed, not at his wrist, but just above his elbow, permitting limited movement. Less than two metres away, he could see another leather strap fastened to another bed. The buckle on this strap was at the extremity of its capacity to contain the large, muscular arm it restrained. Grimacing with pain, Tommaso turned his head to look at the patient beside him. The wolfish grin of Lorenzo Fratelli beamed back.

"So, Tommaso, I have failed, and you have recovered." The Horse flicked his arm against the restraining straps, and the leather creaked and groaned to the point where it must surely give way. "I still have my strength, Tommaso, and I am close to you: very close. I'm sure you would love to tell the good sisters of the true circumstances that brought you here, and how they must move you away from me before I complete the task I have been given. Oh, but you can't, can you?" The grin mocked Tommaso once more, before Lorenzo turned his head away as if preparing for sleep. "Rest easy, di Bova, if you can, knowing that I am beside you."

Tommaso sank back onto the bed and felt a childish urge to seek pitiful refuge beneath the cotton sheets. He could not cry out if he was attacked. He could not tell the sisters of the danger this monster of a patient presented. He could write, however, and the sisters should be educated enough to read. It was doubtful if they would take a message out to the prison population but there must be guards in the infirmary, and they wouldn't want to be held responsible for the death of a block commander. If only he could attract somebody's attention.

Then all hell seemed to break loose.

There were shouts and yells from outside the ward, the sounds of military commands and barking orders. The staccato beat of leather boots on the tiled floor became the vanguard of a posse of armed carabinieri who formed around Tommaso's bed. Beside them, and pointing their carbines uneasily at the new arrivals, were the prison guards. The noisy mob fell silent as all sides contemplated a stand-off. Sabres were drawn and rifles pointed. Frightened faces peeked out from habits as the sisters looked on in shock, joining the precarious silence. In the distance, alarm bells sounded in the main prison. One solitary figure eased his way through the mêlée. His uniform marked him out as a captain in l'arma dei carabinieri, and his confident bearing made it clear he would brook no arguments. Tommaso was sure he had seen him before.

"Lower your carbines and sheath your sabres," commanded the captain. His men did as they were told but the prison guards resisted. He addressed them directly. "I have here full authorisation to take Tommaso di Bova into the protective custody of l'arma di carabinieri in Palermo." A sheaf of papers landed on Tommaso's bed, awaiting the inspection of one of the prison guards. They would wait a while. Tommaso knew few of the guards could read worth a damn and none would be qualified to understand the legal complexities of prison transfer requests, let alone act on them. The uncomfortable stand-off continued, awaiting the presence of the governor, who would undoubtedly arrive with his retinue of lackeys. Tommaso tried again to speak but only succeeded in producing a croak. Why all this furore? And why was he the centre of it?

The carabinieri captain addressed him: "Tommaso di Bova, I am Captain Bruno Fabroni and I am stationed in Favara, with temporary secondment to Palermo. You are to be released into my custody, as the testimony of the main witness who secured your conviction has been withdrawn and your case is under review. Subject to a decision on your guilt or innocence of the charge of serious assault, you will either be returned here or released as a free man. Until that decision is made, you will be placed under the jurisdiction of Carabinieri Provincial Command on Piazza Giuseppe Verdi, where you will remain in custody."

Tommaso's head started to spin with all the information that was being catapulted at his barely conscious mind. He shut himself off from the activities surrounding him and attempted to break down what he had heard. '*..your guilt or innocence of the charge of serious assault…*' He was in Vicaria because he had been found guilty of serious assault, so that made some sense but he had signed a confession and hadn't withdrawn it. So how could he be innocent? '*…the testimony of the main witness who secured your conviction has been withdrawn…*' There had been but one witness: Antonio Ruddini. Why would he withdraw his testimony? Then another recollection jumped into Tommaso's thinking. It wasn't from what Fabroni had announced; it was what Fratelli had said before he tightened the chains around Tommaso's throat – '*Cesare Giuliano gave me the mark…You are the mark, Tommaso.*' He could never forget those words: they were the last ones he had heard before he succumbed to near-death suffocation. Cesare had issued the order for Tommaso's execution. Toto had called that some time ago, so it wasn't such a surprise, but Ruddini's retraction was too much of a coincidence. Something was happening back in Favara – something to threaten Cesare's total control over the fratellanza families.

Tommaso had no way of knowing the truth behind his supposition. If only he could talk to someone he trusted: if only he could talk to Maria. No matter the span of their separation, he believed the fidelity of Maria's love for him was as solid as the walls of Vicaria, and Tommaso held the same in reserve for her. It had been nearly three years: three years with not one word between them, yet he held tightly to the bond they had forged in that shepherd's croft. Maria's father issued the order to execute

Tommaso, but he was sure she would have known nothing of it.

'...you will either be returned here or released as a free man.' Whatever the other doubts assailing him, this was the one statement his mind seized upon as if it was the redeeming blood of Christ his Saviour. There was a chance he would be immediately taken from this infirmary, never to return to Vicaria again. At the very least, he would be held elsewhere and free of Lorenzo Fratelli. There was no reprise for The Horse: he was entombed in Vicaria. Even if the process failed to secure his complete freedom and Tommaso found himself back in Vicaria, he could be sure that Lorenzo would be transferred out of C Block. Tommaso would also leave behind his role as block commander and his new affiliations with Aspromonte. Despite the redemption of freedom, this was a sombre and depressing thought. Tommaso had worked hard over the last few years to build his reputation and his supremacy. One blink and it was all gone. He could hardly ask for his transfer to the carabinieri to be delayed whilst he said goodbye and delegated his many functions to his successors.

With that one talisman of potential freedom, Tommaso whipped his thoughts back to the reality of the exchanges happening around his bed. The governor was there and looking dejected. The prison guards had lowered their carbines and Fabroni's men were preparing a stretcher, placing it on an empty bed pushed tightly against Tommaso's. They were surrounded by nuns, fussing and giving instructions to be careful of their patient's wounds. Tommaso was gently positioned on the stretcher by the nuns and then lifted by the carabinieri before being carried away. As the prison guards stood aside to let them past, the stretcher-bearers paused. Lorenzo Fratelli's face was less than an arm's length from Tommaso, who still couldn't speak, but he could smile. His face lit up in a huge grin which he directed straight at The Horse. His arms now free of the restraints, Tommaso lifted his right hand and gave a small good-bye wave that carried as much of a derisory insult as the mocking smile.

Doors slammed behind him, just as they had when he was first incarcerated, but this time they led Tommaso out towards Piazza Ucciardone: where the small train still stopped and hooted its whistle, where the gulls still swooped into the warm waters of the harbour and where the stevedores still carried homeward smiles as they left their daily toil behind. Eventually the carabinieri contingent emerged from the main gate of Vicaria and Tommaso drank in every new attack on his five senses. Suddenly, he could see more than just a few metres in sunlight so bright he could scarcely believe it wouldn't blind him, and its warmth wouldn't burn his skin. He scrunched up his eyes from the light, remembering back to Ciavallotta and the times he had emerged from the blackness into the midday sun. Yet he could do nothing for the sound that assaulted his ears. It wasn't the volume but the diversity that overwhelmed him. Horses whinnied, gulls squawked, people laughed, trains clattered, and somewhere in the distance dogs barked. The smells of the harbour, when they reached him, were so rich and complex, he could almost taste the sardines. For the first time since Toto had convinced him he would never leave Vicaria alive, Tommaso allowed himself to believe in a future where his horizons extended beyond the dimensions of a cell. Suddenly, his senses luxuriated in past pleasures, confident of a future where they would be reprieved. For the first time in three years he dared to think of the shepherd's croft and the intimacy of Maria's soft skin. Tommaso could feel the warmth of the woollen blanket and smell the burning wax from the tallow candle.

* * *

The smell assaulted Maria like a storm. It didn't build slowly as they were lowered into the inky blackness, it just hit and hit hard.

Umberto had tried to take her mind off the descent and had partly succeeded after the first fifty metres or so, when Maria was blind, deaf and dumb to all but the terror of her alien surroundings. She could look up and see the sanctuary of the surface recede, as the circle of light at the top of the shaft shrank. She could look down and see only a pitch-black emptiness that began just below her feet and ended in hell, for all she knew. The shaft narrowed as the ropes supporting them played out, to the point where Umberto and Maria were barely able to squeeze into the space side-by-side. He called up and commanded that they stop lowering the ropes.

"Signorina, you must change places with me," said Umberto in a whisper.

"I will do no such thing," replied Maria. She had been clutching onto the hand-hold like a drowning man and had no intention of letting go until she had firm ground beneath her feet.

"Signorina Giuliano, please do this. It's easy. The shaft is very narrow here but it widens out in about ten metres. I can wedge myself against the sides and leave my rope free for you to climb onto. I can manoeuvre below you so you cannot fall. I will then take your rope."

"But why take the risk of changing ropes?" Maria feared she knew the answer before the words were out of her mouth. She held the strange cylindrical lamp up to better see the look on Umberto's face. He had told her it was called a Davy lamp. They came from England and were very expensive. Since they had started using them in the sulphur mines, the number of explosions had reduced to virtually zero. Carusi might have been cheap and expendable but a shaft closed because of a rock-fall was lost income on a grand scale, so the Davy lamps were given to the picconieri who worked in the most dangerous depths of Ciavallotta.

"I fear for what Notarbartolo may do," said Umberto, and Maria could see the concern in his eyes. "Accidents happen, especially at times like this, Signorina Giuliano."

"But there are witnesses. The other capos would never support a move against my family. It would be treachery." A small shower of rocks and stones dislodged from somewhere above her and rained down on Maria. The flood gates that held back the sheer terror she was experiencing almost gave way and she grabbed Umberto and clung to him. "Please, call me Maria, and tell me how we can swap ropes."

Umberto explained things quickly and quietly before shouting commands up to the surface about how the ropes would go slack as they negotiated a choke-point in the shaft. When he ordered them to commence lowering, Maria was on the rope he had previously occupied and slightly above him in the shaft.

The smell was now so thick as to be almost tangible. She could feel the bile rise in her throat as her gag reflex threatened to empty the contents of her stomach on the unfortunate Umberto, below. He must have heard her retching and looked up.

"Don't try and fight the smell, Maria. Your senses will start to block it out in a few minutes. We're almost at the bottom of the shaft. You must prepare your other senses for what we'll find."

Maria looked up above and the ropes disappeared into a black void, to reappear again like gossamer threads stuck to the edge of a bright coin, way above her head. Beneath her, the light from the Davy lamps showed the shaft widening into a bell-like structure, from which she and Umberto hung like a pair of clappers ready to strike the sides and ring out a peal of danger. The ropes started to swing, and the glow from the Davy lamps could be seen as two dancing beams, tripping over indistinct bumps and shadows on what she could now perceive as the bottom of the shaft. Her eyes had become accustomed to the darkness, so the lamps' glow took on the brilliance of searchlights as their illumination spread. Maria could see the bell shape gave way to that of a large cavern. Suddenly her fear overtook her again as the dubious comfort of the closed-in walls of the shaft gave way to the vertiginous expanse of a vaulted chamber, in which she hung like a caterpillar on a silken thread. She pulled herself tighter to the rope and the arc of their swing increased. She started to spin slowly and panic welled up to the point where she must have screamed out loud. Umberto started calling her from below but Maria was oblivious to everything but the spinning panic, the vertigo and the suffocating smell. She clung ever tighter to the rope and squeezed her eyes shut. Suddenly there was a loud yell from below.

"Stop lowering," hollered Umberto and Maria's rope halted. Umberto reached up and grabbed her foot to stop the swing. "Maria, you're alright. We are down. I'll move your rope to the side a little. Just climb down the last few metres. Are you fine to do that?"

She looked down at Umberto, who had his lamp held high, dazzling her so she could not see where he stood. She was just grateful that the descent was over and tearfully nodded her acknowledgement of his request. When her feet touched the floor of the cavern, Umberto grabbed her and pulled her close, her head nestled into his shoulder. She clung to him for what seemed like an age as the panic subsided. She made to break free and look around, but suddenly Umberto placed a strong hand on the back of her head, pulling her face closer into his shoulder. His arm tightened around her waist and pressed her closer to his body with amazing and frightening strength. She could not break free and dropped her lamp as she struggled against him. It fell at her feet. She could see its pool of light, but nothing beyond as Umberto's suffocating grasp continued to restrain her. She kicked hard against his shins but still he wouldn't let go. She stepped back to swing a greater kick and stood on something that felt like the dried-up branch of an old tree. The sound it made as it snapped was not dissimilar, and she looked down as best she could to better gauge her footing.

The tree branch was bleached white and its extremity terminated in a skeletal hand, whose bony fingers fell off and dropped to the floor of the cavern like the petals of death's own flower.

Maria gasped and Umberto pulled her even tighter. "Maria," he said, his voice suddenly soothing and betraying nothing of the strength of the vice-like grip with which he held her. "We are on a pile of dead bodies. It's like an open cemetery: as if the earth has suddenly swallowed enough corruption and spat the dead back to the surface. No matter where you step, you'll walk upon a corpse. The dried up bones of the older bodies are towards the edge of the pile, where you are now. When I let you go, turn and walk a few paces away from me."

She felt as if she wanted to leap into the air and away from the bundles of bones and decaying bodies. Maybe she could leap onto the rope and just cling there, but she had made the descent for a reason, and now was not the time to let fear rob her of her fortitude. Umberto released her and then bent down to retrieve her lamp, which she accepted gratefully and walked a few paces away from him. More bones cracked and rattled beneath her feet. Here and there, the odd shoe found itself amongst the skeletal remains. Even the shoes were cast in death: their leather cracked and dried, with heels and soles curling away from uppers to reveal rusty nails, and laces all but turned to powder. Somehow, if she focussed on the shoes, she could avoid thinking about the corpses of their owners. After five paces she stopped and looked back to Umberto. He had removed the strong canvas sack strapped to his back and was pulling out a small bottle of lamp oil and a large sheet that looked like a shroud.

He spoke quietly. "Keep your lamp lit whilst I refill mine."

Maria did as she was told, afraid to move lest her lamp would be extinguished and they would be plunged into total darkness. Eventually Umberto re-lit his lamp and moved towards her to repeat the process with Maria's Davy lamp. "There are two fresh bodies at the top of the pile, Maria," he said softly as he knelt beside her. "One I already recognise as Antonio Ruddini."

Maria's heart sank. All the fear, all the primal terror that went with her descent and standing ankle deep in the bones of the dead was supplanted by the sudden realisation that the end of her quest was possibly a few seconds away. Umberto spoke again: "I can only recognise Ruddini because of the row of gold teeth that still shine from his broken face. He was very proud of his smile. He called it his Midas grin."

"My father has no gold teeth," said Maria, almost apologetically. "In the crook of the thumb of his right hand, there was the tattoo of a snake. With his thumb resting against his forefinger it was barely noticeable, but when he opened his hand it grew to look like a menacing serpent. He never told me of its origins."

"There is a legend amongst the capos that a great knight came to our land and founded the society to which the fratellanza and all the honoured families in Sicily belong. It is said that the knight, who was called Osso, was bitten by a serpent when he first set foot on our shores. He killed the serpent and used its blood as an antidote to the poison by making it the ink for a tattoo: a tattoo of the serpent on the very hand where he received the bite, the same hand that killed the venomous creature. Only those of the status of rappresentante are allowed to wear the tattoo." With that Umberto turned and walked back to the pile of corpses in silence.

Maria tried not to focus on the place where Umberto would make his discovery, but she couldn't help it. The pile stood almost as high as a man's waist. At the bottom, a wide spread of human leg, thigh and arm bones poked out at almost comical angles with the remnants of skeletal hands and feet drooping like wizened fruit from an old vine. Occasionally a shoe would cling valiantly to the remains of a foot, still attached to a leg that was just visible, poking out from the decayed remains of old britches. The pile narrowed towards the top, and the corpses revealed more of their grotesque origins. Eyeless skulls grinned out from the odd confusion of clavicles and scapulas, their toothy smiles partly obscured by wisps of hair that somehow survived the corruption of flesh and tissue. Towards the top of the pile, human remains were more recognisable as having nearly complete torsos and clothing that still betrayed some colour, along with the strength needed to contain their rotting and decaying owners. There were too many bodies to count and Maria tried to convince herself that the pile of corpses must owe its existence to more than just the iniquities of her father. Surely the other capos used this secret tomb to dispose of their enemies? It mattered little. She could not bring justice to the departed.

Umberto wandered around the pile, trying to avoid climbing onto this mound of the dead. He looked over at Maria and she could see the hesitancy in every move of his body. He dropped his gaze and stepped on to the threshold of the deathly pile. Cracking bones sounded off like carbine shots as he climbed higher, to give way to sickening squelches as he reached the top. He was there for no more than a few seconds before carefully descending and making his way to Maria. He stopped half way and kicked some remnants of the dead from his boots before finally kneeling in front of her.

"Signorina Giuliano, it is my unfortunate duty to inform you that your father, Cesare, is dead. His corpse lies at the top of the pile. If you care to turn away, I'll go back to retrieve his mortal remains and prepare them for the journey to the surface."

Without waiting for an answer, he arose and made his way to complete the gruesome task. The command to turn away, Maria accomplished with little difficulty. It was the rest of what Umberto had said that made her head spin. Her father's corpse was at the top of the pile? He was dead then? Yes, that's what Umberto meant. He said it clearly. Maybe she didn't hear him correctly. No, he also said he would retrieve Cesare's mortal remains. An enormous flood of sadness, fear, and loneliness engulfed Maria and she broke down into fits of crying that she was sure could be heard clear across the cavern, let alone at the top of the shaft. All of the terror of making the descent and the fear of what she might find was a gamble, whose winning hand had been beaten by a single black ace. She had lost. Her only task now was to retrieve her father's body and prepare the family for a funeral. Eventually, Umberto approached and announced he had placed the body in the shroud-like sheet he had brought with him. He could have been gone for minutes or hours. Maria's sobbing grief had robbed her of all sense of time. A cry came from up above, barely audible as it reverberated down the shaft from the tiny circle of light over their heads: "Are you safe? What have you found?"

"We are safe," Umberto shouted back.

"Have you found Cesare's body?" echoed the response.

"No," shouted Umberto, and Maria looked at him, astonished. Maybe she had misheard, then? Maybe it wasn't her father? There was silence from above and Umberto spoke to her in a whisper.

"We must do this my way, Maria. If Notarbartolo thinks we have found the corpse then he could throw the ropes over the rim and leave us here to die. He would be rappresentante and his word would be law. You must get to the top. You must take command as soon as you climb over the rim."

Maria went from grief to panic in a heartbeat. Umberto was right. Notarbartolo was a merciless capo who wanted nothing more than complete control of the fratellanza. Only one thing stood in his way: the question of whether Cesare was alive or dead.

More shouts emanated from above, weakened by the depth of the shaft to become almost ghostly wails: "We'll pull you up. Put Maria on her rope first and give two tugs. Then put yourself on the second rope and give one tug. We'll pull you up a few metres apart so you don't get stuck at the choke point of the shaft."

Umberto acknowledged and proceeded to tie Cesare's corpse to the first rope. Maria looked at him, confused and afraid.

"What are you doing?"

"Maria, I'm staying behind. I still fear Notarbartolo and what he might do. They will know the weight on the ropes. They will know if we have added another body. There is only one way to do this. They pull your father's body up, believing it is you, and they pull you up, believing it is me. I trust you will prevail and come back for me."

"No," said Maria. "You cannot stay here. What can I do when I get to the surface and they realise they've been tricked? They could kill me, and you would see my body join this pile of victims."

"There is only one other way to do this, Maria: I make the journey to the surface, and you stay here. I will try and come back for you in a day or two, once they believe you are dead."

Maria could feel the colour drain from her face and her stomach heave. Doomed to spend days alone with the dead was more than she could come to terms with. Her face, when she looked up at Umberto, told him all he needed to know. He tied her father's corpse to the rope and gave it two tugs.

"Is Maria on the rope?" came the question from above.

"Yes," he shouted and the rope began its strained journey to the surface. He then ensured Maria was positioned correctly on the second rope: his rope, as far as those on the surface were concerned. "Quickly, swap your coat and cap with mine. Extinguish your lamp as you ascend over the rim and keep your head down."

She looked once at him, held his face in her hands and kissed him gently on the lips. "I will save you, Umberto, and you will be one of the Giuliano family's greatest friends."

He tugged once on the rope and Maria rose into the blackness, to leave him behind with a single lamp. As she left the horrors of the chamber she could see him many metres below, embedded in a little pool of amber light, like a firefly. Suddenly the rope beside her stopped and she was pulled past the corpse of her father. She had no idea of what was happening. Umberto was too far below to signal and it was too dangerous for her to shout out. She was barely a metre past her father's body when there was a sudden crack from above and the canvas sack carrying his mortal remains plummeted back to the floor of the cavern. The flailing rope whipped past Maria and she watched, horrified, as rope and corpse raced towards the little firefly that was Umberto. It seemed to miss him as the pool of light danced to the side.

He shouted up to the surface: "Wait, Maria has fallen. Lower me back down. I must help her. Lower me back down!"

"We cannot. There has been a rock fall on the lip of the shaft. It is crumbling. We must get you to the surface quickly."

The rope, onto which Maria clung tightly, continued its creaking journey to the top of the shaft.

Part Three

Favara and Palermo. 1868-1875

Chapter 18

"Tommaso di Bova, this is your confession: the very document you signed over three years ago." Captain Bruno Fabroni looked down at Tommaso and waved a few sheets of paper above his head. Tommaso was still recuperating from his wounds but the refuge of Vicaria's infirmary had been replaced by the even more comfortable surroundings of the Caribinieri Provincial Command on Piazza Giuseppe Verdi. He was not secured to his bed; in fact he shared an open ward with a few other patients. He was free to walk around the ward as his strength returned, but his voice was still a useless croak, although there were some signs of being able to form words. For now he sought to keep this to himself.

"I know you cannot speak, Tommaso," continued Fabroni, "but I know you can read. Quite an accomplishment for a former carusi, but then you have made many such exploits during your tenure in Vicaria: musician, poet, storyteller and even block commander. There is much you have to tell Maria Giuliano when you next see her."

Tommaso sat bolt upright and stared at Fabroni. There was no malice in his stare, just confusion, fear and excitement all bundled into one. Fabroni must have divined each emotion at its source and attempted to provide the answers Tommaso sought, but could not put into words.

"And you can be back in Favara within the week, Tommaso. I have here another confession for you to sign. It states that you were threatened and coerced by the fratellanza to plead guilty to the serious assault of the rail-yard boss. Appended to this confession is a true copy of Antonio Ruddini's statement confirming that he was mistaken when he identified you as the assailant. All you have to do is sign what is a retraction of your original statement of guilt, and you should be free within the week. Of course, I don't expect you to sign this without reading it." Fabroni set the documents on Tommaso's bed and turned to walk away. He stopped at the door to the ward and looked back. "I know you may be confused, and perhaps you believe I'm trying to trick you into something. That is understandable, Tommaso. You need someone you know and whom you can trust to help you with your decision. The surgeon tells me your voice will return in a few days. This is Wednesday, so let's go for the same day next week. Set yourself a target, for that is the day Maria Giuliano will join you here. She will be at your bedside and she will help you decide if my motives are sincere and based purely on my concern for the pursuit of justice."

Seven days: seven days to recover and prepare for Maria. Tommaso knew he could do it. His voice would have healed to more than a croak and the pallid skin of his convict existence would be replaced by a healthy bronze glow, corrupted only by the yellow scars: the legacy of his days as a little wagon. Only yesterday, he had clung to the small treasures that he had accumulated in three years of incarceration, and only yesterday those treasures had seemed like all the wealth in Palermo. Yet now, with the passing of only one sunrise, he dared believe that a new treasure-trove of riches awaited him. He would be free, and he would be able to reach out and touch her, see her up close, hear her voice and smell the perfume that had once adorned the letter: the one which started this, so many years ago.

And yet, there was something wrong.

Cesare would never have agreed to let Maria make the trip to Palermo – for her to be here as a guest of the carabinieri would be seen as treason by the rappresentante and all of the capos. Yes, she could make the journey by rail in a few hours, but she could not do so in secret. The fratellanza and the honourable members in Palermo missed nothing. Word would get back to Cesare Giuliano – his daughter was in Palermo and was seen entering the Carabinieri Provincial Command on Piazza Giuseppe Verdi.

Cesare would already know of Tommaso's release into the custody of Captain Bruno Fabroni, and yet this same captain was promising freedom and a meeting so impossible it flew in the face of all Tommaso believed possible. He recalled the doubts he had experienced when Fabroni had taken him from Vicaria. Something was happening back in Favara. Cesare must have lost control of the fratellanza, or was about to. Maybe that was Fabroni's plan after all: have Cesare put away for a crime he truly committed. Having to exchange Tommaso, a mere soldier in the fratellanza, for the *capo di capi* would have been a worthy deal in the eyes of the carabinieri. And why would Tommaso not agree to be part of it? Fratelli was sent to execute him and that sentence was passed by Cesare only a few weeks previously. Then Maria must know. She must be a part of Fabroni's plan, and for that to happen she must have agreed to work with the carabinieri. No, thought Tommaso. Such treachery was impossible. There must be another explanation.

Who then knew of the death sentence passed on Tommaso? Fratelli's confession to being the executioner was only given because he believed his role was about to be fulfilled. If anyone else knew, word would have reached Tommaso, provided the rules for making him a mark had been followed. They obviously hadn't, and Cesare had acted alone: out of personal vengeance. It was doubtful even Fabroni knew. If he did, then Lorenzo Fratelli would have been the one with a ticket out of Vicaria. Taking Cesare down on a charge of murder would have been infinitely preferable to the carabinieri, even if the release of Fratelli would have been more difficult.

The more Tommaso conjured with the elements of his dilemma, the foggier his view became until he had reached the point where none of it made sense. He picked the sheaf of documents from the bed and started reading. It took a while and there were a few terms he didn't understand, but for all his doubts, the documents seemed genuine.

Wednesday it would be then: the day when Tommaso would learn the truth and he would trust only Maria to deliver it. If Fabroni failed to make good on his promises, then there must be other outcomes to his plans that were to Tommaso's detriment. If Maria didn't appear in seven days then Tommaso would be gone in ten. Escaping from the custody of the carabinieri wouldn't be easy but if he tried and failed, then they would have no choice but to return him to Vicaria. At least there he would be safe; assuming the problem of Lorenzo Fratelli had been dealt with.

* * *

The circle of light above Maria's head grew bigger with each jerk of the rope. The ascent was a series of creaking jolts and occasional stops, as the crew above pulled her up, in the mistaken belief they were rescuing Umberto Galli. A few shouts came down seeking answers but Maria just grunted, coughed and spluttered in response. This seemed to work, as the rope ascended slightly faster.

Her intent on reaching the top was to stay at the edge of the shaft for long as possible before she was recognised. Even then, the chances were slim that she would survive. Notarbartolo would try to carry out his plan, and she could well find herself making the descent again, but this time without the benefit of a rope. To do that he had to forcibly throw Maria to her death, and she was willing to bet he wouldn't have the balls for it. Neither would any of the other capos risk murdering Cesare's daughter in cold blood. In fact, the only way Notarbartolo could have conspired to send her to her doom was with the covert assistance of his other pickman. He might have the fortitude to finish her off but would need to risk the pit of hell. Maria had been there and had no wish to return, but she had exorcised the evil spirit that was Cesare's Shaft. Galli had only been partly correct when he said that she would leave the shaft forever different. The real change would be when she left the mine. If she were to do that then she would have defeated Notarbartolo.

Maria held her lamp at waist level so its illumination would not betray her. When she looked to the surface she could make out the faces of the pickmen manning the rope. They had it secured to some sort of pulley system that reduced the effort in raising her weight but seemed to take twice as long as the descent. She kept her head down, hiding her long hair under Galli's borrowed cap. Once again she was to assume the disguise of a working man, but there could be no hiding her true identity when she breeched the rim that was just a few metres above her head.

"Galli, we're about to pull you clear; are you alright?"

Maria coughed and spluttered again, this time with a wheezing rasp she hoped could be heard above.

"He's been poisoned by the gas," came the shout from beyond the rim. "Get him up quickly."

The rope ascended rapidly and the edge of the pit appeared in Maria's view. She grasped the hand reaching out to her and pulled herself clear, whilst knocking her Davy lamp over, causing it to go out. Supine, coughing and spluttering, she peeked out from below her cap to see two pickmen retreating from the edge. Notarbartolo moved forwards just as Maria got to her feet and turned towards him. The look on his face was pure horror as realisation crashed into him. The chatter of confused conversation ran amongst the crowd standing in the cavern, suddenly silenced by Maria's words. "Where is the small locker with the emergency oil lamps and Lundstrom matches?" She got her first question in before Notarbartolo had a chance to bumble his excuses.

Whatever he expected to hear, it wasn't this. "What?" was as much as he could utter.

"Back at the house, after the funerals, you were asked to explain why you'd deserted this very cavern when my father most needed you. You said you'd gone to retrieve lamps and matches. There is no small locker in the tunnel, there never has been. You fled to save your own skin, Notarbartolo. You're a traitor. You tried to kill me because you believe my father may still be alive and you knew I would oppose your appointment as head of the fratellanza."

"You are the traitor, Maria," he shouted back. "Think back to that very same meeting. How'd you know the carabinieri didn't have your father as a prisoner?"

It was Maria's turn to look puzzled and confusion was the partner of fear. She never had the chance to respond before Notarbartolo answered his own question, whilst moving slowly towards her.

"Let me repeat your words: *'you fled and left him to the carabinieri. They don't have him so you must know where he is.'* You could only know that if you had been talking to the hated bastards who ambushed us right here. And who gave them Roberto Carollo as a witness to Galati's death? You did, Maria, and you informed them every time we got close to the Carollo family. They were always one step ahead of us. The capos have known for some time there was a traitor in our midst. We've watched one another like hawks, waiting for any of our number to betray themselves, but the treachery ran deeper than any of us could ever have imagined. You knew, Maria: you knew everything and you betrayed us."

He was closer now, and she could see the evil glint in his eyes, even in the subdued lighting of the oil lamps. She looked around and no one else was moving, or even speaking. There must have been some sort of trial when she was in the bowels of Ciavallotta. The jury had had its say, the sentence was passed and now the executioner had to finish the task. It may have been a majority decision but this was no triumphant mob. They cowed in the shadows, happy to let their new leader exercise his power of life and death. Oh yes, once Maria had joined the corpses below they would all pat him on the back and swear allegiance, but for now they didn't have the balls to tackle her.

"And who watched you like a hawk, Notarbartolo? None other than my father. He could see you were the real traitor, and you knew it." Maria wasn't cowed by the threats and stood her ground, tempting Notarbartolo ever closer to the edge. "How else could Ruddini have been persuaded to change his statement? You concocted the story of the mysterious Pasquale Villabate and agreed it with Ruddini. He was one of your cadre: totally loyal to you, even unto death."

Notarbartolo stopped and a few accusing whispers crept from the darkness of the cavern. He turned momentarily and the quiet chatter stopped. "Ruddini was beaten to a point where no man could have concealed the truth," he said. "Ruddini betrayed only Pasquale Villabate. This phantom was one of your carabinieri stooges, sent to deceive us." The whispering started again, but this time the accusations were undoubtedly directed at Maria. She was losing this fight and her accuser was just a few metres away, and closing. One of them would go over the edge; those remaining must believe the vanquished to be the traitor.

"You argue well, Notarbartolo, like the coward you obviously are. The coward who claims he wasn't given a weapon to guard the tunnel. The coward who claims he only fled to find oil lamps. The coward who couldn't even wait in hiding at the exit of the mine to see if my father escaped, and the coward who wouldn't dare face my father down with this contrived nonsense." Maria's words hit and hit hard. The chattering accusations from the shadows took on a new tone and her accuser's face grew contorted with rage. "Above all, you, Notarbartolo, are the coward who betrayed my father to the carabinieri because you wanted him dead so that you could take his place. How convenient you can place this blame on a mere woman? And how convenient you can arrange for her to fall to her death? If Cesare Giuliano was here, he would shoot you where you stand and all who stand with you."

"Cesare Giuliano is dead!" The response was spat at her with all the vehemence Notarbartolo could muster, but he stopped short, as soon as the words were uttered. Whatever else he wanted to say was suffocated by this revelation that only he could have known.

The stillness in the cavern was suddenly so intense, Maria could hear the fluttering of the *pipistrelli,* flapping leathery wings in preparation for their flight into the oncoming dusk, in search of food.

Cosimo Mutolo broke the silence: "You just told us Cesare perished here: shot by the carabinieri and tipped into the shaft. You claimed to have known all along but waited until now so there could be no doubt about his death or Maria's treachery. Cesare's body isn't there, and yet you carried out the sentence on his daughter; or at least tried to."

"You know nothing of what went on here, you stiff-necked son of a goat," responded Notarbartolo with all the authority he could muster. That currency was being devalued by the second, and insulting one of the capos didn't help, yet he continued with his bluster: "Cesare Giuliano lies at the bottom of this shaft, killed by a carabinieri bullet. The fact his daughter can't find his body is not my concern."

Cosimo Mutolo lifted one of the oil lamps and circled around the rim of the shaft to face Maria across its diameter. "Maria, who was pulled from the depths of the shaft and then dropped to their death? Is Galli dead?" asked Cosimo.

"No," replied Maria. "He is a hero to the true fratellanza. He suspected what Notarbartolo was planning before we made the descent. He swapped ropes with me and put Ruddini's corpse on the other."

"Umberto," hollered Mutolo into the depths. When he heard the cry of acknowledgement from below, he shouted a question: "How do you know Cesare Giuliano is not amongst the deceased?"

It took a few seconds, but Galli's voice echoed faintly up from the depths, explaining how the tattoo of Osso's Serpent would have identified the corpse, even amongst the many who were entombed there.

Mutolo spoke again, glancing from Maria to Notarbartolo as he did so. "One of you is a traitor and one of you is telling the truth. You, Notarbartolo, maintain Cesare Giuliano lies at the bottom of the shaft. Maria and Umberto maintain he doesn't. If he doesn't then your account of what happened here is a lie. You are welcome to make the descent and verify your account."

Maria said nothing, afraid that the fear in her voice at the outcome of Mutolo's suggestion would put the seal on her fate. Yet she knew the usurper to her father's title was a coward and would never agree to be lowered into the depths.

"How dare you accuse me of lying to the families? Cesare is dead. We all know this," screamed Notarbartolo. "If he's not at the bottom of the shaft then there's only one explanation: the carabinieri have his body."

"If that were the case," replied Mutolo, "then why would Maria risk her life to make the descent? She would have known of her father's true resting place because of the treachery you accuse her of. Unless, of course, you wish to change your story and convince us you stayed behind on that fateful night and saw the carabinieri carry the corpse from the mine."

It was plain that Mutolo wasn't happy with whatever decision had been taken after Maria had made her fateful descent. He was brave enough to voice it and clever enough to make it stick. Now the others started to raise their own concerns.

"No one would have asked you to guard the tunnel entrance to this cavern without a weapon." The voice came from the anonymity of the darkness beyond the pool of lights surrounding the mouth of the shaft. Was it just Maria's imagination; or had a few of the oil lamps been snuffed out in the past few seconds?

"I concur," said another voice from the darkness. "You must've had a weapon. How convenient it would've been to take a shot at Cesare and then flee in the confusion?"

"You find comfort in the darkness, you cowards." There was fear now in Notarbartolo's voice. "Step forwards and face me."

Maria had watched Mutolo circling around the perimeter of the shaft. He was right beside the terrified capo as he made his last statement.

"I will face you, Notarbartolo. The stiff-necked son of a goat will face you, to tell you that cowardice and treachery go hand in hand in a merry dance with a desire for power. You wanted to be rappresentante so much you were prepared to betray the man you wished to replace. You lied to us to secure our votes and then tried to murder Maria, so we could never know the truth."

One of Notarbartolo's pickmen stepped forwards, blocking Mutolo.

"Chose carefully," said the man with no neck. "I commend your loyalty but I detect that you are alone. Let's wait to see who joins you."

No one moved, and with that Maria knew Notarbartolo had sensed his impending doom. The bluster and arrogance suddenly disappeared. "My brothers," he said meekly, "I did not betray anyone." A few more oil lamps were put out and the deepening gloom was the harbinger of a death sentence.

"Then why did you try to kill me, Leopoldo?" asked Maria.

"It was an accident: the rope slipped." He looked at his pickman for support but found none.

Mutolo moved ever closer and now stood less than an arm's length away from Notarbartolo. He addressed the pickman with a question: "Did the rope slip by accident? Think carefully before you answer."

"No."

The last oil lamp went out and the blackness was suffocating. There was a sudden grunt and then a yell from beside the shaft.

A Lundstrom was struck and feeble light chased away overwhelming darkness. Maria looked across to the edge of the shaft. Mutolo stood there alone, looking over the lip before stepping back and looking at her.

"I think I speak for all the capos here, Maria. We will wait two months for what we hope will be Cesare's safe return to lead the fratellanza once more. There'll be no more rivalry between us for the leadership until it is time to take a vote, and we will personally guarantee your safety and that of the Giuliano family. If you agree, then please say so, Maria."

Two months should be long enough for her to put the next part of her plan into place. "I agree," she said. "Now let's get Umberto up from that pit of hell before he perishes." Yes, and let me tell him of my plans and thank him for saving my life, she muttered under her breath. There was pain in the outcome of today's events: the family could not bring closure to Cesare's disappearance; indeed it was doubtful they ever would, and Maria would have to bear that cross. Where she found pain, Maria also found pleasure. She would walk from the mine victorious, with Notarbartolo's death to her credit. She had the agreement of all the remaining capos on a two month moratorium before electing a new rappresentante. In that time, if Captain Fabroni held up his end of the bargain, Tommaso would have put himself forwards for the role. He had served a term in Vicaria and done so as a sacrifice to ensure her father's freedom. Those qualities would help, but they wouldn't ensure his success. Maria still had some work to do and Umberto Galli would be an indispensible ally.

Her next stop on leaving the mine would be Chiesa del Purgatorio.

Chapter 19

Captain Bruno Fabroni sat in the pew at Chiesa del Purgatorio and berated himself for his stupidity. The drone of the priest was little more than a distant buzz: all intelligibility blocked out by the turmoil of Fabroni's thoughts. He should have seen this coming: it was obvious now, but hindsight is the only one of God's gifts to be cursed with perfection. All his plans had been executed flawlessly, right up until this moment. Maria had convinced Tommaso to sign the confession on her visit to Palermo, and he was indeed freed within the week. There were those in the judiciary who opposed Bruno in this, and there were those who supported him. The latter he labelled as sympathetic to the honourable societies, and the former he took to be future allies. He could tell neither of his true ambition to wreck the fratellanza by exposing Maria's complicity in his plan and presenting her as a witness in a future trial. Of course, it would be at the hand of one of the capos that Maria would be exposed for the traitor she was; hopefully by Tommaso di Bova, if the information Bruno had was leaked to him in the proper manner.

Bruno always knew Maria's volatile temperament could destroy everything, and he was prepared for this. She was responsible for the note telling the carabinieri what was about to happen to Antonio Ruddini, and by implication she was responsible for the death of her own father. That's how the rest of the capos would see it, and Bruno kept that note safe, along with the rest of Maria's little missives. It would be fatal for her if those notes fell into the wrong hands, which he would ensure happened when the time was right. He would never allow any harm to come to her, however. She would be rescued in timely and dramatic fashion by the carabinieri and presented as a heroine in the fight against the criminal brotherhood that was the fratellanza. Of course, there was another subtle aspect to Bruno's plans for Maria: they would become lovers and wed. That was now impossible.

The announcement of the marriage of Tommaso di Bova and Maria Giuliano had just been read to the congregation.

Bruno had dismissed the fuitina as just a tired old custom, perpetuated by malicious gossip from tired old grandmothers. But the residents of Favara held tightly to their tired old customs. He should have seen it coming, and he didn't; so, now, how much of his plan could be salvaged? As he trudged from the chapel into the bright sunlight of the piazza, he mentally ticked off a list of what he could save and what he had to sacrifice. Outside, a gaggle of women and young girls surrounded Maria, all screaming and whooping with delight at the news. He looked across at her, and their eyes met for just a fraction of a second. There was nothing there: no warmth and no smile; barely even recognition. A more subdued but nonetheless excited group of men and boys gathered around Tommaso, expressing their congratulations with much back-slapping and handshaking. Bruno turned away and finalised his list.

There was no chance of having Maria as a lover. That part of his plan was as void as the gap it left in his life. He thought back to his mother, the rape of the Fabroni land and the murder of his brother. His personal vendetta and the interests of the carabinieri were now one. There was but a single strand to the plan now, and all of the elements were already in place. It was just a matter of timing. As an added bonus, he would take the greatest of pleasure in including Tommaso in the exorcising of the fratellanza capos. If Maria were still to fulfil her role as pentito then she would not sing to the court if Tommaso were to suffer, so there was but one solution to that problem. For the first time in his military career, and in total contravention of everything the carabinieri held dear, Captain Bruno Fabroni considered assassination as a means to an end. Of course, he could not have any personal involvement in this, but he could use the many insidious methods at his disposal to guide others into creating the same outcome. Lorenzo Fratelli had tried to kill Tommaso. It might have been just a typical prison fight, but on the evidence Bruno had unearthed, it was probably something deeper. Either way, Bruno was sure Fratelli would fulfil his destiny if given the opportunity. Returning Tommaso to Vicaria was possible, but once there all Bruno's powers would be impotent, and he was sure Fratelli would never get another opportunity behind Vicaria's walls. There was only one solution: bring the executioner back to Favara. This would take time, and Bruno had no idea how it could be achieved. Fratelli was in for life and the case behind his guilt was rock-solid.

As he mounted his horse and prepared for the journey back to barracks, Bruno straightened his tunic and made sure his sabre was secured at the correct angle by his side. He looked again at the squealing and giggling mob that surrounded Maria. He caught her eye once more but this time he smiled. No, it was more of a sneer, and he was sure she wouldn't miss it. It was a sneer that said – 'I'm going to put an end to your happiness', but he couldn't be sure this message struck home. It would, oh yes it certainly would, but at a time and a place of Captain Bruno Fabroni's choosing.

* * *

They had to go back there: the old shepherd's croft. It looked exactly the same as it had all those years ago, but it was a dilapidated wreck and unlikely to either decay or improve with time. Tommaso knew it would be one of the first places they would visit after his release, he just didn't expect things to happen so quickly, but then lots of things had been a sudden surprise on his first days back in Favara. He only knew of the marriage banns a few minutes before entering Chiesa del Purgatorio on this first Sunday of freedom. Maria had apologised for the rush but asked him to trust her, as there could be no other way ahead for them. The fuitina had seen to that, but she had assured him there were other more powerful forces shaping their destinies. All would be revealed when they once again lay on the rickety old bed and shared a bottle of wine, before surrendering to the passion released by its liberation of their inhibitions. In truth, that was a force so powerful, Tommaso could do little to keep it in check, and longed for the moment when they would consummate what was obviously an assignation driven by the pursuit of the most intimate of pleasures.

Yet, it was clear Maria had other ideas, or at least an agenda that relegated passion to a walk-on part after the main event. Within seconds of their arrival, she had sat beside him on the bed, taken his hand and began with the words: "My dearest Tommaso, I have much to tell you, and for the most part it is of conniving vendettas and untimely deaths."

And so it began. She started with her disguise as Pasquale Villabate and continued through to the death of Cesare and her adventures in the mine. There was a tear in her eye, and her voice croaked with sadness, as she told of the pain of not being able to give her father a burial. Eventually, when Tommaso understood she had depleted her reservoir of stories and the only sound to be heard was the whistle of a rock partridge, he confessed to what he knew. It began with Toto and ended with Lorenzo Fratelli's role as executioner, but Tommaso was careful to omit the role Cesare played in ordering the execution. To burden her now with that knowledge could upset an already fragile relationship and Tommaso feared he could lose Maria. He saw no point in trying to explain the values of the omertá. For all his hatred of Cesare, Tommaso understood, and in that understanding was a complicit agreement to uphold the oath over any and all other relationships. Perhaps, he could make Maria understand this in the future, but it had to be in the future: to venture down that road now would be to court a sudden and bitter separation from the object of his every desire and passion.

Tommaso placed his hand gently on her neck and pulled her close until her warm breath played upon wetness of his lips and tongue. "You have so many memories stored away, Maria. I only want to recall but a few. They are the memories of a piazza on a warm night when the air was pungent with the smell of burning wood. Your hand brushed against my thigh as you reached for the pitcher of wine I had been awarded as 'the slayer of beasts'. I think that's what you called me."

"Yes, yes, it was. You were my hero, Tommaso, and you still are. The passion of those moments was crushed by the guilt of our upbringing. That is a cross we no longer have to bear. You are no longer carusi."

Their mouths met and the rickety old bed creaked and groaned once more. The tallow candle flicked playful shadows on the most intimate curves and mounds of Maria's excited body. The wine loosened their tight grip on reality, and the soft warmth of a woollen blanket cocooned them, as they shared the other thoughts that welled up after the reservoir of their combined passions was emptied.

"Tomorrow," said Maria, "all the fratellanza families will meet. They will gather to honour you, Tommaso. With the announcement of our marriage, they'll have no choice but to accept your nomination as a capo. Cosimo Mutolo has agreed to be your sponsor."

He lay silent for a moment as she played the tips of her fingers delicately over his chest before allowing them to slip below the blanket. "How many of them know the complete truth?" asked Tommaso as the fingers descended further, heralding the discovery of a new and untapped pool of passion.

"None of the capos know," replied Maria, grinning playfully up at him. "Umberto Galli knows more than they do, but he is loyal to me, and I owe him a great deal."

"We will make sure he is rewarded. And what of Captain

Bruno Fabroni?"

The fingers froze momentarily, just below his navel, before beginning their tantalising journey once more. "I can control him," replied Maria. "He is no threat to us."

He was a very big threat, thought Tommaso, but before he could voice his concerns, Maria had thrown back the blanket to fully expose his nakedness. She rested her head gently on his chest and allowed her tongue to follow the teasing fingers to their final destination. Soon he could feel the warm breath once again – a vanguard to the pleasure she would bring to him. Suddenly she stopped, just short of the place he most wanted her to be, and turned her head to look up at him.

"I know you are concerned, Tommaso, but Fabroni really isn't a threat to us. He thinks he is, but he isn't. I can explain more if you wish."

Tommaso placed his hand gently on her neck and guided her back to where he could again sense her warm breath on him. He gave in to her completely, and she took him; gently at first and then without mercy.

* * *

They had a special cell for the drunks and the victims of the fights and stabbings that occurred between rival factions of pickmen. It was almost a nightly occurrence in Favara, and Bruno Fabroni never bothered with this trawl of detritus, which usually never made it beyond the cells of the local polizia. Tonight was a busy night, so some of the overflow of bruised and bleeding combatants was transferred to the carabinieri barracks. Bruno was getting desperate for information on the fratellanza, so he looked through the paperwork relating to the prisoners, hoping to find some glimmer of hope he could exploit in this small harvest of human debris.

It had been almost two months since Tommaso had returned,

and in that time Bruno had heard nothing from Maria. He couldn't approach her, or if he did it would seriously weaken his ability to manage her destiny and that of di Bova. Snippets of news reached Bruno's ears but no one was forthcoming with detailed information. That wasn't a surprise, the allegiance the so-called honourable members had to one another was bound by their stupid oaths and blood ties, but there had always been those in the lower levels of the fratellanza who were prepared to offer some intelligence on the basis of a lenient sentence or charges being dropped. Since di Bova's return, this practice had all but dried up, and it wasn't just a coincidence. What little knowledge Bruno gleaned, told him this new capo had brought much to the existing fratellanza disciplines and their ability to threaten those who were seen as a risk. The violence had increased and selected businesses were increasingly pressured for *pizzi* that had become more and more crippling. Despite this abundant harvest for the men of violence, the meagre pickings of the forces of law were such that questions were being asked of Bruno and his carabinieri.

He picked through the badly-written charge sheets for the five prisoners held in his cells. It was the usual litany of beatings and stabbings, being the outcome of an incestuous fight amongst the pickmen. Typically, this was why these cases never reached the carabinieri. This time it was different: someone had been too vicious with the blade and another corpse was trundled into the local mortuary. The perpetrator could have been any one of five in the cells below and a night of beatings and forced statements would normally have resolved the issue before morning, delivering up a confession. Bruno extracted one charge sheet and held it up to the glow of the lamp. His hand trembled with anticipation, and he made to rush to the cells and drag this particular *picconieri* to the interrogation room, where both the law and the lawless could expect a long night. Then Bruno stopped. It would indeed be a long night, but his prime target would be held for the final interrogation, and then only after he had been deprived of sleep, food and water for many more hours.

The sun's rays were filtering through the skylight above Bruno's head when he finally decided he had enough to put a new strand of his plan into action. Armed with the statements he had been able to extract from the other four prisoners, he descended into the depths of the barracks and drew open the lock on the rusty shackle of the heavy wooden door to the interrogation cell.

"It's been a long night; go get some coffee from the guardhouse and have a smoke. Bring some back when you return, but don't hurry," he said to the guard on duty as he pushed open the door and entered the cell.

His victim sat head down and seemingly oblivious to the noisy creak of rusty hinges. Bruno lifted a bucket of water from the floor and threw it over him. The prisoner jumped in his seat but was restrained by the ropes that bound him. He grunted and looked up. One eye was swollen and completely closed by a congealed bloody mass. The water did nothing to wash this away, so it was undoubtedly the result of the fight that ended in murder. Other cuts and wheals wept diluted blood: these were more recent, the result of the previous few hours' interrogation. Puffed lips concealed a damaged mouth, but there were no signs of a broken jaw. Bruno had been explicit in his commands. Use torture wherever necessary, he had told his comrades, but ensure the prisoner can speak freely.

"Umberto Galli," said Bruno, closing the heavy door behind him. "I trust you've enjoyed your overnight stay at my humble abode?"

Galli said nothing. He just put his head down as if his only purpose in life was to sleep. Bruno selected another bucket; this one filled with a solution of brine and iodine, and threw it over his prisoner. The dousing made him yell in pain. "There, there, my dearest Galli. We must ensure your wounds don't become infected. Yes it stings, but you'll thank me for my care, in time."

"I'll never thank the carabinieri scum for anything," replied Galli, spitting out a broken tooth in the process.

Bruno grabbed a chair and brought it close to his victim. He sat down and removed his scabbard, drawing his sword at the same time. "Damned uniform," he said. "I'm not supposed to take this off in public." He swished the blade in the air a few times. "But then, we are in private; are we not? And I'm sure you won't tell anyone." Bruno waited for a response. There was none. "Right, I'll take your silence as an agreement. Now, where should we begin with your confession to the murder of your esteemed colleague?"

"I murdered no one. I was in a fight, as you can see. I was long gone before anyone was seriously hurt." Another gobbet of blood followed and found its place on the stone floor.

"I believe you, Galli. I really do, and I want to make sure that the record I will send to the magistrate in just a few hours from now says exactly that. Unfortunately, I have four accounts of the murder in my hand and they all seem to agree it was you who delivered the fatal blow."

"Good try, and very intelligent for a Calabrian farmer. I know how this works. I've been told the tricks you carabinieri scum get up to. If you have four statements, then you don't need mine. I will deliver it to the magistrate personally."

Bruno made a play of spinning his sabre slowly on its point, as if checking the balance of the weapon at his disposal. He looked at Galli and then lifted the point of the sabre to press it on his victim's right foot: the one his comrades had dropped the edge of a heavy desk on, just hours before. Bruno spun the sabre again and watched as Galli winced in agony. "Oh dear, a broken bone, I think. That is a shame, especially for a pickman. How will you make your quota now? And how will you support your newborn infant who is due to arrive in the next few weeks? And how is your wife, by the way?"

"Pickmen have a guild, they take care of their own," replied Galli, gobbing another bloody spit on the floor.

"A guild? Ha, is that what it is called, Umberto? No, it's called la fratellanza, but yes it does look after its own."

"I know nothing of la fratellanza."

"Of course you don't. They're a myth. What isn't a myth is what goes to the magistrate this morning. One murder because of a knife-fight. Five arrested – one identified as the murderer and charged. All over as far as I'm concerned, Umberto." Bruno lifted the sword, put it back in its scabbard and strapped it to his side once more.

"I haven't been charged."

"My dearest Umberto, I'm not here to interrogate you. That's been done. I am here to charge you with the murder of Luciano Francenzo. The paperwork is all here. You have to trust me on that, of course."

"Never trust the carabinieri. That's what they told us. They also told us how you twist confessions to force us to turn on our brothers. Fuck off, Captain. I know enough about you and your methods. Try them on someone else."

Bruno stopped and pulled two cheroots from his tunic, lighting both with a Lundstrom. He placed one between Galli's cracked and bloodied lips whilst sitting close to him. After inhaling a satisfying lung-full of the smoke, and allowing Galli to do the same, Bruno continued. "My, my; and where is all of this coming from? You deny the fratellanza yet you recite their training. You also know about me and my family history in Calabria. Do you really expect me to believe your abilities as a man are limited to just swinging a pick-axe?"

"You're wasting your time, Captain Bruno Fabroni. Take your confessions to the magistrate, see how far you get. I'll be out of here and free by tomorrow."

"Ah, yes. Now I understand your contempt. Magistrate Franconi has been a great friend of the fratellanza."

"Magistrate Franconi is a fair and just man," replied Galli, with the assurance of someone who believes they have the upper hand.

"Alas no, that may not be the case," replied Bruno. "Franconi was arrested only yesterday and charged with corruption. I'm sure he will be found innocent of such charges, but whilst he is being investigated, another magistrate will be taking up his duties. It's short notice I know, but I have been able to introduce a trusted friend to the position, here in Favara."

Galli stopped, took a deep draw on the cheroot, and exhaled slowly at the same time as saying, "It's a lie. A good one, yes. But still a lie."

It was a lie: one of Bruno's favourites at times like this in the interrogation of a suspect. The local judiciary were in the pockets of the fratellanza and he had to break his suspects into a confession before handing the case over. However, since it was a well-practiced lie, it was one Bruno could carry off convincingly. He set four sheets of hand-written statements in front of Galli. There was no way the pickman could read them but he could recognise his own name, which Bruno was careful to have introduced into each script. "Umberto, your erstwhile friends seem better informed than you. Here are their four confessions, each naming you as the killer. Look here," said Bruno, pointing at each folio in turn. "That is your name; is it not? These brothers, they already know there is no salvation in Franconi's redemption. The only way out for them is to blame you, which they have done."

"I have made no statement," said Galli, fear now replacing confidence in his voice. "You cannot believe those who were in the fight that cost Francenzo his life. You left me to last because you believe I'm the weakest and will turn on my brothers, making me pentito. You are a poor judge of men, Captain. I will never turn."

Bruno laughed and stubbed out the remains of his smoke

whilst withdrawing the cheroot from Galli's cracked lips. "Umberto, your faith in the impartiality of justice is touching. I really don't care which of you is guilty as long as I have a good chance of one conviction. I have this task to complete and then today brings an end to my duty for the week. I like to leave a clean slate, you understand. Your statement can indeed be given to the new magistrate if you wish, but it will be a waste of time. You might get away with fifteen years in Vicaria Jail if he accepts your plea of manslaughter. I will be writing it up as murder but then my esteemed friend, the new magistrate, always likes me to leave a little room for an agreement on a lesser charge, subject to a full confession. Job done, and we all go home happy, except you, of course." Bruno gathered up his papers and placed a quill pen beside a small inkstand next to the table beside Galli. "Now, it's time to prepare the charge against you. Please listen carefully to all I have to say."

"You'll never make me pentito. You've failed. I'll go to jail and my family will be looked after."

The words were uttered not in triumph but fear, and Bruno had Galli close to where he wanted him. "That may be, Umberto. But you did not commit murder to protect anyone in the fratellanza and fifteen years is a long time to depend on their charity. By the time you see your newborn child, he will either be hauling sulphur on his back, or if it's a girl, she will rubbing its powder on the pox marks on her face. But just so you understand, I'm not looking for pentiti. I've enough of those, but thank you for bringing it up; maybe next time." Bruno pulled his chair up to the desk, took a clean folio of paper and proceeded to write, whilst detailing the charge against Galli. Halfway through the process, he stopped, set down the pen and leaned back in his chair. "You see, my dear Umberto, pentiti have to testify. Then we have to protect them, and their families. It's all very inconvenient and time consuming. We wouldn't go through that for just a pickman. Please take no offence. It's just that you can bring us no more than background information on what's going with the families who control this region. That would be useful but it's not really a fair exchange for me tearing up this document." He lifted the folio and waved it in front of Galli.

"You need an informer, then?"

That arrived sooner in the process than Bruno would have expected, but it was the first overt acknowledgement of his victim's willingness to co-operate. "Well, yes, but all a pickman can tell me is the number of blocks of sulphur pulled from the mine and where the next fight is going to be."

"I am a trusted friend of Maria Giuliano."

Bruno tilted his chair forwards again, picked up the pen and proceeded to write whilst stating, "Maria has no friends; plenty of lovers in the valley, but no friends."

"If that is what you believe, then it is obvious you need informers. Tear up that paper you're writing on. Take these shackles off and arrange my release, along with that of the others so no suspicion falls on me."

"But who then will be charged with Francenzo's murder?" asked Bruno, barely able to keep a self-satisfied smile from his lips.

"I don't care, and neither do you. Four of us go free. One remains. You decide."

Bruno rose from his chair and went to the door. The guard had returned from his enforced break. "Get the medical orderly in here and tidy this man up. Bring some food and water whilst you're at it." The door hinges creaked once again, but Bruno didn't close the lock. He released Galli's shackles and handed him the folio with the murder charge detailed on it. "I won't tear this up, Umberto. I will simply give it to you. There are no copies." He then lifted the four statements from the others and held them in front of his new informer. "And I won't decide who is charged, you will. Choose one."

Galli made his selection and handed it to Bruno to be torn into small pieces.

"Oh dear," said Bruno, "it looks like I will need more statements from your companions, and a confession. Justice will be done but I do have to hurry it along. Please excuse me."

Within the hour, Galli's wounds had been tended and he was still in the process of finishing his meal, when Bruno returned. "Just a few rules, Umberto, now that we are new-found companions. Your communication with the forces of law is only through me in a manner I will describe later. If you get into trouble again, don't attempt to contact me or seek my assistance. If I can help you I will, but you cannot rely on it. Do you understand?"

Galli nodded.

"Very well, then please tell me why Maria Giuliano is not a whore."

Galli's story began at the lip of Cesare's Shaft with the search for Cesare's body and finished with the preparations for the election of the new rappresentante in a few days' time. Tommaso di Bova was likely to be nominated by a majority of the other capos. He had been instrumental in resolving disputes and settling scores amongst them, using much of what he had learned in Vicaria: a place Galli had obviously no desire to see the inside of. A few of the capos still seemed loyal to the memory of Leopoldo Notarbartolo, but they were outnumbered by those supporting Tommaso, and Maria had been instrumental in bringing this about. Galli didn't know how, but Bruno could guess.

The pickman's story continued for almost an hour and some of his revelations were explosive. Bruno had some strategic thinking to do, and he had to act quickly, but the election of di Bova could proceed without intervention. That fitted in neatly with Bruno's plans.

Chapter 20

The illicit taverna on Vicaria Prison's B Block had a window that overlooked Piazza Ucciardone. The window was high up, so no one simply had a casual look to see the world outside. But tonight was different. Lorenzo Fratelli and the other occupants of the taverna listened to the crack of musket fire coming from the hills above Palermo, along with cries and shouts of insurrection from the streets surrounding Vicaria Prison. Tonight, there was a feeling that rapidly unfolding events were leading to a climactic conclusion, and Sicily could once more face the prospect of violent and cataclysmic change.

Lorenzo had been moved from the infirmary straight to B Block after he had recovered from the wounds inflicted on him by Filippo and Tommaso di Bova. He was safe there from the Calabrians, although a few of their number still populated the section of the prison run by Sicilians. Lorenzo's reputation, and his attempt to kill a block commander, had made him a legend in Vicaria. He was feted wherever he went on B Block. It was mooted by Guido, the block commander, that Lorenzo would be his next enforcer, once the current incumbent had earned his release in just a few months' time. Until then, Lorenzo had to keep his head down and not get drawn into the routine vendettas that dictated the lives of many of the inmates. The wound in his leg had healed and his sight had mostly returned in the one damaged eye, both still painful reminders of the unfinished business he had with di Bova and the charge placed on him by Cesare Giuliano. That execution order would have to wait, but sooner or later di Bova would find himself back in Vicaria, and Lorenzo would be there: ever-patient, ever-vengeful, and with the febrile burden of the assassin. Yet, if the growing revolution engulfed Palermo in a civil war once more, then anything was possible for Sicily and Lorenzo's future in it.

What was going on outside the walls of Vicaria had fuelled an atmosphere inside the prison that was a volatile mixture of excitement, frustration and rumour. Lorenzo had watched as it hijacked every conversation between inmates and led to increasing tension with the prison guards. Fights were becoming daily events instead of rare occurrences, and the morgue was becoming more popular than the taverna. The relative peace of the last eight years, since Garibaldi's conquest of Sicily and the unification of Italy, was common knowledge, but this didn't sit well with the current talk of armed rebellion in the streets and piazzas of Palermo. For the price of a tankard of Marsala, Lorenzo would lift one of his companions up to stand on massive shoulders and have a clear view through the bars of the elevated window. Thereby, a running commentary followed, based on what little evidence could be seen and heard.

"Are there warships in the harbour?" asked one from the floor of the taverna.

"No, just a few fishing boats and I can see out into the bay. No navy ships there either, even the British support vessels have gone," was the reply from the inmate standing on Lorenzo's shoulders.

"Are there barricades in the piazza?"

"There is nothing in the piazza." The commentator lifted himself up a little further, with Lorenzo's help. "I can just about see to Corso di Scina. There are barricades there and they are manned."

"Can you see uniforms?"

"No, the men on the barricades don't have uniforms, but they all wear red: either bandanas or shirts, but all have something red. There is a large banner draped over the barricades."

"What's on the banner?"

"La Repubblica."

"Hey, The Horse has drunk your Marsala. It's my turn."

The next paying customer set a tankard down and climbed

nimbly onto Lorenzo's shoulders, just as musket fire ripped through the night air with flashes so bright they lit up the dark interior of the taverna.

"That's from C Block. I can see fires flickering in the windows."

Sudden pandemonium broke amongst the crowd gathered at Lorenzo's feet, and they all tried to climb onto his shoulders for a better view. He beat them off mercilessly and threatened to crack a few heads together if they didn't calm down. Once he had cleared the crowds from around him, he reached down and took a slug of Marsala from the tankard left by the paying customer who was still on his shoulders. The commentary continued: "Listen, you can hear the rioting." They all obeyed and heard the crack of musket fire mingled with shouts and the unmistakable sound of splintering glass. "It's a riot, alright. Wait, I can see some of the red-shirts rushing into the piazza." There was a sudden eruption of gunfire from the battlements of Vicaria, and with it carried a new sound like a hundred carbines firing in quick succession. "My God, the red-shirts are being torn to pieces by the gunfire. The ground all around them looks like Mount Etna spawned a family of evil little children. There must be hundreds of guns on the battlements."

"Not hundreds," came a familiar voice from the crowd at Lorenzo's feet. "Just one: just one gun."

They all turned to look at the old mule-herder just as Toto spoke again. "It's a *mitrailleuse:* a single gun that can fire one hundred slugs in a minute, every minute. It's a gift from the French. If there's one on the battlements of Vicaria, the rebels will never storm the gates of the prison."

The sound of a full-scale riot built to a crescendo outside, but suddenly everyone's attention was focussed on the wizened figure of the old mule-herder, as if he was a soothsayer with some divine insight into what was about to happen.

Lorenzo was first to grasp the depth of what Toto had just

said and asked the question on everybody's lips: "Would the rebels really think it was worth the loss of many lives to storm the prison?"

"They did it before in 1820 and freed 2,500 to join the cause of Sicilian separatism. Then they burnt all the prison records and killed the Governor and all of the prison staff. A few of those who were freed back then might well be out there now: wearing the red of the rebel forces, and they'll be happy to lay down their lives. Don't forget, Vicaria is a fortress that was built to command all access to Palermo by sea. Capture the prison and you control the city."

The sudden clamour amongst the crowd was broken by the arrival of B Wing's commander. "Thank you, Toto," said Guido as he stormed into the taverna, breathless and excited. "I'll take over from here. Gentlemen, what you are hearing from C Block is a planned uprising. Many have died and there'll be more bloodshed before the night is over. All prison guards have been rushed over to put down the rebellion, but soon a contingent will arrive here to put us in lock-down. As soon as you see the guards, you must each pick your target and attack. Fall on the bastards without mercy and kill them all. Take whatever weapons you can, along with any keys you can find, and open every locked door. Now, assemble in the main corridor between the cells but give no ground. Lorenzo, stay with me; you too, Toto."

Lorenzo was as dumbfounded as the rest of his companions, and they all stood stock-still and looked at Guido, as if they'd just woken from a deep sleep and couldn't tell dreams from reality.

"What are you waiting for, you dumb bastards?" shouted the block commander. "This is an uprising, and the rebels on the outside will storm Vicaria within the hour. They cannot do that unless we overrun the defences from the inside. Now go!"

They all scarpered, leaving only Lorenzo and Toto.

"You seem to know about more than just mules, Toto," said Guido, as he approached them – a trace of suspicion in his voice.

"You bribe the guards to get what you want; I befriend them," replied Toto. "They know I'm not a member of the honoured societies, and they think I'm just a harmless old bastard, so they tell me things."

Guido seemed to accept this and turned to Lorenzo. "What the 'harmless old bastard' says is correct. We need to spike the guns on the walls of the prison, or the rebels will never make it across the piazza." An almighty clap of thunder split the night and stopped Guido in mid sentence. There could be no storm, as the sky was crystal clear but nothing else could explain the sound, followed by a wheezing whistle and then an apocalyptic explosion that shook the very floor of the taverna. Lorenzo ran to the window and lifted Toto onto his shoulders before the diminutive mule-herder could object.

"They have cannon," said Toto. "The rebels have artillery pieces." Another blast shook the night followed by the crump of ordnance smashing into Vicaria's walls. "Jesus, they have firepower and they know how to use it. That took out a sentry post on the walls beside C Wing. There must be twenty or more prison guards turned to bloody shreds." The sound of yet more cannon fire reverberated above the noise of fighting; now echoing up from the floor of B Wing.

"The prison guards are here. The fight has begun," said Guido and rushed to join the fray, just as the floor shook again.

"They've hit the main gate," said Toto. "Blown it to bits. I can see the shards of wood all over the piazza."

"Stay here, old man," said Lorenzo as he lifted Toto down. "Help yourself to some free Marsala."

The sight that met Lorenzo as he reached the top of the stairs descending into the main corridor of B Wing was one of a pitched battle between prisoners and jailers. Carbine fire dropped serried rows of inmates, as warders fired in fear of being overwhelmed and beaten to a pulp before they could re-load. With each eruption of cannon fire from outside, Lorenzo could see the resolve of the guards evaporate until their only thought was of escape. More guards joined the mêlée, as they fled evisceration from the cannon fire bombarding the walls, only to be hacked limb from limb as they met heavily-armed inmates commandeering every entrance and exit. Locked doors were thrown open as the out of control mob found their way into every secure area of the block and relieved cowering guards of their keys before slaughtering them with any weapons they had to hand. Some met their Maker quickly, courtesy of a carbine round; others perished in screaming agony as they were beaten to death by the frenzied inmates. It mattered not that guards were formerly on the payroll of the block commander. All allegiances were rendered void by the sudden lust for blood and vengeance that had been hiding behind the thin veil of prison control.

A line of terrified guards ran three flights up the steel staircase to where Lorenzo stood. Their faces displayed a mixture of fear and panic, and it was obvious they would have to kill or be killed in their escape. Lorenzo was the only inmate on the stairs. The first of the guards ran at him screaming, only to be met with the crushing swipe of a ham-sized fist. The second in line clambered over the unconscious body of his comrade but this obstacle slowed him to the point where The Horse simply plucked him from the staircase and threw him onto the floor below, where his skull smashed on the stone floor like an overripe peach. The third attacked with a cutlass, but the killing arc of steel never found its mark. Lorenzo pulled the cutlass from its owner and cut his arm off with it, releasing a fountain of blood over the rest of the line of guards whose hell-bent rush to escape was now a simple but terrifying choice of up or down. They looked up to Lorenzo who swung the cutlass with ever increasing accuracy, further claiming an ear. Then they looked down to the braying mob below, and in an eerie display of blind panic they all jumped to their doom.

Lorenzo ran down the three flights of open stairs just as another almighty explosion of cannon fire blasted into the main corridor of the block, bringing with it clouds of debris and dust. For a few seconds there was silence, as all the combatants reeled from the percussive shock of the blast. When they came to, all were covered in a thick layer of white dust that rendered guard indistinguishable from inmate. The scene was almost comical, as none could identify friend from foe. Then, with an almighty yell, a new cohort joined the fight. They wore red. They were the rebels. They had stormed the prison. The dust-covered inmates rushed to welcome them whilst the few remaining guards tried to flee. They were quickly captured by the victors and herded into one of the open cells. The fight was over, for now. Lorenzo watched as the rebels fell into line on the shouts of orders barked from somewhere in the maelstrom of dust and smoke that continued to swirl around the entrance to the wing. He knew that voice and stood transfixed as the surreal scene below him became even more bizarre. The clouds parted and through the swirling dust a figure strode, as if making an entrance on stage. He wore a dark grey uniform, with the splash of a red sash that crossed his chest. Those long legs, the crisp commanding voice, the overwrought gestures and expressions: it could only be one man – Salvatore di Paolo.

The artist had found his true role and Lorenzo hailed him from the first flight of stairs.

"Lorenzo Fratelli," replied di Paolo. "How fortunate it is I find you so quickly. Please join me on the battlefield and let's finish this before a counter-attack." Di Paolo bowed from the waist in true theatrical style as Lorenzo ran forwards.

Lorenzo grabbed di Paolo in a bear-hug before backing away in embarrassment at his overt display of emotion. "Tell me what we must do," said Lorenzo.

"Why, my dear Girgenti cousin, all that is required of you, is to leave here with my little band of rebels, but please hurry. There are warships entering the bay and they will give us an almighty broadside. But before we go; do you know where the prison records are kept? We need to burn the lot."

Lorenzo was about to explain that he had no understanding of the complexities of Vicaria when a familiar voice piped up from behind him.

"As you entered through the main gate, on the left are the offices of the Governor and the main administration block. Raze them to the ground and all records will be destroyed."

Di Paolo looked down at the one good eye of Toto staring defiantly back. "He is your block commander; maybe?" responded di Paolo as if the stage he was playing on had transformed from the horrors of battle to the subtle drama of a farce.

"No, he is a trusted friend from the depths of Ciavallotta," replied Lorenzo whilst wrapping a meaty arm around Toto's shoulders.

"Very well, any friend of Lorenzo Fratelli's is a friend of mine. Bring him along. But do it now." Di Paolo issued a slew of orders and ten red-shirts peeled off and headed to the Governor's office. He then looked around and raised his voice once more to address the rest of his men. "The prisoners are now the guards and the guards are now the prisoners." He waited for some appreciation of his wit but none was returned. With a sniff of derision, he continued. "Manacle all those we have captured. My personal troops surround me and my two friends here." Six men rushed to his side and Lorenzo and Toto found themselves in the centre of an armed circle. "Now bring the captives and place them in a ring around my group. It is time for me to leave."

Lorenzo suddenly understood the reason for the protective phalanx surrounding them but couldn't comprehend why he and Toto were so privileged. "What about the rest of the inmates?" he asked of di Paolo. "Are they free to go?"

"As soon as we clear the front gate," replied di Paolo. "But for now, I have a mission to deliver you from this stink-hole of a prison."

The tight group of rebels moved forwards with Lorenzo and

Toto at their centre. Wayward fire from corridors and battlements pinged and whizzed around them, with the occasional round thwacking into one of the human shield that protected them. Where the wound was fatal, the victim was left to fall; where it was not so, the victim was forced to continue on and provide a further soft and yielding barrier to any hot lead directed their way.

Lorenzo had some recollections of the journey that brought him through the fortifications of Vicaria: the circular piazza segmented like pieces of a pie, the armoured steel door in the same ubiquitous green paint, the butter-coloured turrets surrounding the large open square and the final small courtyard where flames now blazed in the Governor's office. He was on his way to freedom but liberated as part of an insurrection. How long could he hope to stay free? And could he return to Favara? As rifle-fire and explosions reverberated around him, now was not the time for such deliberation. The tightly-packed scrum burst out into Piazza Ucciardone, and di Paolo issued more orders as fire from ships in the bay was now directed at the gates of Vicaria. This fusillade was instantly fatal to the terrified wretches who provided the human shield, and the grapeshot hurtled into them. Their bodies exploded in eruptions of blood and flesh as thousands of metal balls sliced through yielding bone and tissue to bounce with unbelievable force and speed off the walls of the prison, and ricochet back into Lorenzo's group for a second round of evisceration and decapitation. Lorenzo grabbed Toto and di Paolo as another salvo headed in on a wave of thudding explosions from the cannons of the warships. With his two charges, he fled to the side of the gate and into the shelter of one of the major turrets that formed part of the outer curtain of Vicaria's fortifications. Two of the other rebels in his group managed to escape the first murderous attack of grapeshot and scampered around the turret wall, just as another blizzard of metal balls battered the masonry like the devil's own hail.

Lorenzo set Toto down along with di Paolo. There was the unmistakable look of terror in the old mule-herder's one good eye, but di Paolo's face showed only pain. Lorenzo looked down, and the long legs were smashed and pulverized into limp pieces of bloody shreds, held in place only by the tattered remains of the grey uniform that still smoked from its yielding encounter with hard, hot metal. Di Paolo made to speak but Lorenzo stopped him, then laid his broken body carefully on the ground, before grabbing the two survivors of his group who were about to run and leave them. Di Paolo seemed to understand and took command without giving any quarter to the agony he must have been enduring.

"There's a field hospital on Corso di Scina. One of you take Toto and bring back a stretcher." They looked at their commander and then at one another, trying to decide which draw of the straws would be the shorter: staying here and waiting for the naval guns to target them, or backtracking across the open field of fire that was the piazza.

Toto eventually resolved the dilemma: "Anything that moves in the piazza will be destroyed by grapeshot. The naval gunners have zeroed in on the front gate so no one else can escape the prison. We must skirt all the way around the walls to get to Corso di Scina." He looked down at di Paolo and then up at Lorenzo. "We can't stay here any longer; we all must run."

"I fear that may be a problem for me," said di Paolo, shuddering slightly as bravado overcame agony.

"I've carried hangovers that weighed more than you," said Lorenzo and made to lift him, but the torturous pain would be corralled no longer. Di Paolo screamed and barely stayed conscious.

"The walls of Vicaria are over a kilometre around," said di Paolo. "And then another half to the field hospital. I don't want to die screaming in agony. I'd prefer to just fade away here, if that's acceptable to you all."

"Toto, run and take these two with you. Try and get back with stretcher-bearers. I'll wait," said Lorenzo. He gripped di Paolo's hand as he said it and looked into his eyes to indicate he would brook no argument. When they were alone, save for the continuing bombardment of grapeshot as more prisoners tried to escape, Lorenzo asked, "This could not all have happened just to free one man?"

Di Paolo started to laugh and then curtailed it to a painful smile. "Don't get ahead of yourself, Lorenzo. The struggle to create a republic is what is important and Vicaria is the prize. If we control her, we will hold Palermo against land and sea." The pain was now writ large on di Paolo's pallid face and the puddle of blood he lay in could surely grow no larger. "You, my Girgenti friend, are needed back in Favara, and someone has entrusted me to make sure you were freed when we stormed the prison. The prison records are destroyed and those who have been mown down by the grapeshot are unrecognisable. You are now a ghost, Lorenzo Fratelli."

"Cesare Giuliano hasn't forgotten me," replied Lorenzo.

"No, not Cesare." The once commanding voice was now a rattle that partnered death in a last act. Di Paolo must have been able to sense it. "No time. You are safe to return to Favara. Unfinished business."

In Lorenzo's mind, a line of questions jostled to be first in a fractious queue. Each needed an answer, but there was no one left to ask.

Chapter 21

The piazza in front of Chiesa del Purgatorio looked just the same to Tommaso as it had before his imprisonment in Vicaria. In fact it looked just the same as it had when he slaughtered the Sicilian Black Swine and ate a slice of its heart. The bell tower of the church pierced the blue sky in such a way that the midday sun was directly over the top of the spire. No other building in Favara was allowed to exceed its elevation, so the *campanile* had a commanding view over the entire town. The warm terracotta, and the precious shade offered by the few stunted bushes, made the piazza a popular gathering place. Favoured spots were claimed by those who staked their place early in the day and didn't budge until the arc of the sun transferred desirability to another occupant, whose timely invasion would see off any and all intruders. Today, the individuals who annexed the shadiest spots were evicted by the crowd that had been assembling since morning mass.

Maria clung to Tommaso's arm. They were free to express their affection now they were man and wife, and the crowds in the piazza cheered and applauded when they approached. They had come from all over the region, with some taking two days to reach the festivities. There could be no staying away for anyone who wished to show their allegiance to the fratellanza and its new rappresentante. Tommaso had made the decision that one festival would celebrate both his marriage and his appointment to the head of all the honourable families. It was just one of the actions that won him many supporters from within the capos. No, not every one of them, but enough to ensure his supremacy.

Music chorused through the crowds and the fast upbeat sounds of the Tarantella started to rise to a crescendo. Maria pulled Tommaso into a small troupe of dancers, all dressed in the simple costume of black and white with alternate sashes of red for the girls and blue for the boys. Tommaso felt instantly clumsy and tried to take his leave but Maria was having none of it, and the rapturous applause from the crowds ensured he would have to continue. He knew the simple basics of the choreography; who in Sicily didn't know the Tarantella? But he still felt clumsy.

"Just do what I do, Tommaso," screamed Maria above the spellbinding commotion of the music. "We'll leave when the lead comes on." He could accept that. The main dance was simple, although structured to become more frenetic with the increased tempo before the lead dancer arrived. Finally, just when Tommaso thought he could take no more, a young woman was catapulted into the frenzy and threw herself to the ground, writhing and contorting like a maniac, but still, miraculously, in time with the accelerating tempo. Relieved, Maria dragged him away to the side.

"She's the victim of the spider," exclaimed his new wife. "Only the wild dance of the Tarantella can cure the poisonous bite of the Tarantula." Maria raised her hand in a claw and grasped Tommaso by the neck, in a mock representation of an attacking spider, laughing and teasing as she did so.

Tommaso smiled and swatted her hand away before looking over at the lead, who was now twisting on the ground like she was possessed by demons. Her contortions seemed to become more erotic as the tempo quickened, but this only served to heighten the sense of excitement from the crowd.

"If a tarantula ever bites me, then I'm dead. I could never do that," he said and Maria laughed once more, before pulling him back into the dance troupe, just as the spectacle reached its climactic end. Dancers paused to catch their breath whilst the musicians played on, reverting to something more melodious in the interval between rousing bouts of the Tarantella. This time it was Tommaso's turn to tease, and he dragged Maria to meet the musicians, especially the one who played the zampogna. With a host of smiles and much encouragement, Tommaso was persuaded to take the unwieldy instrument and reprise the mournful wails that once were his signature refrain behind Vicaria's walls. As he played, he looked over the piazza and understood that not everything was as immutable as Chiesa del Purgatorio and its surroundings. Cesare Giuliano had been declared dead, allowing Tommaso's election as the new rappresentante. He understood the necessary subterfuge but this secret was, he hoped, shared only with Maria and Umberto Galli; at least for the time being. Sooner or later his capos would have to know the truth.

For his own part, Tommaso suffered the death of his mother and almost permanent separation from his father who seemed to prefer the hills and pastures of Cammarata to life in Favara. Lucio di Bova couldn't even bring himself to be there for this celebration.

From Palermo there were reports of uprisings and rebellions in a failed attempt to turn Sicily into a republic. They even said Vicaria had been sacked, but any who escaped were mown down by gunfire at the gates. The actions of the rebels had failed and Palermo was in chaos, but life in Girgenti went on without any evidence of rebellions and republics, as it had for centuries.

None of this mattered.

There was a new order in Favara and Tommaso di Bova was the central part of it. With Maria at his side, the fusion of the Giuliano lineage and the provenance bestowed by being a block commander in Vicaria made a powerful combination. There was nothing that could threaten it, and Tommaso was only at the beginning of his reign.

When he had finished his refrain, one of the musicians called over to him and Maria. "You are not forgotten behind the walls of Vicaria, Tommaso di Bova," he said and then pulled a small package from his cloak. It was exquisitely wrapped and carried a label. He handed this to Maria who read the label and looked at Tommaso with a mixture of delight and confusion.

"It says, 'Congratulations on your marriage. From Master Joe.' Can I open it, Tommaso?"

"It's a wedding present. Of course you can open it."

As she did so, Tommaso explained something of the identity of Master Joe and the importance of his support during Tommaso's imprisonment in Vicaria. By the time he had reached the explanation of the ceremony baptising the first-born son into the ranks of the 'ndrangheta, Maria had opened the gift and stared at it, whilst uttering little yelps of pure delight. It was modelled on a simple two-piece hair clasp, with a curved band and a pin, but this was no cheap trinket. The pin was designed to look like a knife and the curved band a key. Both were constructed from silver and gold with the stiletto-like blade of the knife in polished steel. The intricacy of the way the blade locked through the key was undoubtedly the product of one of Calabria's finest jewellers, perhaps even a Vicaria inmate. Maria skilfully bundled up her hair and locked the long blade of the pin into the key. She thanked the musician who had given her Master Joe's present and kissed him once on the cheek, before running off to display this new treasure to her sisters and friends. Tommaso added his thanks and pressed some lire into the hands of the musician who had presented the gift.

"Please enjoy some drinks in Taverna Girandola tonight with your friends," he said, before leaving to catch up with Maria.

The bells in the campanile rang out and nobody paid too much notice, even though the campanologists seemed to be having an off day. The peals were discordant and followed no particular timing. Tommaso looked over at the entrance of Chiesa del Purgatorio and witnessed Father Russo struggling with the heavy door, as if he was locked out of his own chapel. The old priest gave up on the front entrance and ran to the side door, but he encountered the same barrier to his entrance, just as the crescendo from the bells grew to an even more jarring cacophony. Confused looks amongst the revellers in the piazza gave way to concern, as shouts from Father Russo brought more volunteers to the locked doors, where they battered against oak planks as thick as a man's arm, all to no avail. Tommaso noted that some of the fratellanza members had joined the scrum at the doors and he ran to join in, eventually reaching the distressed priest who was seemingly barred from his own place of worship.

"Have you lost your key, Father?" exclaimed Tommaso with a smile. "Perhaps you left it in the taverna or at the bedside of one Favara's finest."

Russo levelled a stark and angry stare at him before relenting, as he recognised the new rappresentante. "Signor di Bova, I'm afraid this is no time for frivolity. All of my congregation have been forced to leave the chapel: the choir, the organist, even the cleaners. They were thrown out by one man and then the doors were locked from inside."

There was a peculiar sense of fear in the priest's eyes but Tommaso didn't really see the nature of the threat. "Why would anyone want to barricade themselves inside the House of the Lord?" he asked. "This must surely be a madman, Father?"

"A madman indeed," replied Father Russo. "One we know as Lorenzo Fratelli."

That hit Tommaso like a cannon ball. How could his nemesis suddenly turn up in Favara and why should he make his appearance now? Russo might have been worried about the relics in the nave or the golden frames on the Stations of the Cross, but the priest wasn't under a death sentence from the madman who had locked himself inside. "How do you know this is Fratelli?" he asked, suddenly panicked.

"No one in Favara could forget him, and besides, he made sure he told everyone his name before he threw them out," replied Russo.

Outside, the discordant ringing stopped, to a piazza full of silent onlookers, all staring up at the top of the campanile.

A commanding voice boomed out into the hush that had

descended on the crowd. "Tommaso di Bova, show yourself! Your audience awaits. Do not hide in the shadows. Surely you do not fear me? What can I do to you from up here?" It wasn't a request, it was a challenge from The Horse and Tommaso walked slowly out of the shadows into the bright glare of the sunlight and the muttering anticipation of the crowd. The unmistakable figure of Fratelli stood on a narrow ledge of the campanile, high above the piazza.

"I fear no man, Fratelli," shouted Tommaso. "Especially one who is a murderer and an escaped convict. You may not be able to harm me from your perch on the campanile, but you will have to come down some time. Then we'll see how fear works."

"So capture me, and hand me in to the carabinieri, if you dare. That would be a fitting first act for the new leader of the fratellanza."

There were a few options open to Tommaso, but overt collusion with the carabinieri wasn't one of them. "I will capture you, but the fratellanza has its own law. You will be subject to it, and later you'll wish you were a prisoner of the carabinieri."

"Signora di Bova, I see you there. You are as beautiful as ever, Maria," continued Fratelli, changing the subject but still holding the attention of the awestruck crowd. "I must congratulate you on your marriage." Tommaso looked across at Maria, who immediately ran to his side as the booming voice continued from its high vantage. "I regret I did not receive an invitation to the wedding. I'm sure you sent one, but the postal service in Vicaria was never that good."

"I would sooner invite a pig to my wedding, and I would have no difficulty choosing one less ugly and repulsive than you, Fratelli," screamed Maria at the top of her voice. This comment produced some laughter from within the crowd, but Tommaso placed a hand on Maria's arm to still her response.

"I am a man of honour," shouted Fratelli in return, "greater than the one you will share your matrimonial bed with, as I did not undertake the fuitina for the sole purpose of overturning your late father's wishes. So, in keeping with my principles, and despite your mean-spirited attack, I will present you both with the wedding present I have taken so much effort in obtaining."

Tommaso watched as Fratelli threw a small package from the top of the campanile. It fell, buffeted by the speed of its descent to land at Maria's feet with a soft plop.

It was a leather pouch.

Maria let out a gasp and made to snatch it. Tommaso stopped her by grabbing her wrist, but she continued to defy his grip. As he looked in her eyes he could detect only anxiety and panic, but his strength prevailed and he grasped the pouch. Whatever it contained was light in weight and rustled slightly inside the soft leather.

"No, do not open it here," whispered Maria. He looked at her again and the same haunting, terrified stare was returned, accompanied by the stuttering fear in her voice.

"What? You decline my gift?" The accusing voice shouted from the top of the campanile, echoing around the still-silent piazza. "You wish to insult a man of honour, Tommaso di Bova?"

There was no choice. Whatever crimes Fratelli had committed, he was still of the brotherhood, first and foremost. Tommaso loosened the draw-string at the top of the pouch. What he saw inside almost made him drop the offering like it was Satan's own sacrament. He looked at Maria, the desperation still writ large on her face, and then he stared at the crowd, their fevered anticipation evidenced by a silence so intense, he could hear the rustle of the breeze in the bushes around the piazza. Slowly, he tipped the leather pouch and allowed its content to tumble onto the sun-bleached stone of the piazza.

A scrawny and decayed hand fell at his feet, palm downwards. The fall almost threatened to turn it to dust, such was the state of putrefaction. It lay on the bleached stone like a dead animal. Maria retched, and then screamed like she was being flayed alive. Those closest in the crowd gasped, and a wave of chatter ran around their number until the entire piazza was alive with murmurs and gasps.

The mortified hand was reduced almost to bone, but some remaining connective tissue and discoloured skin still served to provide a ghostly shroud, giving some detail of the former living entity. For the most part, the wizened skin was black, but in the crook of the thumb, where the living tissue had been richer, a pallid yellow tint allowed the faint outline of Osso's Serpent to show through. Tommaso knew of the legend and he knew Cesare Giuliano was the last to sport the sacred tattoo of the fratellanza: the very one Tommaso was to be adorned with later that day. Swiftly, he grabbed the hand and hid it in the pocket of his hunting-jacket, fervently hoping no one else had seen the identifying mark.

"Men of honour," shouted Fratelli once again from his high vantage. "Tommaso di Bova has been elected rappresentante. So be it, but he is a fraud. He betrayed Cesare Giuliano by kidnapping his daughter for the fuitina, and in so doing he dishonoured her family, and all the families. Yet you accept him back like the prodigal son. I will bring no such dishonour to the fratellanza. There are capos here who did not support his election. Rally to me those who wish to hold fast to Cesare's memories and principles. I will show you how over the next few weeks. Until then, keep your own counsel and be ready."

With that, Fratelli disappeared from view at the top of the campanile, ringing the bell once more as a reminder of his presence and the control he had exerted over the crowd below. Tommaso gathered his men around him and issued a series of orders. They were to surround Chiesa del Purgatorio and block every exit from the building. The main door was to be held by six pickmen and the two doors either side of the nave were to be similarly enforced. Fratelli was a known murderer and a fugitive, but moreover he had insulted the fratellanza and threatened its hegemony. He could not be allowed to escape. After all Tommaso's men were in place, he addressed the expectant crowds in the piazza and told them of his plans in an eloquent address that countermanded the lies he claimed Fratelli had tried to force upon them. There were murmurings of discontent and shouts of support. Thankfully, nobody asked about the skeletal hand, but Tommaso could not expect to be free of that inquisition for too long.

He called Father Russo to his side. "Are there any other exits?" The priest looked troubled at his question but answered that the three doors were the only way out onto the piazza. And so they waited.

Twenty minutes passed and the only thing to change in the piazza was the temperament of the crowd. They grew restless and shouted their demand that the doors to the chapel be broken down and Fratelli executed like one of the pigs on festival days. Tommaso could go along with this and had already sent one of the pickmen to the mine for blasting powder; an action that caused the inevitable protests of sacrilege from Father Russo. Tommaso was having none of it, and when his pickman returned with the barrel of black powder, he was ordered to set a charge sufficient to blow open one of the side doors to the nave. The crowd was ushered away and preparations to invade the building began. Tommaso had watched as Father Russo became increasingly agitated. The priest had no currency to appeal to the crowd, who were rapidly assuming the appearance of a lynch-mob. Eventually Russo called Tommaso to the side, fear and anxiety dripping from every word of an explanation that had Tommaso seething with anger. Chiesa del Purgatorio had a secret crypt. Knowledge of its existence had been hidden from the lay people of Girgenti for hundreds of years. The crypt contained many sacred relics and the mummified bodies of former priests. It was a legacy of the times when Sicily had been attacked by a succession of invaders, and Catholic tradition had ensured its continuing clandestine status. No one should know of it, Russo had explained whilst insisting Tommaso would suffer the pain of excommunication should he breathe a word of this to anyone. Tommaso had but one question: "Is there a secret exit?"

"Yes," said Father Russo, "but I will only tell you if you promise to go alone. The Church will never forgive you the sin of betrayal if you speak of this now, or for as long as you live."

They were in full view of the restless crowd and their whispered conversation could not be overheard. Tommaso's anger was obvious, and he looked across at Maria and the other capos, as he decided what to do with the secret information that the priest had cursed him with. "Light the fuse and blow open the door," he said to his pickman. "Those who are already guarding the other doors; stay where you are in case Fratelli breaks out." Tommaso looked across at Cosimo Mutolo. "Take six trusted men of honour and search everywhere once the door is blown. Take the priest with you. Maria, you are in charge of keeping everyone at a safe distance from the blast. Do it now."

The look she shot him was heavy with a desire to disobey. She took a few seconds but eventually followed his instructions.

The bang of the blasting-powder charge and the thick cloud of white smoke provided Tommaso with the perfect cover as he ran towards the cemetery at the rear of the church. It was surrounded on all sides with a high wall and access was through a metal gate, which was left open during the hours of worship. Once inside the walled graveyard, Tommaso looked across the poorly tended graves to the row of large family vaults, built like small houses with massive ornate doors and heavily adorned with stone carvings of angels and other religious artefacts. The Giuliano vault was here, its capacious interior empty of its main patron. Or was it? If Fratelli had recovered Cesare's hand, then he could have recovered the rest of his corpse and left it in the vault to further condemn Tommaso's first claim to the power of the fratellanza. There would be an answer to that question but it had to be later – after he checked the largest and most adorned vault: the one bearing the name of Caravaggio. This was the secret entrance to the crypt and Tommaso ran to it, hoping against hope that the massive bronze door was still locked. But it was not to be. The heavy door swung, stiff on protesting hinges, as if begrudgingly opening to allow a shaft of light to penetrate a gloomy interior that had sought refuge in the shadows for centuries. There were no caskets here: no stone carvings of supine priests bedecked in all their finery, no death masks and no alcoves where stone sarcophaguses retained the ever-patient dead. The tomb was empty, save for an open metal gate and a narrow stone staircase. Tommaso had seen all he needed to see. Excommunication would have been a problem, so the less he knew, the less he could betray. He pulled the metal gate closed until it locked and then left, hauling the mighty door behind him, to entomb the secret crypt once more.

Fratelli was long gone. He would be back, and he would carry out his threat to win over disgruntled capos in the fratellanza. Those who ran to him would be weak. Tommaso had ways of dealing with weakness, but he wouldn't wait until it showed itself. He would hunt it out and subject every capo to tests of their loyalty, starting this very evening. First would be to question how Fratelli desecrated the body of Cesare. How did he even know its final resting place? If Maria's secret still held good then the only other living soul who knew the truth would have been Umberto Galli…save for one. Captain Bruno Fabroni was there the night Cesare was shot. It was his men who ambushed and killed Cesare's group, allowing only Notarbartolo to escape, but he now lay dead with the rest of the corpses at the bottom of the shaft. If Galli was loyal to Maria, and that supposition had to be tested, then the only link could be between Fabroni and Fratelli, and that was too preposterous to contemplate. No, there had to be another way for The Horse to know where Cesare's mortal remains lay and Galli was the obvious suspect. Tommaso would start with him, but Maria could not be allowed to know; at least for now. After all, if Galli was clean then there would be no point in upsetting the new Signora di Bova.

On his way back to the exit from the walled cemetery, Tommaso passed the Giuliano vault and tried the door. It was firmly locked. He would check again once he had the key. It was unlikely that Fratelli had only brought a hand back from the grisly tomb Cesare's remains shared with the others he had helped put there. If Fratelli had Cesare's body, where better to hide it than in the crypt that Cesare himself had commissioned?

Chapter 22

Taverna Girandola was more than just a Favara drinking den. It was the favoured taverna of the local fratellanza capos and their underlings. The owner was an honoured member, and the small room to the rear was used for initiations and meetings alike. Tommaso could easily remember the first time he had been here, like it was yesterday. His initiation was years in the past but the time in between had been punctuated with life-changing events, starting off with the simple 'gold from fleas' – a concept that was still fundamental to the success of the fratellanza.

The room was laid out differently to Tommaso's recollection of it. This time it was much more informal, but the event had a serious purpose. Four of his most trusted capos sat around a circular table. A deck of cards was being shuffled by Cosimo Mutolo, whilst the rat-faced Alfredo Zagari twitched his nose and sucked on a cheroot, as he dealt out glasses of brandy as fast as No-neck dealt the poker hands. Rocco Nola was the eldest of the group and sported a face-full of grey whiskers, sculpted into perfect shape by the only barber in Favara, but even the accuracy of his scissors couldn't disguise the yellow stains that years of tobacco use had left on the silver moustache. Giacomo Micelli was called the 'donkey', not because of his strength, but due to the fact he laughed like one and was just as stubborn, although the large ears that stuck out like jug-handles probably helped. A pile of lire sat in front of each of the players, with the 'pot' in the middle of the table, all enveloped in thick clouds of cigar smoke, as each player tried to outdo Zagari's Etna-like eruptions of foul-smelling fumes. There was but one empty chair, placed beside Tommaso's, and it told the true reason for this meeting.

Each guest had received an invite from Tommaso that contained the phrase: *Venite sedetevi accanto a me* – 'come sit beside me', and those words would have orchestrated a mixture of fear and anticipation into all who were invited. The fear lay in the potential for a severe disciplinary process associated with this simplest of requests. The anticipation of commendation may have blunted any feelings of anxiety, although not completely, as the fratellanza rappresantante could use the occasion for reward or punishment. Tommaso could have gathered them here for a gamut of reasons, be they sinister or benign. A business deal could have gone wrong, or there could have been an act of treachery against any of the honoured societies. The former could be resolved with a few lire; the latter could see the guilty party slain where he sat. Equally, a reward for services to the fratellanza could be forthcoming, or a new means of extorting more gold from fleas would be introduced, and the gathering would end with much celebration and back slapping. Tommaso kept with tradition: no one would know the reason for the invitation to sit beside him until all were gathered in; save for the last to arrive, as they were the one to be judged, either for their merits or their treachery. So, his four trusted capos continued with their gambling, Micelli's braying laugh a testament to their relaxed mood. The empty chair sat beside Tommaso and awaited its occupant.

A soft knock on the door interrupted the drinking and gambling. The room fell into silence. Tommaso held up his hand and looked at each of his capos in turn. They understood. They were experienced capos. Their judgement could be trusted. He arranged the empty chair beside his and brought a nervous Umberto Galli into the room.

"Umberto, welcome and thank you for attending," said Tommaso as he guided the pickman to his seat. "Cosimo, deal this man in. It's only a friendly game, Umberto. Table limits are fifty lire a bet. Here's some stake money – it's a gift from me for taking you away from the comfort of your home at this hour." Tommaso sat down and dumped a handful of lire in front of Galli. "Hey, Alfredo; where are your manners? Some brandy for our guest and liberate one of those cheroots from your personal stash."

Tommaso could tell Galli was as nervous as a kitten at a dog-fight, so he sought to reassure him once the new hand was dealt, with smokes and brandy duly delivered. "I've much to thank you for, my brother," he said to Galli. "Maria has told me of the assistance you provided in my absence." It was a trick statement. None of the other capos in attendance would know the full depth of Umberto's help because none were supposed to know the true location of Cesare Giuliano's corpse. Tommaso took the cheroot he was smoking and offered the glowing tip to Galli for a light. Galli's hand shook like a leaf as he took the offering. He took a deep draw and a gulp of brandy before replying.

"I am honoured to have been of help," he said. "Maria's life was in danger, threatened by my capodecina. I had a terrible choice to make. Even thinking about it now makes me tremble..." He held out his shaking hand for proof. "To which should I have shown honour on that fateful night? I still lose sleep, thinking I may have made the wrong decision. I still lie awake, trembling at the slightest noise outside my door in case Notarbartolo's cadre have come for me."

Very clever, thought Tommaso, very clever indeed. "You have nothing to fear from Notarbartolo's team," he said in reply.

"Hey, Umberto," said Mutolo from across the table. "You're holding up the game. How many cards?"

Galli looked around as if waking from a dream before looking at his hand. "Two," he said.

"You might want to put some money behind that," said Zagari. "Ante up fifty."

Galli picked at the pile of notes in front of him and placed his stake money. Tommaso stayed silent and let the game progress. There seemed to be a suite of high-stake hands in play – his own included. He could barely contain the smile that acknowledged one of the things his capos knew: never allow Mutolo to deal. He could fix a game as quick as wink. Nonetheless, the betting continued. Even Galli must have believed his hand was a winner, and the pot grew to a sizeable amount.

"Luciano Francenzo was a good friend," said Rocco Nola as he saw the bet of Zagari and raised another fifty, whilst preening his silver moustache. "He was killed in that knife fight you were in a few months ago, Umberto. Tell me – did he die a good death?"

"I do not know," said Galli. "The stabbing happened after I left."

"She must've been some whore," said Micelli, followed by the inevitable braying laugh.

"The fight did not start over a whore," replied Galli in a voice so soft it was barely heard.

Micelli ceased imitating a donkey – "Only a whore with a tongue like a snake could have made a pickman walk away from a fight," he said, suddenly serious.

Tommaso threw another a handful of lire into the pot. "Seen and raised," he said as the play passed to his left. Galli seemed suddenly nonplussed.

"Are you in or out?" said Mutolo, his hand on his own pile of lire.

"In," replied Galli and threw down a hundred lire, leaving virtually nothing of his stake money. Mutolo followed suit and the pot grew.

"The fratellanza are taking care of Francenzo's family," said Tommaso. "He didn't die defending the brotherhood, but I've made an exception."

"What about poor, young Lucania?" asked Nola. "He was charged with Francenzo's murder. Word is he didn't do it. They beat the confession out of him."

Tommaso could detect Galli becoming even more uncomfortable beside him. Zagari replenished the brandy and Galli knocked his back like it was life-saving elixir. "Lucania's family will also be looked after by the fratellanza," said Tommaso. "We believe he was innocent."

"Why so?" said Zagari, as he picked some tobacco out from between his yellowing teeth and looked at it closely before making the decision to follow the bet.

"Because the case was handled by the carabinieri. In particular by one Captain Bruno Fabroni." Tommaso turned and looked at Galli. "I believe you know him, Umberto."

"Yes. He tried to beat a confession out of me. I still walk with a limp from the broken foot he gave me," replied Galli, composing himself a little. He seemed to take strength from redirecting the venom building up in the comments targeted at him. "Sadly, Fabroni picked on the weakest of our number and extracted the confession he needed."

"I visited Lucania in his cell, before they shipped him off to Vicaria," said Tommaso. "He told me he didn't do it. I believe him."

"Did he tell you who did?" asked Nola before throwing down his cards and folding out of the game.

"Yes," replied Tommaso. He paused and shot Galli another glance; the pickman's face seemed to drain of colour. "Looks like it's my bet," continued Tommaso. He looked again at Galli. There was only fifty lire left of his stake. "Fifty seen and fifty raised," said Tommaso.

Galli sat on the edge of his chair, oblivious to the nervous tapping of his own foot on the sawdust covered floor. He stared at a spot on the table and jumped when Tommaso challenged him to bet or fold. "I'm out," he blurted.

"Me too," said Mutolo. "Looks like you win, Tommaso. We're all out of lire. Are you going to show us your hand?"

Tommaso sat in silence. He could almost taste the tension in the room. His capos had followed the question and answer session exactly as he had instructed them. "Yes," he said after a few seconds. "I will show you my hand." He reached into the pocket of his leather coat, pulled out the severed hand from Cesare Giuliano's corpse and threw it into the middle of the table, where it landed palm up.

They all recoiled in horror. Galli was first out of his seat, heading towards the door. Tommaso grabbed him and pulled him back into the chair.

"Holy Mother of God," yelled Mutolo and crossed himself repeatedly. Nola coughed on his cheroot and almost set fire to his moustache, whilst Zagari just sat stunned. Micelli reached a cloth handkerchief from his pocket and threw it over the hand whilst muttering a continuous incantation to God, and all the Saints.

"This is my wedding gift from Lorenzo Fratelli," said Tommaso. "You all saw it in the piazza today, so don't look so shocked." He turned to Galli: "But of course, you weren't in the piazza today."

Both the pickman's hands were flat on the table, as if he was trying to push it and the skeletal vestige of Cesare's corpse away.

"But you have seen it before, haven't you, Umberto?" Tommaso made sure the question was delivered in as menacing a way as he could, and it didn't take much effort.

"No, no, I've never seen that hideous thing before," said Galli, his palms now pressing hard on the table and pushing it from him, as Tommaso stood to his right and pressed down heavily on his shoulder so he couldn't get up.

"Micelli, remove the cloth," said Tommaso. Micelli obeyed, barley touching the seam of the handkerchief as if in fear of disturbing the severed hand beneath.

"Umberto, turn it palm down," shouted Tommaso.

"No, no. Please, do not make me do this. You know I cannot," begged Galli, pressing down so firmly on the table top that the wood creaked in protest.

Tommaso grabbed his knife and plunged it into the back of Galli's right hand, pinning it to the table. Years ago, Tommaso had witnessed a little wagon falling into the boiling sulphur of the calcaroni. Galli made a similar noise. He screamed like his flesh was being broiled off his body. "I say again, Umberto – turn it over. Fail me once more and I will pin your other hand to the table and make you do this with your teeth."

The yelling screams reduced to agonised whimpers as the unfortunate pickman reluctantly obeyed. Only then did the full horror of the disembodied hand inflict itself on those who were unaware of its devastating secret. Had Galli been clever enough and not preoccupied with the heavy steel blade pinning him to the table, he could have swung the other capos away from Tommaso as the doubts in their minds had been fuelled by the revelation of Osso's Serpent. Tommaso was aware of this danger and embarked on a detailed explanation of what really had happened that night when they were gathered around the lip of Cesare's Shaft. He even praised Galli for his actions in defeating Notarbartolo's plans and saving the life of Maria.

When he had finished, Tommaso sat down in his chair, looked at his poker hand and revealed a Royal Flush to the others. He then placed his hand on the knife securing Galli to the table. "The only reason this blade isn't buried in your skull, Umberto, is that you did save Maria's life and steered the fratellanza away from a disastrous period of leadership. I fear you may have undone all of that good work, however. What you tell me next will determine your fate." Tommaso picked the claw-like hand from the table and pushed it into Galli's face. He recoiled in disgust and spat out the bits of putrefied flesh that had been forced into his mouth. "Who told you to bring this to Fratelli?"

"It was Fratelli himself. He turned up at my home in the dead of night and said he knew where Cesare's body lay. I was to descend into the shaft and bring back the hand."

Tommaso grasped the hilt of his knife, ready to pull it free. "Are the rest of Cesare's remains still at the bottom of the shaft?"

"Yes," said the pickman, his voice wracked with fear, pain and grief. "No one would accompany me to the shaft. I had to set up the ropes and make the descent myself. There was no way I could bring his corpse back alone."

Tommaso rocked the blade forwards slightly and Galli howled in pain. "How could Fratelli have known this? It was a secret you shared with Maria, and she with me."

"I don't know. Please believe me. He told me nothing of where he got the information," sobbed Galli.

"So you said – *'Sure, Lorenzo. I'll risk my life to go down the shaft and get this for you'*."

"No. He threatened my children. He said he would kill them one by one and dump their bodies down the shaft until I agreed; starting with my youngest girl."

Tommaso yanked the blade free and Galli clutched his arm to his chest in pain, still sobbing and begging to be believed. He was a liar. Fratelli was many things but he was still a man of honour and threatening anyone of the brotherhood through their children was heretical to the omertá. There would have been no imperative sufficient to defile the oath with such profanity.

"You've desecrated the corpse of Cesare Giuliano. You succumbed to a threat, which you could have brought to me or to anyone here, and we would have protected you," said Tommaso.

"No, no, there wasn't time. This was only last night. Fratelli gave me no time. Please, you must believe me," begged the hapless pickman.

"Gentlemen, going around the table – guilty or innocent?" asked Tommaso, addressing Mutolo first.

Galli pleaded his innocence and clutched Tommaso's arm, sobbing and begging for his life.

"Guilty," said Mutolo.

"Guilty," said Micelli.

"Guilty," said Zagari.

Tommaso held up his hand before the vote reached Nola.

Galli was now on his knees and begging not to be executed. "You have one chance to live, Umberto," said Tommaso. "If you answer honestly to my next question, you will leave here alive but you will be banished from the part of Sicily controlled by the fratellanza. If you are seen here after midnight, you will be instantly executed. You will be stripped of all the protection offered by your oath and you will be expelled forever from this honourable society. Do you agree to this?"

"Yes, but my family...?"

"You can set no conditions," responded Tommaso and Galli agreed to banishment. "Who else knows of this? Who else knows the final resting place of Cesare Giuliano?" asked Tommaso.

Galli looked up like a whipped dog: all pleading-eyes and whimpering-hurt. His mouth moved as if it wanted to respond, but some primitive mechanism of self-preservation prevented the words from coming out. He shook his head. Tommaso took his bloodied knife and pressed the tip of the blade lightly against Galli's throat, where it jiggled slightly as the pickman's Adam's apple bobbed up and down with his sobbing and the pleas for his life.

"Bruno Fabroni," said Galli despondently. "I have told Captain Bruno Fabroni, of the carabinieri, about the events of that night and the location of the corpse."

Tommaso removed the knife. "You did well to tell the truth, Umberto. It's a pity your honour is only packaged in small parcels, to be used when convenient to yourself. You stabbed Francenzo in that fight. Lucania begged for my forgiveness, as he told me how he had signed a confession, only after he himself was beaten half to death by Fabroni. I have spoken to the others involved in the fight, all under the oath of the omertá, and they each gave me the same story: you were the murderer. Yet you walked free, Umberto."

"Guilty," shouted Nola emphatically, and then followed with: "Kill the conniving bastard."

Tommaso held up his hand once more and the room fell silent, save for Galli's sobbing.

"What else have you told Fabroni?"

Galli was still on his knees: a broken man whose life hung by a thread. "There were four statements Fabroni presented to me on that night. He told me they all named me as Francenzo's killer. I understood there was no escape. I offered to become an informer and tell them everything I knew of the fratellanza. I never thought it would come to this. Please believe me. I thought I could get away with just a few snippets of information about the theft of lemons or shipments of sulphur."

Nola jumped to his feet, and seething with anger rushed to where Tommaso stood. "My capo, let me have the honour of putting this traitor to death. I will do it now. I will do it with my bare hands. Lucania is my nephew. He is doomed to spend most of his life in prison because this scum betrayed him and betrayed us all." A chorus of support echoed around the table. Tommaso looked down to the wretch at his feet. The sawdust on the floor had been peppered with spots of blood. It now soaked up a pool of Galli's piss as he soiled himself in anticipation of never leaving the room alive.

"I have made a deal and I will stick to it," said Tommaso. "Umberto Galli is banished, along with his wife and children. Mutolo, take him from my sight and put him on the overnight freight-train to Palermo. The guard is a friend of ours. He will make sure he doesn't leave until the end of the line. Zagari – go to Galli's house and get his family. Only let them take what they can carry. Put them on the same train." Tommaso pulled Galli to his feet by the hair and looked him in the eye. "In time your fear will turn to anguish and then hatred. You will seek to do whatever harm you can to the fratellanza. This is the cross I must bear for letting you live. My redemption is that you will be a living witness to my principles and my vengeance."

He let go of Galli's hair and he dropped to the floor to writhe in his own piss and shit. Tommaso turned to his companions. "I say this to all of you, including this miserable traitor. This is the last example of such forgiveness you will witness from me. Anyone who betrays the fratellanza will suffer death. Anyone who betrays me will suffer death. Punishment will extend to their families, who will be banished from the territories of the fratellanza and they will be cast out with nothing. The fratellanza will strip them of everything they own, because their wealth was given to them by the fratellanza. Anyone who associates with Lorenzo Fratelli will fall foul of these laws. Anyone who reveals such a traitor will be richly rewarded. Now get this fucker out of my sight before I change my mind."

Tommaso kicked Galli hard in the ribs and then left the small room to exit Taverna Girandola. A few of the drinkers stared at him on the way out but none would catch his eye. It was time to take the role of rappresentante to a new level where fear vied with respect to ensure the fratellanza hegemony. It wasn't a case of ego or megalomania. Tommaso knew that the Palermo families were years ahead of the fratellanza in the fealty shown to them and in the total control they exercised over every aspect of life in their fiefdom. Girgenti had to catch up or be overrun by the brotherhoods from the north. Fratelli was part of the same problem.

Chapter 23

Bernardo di Paolo was a dour and taciturn character, who didn't have the flamboyant style of his brother, Salvatore. There was no grace in his tubby short-legged frame and the elegance of the overwrought gestures was replaced by guttural snorts and short chopping gestures from the flabby hands and chubby fingers. Ignorant oaf or not, Bernardo was Salvatore's replacement and he was the Palermo capo that Lorenzo Fratelli had to deal with. Bargaining with him would be hard, difficult and conducted on a precipice, where one slip could result in a fall from being a friend of the Palermo brotherhoods, to being an enemy. Lorenzo had no desire to alienate himself from Bernardo. The plans he had agreed with Bruno Fabroni to usurp Tommaso di Bova could only succeed with the help of Palermo, and the city would provide Lorenzo with a bolt-hole if Fabroni proved treacherous, which he undoubtedly would. Bernardo had responded to Lorenzo's request for a meeting and the ominous phrase 'venite sedetevi accanto a me' had been dropped into the narrative. Lorenzo didn't believe a 'sit beside me' with Bernardo would result in a threat, but that thought was ever-present at the back of his mind, as he stood and looked up at the bullet-strikes on the masonry above the balcony of Taverna Vittime, in Palermo.

The heavy wooden door was still there, and as he stepped inside Lorenzo could detect the *castrati* voice of the colossus behind the bar. Word was he had been gelded when twelve years old for the choir of the Sistine Chapel. The Holy See had undoubtedly exiled him back to Sicily for fear of bringing down the entire painted edifice, if he were to settle his enormous frame on the balcony. The same beaded curtain was parted and the narrow staircase led its creaking route to the lavishly-furnished upstairs room, where the inevitable card game was under way, and the sole empty chair was beside Bernardo di Paolo. Lorenzo shuddered slightly as he was led into the den of the most powerful families in Palermo. They could eat the fratellanza and spit out their bones for the dogs on the streets. This was exactly why Lorenzo needed them, and if he could carry the argument, why they also needed him.

"Lorenzo," beamed di Paolo. "You are a hero to my family and you're most welcome here. Come sit beside me."

Lorenzo did as he was bid and listened to an embellished account of the siege of Vicaria and the bravery he had shown in a vain attempt to save the illustrious Salvatore, all delivered by Bernardo. The assembled capos stood and raised their tankards to Lorenzo in a toast, whereupon the game began anew with cards, stake, brandy and cheroots duly delivered to the space on the table reserved for the honourable member from Favara. Questions about the insurrection at the prison, his escape from it and the brutal attack on Piazza Ucciardone peppered the innocuous chat before the talk turned to the real reason for their gathering.

"Lorenzo," said Bernardo as another round was dealt. "You've asked some favours from the brotherhood here. They're not too difficult to put in place but we would like to know your reasons." Bernardo raised himself slightly from his chair and let out a huge fart, which had the other capos laughing heartily and did nothing to improve Lorenzo's confidence.

"My Palermo brothers, things are changing in Sicily," said Lorenzo with all the gravitas he could muster.

"Hey Bernardo," interjected one of the other players, who looked so fat they must have brought him here on a wagon, "these Girgenti boys are fucking clever guys. I'm not sure I want to play cards with this one."

Bernardo held up his hand to stifle the howls of laughter and begged silence so that Lorenzo could proceed.

"The riches of the sulphur are far from the coffers of Palermo," replied Lorenzo. "I'm here to tell you how to bring those millions of lire back to the true home of Osso. It was what Cesare Giuliano knew, and it was why he sought to establish an agreement with Palermo. His was a mission of fear; mine is a mission of opportunity. I can give you control over the wealth of the Girgenti heartland: wealth that will make the income from oranges and lemons look like nothing in comparison. I have no loyalty to the fratellanza now that Tommaso di Bova has taken control. I seek a place in Palermo: a place at this table, on equal standing with those here. In exchange, I will bring you the wealth from the devil's gold."

Bernardo took a slug of brandy and practiced some more sonorous venting of bodily gasses before replying. None of the others dared interrupt, save for more raucous laughter, which abated on cue. "These are brave claims, young Fratelli. I was told you only wanted to make some changes to the way we control the rail link from Palermo to Girgenti, yet you promise much wealth and influence. If you can deliver, we'll make a place for you in Palermo. If you fail, Girgenti is your only place of sanctuary. So where do we start on this plan of yours?"

"We start in America," replied Lorenzo.

* * *

They were all tied together and dumped at the side of the railway track that led into Girgenti. The corpse of Umberto Galli was amongst them but the others were alive, if badly beaten. The survivors were all employees of the *Società per le Strade Ferrate del Mediterraneo,* the local railway franchise, and their blood-spattered uniforms were ripped and covered in dirt as if their occupants had been dragged behind one of their own freight cars for the last few kilometres of the track. Tommaso had been brought to the scene quickly, and before the local polizia had been informed. He had been visiting the rail-yard boss in Girgenti amidst growing rebellion against the fratellanza from all who worked for the railway. The mood had been tense and threatening as Tommaso dealt with the intransigence the same way he dealt with treachery: without mercy. Only the sudden news of this blood-letting by the Palermo brotherhoods had prevented the fratellanza from claiming another victim.

Galli's corpse was bloated and the swollen face was a testimony to the beatings that killed him. Tommaso hadn't seen anything of him or his family in the six months since he had been exiled to Palermo. Around his neck was tied a rough piece of card with the words "Look after your own traitors", scrawled in what Tommaso assumed was Galli's own blood. Whoever had killed the odious pickman had done Tommaso a favour, and he approached one of the badly-beaten railway workers to inquire what had happened.

The story was as he had expected. The Palermo brotherhoods were exerting tighter control over all the freight that was carried between the sulphur-rich south west and the port of Palermo. Porto Empodocle was the closest shipping port, just a few kilometres from Girgenti, and had prospered thanks to the sulphur exports. The completed rail link to Palermo had led to competition for this valuable freight, and where there was competition for business, there was competition between the brotherhoods and the families who controlled them. The message to the local railway workers was simple: the honourable families in Palermo would provide all of the staff who worked the line to Girgenti. There would be no more warnings. The axis of power between the Sicilian brotherhoods was shifting and the direction was Palermo. The other capos in the fratellanza could see it but didn't understand the true message. Tommaso did, and as he personally untied the victims of this attack, his mind was buzzing with thoughts of how he might best counter it. He trudged back to the small wooden cabin where the rail yard boss still waited, guarded by Mutolo. Tommaso's mood had changed from one of aggressive belligerence to one of submission. He couldn't deny the threat from Palermo and he couldn't use innocent Girgenti workers to push back against it.

The rail-yard boss was called Giancarlo and he looked nervously at Tommaso, anticipating a continuance of the threats and aggression that had been evident before their meeting was interrupted by the discovery of the victims of the latest Palermo attack. After explaining things to Giancarlo, Tommaso sat down on the desk facing him and asked Mutolo to leave.

"How many Girgenti workers do you have for the line to Palermo?" asked Tommaso.

"Ten men," replied Giancarlo. "Four for the daily passenger return, four for the overnight freight and two on rota."

"They can no longer work the Palermo line. Can you find them other jobs?"

The rail yard boss rummaged amongst some papers on his desk before making a few pencil marks on one and consulting a chart pinned to the wall. "I can use four," he said. "The rest I will have to let go."

"Send the other six to me. The fratellanza will ensure they have work and an income equal to what they have lost. The Palermo brotherhoods will approach you," said Tommaso. "They might threaten you, they might bribe you. Either way, they'll want you on their side to ensure control of this rail yard. You'll go along with them, but your real loyalty will be to me. Only we two will know of this arrangement, but I will ensure you and your family come to no harm as long as you stay loyal to me. Do you accept this condition?"

"What do I have to do?" asked Giancarlo.

"The fratellanza has many business interests. Palermo will seek these interests out and try to destroy them. Where you see this: do nothing to stop them. You and I will meet regularly. You'll tell me all the details of every move Palermo makes to control the freight out of Girgenti."

"And that is all?"

"Save for one thing," replied Tommaso. "You know Lorenzo Fratelli?"

"All of Girgenti knows The Horse."

"He is the enemy: a traitor to Girgenti. If you see him, get word to my home using a fake telegram. Just tell me where he is. If I find him where you have said, I will make you a rich man."

"You are very generous, Tommaso di Bova. I will do all that you have asked and I will ensure the word is spread that the fratellanza look after the innocent victims of Palermo's war against us."

"Do no such thing," said Tommaso. "Let the other victims do that. You say nothing for us and nothing against us."

"I understand," said an enlightened Giancarlo.

"Good, now tell me: how does it make sense to move all that sulphur across the width of Sicily when we have Porto Empodocle just a few minutes away?"

Giancarlo ruminated on the question for a few seconds. Tommaso could see he was no longer nervous and he sat comfortably in his chair, looking again at the pile of papers on his desk. He lifted a thick sheaf and held it out to Tommaso. "These are the shipping-orders for the sulphur from the biggest customer the mines have. All of this is headed for one distributor, in America." Giancarlo then lifted another sheaf – this one just a few pages thick. "These are the orders for the sulphur from all of the customers outside America: the rest of the world, if you like. Even six months ago, the quantity of those shipping-orders was the other way about. Palermo has always shipped to America. Porto Empodocle has always shipped to everywhere else, and the fratellanza don't control Palermo."

Tommaso felt a sudden chill, despite the heat of the day. "Why has it changed?" he asked.

"I only know coal and steam," replied Giancarlo. "But I hear stories about the sulphur and what it is used for. In Germany and Austria, they have developed new processes of getting what they want without the need for our devil's gold. The price has dropped and the Girgenti miners are making less on every slab of processed mineral they ship from Porto Empodocle."

That rang true for Tommaso. It wasn't only the railways that were rebelling against the demands of the fratellanza. The mines were closing down and the value of their pizzi was dwindling. "So why does America still need so much?"

"It isn't only the sulphur that leaves Palermo for America. The families there have sent those they trust to ensure the Americans don't adopt the processes everyone else is using. The brotherhoods from Palermo control the yellow gold in that land. They now want to control every last bit of it in this."

The information from Giancarlo was invaluable but distressing. Tommaso looked at the shipping orders from the two piles of paper, and his anxiety rose to another level. "America pays more for its sulphur?"

"Yes," said Giancarlo. "Palermo buys it at source and sets the price. Now you can see why we send the devil's gold across the width of Sicily."

* * *

Captain Bruno Fabroni knew a little bit about sulphur mining, but he did know much more about the huge sums of money behind it and the associated larceny practiced, on the grandest of scales, by the brotherhoods in the mining regions. Every day he dealt with fights and stabbings as rival clans of pickmen fought over their respective claims and crews of carusi. What was laid out before him this morning, in a murky siding of the Girgenti rail yard, would make such petty bickering pale into insignificance. Brotherhood on brotherhood murders were usually vicious, but this execution transcended conventional brutality in a way that he had never before experienced. Something told him he might have to get used to it.

Fabroni knew of the calcaroni and how their furnace-like construction would melt the sulphur into a sticky mass that boiled like Etna's lava. This searing liquid was poured directly from the furnace into wooden moulds making *balàti di zolfo*. These blocks of sulphur were a standard weight and shape: easy to load, easy to count and easy to carry. They were traditionally built into rows on each railway carriage: six blocks high by ten blocks long, with five rows per carriage. The carriage that Fabroni stood beside with his men had some cargo that wasn't on the manifest however, and its inclusion was a clear warning from someone to the fratellanza. The warning, if the fratellanza heeded it, would close down their income from the mines. The 'someone', Fabroni feared he knew only too well. This attack followed some of the pattern of the previous one on the workers of *Società per le Strade Ferrate del Mediterraneo*, but its differences were calculated to carry a level of threat way beyond simple intimidation. Of the four victims in this case, only one had been left alive to tell the tale. This time the carabinieri and polizia had arrived before any member of the fratellanza could corrupt the evidence and destroy the investigation, not that Fabroni needed an investigation to know who was behind this hideous multiple-murder.

The eyes of the one poor wretch who had been left alive to tell the tale stood out on stalks, and his pallor was that of a ghost. Like a ghost, his wailing cries had alerted the shunting-crew at Girgenti station, and they had pulled at the balàti di zolfo to reveal a large, amorphous yellow mass, carefully hidden in the middle of the freight-wagon's cargo of sulphur blocks. That the sluice had been opened on a calcarone, with all of its molten contents allowed to flow and harden where it fell, was obvious. For the survivor, the physical torture had been limited to his right hand. This was encased in the dirty yellow cast of the hardened brimstone, revealing skeletal fingers where the flesh had been boiled off when the molten sulphur flowed freely from the calcarone. There was also the clear outline of a rope that tied his arm to whatever else was under the rest of the mound of solidified yellow ore.

On close inspection, this mound showed three separate peaks that could be discerned as human heads. Two heads tilted to the side on necks that had tried to force a way out of the molten torrent pouring down on them from above, but they were defeated and turned to columns of brittle yellow. One head seemed crushed down into what must have been the shoulders of the scorched body that once supported it. Eyes were visible as bulging red blisters in the yellow cascade of the deadly shroud. Nose-cavities could be discerned above the gaping maws of mouths, shaped by indescribable agony and terror. Once his mind had reluctantly accepted the evidence of his own eyes, Bruno could begin to perceive the screaming horror of the victims etched in their boiled faces – visible, despite the now-solidified cover of molten sulphur. Here and there, blood-red eruptions burst through the yellow lava, all the way down the tortured bodies. Ropes, fossilised in the hardened mass, stood out as taut bindings, stretched under the last-seconds of dying panic as the victims fought with their final agonising breaths to be free of the molten shroud of death.

A doctor had appeared and asked to be allowed to attend the victims. Bruno let him through, but it was obvious nothing could be done for the three who were entombed under the contents of the calcarone. The living survivor was showing signs of the obvious shock to which he had been subjected, and Bruno climbed up on to the bed of the wagon so he could be close enough to ask some questions. The doctor fussed and objected but Bruno pressed on.

"I'm Bruno," he said to the terrified living witness. "I don't believe we have met. May I know your name?"

"It's Giovanni," came the timorous reply. "Giovanni Farina."

"Giovanni, you are safe now. The doctor will look after you, and we will get you to his clinic. I will post a guard there so no one can cause you further harm. Are you in pain?"

"I can feel nothing," he said, all the while shivering and staring at a spot on the wagon to his left – anywhere but at the horror fused to his right hand.

Bruno shot the doctor a look and he nodded in return. His patient was minutes, or even seconds away from going into shock and collapsing.

"Do you know who did this, Giovanni?"

"They…they were from Palermo," he replied, his eyes now rolling in his head and his breathing becoming shallower. "I've never seen them before. Some wore hoods over their heads, but they told me to tell everyone they were from Palermo. Yes, that's what they said. 'Tell them, Giovanni. Tell them we are from Palermo'."

Bruno removed his tunic and placed it over Giovanni's trembling shoulders. "You would look good as carabinieri," he said.

Giovanni blinked and secured a few seconds of clarity; he even seemed to be trying to smile. "They let me live because I hadn't taken the oath," he said, and this memory seemed to recall all of his circling demons. His pallor whitened even further and his eyes rolled momentarily towards the back of his head, but he held on as if there was something else he had to impart.

"These murderers from Palermo; who did they kill?" asked Bruno. Giovanni looked to his right for the first time, and the physical pain seemed to hit him along with the terror. His mouth moved, but his words were barely audible. Bruno put his ear close to Giovanni and was rewarded with an answer, just before the poor wretch passed out.

"He will lose most of his hand," said the doctor, "but for now I will have to cut him from the mound. This may damage your evidence, Captain, but there is no choice."

"Do it," replied Bruno, as he made to go about the standard

protocols for investigating a murder.

Lorenzo Fratelli had told Bruno he would deliver Tommaso di Bova to his own capos and they would kill him. Bruno had no idea of how The Horse would achieve this, but it sounded wonderfully elegant. There was nothing elegant about this slaughter. Bruno had made his pact with Mephistopheles, and in true Faustian style seemed doomed to be deceived and humbled for little reward, but Bruno would not be blind to his own salvation. If the arrangement with Fratelli delivered only corpses of little value then there was an alternative to destroying Tommaso di Bova. It lay with a bundle of letters written by Maria di Bova in the days when she had used Bruno to further her own ends; in the mistaken belief he would not demand restitution.

Still, Bruno had to give the devil his due. Fratelli had begun by closing off the lifeblood of the fratellanza and now he had started to murder their senior capos. The loss of Cosimo Mutolo, Alfredo Zagari and Rocco Nolo would be a bitter blow to Tommaso di Bova.

Chapter 24

The railway bridge over the River Platani was twenty-five metres wide and made of wood. Its three supports were bedded in concrete columns, anchored in the river bed, and it found itself in a desolate part of the single-track line's sinuous traverse of Sicily. The pale wash of the moon cast over this barren landscape, deserted save for a few snakes and other nocturnal hunters looking for food. Tonight there were some new predators, in the form of Tommaso di Bova with a team of his most trusted and capable men. They were awaiting the midnight freight-train from Girgenti to Palermo, which Tommaso knew would consist of fifteen wagons loaded with balàti di zolfo and one wagon loaded with barrels of lamp oil. The last passenger train had passed through about three hours previously, and the freight train was due soon: at about thirty minutes past midnight. The intervening time had been used to build an oil-soaked wooden barricade across the track, at the exit from the bridge. Tommaso looked at his pocket watch. In another few minutes they would light the barricade, which should be well ablaze by the time the freight-train arrived, forcing it to stop.

Tommaso spoke to his team. "I promised the fratellanza I would avenge the deaths of Mutolo, Zagari and Nolo. The action we take tonight is only the start, but we'll do no physical harm to anyone on the train. You have all besieged me with appeals for retribution, and I'll give you that vengeance, but in a way that does the most damage to Palermo. We'll hurt them by destroying the income they have robbed from us. They struck fear into the mine owners and our crews by what they did. They believe we cannot touch them because we are simple peasants from the forgotten bad-lands of Sicily. They're wrong, and they'll forever regret attacking Tommaso di Bova and the fratellanza, starting tonight. In a few minutes we'll light the fire under that barricade and also light a fire that will burn those who have harmed us. You all know what to do."

"My capo, forgive me," said one of his men, "I mean no disrespect; but how will just stopping a train hurt those who have robbed us and taken the lives of our brothers?"

"There is no insult in your question," replied Tommaso. "We need to attack our enemies where they are weakest, and in places they believe they cannot be harmed. I haven't picked this spot just to stop a train. We will do more than that – much more. Light the barricade."

The wooden sleepers stacked on the track burned brightly as the sound of the approaching train reached the place where Tommaso had set the ambush. The driver couldn't miss the blazing barricade, providing he was looking. This could have been a fatal flaw in Tommaso's plan, but the shrill blasts of the whistle on the train, as it rounded the broad curve ahead of the bridge, confirmed the driver had seen the danger. Squeals of metal on metal accompanied juddering clunks and bangs from the freight cars, as the crew on the footplate struggled to bring the engine and its load to a halt. They did so perfectly: square on the bridge, exactly as Tommaso had planned. His first team were on the footplate in seconds, whilst the second group sought out the guard. All the captives were bundled off the bridge and herded together at the side of the track as Tommaso strode forwards and issued the orders to his men. "Go to the end freight-car and take the barrels of lamp oil. Douse the sulphur in every car and then set light to it all."

His men looked at him dumbfounded. They had all served time in the mines and knew that the calcaroni were often fired by burning sulphur below them. It was a practice that was forbidden because of the noxious gasses produced, but sulphur was more plentiful than coal and the mining inspectors could be paid to look the other way.

"The fumes will kill everything as far as the eye can see," said one of his team.

"It will burn for days and take the bridge with it," said another.

"No crops are farmed here," replied Tommaso, "and there is no livestock. The nearest town is Capofranco and it is five kilometres away. Let them experience what life is like in Favara when the calcaroni burn. It'll do them no harm. Etna puts out more fumes in a day, and we still drink the wine from the vineyards on her slopes. Yes, the bridge will be destroyed, and the line will be compromised for months, but the cargo of sulphur will be utterly consumed by the fire. It's worth millions of lire, and it's been bought and paid for by our enemies in Palermo. They will suffer a huge loss, but this will be nothing to what I'll do to them next."

All of this was within earshot of the frightened train-crew, who cowered at the side of the track. Tommaso addressed them directly. "When the fire has taken hold, you'll be free to get back on the foot-plate of the engine. We will de-couple it, and you'll be allowed to continue on your way to Palermo, unharmed, but without your cargo, which will be reduced to ashes. Tell Bernardo di Paolo it was the fratellanza." Tommaso took off his glove and held his right hand up to face them. "Be sure to tell the fat pig that he cannot defeat those who follow Osso's Serpent. Di Paolo has picked his fight but we'll pick the battles. This one attacks the sulphur; the next one attacks the Conca D'Oro and the citrus harvest. I will bleed di Paolo's coffers dry, starting now."

* * *

The hilltop town of Bova was as inaccessible as it was majestic. Tommaso had been taken from the town of his birth when he was an infant and had never returned. Today would change the course of his association with the brotherhoods of Calabria in ways that were only dreamed of behind the walls of Vicaria. He had been told of Bova's beauty, its majesty, its music and its people. Now, he would experience these wonders for himself, and his anticipation grew with each minute the voyage continued. He was still in awe at how quickly the journey had passed: from Girgenti to Messina and across the narrow straits in the steamer to Villa san Giovanni, before another train to San Pasquale. It would have been quicker had the train journey not been broken just outside Campofranco by the destroyed railway bridge, courtesy of Tommaso's actions. A small footbridge had been constructed and passengers walked across to join a second train that completed the journey. All of that in less than two days, with an overnight stop in Messina, where he had slept beneath the stars on Spiaggia del Faro and watched the mighty beam from the lighthouse at Montorsoli illuminate the Straits of Messina, all the way over to Concessa on the Calabrian Coast.

Now he was on the final few hours of his journey. As the small train left the station at Straci, the Aspromonte hills grew steeper as they shot up in towering, rocky precipices away from the azure waters of the Calabrian coast. In the distance, Tommaso could see the rocky outcrop on which Bova stood: its isolation its strength. Up there, one thousand metres above him, the only language was Grecanico, defended by a fiercely independent colony who shunned any association with the rest of Italy, yet whose hospitality was renowned by all who came to them with open hearts and minds. Like in his native Sicily, the inhabitants of these remote rocky outcrops had suffered generations of sieges from Saracens, Normans, Turks and Bourbons, and like Tommaso's Sicilian population, they had endured. He had wondered and marvelled at these stories as they were recited to him by Master Joe in the isolation of Vicaria. Now that Tommaso was close to his spiritual and ancestral homeland he could feel the pull of this attraction. His only fear was that he may never want to leave.

San Pasquale was little more than a dusty patch of ground at the side of the rail-line; there wasn't even a platform. Tommaso descended and the train pulled away as if grateful to be rid of one of the hill-people. He had dressed in the manner he knew in Vicaria, accompanied by a red-silk handkerchief tied around his neck and sporting three small metal pins, in the shape of flowers, sticking out from his leather waistcoat.

"You seek a path to Vua?"

The stranger appeared as if from nowhere and spoke Grecanico, even using the traditional name of Vua, rather than Bova. He was dressed in the same style as Tommaso, sporting the same red silk at his throat but with four flowers adorning his waistcoat.

"I seek a path to the town of my birth," replied Tommaso, also in the Greek dialect that formed the basis of the language of Aspromonte. "I am known as Tommaso di Bova in Sicily, but here I will be Tommaso di Vua."

"You are welcome, Tommaso di Vua. I am Don Nucera. The brotherhood of Carcagnosso welcomes one of the brotherhood of Osso as an honoured guest. Master Joe has instructed us to offer you all hospitality and assistance. We will walk to Vua. There is no other way, unless you brought a mule?"

Tommaso looked around and smiled. No mules were in evidence. "How far is it? And how high will we climb?" he asked.

"Three hours is the distance," replied Don Nucera, "above the clouds is the height."

"There are no clouds today."

"There are always clouds, and Vua always rises above them."

The first thirty minutes' walk was uneventful, and followed a small river valley north, before Don Nucera led the way to the left and began a steep and sinuous ascent that climbed through old olive groves and citrus orchards. After a climb that would have left a goat breathless, they topped a ridge and left the green world of cultivated plantations behind for stunted shrubs, in a landscape largely devoid of colour, save for the natural rock of

Aspromonte. Now that Tommaso was clear of any plants taller than knee-height, he could see the twisting spine of the ridge they were following and the vertiginous town at its head. And still they climbed – through the thinning air and the piercing sunlight. Don Nucera stopped and Tommaso caught up to stand breathless beside him. He could see his guide had barely broken sweat and smiled benignly at Tommaso's discomfort.

"You need some refreshment," he said, and pointed to a small gushing stream that gurgled noisily beside the path, in its tumbling descent to the sea. Tommaso scooped up some of the mountain-cold water and poured it over his head before drinking his fill.

By the time the first terracotta tiled cottages of Bova appeared beside the path, the water had dried from Tommaso's dark hair and he had become more accustomed to the altitude, so had stopped panting like an excited puppy as he walked beside Don Nucera. A few residents went about their daily activities, chastising wayward livestock and ushering strutting roosters and chickens into their respective enclosures. All looked up and acknowledged Nucera but any attempt at eye-contact made by Tommaso was rebuffed.

"They will welcome you as a guest, in their own time and their own way," said his guide, aware of Tommaso's concern. "Word will go out that Master Joe's guest has arrived and been accepted. Then you will barely be able to walk past even the least of these simple dwellings without an invitation to eat and drink with the family."

Master Joe had served his sentence in Vicaria and had returned to the eyrie that was his home. It had taken Tommaso many days to send a message to him and receive one in return. He had requested the assistance of his 'ndrangheta brothers in his battle with Palermo. There was no guarantee the men of Bova and the brotherhoods of Calabria would agree to become involved; in fact it was likely they wouldn't. Nonetheless, the journey was worth the effort, even if Tommaso returned empty-handed. He knew he would be treated with respect throughout his stay, whatever the outcome, and his visit would, at the very least, strengthen the bonds made behind the butter-coloured walls of the prison he shared with the rappresentante of the Calabrian Brotherhoods.

* * *

"I'm late." Maria di Bova looked across at her sister, Cristina, as they sat on the terrace of the family home and took in the late evening sun. Her sister's eyes opened wide; almost as wide as her mouth, and she screamed in delight before flinging herself across the terrace and hugging Maria like an excited bear.

Maria gently prized Cristina's smothering arms from around her neck. "I haven't told Mama, yet," she said.

"She's across in the barn," replied Cristina, dragging Maria by the arm and pulling her out of her chair.

"Not just yet," replied Maria. "I don't know how to work out the dates and she might figure we conceived before the wedding."

"Don't be stupid," said her sister. "She will be too delighted to think anything of the sort."

"Tommaso doesn't know; he's still in Calabria. I want to keep it a secret."

"You told me," replied Cristina, gleefully.

"I had to tell someone," said Maria, smiling so much her face hurt.

The next ten minutes were a whirlwind of excited chatter, questions without answers and preferred names for boys and girls before their happiness was shattered by the sound of galloping horses, shouts and carbine fire. All around there was noise and confusion as a dozen armed carabinieri invaded the Giuliano farm and galloped across the yard to surround the house and outbuildings in a cloud of dust, gun-smoke and brandished sabres. As the dust settled, one lone mounted figure trotted forwards to where Maria and Cristina crouched in fear.

"We're here for Tommaso di Bova," said Captain Bruno Fabroni. "He's wanted for questioning about the attack on the rail line near Campofranco. If you know where he is, then lead us to him to avoid any bloodshed."

Maria stood up and brushed herself down, fear being replaced by incandescent anger, which burned on her cheeks. She hoped Fabroni wouldn't miss it. He certainly wouldn't miss the fury of her response.

"How dare you arrive here like a horde of barbarians, Captain Fabroni? You know fine well Tommaso isn't even in Sicily, let alone on this farmland. Only three frightened women and an eleven-year-old boy occupy the house. Are you so terrified by our presence, you are afraid to walk up to our door alone? You should be ashamed of yourself. You make a mockery of the uniform you wear."

The silence that followed Maria's condemnation was so overpowering that the few bellows and snorts from exhausted horses were quickly stifled by their riders. Cristina looked at her dumbfounded, as Fabroni dismounted and strode over to them both. He looked Maria up and down but said nothing, before walking back to his troops and barking a few orders.

"Commandeer that wagon!" he shouted at one of the men, pointing in the direction of the main yard. "Bring a horse from the stables and hitch it to the shafts," was the following instruction to another.

Maria watched, her ire rising with every desecration of her family home and farm. When the wagon was hitched, Fabroni strutted back and grabbed her by the arm. She screamed and pulled against him, joined by Cristina who was instantly knocked back by a cruel backhanded slap from the carabinieri captain. The sound of the assault and Cristina's subsequent crash to the ground froze Maria in shock and she found herself being dragged to the wagon where she was thrown onto its bed and tied by the wrists and ankles to its inner sides. By now the shock of the violence used against her and her sister had provided an even more aggressive catalyst to her anger. She pulled at the bindings and screamed at Fabroni but was powerless to do anything else. Fabroni hitched his stallion to the wagon, jumped on the seat and whipped the horse between the shafts. The wagon jolted forwards, catapulting Maria off her feet, but she was unable to brace herself because of the restraints and fell to land with a thump. She lay like a trussed animal in the back of the wagon as Fabroni issued further commands to his troops, who departed with him and Maria. Fear was now rising to the forefront of her gamut of emotions. She hadn't been arrested, just dragged off like a fighting drunk from a bar-room brawl. But more than that, there was a history of collusion with Fabroni that no one must ever know. Her life depended on it, and if he chose to betray this then she was doomed.

Their route back to the carabinieri compound was not the most direct. Maria was forced to undergo the ridicule of being paraded through the town like a common criminal as she kicked, pulled, fought and spat her way through the uncomfortable and humiliating odyssey. Finally, just as daylight handed over night-time duties to the pale wash of the moon, Maria found herself tied to a chair in Fabroni's office, awaiting his return and further episodes of the degrading treatment she was being forced to endure.

He arrived in a swish of pristine uniform and rattling sabre, having obviously taken the time to brush away the dust of the ride and polish the black leather of his boots. Fabroni placed himself on bended knee in front of Maria, a self-satisfied grin on his face.

She gobbed a large spit straight at him.

She had been saving it in the hope of just such an opportunity, and it found its target. The grin morphed to an angry scowl and he rose to tower above her. She half expected the stinging back-hand to claim another strike and she was prepared for it. In fact, a bruise or a laceration would be further proof of her ill-treatment at the hands of the carabinieri, allaying any fears amongst her peers that her temporary incarceration had compromised the secrets of the fratellanza. Fabroni was angry but she knew he was also cunning. He ripped the sleeve of her bodice and used it to mop the spit from his face before kneeling in front of her again. He pulled a familiar leather pouch from his tunic and tossed it in her lap.

"How convenient Tommaso discarded this little pouch in the piazza after he had emptied it of your wedding gift. It's such a treasured memento; is it not?"

Maria just glared back at him. They both knew where this was going but she wasn't about to show any fear.

"Of course," continued Fabroni, "the content is now completely original. I've saved up all of your little epistles on the fratellanza and put them together. They make fascinating reading, don't you think?"

"You bastard, Fabroni. You are in league with Fratelli. You are as guilty of the murders of Mutolo, Zagari and Nolo as he is. So don't try and blackmail me, or I'll make sure your treachery to the carabinieri is exposed."

"My, my – we are getting ahead of ourselves. Who said anything about using your sneaky little letters as blackmail?" He paused and pursed his lips. "Although, now you come to mention it…"

"If I go down then so do you, Fabroni," said Maria, her anger hissing through gritted teeth.

"So, let's think about how that works," he replied. "Disgraced traitor to the fratellanza accuses carabinieri officer of being complicit in murder. I wonder which story the courts would believe. Perhaps you could call Fratelli as a witness?"

I might just do that, thought Maria. It wouldn't be as irrational as Fabroni imagined. In fact, it would be relatively easy.

"But as I said – we're getting ahead of ourselves, Signora di Bova. I'm not here to blackmail you over these letters. Did I mention your handwriting is exquisite by the way? No, I just wanted to remind you that we have unfinished business, you and I."

"After this? You flatter yourself, Captain. I want nothing more to do with you."

"My, how your tone has changed since you begged me to help rid you of Fratelli and free Tommaso. You think that debt's been discharged? No, Maria. You haven't even made the first payment."

"Who pushed my father's body down the shaft?" Maria had been saving this weapon until it could be most effective. That time was now and it hit Fabroni like a cannon-ball.

He turned his back on her for a few seconds before responding: "I believe you have found it was Notarbartolo who did that."

"Notarbartolo was nowhere near the shaft," replied Maria. "He might have been guilty of firing the shot which killed Cesare, but he could not have pushed him over the edge."

"We are wasting time…"

"It's my time to waste, Captain, as you have me tied to this chair and I can go nowhere. Galli was one of Notarbartolo's pickmen, so he knew what really happened because Notarbartolo told him: he told him he was the only fratellanza survivor, and he fled to save his own skin. The only people who could have tipped my father's body over the edge were carabinieri. You were in command. You are responsible." Maria watched her words rip into Fabroni and his cheeks glow with rage and frustration. Strike me you bastard, she implored under her breath but he wasn't yet at the point of losing control.

Maria pushed on. "The carabinieri desecrated my father's

corpse and that's enough to see you kicked out if proven. Let's take it to the courts, you bastard. Let's see who they'll believe. And once I can sow the seeds of doubt about that, I can ask if you executed Cesare Giuliano in cold blood."

The flaming anger burning in Fabroni lit a fuse and his self-control was blown to smithereens in the resultant explosion. "Your father had a hole in his head big enough to ride a horse through," he screamed and grabbed her by the throat with one hand. Maria gasped for breath and pulled against the ropes binding her to the chair, but to no avail. Her ankles were also tied so she couldn't kick out. Fabroni wrapped his other hand around her neck and Maria squirmed and fought as she started to panic. All she could see were Fabroni's bulging, blood-shot eyes and the maniacal look on his face. He was standing, bending over her, his body weight pushing against her and the chair. She struggled and managed to loosen enough of the binding on her right ankle to allow her leg to move. With all her strength, Maria thrust her right leg upwards into Fabroni's groin and felt the sweet, gelatinous crush of his testicles against her kneecap. His face turned white and his grip failed. The chair rocked back and toppled to the floor, taking Maria with it. Fabroni was hunched over and retching like he was about to vomit. Maria gasped as if she had just surfaced from drowning. Her breathing slowly returned to normal as Fabroni continued to heave and splutter. He clutched his squashed testicles and hobbled about the room like an aged cripple then turned towards her with his face showing a comical, quizzical look that somehow surfaced through the pain.

It was totally incongruous, but Maria started to laugh. She couldn't help herself. Seconds ago she was gasping because she was being choked; now she was gasping because of uncontrollable hysterics. The more she hooted and guffawed, the more Fabroni stared at her with that mad look of agony, overwritten with confusion and topped off with pathos. He was still doubled over with his hand now down the front of his open riding-britches, gently massaging his scrotum. Tears started to stream down Maria's face and the contagious laughter finally infected Fabroni, making the comedy even more surreal. He moved towards her, now crawling on hands and knees, looking and sounding like a sow in heat. Some colour had returned to his face, which looked less like that of an alabaster statue and more like one of the stone gargoyles decorating Chiesa del Purgatorio.

Fabroni opened the door of his desk and pulled out a bottle of grappa and two glasses before pulling himself to a standing position. He released Maria's bindings before speaking his first words since her assault on his testicles. "Signora, I should help you to your feet but I'm barely able to hold myself upright." He poured two generous measures of grappa and reached one over to Maria, who rose from the floor and curtailed her fits of laughing to a few breakthrough sniggers. "Please forgive me," continued Fabroni with a grin, "but I would prefer to keep this desk between us, at least until my gonads recover."

"The fratellanza have a saying, Captain – '*you never know what's in a man, until you kick him in the balls*'. Who knows what I will now find in you?"

Chapter 25

It had been four days since Tommaso had made the climb up to the town of his birth. Despite the welcome and the hospitality, he longed to be back in Sicily. There was much in Favara that needed his attention, not least his new wife, but Master Joe had insisted on keeping him waiting whilst the families he controlled debated Tommaso's request for help. It had been explained that organising a meeting amongst the Calabrian brotherhoods was no simple matter, as reaching out to them and getting a response could take days, and that was even before anything was agreed. It was with some surprise, therefore, that Tommaso's final sit down, in a small taverna on Piazza Roma, produced a result. Not just an agreement, but the fulfilment of one of his requests: to obtain retribution for the deaths of Mutolo, Zagari and Nolo.

This 'sit beside me' with Master Joe had started off differently to the others. There were more people there and quite a few faces were new to Tommaso. The atmosphere seemed tense and some of the new arrivals fidgeted and scanned the open piazza with furtive glances, as if they had a genuine discomfort at being present. Some things never changed, however, and the smell of roasted goat soon permeated the thin air. The *capra alla pecurara* was cooked in its skin and served with copious quantities of the local wine, made with fermented honey. Food and drink softened the mood, as did Master Joe's invocation of the *philoxenia:* the ancient Greek tradition of hospitality that made these gatherings so unique. Bova and the men of Carcagnosso followed the tradition of the 'sit beside me', but there was never the overbearing threat associated with the same convention in the other brotherhoods. The Calabrians never violated the sanctity of the dinner table.

They did talk about their conquests and their killings, however, and it was the account of one of the strangers that held their attention. The story started back in Vicaria. Three Calabrians had been slaughtered by a Palermitan just before he was due to be released, thus the perpetrator was freed without retribution. That Palermitan had been one of Bernardo di Paolo's crew.

Rumblings of anger had surfaced amongst the gathering as this was recounted, and Master Joe had placed his arm around Tommaso's shoulders whilst the next part of the tale was revealed. For Sicily to ask the men of Aspromonte for help was made all the more poignant because the request chimed in with a debt that had to be paid. There was no need for an agreement to do so. There was only the imperative for action. Those responsible for the lives taken in Vicaria must be made to pay, and not just by the execution of the guilty. Three of Aspromonte's finest had been murdered. The same number of Palermo's best would be slaughtered. That was why Master Joe had insisted on Tommaso staying: he wanted to show the job had been done.

It was now obvious that the man telling the tale was also the executioner, and he was one of a number of Calabrians living and working in Palermo, who would never forget their true roots. He continued with his story, recounting how, in one night, he and two of his crew had executed three of Bernardo di Paolo's most trusted family heads, and strung their bodies from lemon trees on their respective farms. In true Aspromonte style, the victims had died by the knife. Along with the noose around each of their necks, a single red silk handkerchief had been added to ensure the brotherhoods in Palermo understood the retribution was delivered from Aspromonte. But the killers had added one final touch, which would strike fear into the families who controlled the wealth of the Conca D'Oro. Into the mouth of each of the victims, they had inserted a small chunk of sulphur. The implications were clear. These killings were also retribution for the recent executions of the fratellanza, and more importantly – Girgenti and Aspromonte were now working together against

Palermo.

It was now clear to Tommaso why the new arrivals seemed so nervous – they were Aspromonte true-bloods who lived in Palermo and carried out their work under the noses of di Paolo and the families he controlled. Their lives were constantly at risk, but for as long as they remained just anonymous labourers, they could strike without warning and just disappear back into the fold of itinerants. It was a bold and dangerous strategy that seemed to be masterminded by Master Joe himself. Tommaso wondered if this could ever be a tactic the fratellanza could adopt. He turned to Master Joe, whose face lit up in a wide smile.

"There is an added bonus," replied the Calabrian. "All of Palermo's citrus exports from the Conca D'Oro to Calabria arrive in the port of Villa san Giovanni before they are sent onwards by rail. The men of Carcagnosso control the port and the entire rail line, all the way to Siderno. Right now, wagon-loads of lemons, oranges and grapes lie rotting on the quay side."

"I think we may have started a war," said Tommaso. "There will be blood flowing on our streets."

"No more than normal, my Sicilian friend. One of the things Vicaria didn't teach you was the value the brotherhoods in Palermo place on their anonymity. The mass uprisings were fine for the separatist rebels and before them for Garibaldi's mobs. Yes, the di Paolo family changed their allegiances as quick as the autumn winds, but when it all died down, they went back to being invisible. In Vua and in Favara, we have but a few officials to bribe and control; in Palermo they have many and all are ghosts. They do not know who is with them and who is against them, and that's how di Paolo likes to keep it. Open warfare on the streets would upset the city dwellers and force those in power to take sides against the brotherhoods."

"Di Paolo won't just let this go," replied Tommaso.

"No, he won't. We've acted on our own account, and on yours, my friend. Di Paolo will keep it personal. He'll come after us and our families. In Vua, our isolation is our strength and my personal guarantee of safety."

"Favara has no such strategic advantage."

"This is why you must leave us now and return to the fratellanza, Tommaso. Prepare for the vendetta."

* * *

Maria di Bova's hand trembled, and the solid silver dip-pen she was holding spattered little drops of black ink onto the clean paper. For the third time she screwed up a spoiled sheet and pulled a new one from the drawer of the letter rack in front of her. It wasn't as if she didn't know who she was writing to. Captain Bruno Fabroni was to be the recipient of this most secret of missives. It wasn't even that she didn't know the content of what she must scratch into flowing inky trails across the bleached white of the paper – the script was already burnt into her conscience. If anything, it was that same conscience which pulled the trigger on her fears and made her tremble.

A simple letter had changed her life when she delivered it to Tommaso's mother many years past. Just words on a page from one person to another – insignificant on their own, but coupled with the actions they mandated, those words were powerful enough to forever change Maria's fate and that of the fratellanza. The words she must now write would provoke similar changes, and as in the past, she put them together without recourse to those who would be most affected. Tommaso knew nothing of what she was about to do, nor did anyone in the fratellanza. Like the ash and pumice that blew from Etna after a major eruption, all would feel the fallout from her explosive actions.

She steadied her hand once more and dipped the pen into the ink-well before returning it to the paper. This time she was resolute, and the words flowed like a fountain of sparks from a firework.

'My Dearest Captain Fabroni...

No, scrub that, she thought, reaching for another clean sheet.

'My Dearest Bruno,
I trust the injury I inflicted on you at our last meeting has repaired itself. I would hate to think I had caused you any lasting damage. I would consider that most unfortunate on a personal level. My actions then have troubled me greatly and I sought to apologise, yet mere words are not enough to ascertain if you have recovered. More on that later.

These times are troubling for me as I begin to understand that being the wife of the rappresentante is mostly to do with the pursuit of duty, and not of happiness. Tommaso spends so many days away from the family home that I feel like he is a stranger, and when he is with me, he seems distant and unconcerned about my happiness or the future of our child. Yes, I'm sure you have heard that I'm pregnant – it's the talk of all Favara, even though it's only a month or so and nothing is visible, even on very close inspection. I examine myself naked in front of the mirror every morning – half pleased to see the slim tightness of my body has not yet changed, and half disappointed that no little bulge is yet evident.

The actions of the fratellanza families are becoming even more callous in the face of the threats from Palermo. The heads of the families have undertaken many changes under Tommaso's leadership, tightening the already suffocating stranglehold of the omertá. I know the wives of the other capos feel the same way, but I barely get to meet with them or talk to them. It's as if Tommaso doesn't want me to have any recourse to the families that I held together so tightly whilst all awaited his return. My only understanding of what is happening outside the family home is through my sister, Cristina. Tommaso is unaware of this; I hope he never finds out. The bruise on Cristina's cheek has all but gone now. Nonetheless, I don't think she will ever forgive you for striking her in the way that you did.

Between the carabinieri and the fratellanza, I believe I have constructed the full story of my father's passing. I hold no individual or group responsible for his demise. I cannot do so, in truth, lest I am forced to admit my actions on that night also contributed to the debacle of his death. I will not, however, forgive the Nortabartolos for exploiting his disappearance, and it pains me now to see that same family sit down with Tommaso and take their share of the copious amounts of money made from the fratellanza activities in the regions they control.

I fear I am at a crossroads, and I wish I could sit down and pore over the map that brought me here. Perhaps the answer lies in the many letters I have written to you previously. Regrettably, I kept no copies, and I can remember little of what I said. Yes, I can recall the themes, but not the intimate details that may help me decide which road to take at this confusing juncture of my life. I know I have some important decisions to make, and I must do so before I make Tommaso a father. After that, there is no going back.

You once told me the carabinieri would take care of me if I became pentito, and I rebuked you sternly for even thinking I could do so. I still abhor the betrayal this would mean, but my unborn child deserves more than a life of murder and corruption. The decision is no longer mine alone but the unborn do not have a say, and I cannot turn to the father for guidance. You are the only man I have ever confided in, outside the family. That relationship is far from perfect but it could have promise if I truly believed I could place my trust in you. And by this I mean a trust that extends beyond the uniform you wear.

On Friday evening I will take my usual solitary ride into the countryside, as is my wont. Tommaso will think nothing of it. My horse will trot along Via Ugo la Malfa, until it intersects with the steep, rocky lane that leads to Monte Caltafaraci. Just off that lane is a deserted shepherd's croft. Please join me there. We can discuss all I have raised in this letter and I can decide my future. Perhaps, I can also satisfy myself that my assault on your manhood has in no way led to any permanent disability.

Sincerely Yours
Maria di Bova

* * *

Lorenzo Fratelli knew there would be an empty chair beside Bernardo di Paolo in Taverna Vittime. If Lorenzo failed to honour the request for a 'sit beside me', he would have condemned himself to death. Nowhere in Palermo was safe for him now. The loss of an entire freight train of sulphur was bad, especially since Lorenzo had suggested the plan to own and control the American shipments, but the executions in Conca D'Oro brought judgment day for The Horse.

There was no future in trying to be inconspicuous on di Paolo's turf. Every street urchin and every pimp in Palermo had been told to find the big man from Favara. There would be rewards worth a king's ransom for the first to send di Paolo's henchmen to Fratelli's sanctuary. However, if they couldn't find him, they couldn't make him fill that empty chair. So, Lorenzo had hidden himself amongst some bales of cotton on a late-night freight train from Palermo to Girgenti and used the time to figure out his salvation. It didn't take long. Di Paolo wanted Tommaso di Bova dead. Captain Bruno Fabroni wanted di Bova dead. Cesare Giuliano had gone to his Maker wanting di Bova dead. There was no longer any time for stupid games and attempts to foment murderous rebellion within the ranks of the fratellanza. Lorenzo had to finish off what he started in Vicaria and he had to do it on his own. He would return to Palermo with di Bova's head in a bag and dump it on the table at Taverna Vittime. That would bring vengeance, and the soul of this enemy was worth more than all the lire he had cost the brotherhoods whilst he lived. Only then could Lorenzo could ask for forgiveness and the sanction to go after the Calabrian assassins and their capo. There was no guarantee this would put him back in favour with di Paolo, but he had no other option.

As the train completed its final run in to Girgenti, the sun had come up and removed the cover of darkness that would have allowed Lorenzo to leave his hiding place unnoticed. The rail yard would be busy with the morning grunts of the shunters adding to the soft clanking of the wagons, jinking and shuddering through a labyrinth of sidings. The Horse was hardly inconspicuous. His notoriety could be his downfall. If di Paolo had anyone in Girgenti on his payroll then word would reach Palermo in minutes, but they could do nothing quickly. They knew di Bova governed the fratellanza families with a military discipline. Favara and the entire Girgenti valley had its own street urchins, and even its pimps, who were the eyes and ears of the fratellanza. All outsiders who arrived from Palermo had their every move scrutinised, like a cat watching a mouse. Even the carabinieri couldn't match the way di Bova's network of informers covered the ground like a rampant weed. Lorenzo had no intention of staying in Tommaso's domain for a minute longer than would be necessary to kill him, but he would have to hide until darkness descended on the valley again.

It would be the Sabbath in four days. If di Bova was in Favara, he would take the Sacrament from Father Russo in Chiesa del Purgatorio, as he always did when he felt secure enough to show himself with his new wife. The blood and body of Christ would be the last thing to touch di Bova's lips before Lorenzo killed him, and he would do it in front of Maria and the rest of the family. It mattered not that he would commit murder in the House of the Lord. That sanctity had been defiled by what Lorenzo had seen stored in the crypt. There was wealth enough there to relieve all the suffering and hunger of the poor in the valley. If Father Russo decided to do so, the usury and slavery of the little wagons could be wiped out overnight. From the day his mother sold him into the mines, Lorenzo's life had been fashioned by the sulphur and its link to poverty and despair. He had lived those painful years believing that link was unbreakable, and his only exit from the brimstone hell was through corruption and murder. He wasn't a little wagon by choice. He never had the chance to comb olives from the trees above Ragazzi or pull fishing nets from a small boat, bobbing in the plentiful waters off Porto Empedocle. That life was closed to him because he was a slave to the twin evils of poverty and vice. Even now, even as he planned di Bova's execution, a small voice in Lorenzo's soul cried out. He ignored it. His soul's only route to redemption was through the oppressive doctrine of the Church that hoarded enough wealth and influence to smash the brotherhoods and the penury that empowered them. Father Russo could have saved him – could have saved them all, and not just their souls. No, Lorenzo couldn't feel compassion for the sanctity of the Church. He would execute Tommaso in front of the congregation and drag his body into the crypt before beheading it.

Equally, it was of no consequence that Maria would hound him through this life and the next for killing her beloved Tommaso. Cesare had promised her as a wife to Lorenzo, but she was now sullied by the filth of this usurper to the fratellanza crown. Maria had rendered Lorenzo cuckold. His only salvation from the ultimate shame of being ridiculed for her infidelity was that only he and Tommaso knew of the betrothal Cesare had promised. If Tommaso died, the secret died with him, and Lorenzo would be free of the indelible shame that only a woman's betrayal could stamp with such potent authority.

The train clanked to a halt, right in the middle of the yard, and Lorenzo poked his head over the side of the wagon. He gathered up and checked the few possessions he had managed to secure before he fled Palermo. He had a bundle of lire, a Carcano M91 rifle with forty rounds and two keys. The keys were the most important items in his limited inventory. They were the ones given to him by Bruno Fabroni; the keys to the secret crypt below Chiesa del Purgatorio.

There was nobody about, but he was directly across the tracks from the office of the rail-yard boss. He could see him sitting at his desk: the same Giancarlo who had been there when Lorenzo had dumped Ruddini's body at the side of the tracks. Giancarlo only had to lift his head and look out of the window to see the unmistakable frame of The Horse climb from the wagon and run into the shadows. Lorenzo took the risk and made his move.

* * *

Captain Bruno Fabroni was a bag of nerves. His mouth was dry and his hand shook. He was mystified as to why. He could face down a couple of brigands, sabres drawn, and fight them to the death without flinching. As a mounted cavalry officer, he could charge a skirmish line of musket-firing rebels and salivate at the thought of running at least one of them through. Yet here he was, clutching nothing more than a piece of paper and behaving like a pubescent teenager on the verge of his first fumbling foray into a girl's undergarments.

He consoled his delicate ego by confirming the folio he clutched was no simple sheaf of fine paper. It was a personal letter to him, delivered by the postman – the same trusted carabinieri officer who had been invalided out of the service and now delivered the mail to Church and State, without fear or favour. And he still undertook the personal service of transporting letters from Maria di Bova.

Bruno had been uneasy and repentant since his clumsy invasion of the di Bova estate and the arrest of Maria. Looking back at it now, he could see it was a stupid attempt to demonstrate his authority, but all it succeeded in doing was making him look a fool and earning a serious kick in the bollocks for his efforts. He had struggled with how he might repair the damaged bridges back to Maria and had given up hope. They were burnt beyond his ability to restore them, but Maria could accomplish what he could not. The letter could be a final demand to leave her alone, yet she must know the power of the other letters Bruno had in his possession. Why would she want to compound her dilemma by adding to this damning inventory? It could be a simple apology for the pain and humiliation her right knee had inflicted on him. But would Maria seek his forgiveness for lashing out against his violation of her freedom; not to mention almost throttling the life out of her? What mysteries would be revealed when the words scratched onto the paper by Maria's own hand were delivered in all their intimacy?

The solution to Bruno's quandary was obvious: open the letter and read it. And yet, it wasn't so simple. The whole episode with Maria smacked of failure. On its own that failure was crippling enough, but allied to the disastrous liaison with Fratelli and the hopeless attempts at controlling the fratellanza, it was damning. Bruno had promised his mother he would avenge the assaults on the Fabronis with nobility and justice, but he had made that promise at her graveside, on a lonely cemetery, on a hillside near Reggio, long after she was as cold and desiccated as the bitter earth she was buried in. The carabinieri had come first: even ahead of his dying mother's last breaths. He had given up that sacred rite, to be part of something he believed in: something that could defeat the power of the brotherhoods and avenge her death. Oh yes, if she had been alive to see him graduate and wear the uniform, then her heart would have swelled with pride and he would have had her blessing. She died alone, in complete ignorance of the values Bruno bestowed on her by proxy. By his failures, he had condemned himself to a torment of biblical proportions and sacrificed the comfort of tending to a dying mother on the altar of justice.

There was no justice. The Fabroni lands were long since divided up amongst the scum who had annexed them from their rightful owners. The only land the Fabronis could now lay claim to comprised three burial plots: his mother's, his brother's and his father's. Bruno had failed. His grand plan was in tatters. He could not stand at those gravesides and weep with the purity of grief; only with the burden of shame. The Calabrian

Brotherhoods grew stronger with each passing month, and he was powerless to stop them. The families of the fratellanza flourished under the new stewardship of the rising star who was Tommaso di Bova, the same Tommaso di Bova whom Bruno had worked so hard to free from his incarceration in Vicaria.

All of these failures led to a litany of problems that Bruno was ill-equipped to solve. He had to face up to the facts: Machiavelli he was not. Within the confines of his oath to the carabinieri, he was just as duty bound as those who swore the omertá. Yes, the values were different but the principles were the same: sacrifice your personal ambitions for that of the greater good. So what value the letter he now held in his hand? Could it bring back a mother, father and brother? Could it restore the Fabroni lands to await another baptism from the fertile silt washed down from Lago Constantino in the foothills of Aspromonte? Could it restore his battered credibility amongst the ranks of his peers?

It could do none of these things. Its only value was the paper it was written on and the coating of expensive perfume, whose smell permeated the dank atmosphere surrounding his desk. Bruno crumpled the letter into a tight ball and threw it into the wicker basket with the rest of the day's rubbish. He stood, straightened his uniform, and made to march out into another morning's baking sun to immerse himself in the minutiae of another day. It was time to forget about grand plans and conquests. To gain any reward from the burden of honour his life demanded, meant dwelling on the dull and boring routine of investigation, arrest and conviction. There were no shortcuts. In time, he might build a case against Tommaso and the fratellanza but victories easily-won brought feeble rewards. The crumpled-up letter in his waste bin crackled slightly as the tightly scrunched paper began to expand. He looked down at it, as if it was calling to him; he sniffed the perfume once more, then turned his back on it and walked away.

Chapter 26

The sulphur burned with a pale-blue flame that barely illuminated the ground around him. It was a pitch-black night, and the silver splash of stars in the heavens above him looked like the vanguard of the second coming. He could have thrown a few twigs on the fire and lit up the desolation of the hillside on which he would bivouac for one, maybe two more days. The gloom didn't bother him, however; nor had he any desire to brighten his surroundings. What would be the point? He could hear well enough, and this was the only sense he needed to ensure his safety. There was a rustling family of hedgehogs to his left, and another further down the slope to his right. Just behind him, a few geckos scampered across sharp pebbles, seeking sanctuary in the cooling rocks. The sulphur burnt without a whisper, so he could concentrate on the faint sound of a red fox, just downwind. Yes, it was there alright. It raised its head, and the faint glow of the blue fire was reflected back in its golden eyes. For sure, it was watching him, but its passion lay in the value of a few scrawny geckos and a fat hedgehog or two.

Through the years, he had learnt to understand many of Sicily's hidden treasures. Some were blessed with an incalculable worth, but others held all the merit of a poisoned chalice. From the day he was born, poverty had been the only coin by which he could calculate the value of his own life. Hard work, cunning; even the ability to read and write could never break the circle that hemmed him in to a life of misery, and of course he wasn't alone. His father and his grandfather had existed on little more than the meagre harvest they scratched from the unforgiving ground. Of course, had they been able to keep all they cultivated, then their lot would have been more fruitful and capable of returning some small amount of wealth to the land that spawned them.

Family recollections were from an age long past, and he could not remember how many years had gone by since the last of his kin had been lost to the dark shepherd. Their graves were out there somewhere on the hillside above Favara. He hadn't visited them in decades. All he had of value now was the oath – the omertá, but even that had been corrupted. He was one of Osso's true sons; not the stinking offspring of the fratellanza. He had rejected the families of Girgenti many years ago, and would never reveal to any of their evil brood that he was bound by the same oath they had turned into an excuse for murder and corruption. He was one of only six: six old survivors who had taken their oath decades ago, shunning its recent interlopers. Yes, it was the same oath Tommaso di Bova now spouted to his new recruits in the dark corners of Taverna Girandola. And why did the fratellanza swear to the omertá in darkness and secrecy? The original descendants of Osso had made their vows in front of an adoring crowd.

He threw another piece of sulphur on the fire as he recalled the day he was made one of the brotherhood, in the small piazza in front of Chiesa del Purgatorio. There was no need to slaughter wild pigs or gather families to an orgy of food and wine. Back then, taking the oath was reserved for those who could demonstrate a passion to care for the poor and the oppressed; to fight against the corruption of the landowners and barons, and to push back against the tyranny of the local polizia who served only the oppressors.

There were but a few ways to be chosen for the honour he now still carried. One was through the loss of a loved one to the forces of the corrupt and the rich. Somewhere amongst the graves on that hillside were those of a loving wife, an honourable son and a beautiful daughter. They had all died on one fateful night.

The red fox tracked right, still keeping downwind of the fat hedgehogs and undoubtedly using the noxious vapours of the sulphur fire to mask any of his own scent that might be picked up by his prey. The prickly spines would prove a small problem, but hunger and cunning could overcome pain. The fox would prevail. Sadly, the seminal upholders of the oath could not. They were overcome by the violence and corruption of the fratellanza. And it wasn't just the families of the Girgenti valley. He had been to Palermo and even made it across to Calabria. They were all the same: murderers and villains, in league with the very forces of the law that were anathema to the pure sons of Osso.

Six old men to keep alive the true values of the Spanish Knights, who endured thirty years in isolation before they could establish a society they believed would overcome the evils of nepotism and corrupting wealth. Six old men with poignant and distant memories of friends and family. What could six old men do?

What could the red fox do to overcome the compact defences of a prickly ball of spines? The red fox was clever and only picked a fight it could win. He had watched them hunt hedgehogs before. Their tactics were simple and devastating but reliant on the intimate knowledge of their domain, which needed a gently sloping hill and a stream. He looked down the hill to the stream and smiled.

The fox would approach from above, making no secret of his presence once his victims were perfectly aligned on the hillside. The hedgehogs would roll into their defensive spiky ball, whereupon the red fox would run down, turn, and with his back legs kick them down the hill until they rolled into the stream. The very posture that the hedgehogs used to defend themselves would be the one that rushed them to their doom. Once in the water they would drown and open up, or open up to try and flee from a watery grave. Either way: foxy would have them. A lesson, yes: a lesson from the school of hunger. He had been there, but his qualifications were bestowed by a much greater pain than an empty stomach.

They had called him 'The Rebel'. His real name ceased to be

important once he had taken the oath. The brotherhood all liked their unique identities and his was justified. He had rebelled against the oppression from an early age, coming to the attention of the local polizia even before he was into his teens. What started as throwing stones at the landowners' horses, progressed through destroying drainage ditches in the lemon groves, to lighting fires in town halls and offices. He was a constant thorn in the side of the baronial Bourbon families, who owned and controlled the land. He railed against all of the instruments they used to perpetrate their hegemony. But he could only have remained an enigma for so long. He knew the oppressive and corrupt forces of law and order would catch up with him, and it didn't matter a damn that they would never have enough to convict him. What they didn't have, they made up with coerced confessions and paid-for witnesses.

The kidnapping hadn't been his idea. Even now, forty-five years later, he still deplored it and said so every time his group of six met to discuss past history and how ineffectual they were in the present. "Yes, Salvatore," they would exclaim in frustration. "You remind us of the kidnapping every time we meet, and every time we say the same thing: it wasn't our idea either." But still they went along with it, save for Ciro Terranova, of course. It seemed so perfect.

The baronial rich liked their homes in Palermo and only retreated to their estates in Girgenti if the talk of rebellion in the capital city made life too uncomfortable. Then there would be a party in the valley and all were invited, including the poor and oppressed who were too downtrodden to realise their pernicious tax receipts had paid for it all. Firework displays would hold them all in awe whilst a few scrawny goats would be roasted and distributed to the fawning masses along with bread and some wine. All that was distributed as a testament to the largesse of the rich was, in fact, a small slice of the recent bounty raked in from the underprivileged. Where such bounty was given back it was only the sub-standard stuff, for which the producers were punished by an increase in their taxes.

And they called him the rebel! Who could not rebel against such an iniquitous manipulation of the downtrodden?

And, yes, he had agreed with the kidnapping. And yes, he had forever lived to regret it. She was the daughter of the biggest landowner in Girgenti. Her name was Mariana and she was as beautiful as she was delicate. Neither of those qualities could save her from being a victim. The plan was never to ransom her back for money. The demand was simply for a guarantee that taxes would be reduced and held at such a rate for the next five years. Then it all went wrong. The nascent brotherhood trusted junior members with her care. They might as well have trusted chickens to the red fox who was now completing his flanking move on a bunch of succulent hedgehogs. Mariana was raped repeatedly and her tortured body dumped in the Ciavallotta mine, where it was discovered by the overseer.

Revenge was swift.

On a winter's night, when all were indoors, five hovels were torched on the outskirts of Favara, but not before their doors were barricaded from the outside. He hadn't gone home that night because he feared they would seek him out, but he never believed they would inflict their vendetta on his wife, his daughter and his son. Three of his compatriots shared a similar fate and all of their tears splashed in the dust of the same Favara hillside, as canvas-wrapped bodies were lowered into their earthly cocoon. No wood for the coffins; not even a simple cross to mark the grave. Wood was too precious and the poor couldn't pay. They had used blocks of sulphur for headstones and burnt some markings on with branding irons, borrowed from the forges deep below ground.

Mariana's death had focussed a terrible vengeance on those suspected of being sons of Osso. In many ways that fashioned the fratellanza into what it now was, as the revenge meted out by the establishment became a rallying cry to all of those who felt oppressed and were willing to do something about it. In as much as it could, time had healed his pain, but not his desire for vengeance. In the few years after the massacre, that hunger was fed but not satisfied. The forces raging against the landowners and moneyed elite became corrupted by the allure of easy rewards, and the struggle for a fairer distribution of wealth was forgotten. Likewise, his group of six became forgotten, and that was how they preferred it. To the young bloods of the fratellanza they were relics from a past age. The omertá protected them; their anonymity protected them even more – they just faded from view.

Four of the six still met every week, in one of five tavernas throughout the valley. They still plotted and schemed, convinced they would once again re-ignite the values that had spurred the Spanish Knights to create an entire society based on equality and brotherhood; not wealth. In forty years of such scheming they had achieved exactly nothing. Yes, the Bourbons had been deposed by rolling revolutions, only to be replaced by others who concentrated their wealth in corrupt silos that could only exist on the backs of the poor and oppressed. Every week, Salvatore and his old companions met and trotted out their excuses for doing nothing. The fratellanza were too strong, they would exclaim. They were only six and frail, they would sigh. Violence was a tool to be used with precision, they would agree. The true values of the Spanish Knights would prevail, they would acquiesce. And so their delusion trotted along like a hobbled pit-pony, doomed to deplete all of its energy in the gloom of a forgotten and merciless underworld.

Until now.

Old and forgotten they may have been, but they knew how to tap into the rich seam of rumour and gossip that permeated the Girgenti valley along with the news that travelled down the rail line from Palermo. It took skill and guile to sift the reality from the nonsense, and these were qualities honed, not blunted, by age. The di Paolos and the di Bovas were on a collision course, as the families they controlled became ever more entwined in their own manic Tarantella that would eventually lead to open warfare amongst the sons of Osso. The blood-letting had already started. Mutolo, Zagari and Nolo perished under an avalanche of boiling sulphur. Revenge was meted out on the rail line to Palermo and in the lemon groves of the Conca D'Oro, but now the continuing vendetta targeted Tommaso di Bova. Fratelli was back from Palermo and he could have but one mission: to kill the rappresentante. The hated carabinieri were in the thick of it, as always. Why did so many believe they were more honourable than the sons of Osso? Captain Fabroni was investigating the murder of three of the fratellanza when he already knew the culprit and chose to turn a blind eye. Tight as the carabinieri's ranks might have been, not much escaped the old men's notice. Of the six, only four had been made to bury their dead and mark their graves with sulphur headstones all those years past. The other two had taken a different route to the brotherhood and one was a recent recruit, albeit with the loss of a loved one in conditions the others could sympathise with. That aside, Salvatore would have murdered him with his bare hands under normal circumstances, but this newest member, Ciro Terranova, had an interesting story.

Fifteen years ago, in 1860, Sicily was in the process of either tearing itself apart or emerging as a small region, fit to be part of the new Italy. The carabinieri hadn't yet celebrated their 50th anniversary but were universally hated and detested by Salvatore and all the brotherhoods, as if they had been the serpent in Sicily's own Garden of Eden. On the 14th September of that year, under the command of General de Sonnaz, a carabinieri unit charged St Anthony's Gate in Perugia to free the city from the invading armies of Pope Pious IX. The ensuing battle was a victory for Sonnaz but the general was a pompous and arrogant idiot, who threw the men under his command at death and danger with reckless abandon. St Anthony's Gate would have easily fallen to a few rounds from the Armstrong Field-Guns provided by the British. They were less than an hour away when Sonnaz decided his brave carabinieri could take the gate with only muskets and brio. Ciro Terranova was in that first charge and lost an arm as a result. He had watched it ripped from his body by a piece of grapeshot, fired from the parapet above the Gate at virtually point-blank range. It twirled its bloody flight into the air and landed at the feet of Sonnaz, who skulked in a narrow passage out of harm's way. Ciro would have gladly given up any other limb if he could have prevented the second charge at the heavily defended gate. That second charge claimed his son, Enrico.

It was madness, and for nothing more than the twisted vanity of an arrogant general who only wanted battle honours for his company. Ciro was invalided back to his regiment in Favara, a bitter and disillusioned man. He had been crippled and had lost his only son so that the carabinieri could add new colours to their pennant, in celebration of a great victory. With only one arm, Ciro was no use in active service so they had stuck him behind a desk where his acrimony had boiled away until it condensed into a caustic paste that corroded every value he had once nailed to his regimental colours. In 1864, he sought out Salvatore and the other four. Across Ciro's desk, every scrap of information about the Sons of Osso passed. Once he had made up his mind about the future course of his life, Ciro decided what information would be filed and what would be burnt, but the burning would only take place once he had sworn the omertá. At first, Salvatore suspected a trap, but he could read, and the documents presented by Ciro were devastating. His knowledge of the brotherhoods was unsurpassed, as was his new-found devotion to the principles of Osso. Ciro knew enough to claim the right of the omertá based on the earliest of the values by which it was awarded: the loss of a loved one to the forces of the law. Salvatore couldn't fault his claim, regardless of the origins of the claimant. And so Ciro Terranova was sworn into the brotherhood, in total secrecy. The subterfuge was necessary as Ciro was to return to the demeaning task the carabinieri had finally retired him to: that of postman for Favara and the surrounding district. He was an exceptionally good postman, and his devotion to delivering the mail without fear or favour was praised by all who knew him. What they didn't know was his skill at breaking a wax seal without leaving a trace on the paper and then re-attaching it after reading the contents of every missive that found its way into his satchel.

So, what could six old men do? They could let Palermo and Favara lock horns and hope that the destruction of the fratellanza would allow a resurgence of the seminal values of the brotherhood. Perhaps, once again, those who swore the oath could do so in front of an adoring crowd, for whom the omertá could provide a talisman to fight the oppression of nepotism and privilege. That was but a dream. It hadn't become reality in Salvatore's forty-five years of allegiance to the oath, and it never would. The fratellanza could be destroyed by the brotherhoods of Palermo. The spawn of one devil would thus be replaced by another, and Osso's bones would shudder wherever they were interred.

If Tommaso di Bova was assassinated by Fratelli, in league with the di Paolos, there would be an empty space in the control of the fratellanza families. If the history of Sicily had taught Salvatore anything, it had taught him that wickedness expands faster than righteousness, and fills empty spaces with impermeable evil.

So, stop it from happening, then. And how the hell were Salvatore and his five old comrades supposed to tackle Fratelli?

Just down the hill there was a sudden clattering of pebbles followed by a small splash, then more rattling pebbles and bigger splashes as foxy overcame his prey. The young cubs would go to their lair on full bellies tonight but the baby hedgehogs would starve and die in the next days. Salvatore didn't believe in omens, but perhaps Mother Nature was giving lessons, as she always did. One only had to turn up for class and pay attention to learn.

Salvatore Morello groaned as he raised his creaking bones from the dwindling warmth of the sulphur fire. It was time for sleep. He walked down to the stream and pulled a rag from his pocket to soak it, before returning to throw it on the pieces of yellow rock that burnt with the blue flame. There was enough fuel there for at least another night. Close to the water's edge, he could just about make out the dark stain on the pebbles. He could smell the blood of foxy's evening banquet.

He was a proud man, and despite his years and his wisdom, he still had a primal hunger for vengeance. But how to satisfy it? He would sleep on it, out here in the open, beneath the silver splash of stars; not in the stinking blackness of Ciavallotta's brimstone caverns. Out here he was Salvatore Morello, one of the founding fathers of the Osso Brotherhood in Girgenti. In the yellow hell of the sulphur mines, he was merely Toto: the mule-keeper.

Chapter 27

"You never adorned any of your previous letters with perfume."

Captain Bruno Fabroni leaned against the decaying timber prop that formed the door frame of the old shepherd's croft and stared down at Maria. She looked up on hearing the sound of his voice and a plethora of confusing emotions scrambled to fight their way to the front of a disorderly queue. Part of her hoped he would not turn up for this most salacious of meetings, but a more primal and disobedient part salivated in the darkness. She had arrived early and tried to prepare herself for the task that would shape her destiny. More than once, she had stepped past the dried-up timbers of the door frame and made her way back to her mount; only to allow her base instincts to take over – driving her back to sit on the remains of the bed and wait. The soft clatter of hooves on broken stone had announced his arrival, long before the carabinieri captain was visible on his mount, as he rode up the rocky lane. Nonetheless, she had watched intensely in case the planned assignation would be threatened by the arrival of someone else, perhaps even Tommaso. And that potential threat was still there. Discovery by her husband would surely lead to two corpses in the old shepherd's croft.

She stood up to face him and allowed her heavy cloak to fall on the bed, revealing a simple cotton chemise that was so light, it could have been woven by a spider. The hem barely reached the top of her thighs as she stood facing him, with one hand hidden behind her back, lightly pulling the sheer cotton to her otherwise naked breasts and hips.

"The other letters weren't so important," she replied, betraying a quiver in her voice that she hoped he would divine as one of nervous, sensual anticipation.

"You mean these?" said Fabroni, as he dangled the familiar leather pouch off an elongated and rigid index finger. He threw the pouch towards the bed as he moved from the doorway into the ramshackle shambles of the gloomy interior. "It was the perfume that made me retrieve this from the bin beside my desk," he continued, gripping her final letter to him between thumb and forefinger, and waving it gently, as if it was a holy sacrament. "I don't understand this sudden change of heart, Maria. You need to convince me of a future that you've described so vividly and so enticingly."

"I can spend all of our time together plying you with words and reason, Bruno. Yet, you must know that such explanations would be worthless without the conviction of my emotions. That is why we're both here; otherwise the postman would've been the only bond between us." She took the leather pouch from the bed and looked inside. Satisfied it contained all of her other letters to him, she placed it carefully on the window ledge beside the bed. Looking directly at Fabroni, and reading the eager anticipation in his eyes, Maria slowly slipped the top of the chemise over her right shoulder, doing the same with the left until the flimsy cotton was only stayed in its descent to the dusty floor by the pout of her breasts.

He moved towards her, and she could smell his freshly-washed skin, adulterated ever so slightly by the aroma of glistening sweat that beaded on his chest, visible through the open neck of his unbuttoned uniform. The chemise put up no further effort in defying gravity and fell to the floor. His eyes danced all over her body, tarrying where they found the most intense reward. Maria widened her stance to deliver even more gratification. Suddenly he was on her like a wild animal, grabbing her from behind to pull her yielding body against him.

She protested, just a little, kissing his cheek and whispering in his ear. "Be gentle, please, Bruno. Understand this is difficult for me. I want to feel comfortable so that I may please both of us." He relaxed his grip and Maria responded by pushing her hips firmly towards him and allowing her upper body to arch back slightly, using his arm for support. His hungry eyes fixated on her breasts as she worked her groin against his. "I am relieved to feel that you have fully recovered from our last encounter, but a closer examination may be in order." The smile arrived on her lips more easily this time, and she could feel the warm flush of her excitement bringing a pink glow to her chest and neck. Within seconds the carabinieri uniform had joined the chemise on the floor. Maria shuddered against the hard nakedness of his body and little sighs of pleasure escaped her lips as she leaned on his shoulder before letting her mouth find his. She allowed the exploration of his tongue but pulled away if he thrust too forcefully. Deftly, she also managed the same teasing with his finger, as it took delight in being the vanguard of his next fervent intrusion into her body.

Her knees started to buckle with pleasure, and she knew he could sense it. He picked her up from the floor, and she wrapped her legs around his hips. Once again the wild animal flared in him. She almost gave in. This was too soon. She had to control him but was so close to just capitulating. She could more than match his passion if the wild creature locked away in the dark and unredeemed caverns of her own soul escaped. It fed on primal desire, not common sense, and its strength all but overwhelmed her, as she squirmed against Bruno's persistent attempts at entering her.

"No, not like this," she gasped and raised herself up ever so slightly to break the bond that was so close to deep and warm fulfilment. "Please, lie down on the bed. Let me sit on top of you." She could barely get the words out without a shudder, but he dutifully obeyed and stretched himself out on the coat she had carefully placed on top of the old straw mattress. She straddled him and sat on his chest. He reached behind her and gently pulled her open before pushing her down towards the union they had been at the threshold of just a few seconds previously. Once again the demon possessed Maria, and her hips swayed and danced to its tune. Her willpower was diminishing with every gyration of their bodies but she couldn't just give in to the final coupling. She pushed forwards, away from the ultimate indulgence that beckoned with such intensity. He responded by guiding her gently up the length of his torso to where he could administer a new and intense pleasure. She smothered his mouth and succumbed to another attempt at breaching those last crumbling bulwarks of fidelity and decency.

Just one small clench of pure physical pleasure and she would break free. She promised herself this, but the token pledge disappeared like smoke in the storm of her passion. She stayed on his mouth like a limpet on a wet rock until she climaxed with a yell so loud it startled her. The sudden shock brought her back to reality. Her breath exhaled noisily and sweat glistened on her body, as if she had been consumed with a fever. She drew back from his mouth and rested her warm wetness on the hard muscles of his stomach whilst holding up her hand in a plea for him to wait. She could feel every moist ripple of his solar plexus beneath her, as tiny little aftershocks from her orgasm made her shudder. Taking a deep breath, she reached up to the golden clasp that held her hair: the same clasp that had arrived as a wedding present from the Calabrian brotherhood. Unlocking the key from the knife allowed her dark tresses to tumble about her shoulders, and she could sense Bruno's eyes on her once again, but this time the look was of admiration; not lust.

"There's a legend in Calabria," she said as she regained her composure and held the two parts of the hair-clasp: one in each hand. "A new-born is laid between a knife and a key. If they touch the key, they will grow to be a servant of the law. Touching the knife means growing up to become a rebel and a bandit." With her left hand she reached the part of the hair clasp to him that was fashioned like a key. He took it and smiled. With her right hand she took the part that was fashioned like a knife. "This must be mine, then." The small stiletto-like blade twinkled once in the light coming in from the doorway.

She smiled, and then plunged the blade deep into his heart.

His body convulsed and he fought to defend himself, but she stabbed again with a speed and ferocity that had no place in the same world where their love-making had dominated just seconds before. The demon that had sought to control Maria through the pleasure of lust, now gleefully accepted its new role, and a third strike delivered another deadly puncture to Bruno Fabroni's heart. His eyes bulged; he gasped for breath; he tried to speak, but all he could do was acknowledge to himself that he had but seconds left. They were the seconds Maria used to deliver her final message.

"A kick in the balls would never have evened the score, Fabroni. You humiliated the wife of the rappresentante and you heaped ridicule on the di Bova family. The letters were a mistake. I had to retrieve them. You served your purpose but you were never going to just go away and leave us alone. I started this, and yes I was foolish to do so. It needs to be finished. I told Tommaso you wouldn't be a problem. In the end; you weren't."

The rattle in his throat was the last sound he made as the venom of Maria's final riposte faded, but the eyes were still wide-open as they bulged from their sockets. Maria arose and threw his tunic across his corpse, hiding his face. Then she dressed, after wiping the blood from the pieces of the clasp and pinning her hair back. It was time for the next phase in her plan. She left the croft, walked a few paces away and recovered a small barrel of lamp oil from its hiding place. It took her about a minute to retrieve it and retrace her steps. She walked from the brightness of the evening sun into the gloom of Fabroni's final resting place. It would be his funeral pyre. She would flee with his stallion and release it somewhere on the hillside. By the time anyone reached the conflagration, Fabroni's body would be reduced to ashes. She looked around for the leather pouch. There was no point in taking any chances it might survive the fire. The letters it contained were coming with her. Stumbling in the murky interior, Maria went to the window ledge beside the bed, but the pouch was nowhere to be seen. She let her eyes become accustomed to the gloom and searched again, slightly more frantic this time.

"Maybe this is what you're looking for?"

Maria let out an involuntary yell and jumped. She peered into the shadows and an old man stepped forwards, holding the leather purse in his hand. Who was he? Had he seen what happened? Would he have to die as well to protect her awful secret? She calmed her racing thoughts and tried to find the answers.

"Forgive me," Maria said nervously. "I didn't know the shepherds still used this croft. I am the wife of Tommaso di Bova." She hoped the name, and its fearsome reputation, would stay any stupid ideas the old man might have.

"Oh, I know who you are," he replied. "I even know why you're here." He looked down at the corpse on the bed, and for a reason Maria couldn't understand – he smiled. "I'm not a shepherd, but I do have a purpose in life. It's one I share passionately with my friends. Please meet some of them."

He gestured towards the door, and more old men shuffled in. Maria suddenly felt vulnerable. Whoever they were; they had a purpose, and it involved her. She was no longer in control. She looked again at the strangers who crowded around the doorway like sheep in a pen. The old man with only one arm was instantly recognisable. He was the trusted postman who had delivered her letters to Fabroni.

* * *

"You said kidnapping was a bad idea, Salvatore. You've been telling us this for the last forty-five years. So tell me again: why we have kidnapped the wife of the most powerful and deadly man in the region?"

Toto listened to the protests of Ciro Terranova and threw another few bits of wood on the fire: precious fuel ripped from desiccated timber props supporting the cavern roof. Burning the sulphur was not an option – not down here in the bowels of the deserted mine at Portella. Maria sulked in a far corner of the cavern, out of earshot, manacled loosely by the ankle to a stake in the ground. He wasn't comfortable about keeping her as a hostage. It had been a long time since he had any need to understand a woman; not that he really ever could, and they might both be here for a while, but he had a plan. It wasn't a great plan; at least not yet, but it could work with a bit of good fortune.

Terranova chimed in again, before Toto could answer. "And kidnapping a woman belonging to one of our brotherhood; isn't that against the omertá?"

"I don't recognise the fratellanza as being of the same brotherhood that we swore the oath to," replied Toto whilst he had the chance. "Anyway, she'll come to no harm, no matter what we achieve. Forty-five years ago, it wasn't the kidnapping; it was leaving that Mariana woman in the custody of young hot-blooded idiots who could only function when their dicks were hard, and then only like animals. Look around you, Ciro. Do you believe that's a problem any of us will have? I bet you wish it was!"

Ciro hung his head in embarrassment and the other old men looked away as if to acknowledge an uncomfortable truth. Ciro leant closer to the fire, his voice a conspiratorial whisper. "For a minute, back there in the shepherd's croft, I thought the old pit prop might have come back to life." He wheezed a quiet laugh and the others cackled in unison.

"Fabroni had one on him like a stallion," replied Toto, remembering the view through the open doorway and suppressing an evil snigger. "Pity he never got to use it. Would've liked to have seen that."

"I reckon he'd learnt to breathe through his ears," said Ciro, slapping his thigh for effect and causing the others to chorus with uncontrolled laughter. Maria stirred across the cavern and they all smothered their outbursts, leaving only a few reckless giggles to break through the crackling of the burning wood fire.

"We should've stopped her," said Toto, suddenly serious. "That was our plan and Fabroni would have been just as dead, only at our hands. Think of what we could've done with a threat to expose a cuckold Tommaso di Bova. We could've been at the top table, bringing the true values of Osso back to those murdering bastards."

"Her letter to Fabroni was clever," replied Ciro. "In fact, we wouldn't have believed her real mission if we hadn't seen it with our own eyes."

"Murdering little bitch," said Toto, looking over to the far corner of the cavern and smiling. "But any slaughter of carabinieri is justified in my eyes. Still, we mustn't underestimate her. Where's her horse?"

"In the old mule-pens, off the main shaft," replied Ciro. "I managed to bring some fresh straw."

"Good. Keep it tied up there and make sure it can't be heard from above ground."

"So what do we do, Salvatore? What's the ransom?"

"Nothing," replied Toto. "All Favara knows she is missing. Tommaso knows she has been kidnapped but not by whom, or for what reason. If he doesn't know what the ransom is, he will blame Palermo. We don't care. What we really need, is to drag Fratelli out into the open. He's in Favara. His mission is to kill Tommaso. If he does this, he'll open the door to di Paolo and his mob of scum. They'll rape Girgenti of every last balàti di zolfo and basket of lemons."

"So we raid Fratelli's hiding place and kill him?" asked Ciro with a mocking tone that couldn't be missed.

"No need. I know what Lorenzo and Tommaso will do next.

They'll act like they always do when faced with a pissing contest." Toto paused before standing up in the flickering light of the fire. "Gentlemen, you must all leave now and go about your business. Follow the routines you have always followed." He looked around the old faces, their heavy, wrinkled features cruelly accentuated because of the shadows conjured up by the wood fire. "Ciro, you must break many wax seals over the next few days." He gave Terranova a broad smile and was rewarded with an equally toothless one in return. "Massimo, keep those *pizzini* coming. Your 'little notes', copied from the telegraph-office manifest, are very valuable." Toto reached over and patted the nodding Railway Telegrapher on the shoulder. "Giancarlo, continue to watch the rail yard. Thanks to you, we know Fratelli is here and we know where he is. Father Russo is one of us and the foremost member of our group. He knows he has a big rat in the crypt below Chiesa del Purgatorio, but he'll keep his own counsel on that, as we have asked. I'll look after our guest. No one will find us here. Be careful to brush over your footprints on the way out. What taverna are we meeting in tomorrow night?"

"Girandola," replied Massimo. "But maybe that's too risky."

"It's what we normally do," responded Toto. "Don't forget, I should still be locked up in Vicaria Prison and that risk hasn't made me change where I drink my ale."

"I would rather face arrest by the carabinieri than a beating from a murderous di Bova," said Massimo. "But anyway, Toto, who cares about an old bastard like you? When you die, you'll be in hell for months before the Devil can be bothered to stick his pitchfork up your arse."

"Maybe," said Toto, "but I'll be too busy celebrating with my friends to give a shit."

More childish laughter erupted on cue as they all shuffled out, leaving Toto alone in the cavern with his hostage. Taking her had been spur-of-the-moment, but he reckoned they had little choice, and there was a bonus: one that would ensure his little group's continuing safety after this was all over. He gathered up what they had been able to pull together at short notice to make Maria comfortable and shuffled across the rough floor of the cavern to where she was tethered. Carefully, he lit the hurricane lamp brought by Ciro. It was a hideous thing in pink glass and had no place in a sulphur mine, but it gave out more light than the crude devices used by carusi, and its large oil reservoir would last for many hours. He reached across and pulled the burlap sack off Maria's head. Two green eyes reflected the lamp's glow and burnt through the gloom to fix him with a stare that would have terrified a pack of ravenous wolves.

"You're a dead man," hissed Maria. "You're all dead men. You've kidnapped the wife of…"

"I know who you are," snapped Toto, "and I know what Tommaso di Bova is capable of. We spent time together in Vicaria. I am Salvatore Morello, better known as Toto, and I probably understand Tommaso better than you do."

"Then you know you're a walking corpse," screamed Maria as she yanked at her bindings and made to fling herself towards him.

Toto didn't flinch. "There are two things that will protect me and my friends. The first is that you cannot leave here without one of us guiding you to the surface. You are deep below ground and the mine is abandoned. One wrong turn and you will either fall to your death or spend eternity in this labyrinth. The second is that we have all of your little love notes to the late and not very lamented Bruno Fabroni. Tommaso would be very interested in reading them: now, or at any time in the future. Or we could send them to the di Paolo family in Palermo, or even just pick one of the other fratellanza capos who were close to Notarbartolo. Do you have a preference? Of course, you don't need to decide right away."

Maria coiled back like a snake waiting to strike, but Toto knew her venom was impotent. He opened up a new bedroll and pushed it towards her with a parcel of food and a jug of fresh water. "If you look across to the far end of the cavern, you'll see the ladder by which you came down. I will leave shortly and pull the ladder up behind me, before throwing down the key to the manacle on your ankle. Feel free to explore, but I can assure you there is no way out."

"You can't leave me here alone." The tenor of her voice now carried a note of anxiety that eclipsed the previous malice.

"One of us will return before the lamp runs dry. Who knows? We might even release you if our plans work."

"The fratellanza will never allow you to enjoy a ransom. They'll hunt you down, and they will free me."

Toto fixed her with his one good eye. "Maria, you may not believe me, but all of this is to save Tommaso from being murdered by the di Paolo family, or should I say by Lorenzo Fratelli – their executioner. The Horse almost succeeded last time, and it was your own father who put him up to it. Cesare ordered Tommaso's killing in Vicaria. I was there. I know it to be a fact."

The hostile blaze in the green eyes faded. Maria looked away and stared at the ground. "My father would never do such a thing," she replied in a voice so soft it was barely audible.

"It's not the first time you've been kidnapped, Maria. Remember the fuitina? Your father promised you to Fratelli but Tommaso sullied your honour and publicly defied Cesare Giuliano. How did you think he was going to react to such an insult?" She sat in stony silence as the truth started to do what uncomfortable veracity often does.

Toto arose and made to leave. Maria looked up at him. Now cowed and confused, she looked suddenly helpless. He harrumphed and turned his back. She was still a cold-blooded killer. "You have time alone to think on these things." Toto climbed the rickety wooden ladder and pulled it up behind him, before tossing the key down to where Maria sat. She made no attempt to free herself.

* * *

"Fratelli must have her."

Tommaso di Bova looked down the table at Giovanni Farina, his deformed hand forever a reminder of the terrors he had been subjected to when he was made to witness the boiling sulphur executions. Of all those gathered in the di Bova house that night, Farina was the newest member of the fratellanza. He wasn't a capo, but he was above the level of a pickman.

"How can you be sure, my good friend? Wives and children are never to be used in our disagreements and struggles. How do you know Fratelli has my Maria?" asked Tommaso.

"Fratelli was seen in the Girgenti Rail Yard last night. He is desperate and prepared to do desperate things, Tommaso. If he shows up here for a fight, you will kill him, and we will watch with pleasure. If he shows up in Palermo without your head in a sack, di Paolo will kill him. If he shows his face anywhere in Calabria, the 'ndranghetta will turn him into food for their dogs. Even Naples is out of bounds. Here is where he has chosen make his last stand. He will use Maria to draw you out."

A wise head on such young shoulders, thought Tommaso. He had looked at each in turn when he gathered them in to announce that Maria was missing, and he had read only expressions of confusion and desperation. Now, there was grit and determination in their resolve. They knew their enemy; they knew his crime and they had the full sanction of the omertá to hunt him down and destroy him, but only when Maria was safely back in Tommaso's arms. "Then he has her in the crypt of Chiesa del Purgatorio," said Tommaso with newly-found enthusiasm, like a drowning man clutching a rope.

"We've checked with Father Russo," replied Giacomo Micelli, his braying donkey laugh absent from the proceedings. "He refused to let us down there, but he assured us the crypt is empty, and there are no signs Fratelli has been there since his last visit. He could be hiding in one of the abandoned mines. A hundred of us could search for months and turn up nothing."

Tommaso let go of the rope and sank beneath a sea of despair.

"There is one other thing, and it is difficult for me to report," continued Micelli.

"Giacomo, you should have no fear of bringing me news that could ensure the safe return of my wife."

"Captain Bruno Fabroni went missing about the same time as Maria was last seen. His stallion was found wandering on Monte Caltafaraci."

There was a gasp from the other fratellanza brothers assembled in the room. Nothing was said, but the spectre of some sort of illicit liaison between Maria di Bova and a carabinieri officer arrived to haunt them. Tommaso had to do something to exorcise its presence. "Has my wife's mare been found?" he asked, his emotions simmering in a cauldron of confusion.

"No," replied Micelli, "but there is further troubling news."

Tommaso looked at him, as if he was Satan turning up for Communion. "Continue," he said whilst taking a seat at the top of the table. He lowered himself into the chair as if he had aged thirty years in the last few seconds.

"The old shepherd's croft, the one on the lane off Via Ugo la Malfa, was set ablaze earlier today. The remains of a body were retrieved from the ashes. They are with the physician in Girgenti. He is trying to identify the victim."

Mouths and eyes all opened wide amongst those gathered round the table. Gradually they settled and everyone looked to Tommaso. "Who knows the physician from Girgenti?" he asked. Farina volunteered that the physician was a family friend. "Get to him now, Giovanni. I don't care he has to work through the night. I want an answer on that corpse. Find out if it might be

Maria. Don't come back until you have something." The young Farina arose and left as quickly as his legs could carry him.

"What should we do, Tommaso?" asked Micelli.

"We scour the hillsides and the valley looking for Maria and her mount, Giacomo. What else do you suggest?" There was anger in Tommaso's response, largely borne of frustration, but stupid questions did nothing to temper it. "Maria may be injured or simply lost. She could have departed from her routine for any number of reasons. She could have fallen and be lying helpless somewhere. Go, all of you, and return here at first light. If someone has kidnapped her, they will have to let us know their ransom. And you Giacomo – start with the abandoned mines." They all rose as one amid a noisy clattering of tables and chairs, afraid inactivity would make them a target for Tommaso's wrath. "Take this message with you," said Tommaso, and the room fell silent. "I make this solemn vow to you all: if someone has taken Maria, they will suffer untold agony before they die."

Chapter 28

The small bottle of oil and the battered lamp were still in the place that Lorenzo Fratelli had hidden them on his last covert stay in the crypt below Chiesa del Purgatorio. He was relieved to find both with a dry pack of Lundstrom matches, but it wasn't completely dark down there during daytime. The crypt had been both a secure hiding place for the clergy and a repository for the dubious wealth of the diocesan treasures. In the past, hidden passageways had been created to allow priests and clergy to escape and hide away from any pillaging and killing. Whilst the entrances to all but one of these had been bricked up, the passageways themselves still remained and small ventilation grilles allowed light and sound to permeate the gloom.

Lorenzo had time to plan Tommaso's execution. From one passageway he had a clear view of the nave through the vent, and from another passageway he could position himself right behind the confessional. A third passageway was still accessible from a locked door that led to the vestibule, where narrow stone steps climbed a spiral column to the bell-tower. He had used this in the past and one of the keys in his possession still worked as before.

With one day to go, he rehearsed his plan and waited for a member of the congregation to take a pew, close to where Tommaso was likely to sit. To Lorenzo's astonishment, he watched as the shuffling figure of Toto appeared in the nave and made his way to the front. The old bastard was still alive and had somehow survived the murderous grapeshot when they had both escaped from Vicaria. Curiosity and admiration for the old mule-herder caused Lorenzo to observe closely as Father Russo was summoned to the confessional where Toto joined him. There was something unusual about the furtive way this happened and Lorenzo quickly squeezed through the narrow stone corridors until he was right behind the confessional, where he could hear every word through the ventilation grille. Father Russo and Toto talked openly, but this was no appeal for absolution; it was an account of the kidnapping of Maria di Bova. Lorenzo listened in astonishment and witnessed his plans turn to dust. Tommaso would be on the hunt for Maria and his appearance at mass was as good as over unless he found his wife in the next day.

Tommaso di Bova would rush to blame Palermo for the kidnap, and the crypt would be the first place he would look. There was no time for Lorenzo to figure out why Toto would be a part of such a suicidal plot and even less time to sit around and come up with an alternative plan. He had to leave, and he had to do so immediately. As Lorenzo's jumbled thoughts came together, despite blind panic trying to scatter them like sheep, he could envisage a situation where he could turn Maria's kidnapping to his advantage. He listened intently as the discussion between priest and mule-herder drew to an end, silently besieging either to give up the one piece of information he needed: where they were keeping Maria. As if on cue, Toto closed the conversation with: *"She is safe in the cavern used as a store-room for blasting powder, in the abandoned mine at Portella. She is alone with enough to sustain her until tomorrow night, when we will decide the ransom and send the letter to Tommaso. If anything should happen to me, then we will have failed. It falls to you, Father Russo, to look after her well-being and ensure her release. It was never our intention to harm her, however things turn out."*

It was a good hour to Portella, on foot across paths rarely travelled. Lorenzo was familiar with the old mine; he had been caruso there before moving to Ciavallotta. Maria di Bova was his prize and what a prize she would be. How he would use this and what Toto's plans consisted of, would occupy Lorenzo's thoughts for that hour and beyond. All that was important now was his escape and his capture of Maria.

* * *

His crude lamp had barely enough of a wick left to enable Lorenzo's descent into the Portella mine. He could hardly remember the complex layout of tunnels, but the underground store-room for the blasting powder was directly off the main shaft and deep down in the bowels of the earth. This was true of all the mines. If something set off the powder, it was safer to be above the explosion than below. Finally, he could see a faint glow in the maw of one of the shafts, and he followed it like a moth to a flame. The shaft opened up to a rocky gallery that looked down on a hollowed-out cavern, still betraying its brimstone-coloured origins in the light from the lamp left for Maria. Lorenzo had extinguished his own lamp, long before he reached the cavern. He had made his final approach as silently as his huge frame and the rubble-strewn floor of the shaft would allow. Staying concealed below the rim, he peered over the edge and could see Maria sitting in the pool of light. She seemed motionless, and if he listened carefully he could hear sobbing.

Lorenzo sat that way for a long time and just stared. He had last seen her from a distance, as he challenged Tommaso from the campanile of Chiesa del Purgatorio. Now he was less than a few metres away from Maria, he could drink in the beauty of her face as she wiped away the tears and looked around, hoping to find something that might help her escape this hell-hole of a prison. Here was the woman he had been promised as a bride: his reward; his gift from Cesare. How different things would have been if only he had been allowed to consummate that relationship. Even now, after all that had happened, dare he believe the clock could be turned back and she could rightfully be his? For that to happen, Tommaso di Bova had to die. If by Lorenzo's hands then nowhere would be safe for him outside of Palermo, and Maria would never make that move. If Tommaso lived then Lorenzo had nowhere to go. He could never return to the di Paolo's domain or they would execute him on sight. The same held true for Calabria and Naples: too many corpses had piled up in Vicaria for Lorenzo to ever seek refuge there. So the only woman he had ever loved, the one object of his desire, his infatuation and his rightful prize, had to be the hook on which he could land his prey. Lorenzo couldn't conceive of a way to conjure the ingredients of that spell into a happy ending. The best thing he could do was let Toto continue with whatever nefarious plan he had hatched and await the outcome. Lorenzo was an opportunist, not a trailblazer. He knew the limits of his own abilities, and life had taught him that he could grow fatter on carrion than he could on husbandry.

He turned his back on Maria and crept away from the rim of the cavern.

* * *

It was one o'clock in the morning, and Tommaso sat alone on the veranda of the di Bova family home. He had returned exhausted from the search when darkness made it impossible to look further. Sunrise was still hours away but sleep was elusive and pointless. His mind was a box full of firecrackers, each detonating on sudden ideas of where Maria might be, and then fizzing out in showers of sparks and charred remains. He had no idea of where else to look, and the thought of her being taken against her will continued to haunt him. Then there was Bardoni, and he had always been a threat. Tommaso berated himself for even thinking that his beloved could have somehow run off with him. If that were true, the carabinieri would have arrived like a pack of wolves by now and taken their prey. Or would they? Yes, if Maria had turned pentito; but no if she had simply run off with Bardoni in a tryst where each had agreed to start life anew. He continued to torture himself with this conundrum until the silence of the night was interrupted by the sound of galloping hooves.

Tommaso jumped from the chair and grabbed a carbine from a pile of weapons placed close at hand. Could this be the raid by Bardoni's men? Not unless they were all arriving on one horse. Tommaso relaxed a little, then his agitation returned as he realised it was Farina, the messenger he had sent to the physician in Girgenti.

"You have news of the corpse in the shepherd's hut?" asked Tommaso before the breathless Farina could even rein in his mount.

"It wasn't Maria," came the reply. "The charred remains were that of a man, impossible to identify, but they did find these."

Farina dismounted, flicking froth from his exhausted stallion. He handed Tommaso two pieces of metal, so twisted and deformed by the heat as to be barely recognisable. "They are spurs. Spurs from the riding boots of a carabinieri officer's uniform."

"Fabroni?" asked Tommaso.

"The physician can't be sure, but the charred bones and teeth match those of a man aged about the same as Fabroni and of the same build. The teeth are sound, indicating this was not a poor shepherd."

"But we found Fabroni's horse wandering far away from the croft," said Tommaso, perplexed.

"If Fabroni took off on his horse, then he did so barefoot. The spurs weren't found on the body but nearby, and there was something else noted by the physician. The fire was intense, but the skeleton was not entirely reduced to ash, probably because it had, for the most part, been covered by some sort of heavy cloak. This protected the upper torso. There were three puncture wounds to the breast-bone made by a fine stiletto-like blade. Whoever the victim was, they didn't die by burning or suffocation. They were stabbed and died before the fire was lit."

Tommaso sighed and embraced Farina. "Thank you,

Giovanni. Go into the house and take some refreshment. You can rest here until morning." He weighed the two twisted spurs in his hand and waited for the exploding fireworks in his head to die down. There were many possible explanations for the chain of events leading to Maria's disappearance. Tommaso chose to fixate on one link that could explain some of the bizarre episodes. He believed the charred corpse was in fact Fabroni's. Why then was he found at the very place where Maria habitually rode to on her Friday excursions? *"Three puncture wounds by a fine stiletto-like blade."* The same sort of blade contained in Maria's hair clasp. No, the next link in the chain was inconceivable: Maria had killed Fabroni. Inconceivable, thought Tommaso, but not impossible. But why then would she disappear? She knew enough about the workings of the fratellanza to know they could protect her, and confessing to murdering one of the carabinieri would have been a badge she could have worn with pride. Besides, the Maria he knew, indeed the Maria all of the fratellanza knew, never ran away and hid from danger.

Tommaso slumped back in the chair and looked up, besieging the night sky for once, just once in time immemorial, to order night's regiment of perpetual soldiers off the parade ground before the day's bright new recruits had left their barracks. The dark mass sprinkled with silver looked down, and with the stoicism of aeons continued its unhurried circuit of the firmament. Way off to the east, the inky blackness was just starting to fringe with a deep blue. Sunrise would not be rushed. Tommaso let his head fall forwards and sleep ambushed him.

* * *

"Toto, you lying little shit. My father never told Fratelli to kill Tommaso. Get back here and don't you dare leave me. Face me and tell me the truth."

The tirade from Maria was delivered with a barrage of stones, one of which hit Lorenzo on the back of the head as he crept away from the edge of the cavern where she was held captive. The ability to move with the stealth of a cat was not a gift bestowed on Lorenzo's large frame. He had all the grace of a lumbering ox and Maria had obviously been alerted to his presence; or the presence of someone she assumed to be Toto. Staying his course and leaving would have been the sensible thing to do, but the large lump already rising on the back of his skull and the disturbing admission that Maria now knew of her father's execution order, forced him to turn back. If she knew all she claimed by her last exclamation, then slaying Tommaso alone wouldn't exorcise the shame bestowed by her infidelity to her father's promise. Lorenzo would have to kill her and Toto. The death of the old mule-herder would weigh heavily on his conscience, but could he muster up the wherewithal to execute Maria?

Keeping below the lip of the rim on the cavern-edge allowed Lorenzo to reach the ladder giving access to Maria. She wouldn't see him until it was too late. He didn't trust her not to launch the oil-filled lantern at him when his back was turned. Feline stealth may not have been one of his qualities, but he could move quickly when it suited him. Before Maria could react, Lorenzo was down on the floor of the cavern and moving towards her, his Carcano rifle pointed menacingly at her head. The shock on her face was visible across the ever-decreasing gap between them, and Lorenzo stayed silent, waiting for her first words to determine how he would react to the new layer of difficulty her admission had introduced. Perhaps he would just kill her on the spot and await Toto's return to complete the slaughter. Steady as his aim was, he knew there was no chance he would pull the trigger.

"You bastard, Fratelli. You're in league with that smelly little fucker, Toto," screamed Maria as she stared him down, despite the menace of the Carcano. "Tommaso will take great delight in seeing you both go to hell together."

Lorenzo couldn't put together a lie quickly or convincingly. If he had a few hours to think through things as Maria saw them, then he could probably come up with a strategy he could use to his advantage. Best just to say it as he found it. "I've nothing to do with Toto or the reason you are here," he replied, hoping that Maria wouldn't detect the slight tremor in his voice arising from his first close proximity to her since their last meeting. He could almost smell the aroma of roast goat and taste the fine Ragusa as the memories flooded back. But this was no flower-filled meadow on the edge of Favara.

"Then get me out of here, and you can be sure Tommaso will reward you," said Maria with a sudden lightness in her voice and a fresh look in her eyes that Lorenzo could have succumbed to in an instant, were the circumstances any different.

"Maria di Bova, you talk with such authority on things you know nothing about," he replied, dropping the Carcano just a little and flashing a wolfish smile in her direction. "Yes, I will take you from here to a place where you'll meet up again with Tommaso, but on my terms. Now move away from the oil lamp." She did as she was told. The lamp was a weapon. Lorenzo's instincts told him Maria and weapons were a dangerous combination at any time.

"You're hardly in a place to dictate terms, Lorenzo." Maria's voice was softer now but her venom was just as focussed.

Lorenzo knew he was no match for her guile and cunning, but he had to put up a good show of superiority. "Really? Can you walk free from here, Maria? Can you run to the welcoming embrace of the fratellanza and demand vengeance for all of the ills inflicted on you? I think not. You're mine, to do with as I please."

"Then take me, Lorenzo. Defile me, and then run away. Tommaso will hunt you down and kill you anyway. You might as well add rape to your transgressions."

With that, Maria started to pull at her clothing. Lorenzo watched, dumbfounded initially and then with rampant sensual excitement as she stripped down in front of him until she stood naked in the warm glow of the oil lamp. The Carcano dropped as his arousal rose until he stared open-mouthed at the sight before him. He was speechless, and she taunted him with her body before adding a further spark to his tinder-dry ardour. "Take me, Lorenzo, and who will know?" Maria lay down on the pile of clothes she had discarded. She opened her legs wide and thrust her hips straight at him. "Fuck me and then run away. You can do it and get away with it. Who would believe that you just turned up here and took me before escaping?"

Lorenzo watched as his passion overcame what little resolve he had left. A small voice told him she was just playing with him. He didn't doubt it, but play like this was as powerful as it was tempting. He could have her: not forever, but just once. Surely that would be just reward for the years in Vicaria, for the ridicule of the fuitina, for the cuckold way in which Tommaso luxuriated in the pleasure of her sex and for the unfulfilled promise of Cesare. Without thinking, he was slowly walking closer to her. The Carcano was pointed at the ground.

He wanted her so much it hurt.

"Lorenzo, it wouldn't really be rape," said Maria in a tone that was at once comforting and heavy with desire. She sat up and undid the clasp on her hair to let it fall around her shoulders. "Don't you know that all of the young girls, and many of the married women in the valley, go to their beds at night dreaming of encircling your muscled torso between their legs and pulling you into them? We all believe you are called The Horse because you are endowed like one." She giggled as she said it and followed up with a smile that was as open as the invitation to her sex.

Lorenzo was powerless to resist. He set the rifle on the ground and pulled his shirt over his head. He flew to the object of his desire and knelt in front of her. He could see her arousal and smell the warm fragrance of a lingering perfume that had been resurrected by the heat from her body. Tentatively, he reached out and let the tips of his fingers caress the inside of her thigh. He ripped at the remainder of his clothes until he was naked and rampant between her open legs. Every part of her body beckoned, and every part of him made ready to thrust forwards in response. She lay back, legs opened wide and ready to wrap around him, arms ready to embrace him and hands still clutching the hair clasp she had released only moments before.

Somewhere in the distance, a horse whinnied.

In an instant, Lorenzo's emotional state went from passion to fear. He jumped up and away from Maria, grabbing his Carcano from the ground.

"It's alright," said Maria. "It's my mare. Toto and his gang tied her up in the old stables."

Lorenzo looked back at her, still open-legged and still beckoning with her arousal, but the moment was gone. "Put your clothes on, and do it quickly." He went to the oil lamp, and after checking he had spare Lundstroms, he turned the wick down until there was just a glimmer of light.

"Lorenzo, it's just my mare. There's no one else here. Please come back to me."

"Toto and his gang?" questioned Lorenzo as he quickly dressed himself. "What gang?"

Maria started to cover her nakedness, suddenly ashamed of what had been a beacon of desire only seconds previously. "I saw three here with him. I think there may be more."

Lorenzo said nothing and continued to listen for even the slightest sound of someone approaching. The horse whinnied again. It seemed no closer than last time. Carefully, he took the hideous glass oil lamp and climbed the ladder before pulling it up behind him. Ignoring the protests from Maria, he left her in darkness and made his way to where he remembered the stables should be. Sure enough, Maria's mare was tied up where she said he would find it. He checked the saddle-bags and found some paper and a few pencils, which he retrieved and brought back with him.

He found Maria whimpering once again, but this time there was real fear in her shuddering sobs. The light from the oil lamp seemed to soothe her. Lorenzo sought to mock her for her childish terror of the darkness, and then thought better of it. She continued to arrange her clothing until she was satisfied her modesty had been restored. "You won't get another chance like that one, Fratelli. I told you it was just my mare, but you didn't trust me. Remember this as the time Maria di Bova offered herself to you and you turned her down. You'll never feast your eyes on my naked body again."

"There will be another time and it'll be at my choosing. You're not free of this by a long way, Maria, and until you are, consider yourself my prisoner. As you said before: Tommaso will kill me anyway, and rape can't make the punishment any less."

"I will personally cut your bollocks off, Fratelli."

"Not before I have used them on you, Maria, and only if Tommaso lives to defeat me, which he won't."

She spat at him and turned away to skulk in a corner. He followed her, keeping the lamp out of reach and grabbed her by the shoulder to face him. "Write the word '*Sunday*' on this." He held out a piece of paper and a pencil, retrieved from the saddlebags of her mare. She looked at him, puzzled. "Do it," said Lorenzo and grabbed her bodice, ripping two buttons from it. She took the paper and wrote one word. He looked at it. It seemed to say Sunday. Another piece of paper followed with the request for another word – '*alone*'.

Maria did as she was asked and then commenced a mocking snigger, as she looked at him like he was a lost child. "You don't know how to read or write and you're trying to put together a ransom note, one word at a time. You dumb bastard. I could write anything and you wouldn't know." The laughter continued but stopped suddenly when she saw that he was making constructive use of the other pencil and paper.

"No, I was never taught how to speak on paper; at least not with the words you seem to know so well," replied Lorenzo with a confidence that countered the scorn levelled at his lack of education. "What I can do is draw. I was always good at it. No one needed to teach me." He had quickly sketched a head and shoulders portrait of Maria, which he turned towards her. The look on her face was a mixture of confusion and awe. It wasn't one of Lorenzo's best drawings but it was undeniably a portrait of the missing Signora di Bova. "I only needed the two words; the rest I can draw." He looked at Maria, rummaged through the few items scattered around and watched her expression. "Give me the hair clasp. It will provide proof you are my hostage."

Maria protested and pushed away from him, but Lorenzo was in no mood for compromise. The more she protested the more he was determined to have what he wanted. He grabbed her by the hair and pulled her towards him. Maria's arms wind-milled in fury as she lashed out, but Lorenzo held on, keeping her at a distance. Then she struck a vicious blow which made him leave go and instantly pull back. Sticking out of Lorenzo's forearm was the top of a stiletto-like blade with some sort of gold handle. Instantly she came at him again, trying to reach the blade before he did.

She lost.

Lorenzo's back-handed swipe struck her upper body and sent her flying across the cavern like a broken doll. Maria lay where she fell, winded and whimpering. Lorenzo pulled the blade from his arm, wincing at the pain and incredulous at the ferocity of her attack. At first he was puzzled as to how she had been able to find a knife, but examining the weapon pulled from his arm answered that question. The stiletto was part of the hair clasp, the one she had released minutes previously and held in her open arms as she beckoned him into her body.

Blood dripped from the puncture in his forearm and he wondered how far *he* would have penetrated *her* before she had brought the same blade down on his neck. Perhaps she would have let him thrust deep inside her so that her climax would have been a screaming convergence of physical pleasure and bloody vengeance. Either way, he now knew of the murderous intent of her seduction. She was willing to use her body like the dark shepherd's pet whore: luring all who succumbed into the pen, from where the only escape was straight to bright Lucifer's open embrace.

Maria pushed herself up to a sitting position and glared over at him. The green eyes blazed in fury, not in pain. The swipe from his arm had winded but not damaged. He walked over and kicked her shoulder, knocking her back down. Then he ripped the dress from her waist and cast it aside. She closed her knees tightly and squirmed, trying to prevent the inevitable, but he grabbed her legs and forced them apart. He pulled more clothing away until the intimate exposure of her sex took him back to where their erstwhile coupling had been interrupted, minutes previously. He was between her legs now and ripped her bodice off to hold her down by her exposed breasts. There was no intimacy, only violence and the panic in her green-eyed stare matching the rising ardour in his. He could smell her fear as he raised his bloodied hand from her breast and took the small stiletto to hold it in front of her terrified gaze. Slowly, he traced the point of the blade across her throat and then down her breastbone to hover expectantly just over her heart. She struggled in vain, and terror overwrote fear on her face. The tip of the blade continued its journey from a place of instant death to one of murderous disembowelment, as its point pressed menacingly into the soft opening of her navel. She spoke once, calm now and with the reluctant acceptance of her fate. "I am with child. Take whatever you want from me, but do not take the life of the unborn."

Lorenzo said nothing and let the blade continue. Its tip rasped lightly over her pubic hair before gently touching the softly yielding flower that had promised so much and delivered so little. Lorenzo pulled his shirt off with one hand and bent over her until he could feel the cold press of her nipples against his skin. The blade threatened to move deeper into her. He could feel her move slightly beneath him in a panic-stricken attempt to be a benevolent guide to its progress. There were tears now and shuddering sobs. He withdrew the stiletto and leaned back. Keeping his body between her legs, he once again used the menace of the blade. He pressed its tip against her throat and applied enough pressure to draw a little trickle of blood. "Remember this as the time Lorenzo Fratelli had you at his mercy and then gave you back your dignity and your chastity. You deserve neither. You are just the fratellanza's whore, and I can buy better in any taverna in the valley. I wanted you so much when your father promised you to me. You were his to give. And yes, he instructed me to execute Tommaso because of the shame that little caruso had brought to the Giuliano family." He looked at her and tried to read the unspoken response in her eyes. He divined it as some sort of infatuation and immediately dismissed this as just another deception. "Put your clothes on. You disgust me, Maria."

Lorenzo gathered what he needed and made his way to where her mare was stabled. He left Maria with the battered old carusi oil lamp. He needed the hideous glass thing for its additional light but he assured her he would come back and change them over. The drawing would provide some proof he had Maria, the hair clasp would make it indisputable, and her mare would be the way to deliver both. The mare would find its way home and Tommaso di Bova would find Lorenzo's ultimatum and proof he had Maria. He had carefully copied the two words she had written and also drawn the hands of a clock, along with a detailed vista of where he wanted Tommaso to turn up alone and claim his wife. The building and the landscape on the drawing were unmistakable to anyone who lived in Girgenti. The time on the clock and the position of the sun in Lorenzo's drawing clearly indicated that the fateful assignation would be one hour after dawn. Already the eastern sky was tipping an indigo wink to the approaches of the rising sun. Tommaso would have no time to prepare and Lorenzo would be in position, with Maria, long before the first shadows enjoyed their short westward journey.

Killing Tommaso in front of Maria was still Lorenzo's mission, only now he could do it with impunity and keep her as hostage for as long as it suited him. If he had Tommaso's head in a bag for Bernardo di Paolo then many things were possible: perhaps even a return to Palermo with the widow di Bova in tow.

Lorenzo made it back to the mine just as the sun pushed a glowing rim above the eastern horizon. The timing was critical, and he had no way of knowing for sure when Maria's mare would make it back to the di Bova home. It would take Tommaso at least an hour to get to the venue chosen for the showdown, but it would take Lorenzo only a few minutes, and once in place, no one could approach it without being seen way in the distance. As Lorenzo dropped the ladder down to get Maria, he felt that at last his plan was starting to look as if it might be successful – right up until the second he heard the braying donkey laugh of Giacomo Micelli behind him. The triumphant blaze of Maria's green eyes met Lorenzo in the same instant, and he turned in response to the sound of a carbine being cocked. Its barrel was pointed steadfastly at his head. He dropped his own weapon as Micelli issued his ultimatum.

"I don't have to let you live, Lorenzo. Maria has told of your plans and the place you have suggested to entice Tommaso di Bova to his doom. Give me one excuse, just one, and I will drop you like a diseased dog. I prefer to give that pleasure to Tommaso. I suggest we follow your plan, Lorenzo. It'll be easier to meet him where you suggested. He's surely on his way."

Chapter 29

Tommaso had fallen asleep wishing he could force the sun to cut short the darkness and quickly usher in a new day: one where he would find Maria safe and well. The arrival of her mare changed all that. Now he wished the heavenly spheres would stop turning just long enough for him to gather his loyal brothers together and be better prepared for the moment he must face Lorenzo Fratelli and bargain for Maria's life.

Giovanni Farina had surfaced from his sleep and emerged from the house on hearing the commotion. He joined Tommaso and examined the drawing sent by Fratelli. Tommaso knew Farina couldn't read, but he didn't need to. The drawing conveyed everything that Tommaso was required to do.

"The sun is already up, Tommaso," said Farina, shrugging his shoulders and looking helplessly at Tommaso. "There is no way of making an approach without being seen, and it would take us time to get there – maybe an hour; probably more."

"That's all the time I have, Giovanni. Fratelli is a clever bastard, I'll give him that. He has timed things to suit his own ends. We are not prepared for this."

"He has the high ground, but how can he hope to leave it?" questioned Farina. "We can have the site surrounded within two hours. You may need to drag things out before we can muster enough men and get there."

"Fratelli will have thought of that. Whatever he has called me to, won't last for long." Tommaso mounted his horse and made to go. "Giovanni, I leave you in charge. Gather however many you can and surround the site, but at a distance. Don't let yourselves be seen. If Fratelli attempts to leave without Maria and me, then kill him." Tommaso knew there was despair written all over his face, and try as he might; he couldn't hide it. If he could pull together a plan then he could inspire those who looked up to him, but he was bereft of ideas.

"And if he attempts to leave with only one of you?" asked Farina.

"Use your best judgement," replied Tommaso, as he flicked the reins on his mount and galloped off.

Less than an hour later his mount was tiring but Tommaso kicked the stallion's flanks hard and rode through the early morning light with a reckless pace that left a trail of dust behind him. He could see his destination in the distance, high on the crest of the hill, the morning sun rendering its magnificence in stark relief against the southern sky. The drawing Fratelli had made was clear as crystal. In fact a five-year-old child could have made similar in a shaky and immature hand, but everyone in Girgenti would still have recognised it. Many had invaded Sicily and most had taken what she had to offer, leaving nothing but despair and chaos. Just a few had left a legacy. The hilltop town of Bova had just such a legacy. It was Greek and as deeply ingrained into Tommaso as the legacy of touching the knife at his birth. To the occupants of that high, Calabrian eyrie, the temples of Girgenti were the one place of pilgrimage that all of her citizens wished to make. To the locals in Sicily, the temples were just strange relics of a civilization that came and went along with all of the others.

The Temple of Concordia was Tommaso's destination and was one of the greatest of the Greek ruins that lay scattered along the floor of the Girgenti valley and up onto the northern ridge. For the most part, the ancient buildings and statues were just the disjointed and tumble-down legacy of long-forgotten stonemasons and artists. Thousands of years ago the entire site must have been something of wonder but it now lay derelict and looted of any treasures that could be picked up and carried away. Concordia still stood magnificent, however, and Tommaso spurred his mount on with ever increasing anxiety towards a destiny governed jointly by his greatest enemy and his only true love. The eastern portico of the temple lit up in the glow of the rising sun. Its six massive stone columns presented themselves to the morning as they were designed to do and had done for aeons. The entire magnificent edifice threw long shadows west along the ridge. Slowly, the brightness of the new day lit up the sides of the temple and more massive columns were thrown into sharp relief against the dawning blue of another morning sky. The outer walls of the temple were all great columns, atop which sat the remains of what must have been a substantial roof. As the light chased intricate shadows from the inner curtain walls, Tommaso was now close enough to see between the columns and into the innermost part of the temple ruins. He was close now and Lorenzo must have stood gloating as Tommaso raced from behind the final ridge that separated him from his destiny and that of Maria.

Finally, he rested his mount where he could ride no further. A bronze statue lay on its side, where it had fallen, over a thousand years ago. Part warrior, part angel it would have towered like a giant colossus above the entrance to Concordia. Legs and arms truncated by time and plunder, now it just lay impotent: a symbol of what was gained and then lost as the inexorable march of civilisations laid down another victim to history. Tommaso tied the reins to what was left of a bronze wing and stood twenty paces from the four stone plinths, each as tall as a man, providing the foundations for the entire Temple of Concordia. It was an even more awesome sight up close, but his only interest was bringing this assignation to a close and escaping with Maria. He had no idea how he was going to do that, nor had he any idea of Lorenzo's demands. Whatever they were, one thing was for sure: Tommaso could give up anything except his life and that of Maria. Even if they were both reduced to destitution and banished from Girgenti, they had the chance, skills and the loyalty of the fratellanza to come back and take what was rightfully theirs. That could be Tommaso's only aim: to survive unharmed and ensure the same for his wife.

"Show yourself, Fratelli. I'm here for Maria, and I'm alone." Nothing moved and no one responded. Tommaso walked closer and made his way to the rough cut steps, leading between the two central columns of the eastern portico. A short, stocky man appeared from the interior and stood looking down, whilst chewing on a piece of meat. Tommaso had never seen him before in his life and suddenly panicked at the thought of this entire process being ruined by the interruption of some fat oaf, who had decided to sleep off his drunken state in the shadows of the temple.

"It's a long way from Palermo," said the oaf, before breaking wind and examining the remains of his early morning meal. "Travelling makes me hungry. Sitting around doing nothing makes me hungry. In fact, the only thing that doesn't make me hungry is eating."

Tommaso swore he could hear laughter coming from inside the temple. Something had gone badly wrong. He wanted to speak out – to say something, but his mouth was as dry as the hard stone of the temple steps on which he stood.

The fat oaf examined the remains of what he was chewing. It was now a denuded bone, so he cast it aside before wiping his greasy hands down the front of his tunic. "Forgive my manners, Tommaso. The name is di Paolo; Bernardo di Paolo. Perhaps you have heard of me?"

Tommaso ran at him like a charging bull. There could be no other action to take. All that Fratelli laid out had suddenly fallen apart and there was only one solution: hit the enemy with everything at his disposal. That was precious little, and it was rendered useless by the appearance of one of di Paolo's henchmen; bearing a carbine pointing at Tommaso. The threat he presented was obvious. What was just as potent was the threat from another two armed men who stood over the kneeling figure of Maria, just inside the entrance to the temple. Maria looked up at him, her face a picture of confusion and fear. She wasn't alone in making those feelings manifest. Tommaso felt exactly the same but tried to hide it. What he saw next would only add to the bewilderment. Beside Maria knelt the unmistakable figure of Lorenzo Fratelli. His hands were bound and he was chained to a large block of the ancient stone. His bruised and battered face made him look like he had been a sparring partner to every bare-knuckle fighter in Girgenti. He also had a carbine pointed at his head.

"They are all unharmed, for now, but you don't deserve any mercy from us, di Bova," said di Paolo. "Your actions cost Palermo many lire and the lives of our brothers. Still, it might just please those of us who made this journey to the badlands if I was to make you aware of what an insignificant little fucker you are." He turned and faced his own men. "Should I tell him?"

A raucous chorus of approval answered his question.

"The rappresentante. That's what they call you, isn't it? The leader of all the fratellanza."

"And you are in my domain, di Paolo," replied Tommaso. "You'll never leave it alive."

"Well, I think we've done pretty well so far," bellowed di Paolo, to much laughter from his mob. "We have you, your lovely lady wife, and as an added bonus, another Favara caruso who has caused us much financial pain." Di Paolo shot a glance at Fratelli who looked back once and then hung his bruised and bleeding head, as if in shame. "And this is not our first visit. Last time, we left you with a little delicacy to savour. Did you bury Zagari, Mutolo and Nolo; or did you serve up their cooked flesh on a tin plate with some roast goat?"

The reference to the murder of three of Tommaso's best by pouring the molten contents of a calcaroni over their naked bodies made him seethe with impotent anger. "I think we have Fratelli to thank for that," replied Tommaso.

"I wasn't there, Tommaso. I didn't kill them. Micelli was the executioner. He led the others to their death." The exclamation came just ahead of a vicious swipe from the butt of a carbine, creating a resounding thwack that echoed through the ancient stone walls. Lorenzo took the punishment and looked up at his attacker before glancing back to Tommaso.

"Do listen to your caruso friend, Tommaso," said di Paolo. There was a smirk on his face that prefaced something the Palermo thugs would also find amusing. "You see, Tommaso, you are not of fratellanza nobility. You are just carusi. You do not deserve your place in this dynasty and neither does your fat friend here. Notarbartolo knew that and his memory lives on." Di Paolo walked over to where Maria knelt. He lifted some of the dark tresses from her shoulder and caressed them gently between his chubby fingers. "You must understand, this fine treasure of a Favara woman should never have been given to carusi. Cesare made many enemies when he promised her to Fratelli and then you made more enemies when you took her in the fuitina."

"Take your hands off her, you steaming pile of Palermo shit," yelled Tommaso. "Call your in-breds off and we will settle this. Just you and me. Or are you afraid you might get your fat arse kicked by a Favara caruso?"

Di Paolo let go Maria's hair and walked to where Tommaso stood before delivering a punch to the side of his head that knocked him to the floor. Barely conscious, Tommaso could hear Maria screaming from across the cavern before the sound of a smack rendered her silent. Tommaso staggered to his feet, determined not to let di Paolo better him, but carbines at point-blank limited his ability to respond.

"Enough of this," said di Paolo, as if he had tired of some game which was too easy to win. "We have to leave. I know all about what you have in place, Tommaso. I know the number of men and the time they will take to get here. I know these things because you do not command the loyalty you need to survive. I killed the only ones who were really loyal to you. The ones who aren't remain alive and loyal to me; to Palermo." He hit Tommaso again and forced him to kneel on the floor. The carbine was now right behind Tommaso's ear. This might be the end. Di Paolo knelt beside him and pulled his hair back to force Tommaso to look up. Standing over him was Giacomo Micelli, the grin on his face a vanguard to the braying donkey laugh that would surely follow.

"Crawling on hands and knees is the way a caruso should die," said Micelli. "You are Calabrian scum, Tommaso. You don't belong in Girgenti and you don't belong in the fratellanza."

Tommaso knew it would lead to another battering but he said it anyway: "And you are a traitor to the omertá. Wherever you go and however you try to hide, Micelli, someone will find you and kill you for this." Micelli kicked him in the face and put his own carbine to Tommaso's head.

"Not here," said di Paolo. "We didn't bring anything to cut your head off, Tommaso. How very stupid of me. It's the only piece I need to take back to Palermo. You can carry it around like you used to carry the sulphur, until we can find something sharp enough. The same for you, Fratelli. Don't they call you The Horse? Well, let's see how far you can gallop without your head."

Micelli backed away and his place was taken by di Paolo who stood in the puddle of blood fed by the wounds inflicted on Tommaso's face. Across what seemed like the vast emptiness of the floor of the temple, Maria begged for their lives, only to be silenced with another smack. Even Fratelli tried to use his formidable strength, but he was chained down, and a scrum of bodies beat him into submission. Tommaso entered into this expecting to deal with Fratelli, and even at that he was bereft of ideas. Help from Favara was at least half an hour away, and now he didn't even know who he could trust. If Micelli had betrayed him, then there must be others. As if on cue, di Paolo lanced another sword into Tommaso's helpless dilemma.

"Giacomo is not the only one, Tommaso." The triumphant

note of victory was heavy in his voice. "How do you think we knew to be here? Fratelli didn't tell us and your good friend Giacomo didn't know which deserted mine to search first. Your brotherhood is riddled with those loyal to Palermo. They know the future, and once we kill you, they'll join us and swear their loyalty to me. And I'll reward them. I've already given Maria to Giacomo to do with as he pleases."

Tommaso's thoughts were doing the firework thing again, but this time everything was going off at once. He had to escape and save Maria. His only ally was Fratelli. If they could just work together they might be able to do something. He had no idea how he could communicate that to The Horse, or work out a plan.

"It's time to go," commanded di Paolo. "Back to the mine until nightfall. Micelli, find an axe and join us. You can have Maria when we cut the heads off these two fuckers."

Within minutes they were in a cavern in the Portella mine. On the short journey, Tommaso tried to talk to Lorenzo, and more importantly to Maria, but di Paolo's henchmen kept them separated. The cavern showed some signs of previous occupation. There was a garish oil lamp in one corner and a bed-roll with some food and water in another. Maria went straight to the bed-roll and sat down on the ground without waiting for an invitation from her captors. Di Paolo instructed his men to put Tommaso side by side with Fratelli and make them both kneel on the floor. A quick attempt at talking to The Horse earned Tommaso a side swipe from the butt of a carbine, which opened up the wounds he had taken some minutes previously, when they were at the temple. Maria screamed again and begged for them to stop the beatings but all she received was another smack to the side of the face. Tommaso looked once at Lorenzo. He shook his massive head slowly as if to say: 'this isn't how it was meant to be'. That was little comfort and their joint anxiety only increased as Micelli returned with an axe, much to the delight of di Paolo. He weighed the axe carefully in his hands and ran his thumb over the blade, whilst pacing around his kneeling victims. Micelli went over and grabbed Maria, making to leave, but di Paolo stopped him in his tracks. "Hey, Giacomo. Why don't you just fuck her here, and we can all watch?"

"We agreed, Bernardo," replied the traitorous Micelli through a chorus of evil laughter. "You gave me Maria as my reward. It's time for me to go."

"I'm your capo now, Micelli. I'll tell you when to go, and if I want to give my crew the reward of watching you make noisy sex with this fratellanza whore, then that's what you'll do." On cue, one of di Paolo's thugs moved between Micelli and the ladder. "I was never very good at chopping logs," continued di Paolo, swinging the axe so close to Tommaso's head, he could feel the swish of air on his bruised face. "Micelli, you do it. You get to cut the head off the Calabrian scum who has dishonoured the fratellanza. Then you can follow up with a swipe at Fratelli. He has a neck like an ox so it might need a few swings. Then you get to enjoy your reward. I bet she fucks like a taverna whore."

Micelli didn't move. Tommaso looked up and he could see the hesitation in responding to di Paolo. "That's not what we agreed," replied Micelli.

"Get over here, Giacomo." The command was bolstered with a firm shove from the thug who had blocked his way. Tommaso sensed now was the only chance he and Fratelli were likely to have. There was confusion and dissent, so di Paolo's mob weren't paying too much attention to their captives. He looked once at The Horse and tried to convey what was obviously in both their minds: escape. Lorenzo looked over his shoulder to where di Paolo stood and then back at the sole oil lamp illuminating the cavern. Tommaso could see his exaggerated actions and understood. He looked directly at Micelli and then back. Fratelli nodded once. Tommaso replied likewise. They both knew the plan and not a word was spoken. The Horse would take down di

Paolo and then go for the lamp, plunging the cavern into darkness. Tommaso would target Micelli, who still carried his carbine, and be hurtling towards him in the darkness. Carusi weren't helpless and frightened in the total blackout of a sulphur mine. They could immediately fall back on their other senses. This was the only advantage they had: Tommaso could only hope it was enough.

The volley of shots blasted through the cavern as if a hundred thunderstorms had been pent up in a strongbox and suddenly released.

There was only one volley, but it was devastating and accurate. When the smoke settled only four people in the cavern had missed being struck by gunfire: Lorenzo, Tommaso, Maria and Micelli. A shout from up in the rocky gallery commanded Micelli to throw his carbine away, which he did with alacrity. Tommaso and Lorenzo exchanged nonplussed glances at each other, unsure of anything except a belief that it was best not to move in case another round of musket fire found them. And it was musket fire. Accuracy wasn't an issue at the distances involved and only a lead ball could inflict such devastation on human flesh at close range. Di Paolo had fallen in front of Tommaso. Most of his head was missing but the axe was still gripped tightly in his hands. Across the floor of the cavern, Maria raised herself up slightly and looked over the dead bodies.

"I'm fine, Maria," said Tommaso in what was a frightened whisper that carried across the silence of the cavern.

"Ah Lorenzo," said a voice from the gallery above the cavern, where the murderous fusillade had started. "If only the good Lord was as attentive to everything said in the confessional of Chiesa del Purgatorio, then the world would be a better place." Tommaso knew that voice and he looked at Lorenzo in bewilderment. The Horse just shook his head and smiled.

Toto was the first one down the rickety ladder in the corner of the cavern. He stood and surveyed the destruction before taking the time to re-load a musket that must have been older than the Greeks who built the Temple of Concordia. Three others followed him down the ladder, two of them sporting a musket in each hand. They spread out, kicking bodies to make sure they were dead and retrieving carbines and any other booty they thought valuable. After a few seconds, keys were found and the heavy manacles securing Lorenzo and Tommaso were undone. Maria ran to him and clung so tightly to Tommaso, he struggled for breath. He gently prized her arms away as Toto wandered across with that unmistakable gait and fixed Tommaso with his one good eye.

"Hah, you should know the mines are full of surprises, young di Bova," said the old mule-herder. "Don't waste your time trying to figure this out. I'll explain later, but all is not what it seems."

Tommaso looked at Toto and then down at the flintlock musket he held in his hands. He knew it was loaded and would only provide one shot. That was all he needed. He looked once at Lorenzo and grabbed the musket. Lorenzo stepped back, a look of resignation on his face. Tommaso cocked the rusting old hammer, lifted the musket to shoulder height, turned, and blew a hole in Giacomo Micelli's chest. Tommaso faced Lorenzo once again.

"Would you like me to re-load for you?" asked Toto.

"No," said Tommaso whilst holding his gaze on Lorenzo. "I've done all of the killing I need to do here today. What about you, Maria?" Tommaso turned to his wife. She looked once at him, and then at Lorenzo. There seemed to be something conveyed in that look Tommaso didn't understand, but then there was a lot he didn't understand.

"No," said Maria. "All who are left here deserve to live on, whatever their previous transgressions."

"Perhaps you should ask Signor Fratelli the same question," said Tommaso.

Toto repeated himself but Lorenzo just shook his head slowly before saying, "I don't see anyone here who deserves to die at my hands."

"You may still want that one shot," said Toto, re-loading. When he finished, he handed the musket back to Tommaso. "I kidnapped Maria," he said. "But before you finish off my sad old bones, let me explain why."

* * *

Toto made himself comfortable on the bed roll Maria had vacated and called her over, along with Tommaso and Lorenzo. How was he going to explain that he had found Maria and Bruno Fabroni naked and breathless in the old shepherd's hut? How could he cover up knowing the content of all the secret letters sent to the carabinieri captain? Toto decided he couldn't, and so he began his tale on finding Maria setting the fire that attempted to cover up her crime. She could explain her own way out of that dilemma in her own time. He had left her all of the room she needed to do so, and they both knew he still held on to the damning letters she had written.

Interspersed with his abridged account, Toto threw in the historic details of his and his comrades' fealty to the original omertá, when it was in its purest form. He explained how Ciro Terranova had copied letters going back and forth and how they knew the carabinieri's every move. Maria squirmed uncomfortably at this but said nothing. The telegrams between Palermo and Favara were snooped on courtesy of Massimo, and Giancarlo ensured the identity of every one of the di Paolo clan was exposed as soon as they got off the train, and that included Lorenzo Fratelli. Micelli had been stupid enough to use the telegraph to send messages to di Paolo, who was so convinced Palermo had total control over the system that he sent messages back. Toto pieced together the jagged and broken shapes of confusion to form a smooth account of how he knew Fratelli would try to kill Tommaso, mainly to appease di Paolo. Yes, Maria was part of the reason for his motivation but Fratelli couldn't have been aware of the role of Micelli, nor of the futility of any future deal with Palermo.

So, Toto and his friends kidnapped Maria. They knew Fratelli was hiding in the crypt of Chiesa del Purgatorio and they knew he could hear any conversation happening in the confessional. Toto was careful to hide the full details of Father Russo's part in this, and the identity of the sixth member of Toto's group could never be divulged to anyone outside their number. Massimo sent a telegram to di Paolo, pretending it came from another unknown traitor in the ranks of the fratellanza and gave details of the kidnap and the location for the handover.

Tommaso interrupted the account: "So Micelli was the only traitor?"

"The only one we know of, Tommaso," replied Toto.

"How did you know the time and place for the exchange?" asked Tommaso.

Toto smiled and addressed Maria. "Do you normally carry paper and pencils in the saddlebags of your mare?"

"No." She looked at Lorenzo. "He never said where he got those, and I never thought to ask."

Toto reached into a bag he carried with him and produced a rolled-up, yellow piece of paper. "You might remember this, Lorenzo," he said as he rolled it out. It was an almost exact copy of the drawing of the Temple of Concordia that Lorenzo had used as his message to Tommaso. "It came from the wall of your cell in Vicaria," explained Toto. "I often admired it and you said you'd draw me a copy. You never got the chance, but this was given to me by another inmate who was released some time after our escape. Portella, where we are now, is just a short walk away. Before you departed from this mine to use the mare as a messenger, you went back to give Maria the lamp. That gave Giancarlo enough time to look at the message. You see, Maria, all four of us have been in this mine the entire time. We have sought to protect you, and we never left you alone."

Maria's face turned white and then quickly to red. Toto knew why, but that was another secret he held in abeyance. The Horse just grinned at them all in turn, whilst reserving a special look for Maria. Toto didn't miss it but went on to explain the most dangerous part of the plan: putting them all together in the same place. Only then could Lorenzo be made to realise that di Paolo would kill him, even if he returned with Tommaso's head. Only then could Tommaso begin to realise that he couldn't keep fighting di Paolo with one hand and Fratelli with the other, and only then could the two former carusi understand that the reasons behind their enmity could all be traced back to one woman. (And a treacherous one at that, thought Toto, but decided to keep his own counsel.) Yes, his plan was a litany of risks tied together with a gossamer-thin strand of hope, and it could so easily have resulted in fratellanza bodies littering the cavern floor. Sooner or later, word would get back to the rump of the di Paolo-controlled families and they would re-group. A weak fratellanza would just roll over in the face of Palermo's might, but the defeat of Bernardo had stymied that ambition, if only for a while.

Toto looked at Tommaso and Lorenzo. "You are carusi, little wagons who pushed, fought and clawed their way out of this shit." Toto waved his arm at the deserted cavern they now sat in. "Cesare Giuliano was manipulative and cared nothing for either of you. Tommaso, he wanted you dead and issued the order to make it happen. Lorenzo, he wanted you to marry Maria because he needed the link to Palermo. Yes, you killed Galati and were sentenced, but you must know that Cesare could have interfered with that trial and produced a different result. He had others he could use to influence the di Paolo families, so he kicked you into Vicaria to kill Tommaso. After that you would have been left to rot."

He watched as Tommaso and Lorenzo exchanged glances. They both knew there could be but two inevitable outcomes. Toto sought to move them towards the one he wanted. "Right now, in tavernas all over the valley, the gossip is about you, Tommaso. It's about a missing Maria and the disappearance of a Carabinieri Captain. It's about how Lorenzo Fratelli has been a traitor to Favara and has thrown in his lot with the men from Palermo. So, let's go to Taverna Girandola – all of us. Let's sit and drink together until we fall down drunk. And let's do it where all can see and witness the new order."

Chapter 30

Father Carl Russo had always seen it as one of the great testaments to his faith, and his pastoral care, that he could preach a sermon baptising a new child into God's flock on the same morning he had to say a funeral mass for those that had departed. This was a day that tested such fortitude. There was much for his congregation to feel happy about when Tommaso and Maria di Bova brought the infant Lucio to the baptismal font. The proud parents had prepared well, and the invocation of *Comparatico* was, Russo had to admit, a work of genius. Lorenzo Fratelli was named as the godfather of the infant di Bova and stood smiling through the ceremony, as if the young child was his own. Tommaso and Lorenzo had become *Compari*: co-fathers; bound not only by the omertá but by the oath of Comparatico. Individually, neither was an oath they could break; collectively the power of the public and secret codes of honour would bind the two former enemies together irrevocably. The strength of the fratellanza was bolstered and the wagging tongues were silenced. It was clever, and undoubtedly a product of Maria di Bova's connivance and control.

As were, Russo suspected, the four funeral masses he had held later.

The tomb that had been the hidden entrance to the secret vault below Chiesa del Purgatorio was now just that: a tomb. Russo had, with help from diocesan funds, undertaken a program of works to seal up the entrance and brick up the stairway that led down to the secret crypt. The most adorned vault in the cemetery no longer carried the name 'Caravaggio'. Above the great bronze door there was simply the legend 'Osso'. It was an inspired move on Russo's part. There were now six burial chambers in the vault. Four were filled with recently-added coffins, awaiting final closure when the alcoves containing them would be sealed in stone. The coarse and plain timbers, along with the mortal remains of their occupants, would forever after be concealed from the light, whilst the prayers of those who remained would speed four immortal souls to God's good grace. The marble plaques were already carved with the individual names and laid carefully below each of the burial chambers.

The congregation had departed and recollections of the dead were reduced to flickering remembrances back in the Chapel. Candles had been lit with irreverent haste. Transient mourners hurried away to celebrate new life and cast aside thoughts of immortal souls, patiently tapping their feet in purgatory. Yes, because of the christening, there would be long celebrations in the piazza and wild pigs would be slaughtered. Hordes of visitors had already descended on the town, and the tavernas had echoed with their carousing, long into the previous night. There would be new carusi elevated to the ranks of pickmen and there could well be more corpses on the streets in the morning, as smouldering vendettas burst into flames. None of that mattered to Russo, nor to the single mourner he shared the tomb with.

"I fear for my own life," said Russo, but this did not elicit an answer. The mourner just knelt in prayer at each of the caskets in turn and spoke once to say aloud the name carved onto the individual marble plaques. Giancarlo, Massimo, and Ciro lay cold and stiff in their coffins as the mourner spoke, before falling silent in prayers for each. Father Russo respected the reverence shown and stood in quiet supplication before moving on to the last coffin.

"Toto," said the mourner as he knelt before the final casket. "You were the first of the few of Osso's true believers. I will miss you, my friend. May you soon be with the souls of the family you lost."

Father Russo said the prayer this time and then waited for the inevitable questions.

"How did they die, Father?"

"In a rock collapse in Ciavallotta. Their bodies were pulled from the rubble but there was nothing that could have been done to save them."

"Who else died in the collapse?

"No one."

"Were you supposed to be with them?"

"No. Like you, I would rarely join with them. We six last met together over a year ago, as you will recall. My only contact since then has been when they came to the church, either on the business of the brotherhood or just as members of my flock."

"Why were they in Ciavallotta? Toto, maybe; but what reason for the others to be there?"

"There was no reason."

The mourner pulled the small leather pouch with Maria di Bova's letters from the pocket of his coat and handed it back. "This was the reason. They were taken down to their deaths. This is what I believe."

"I've spoken to some of the pickmen who found their bodies," said Russo. "There was a smell of blasting powder in the collapsed cavern and some powder burns on their clothing. It was no accident."

"They were a threat to Maria. The letters, the treachery, the illicit sex, the infidelity – Toto knew it all and that harlot killed him for it. She will still be searching for the letters. Does she suspect you might have them?"

"I don't know," replied Father Russo. "It's why I said I feared for my life."

There was a moment of silence before a reply, which asked another impossible question, rather than calming Russo's fears.

"Could she have done all of this without Tommaso knowing?"

"With Maria; anything is possible. I know you hope that will prove to be the case, and there are grounds for believing it.

Tommaso held no bad feelings for our brothers after the kidnap. Indeed, both he and Fratelli have benefitted from what followed. However, it'll be difficult for me to unearth the truth without increasing my exposure to danger."

"There are only two of us left, Father Russo. I have no intention of letting you stay within the reach of that maiden of Satan. I suggest you quickly put your affairs in order. I'll arrange for you to be sent to a new parish in Calabria."

"You can do that?" asked Russo, trying to keep the tenor of disbelief from his voice.

"I am that rarest of honourable men. I've taken the oath of both Osso and Carcagnosso. I am of both Calabria and Sicily. I've succeeded in upholding the true values of the oath in Calabria, and we have many friends there. But I regret I have failed in Sicily."

"We've all failed in Sicily," interrupted Russo, as if to acknowledge that those who lay in the coffins paid with their life but didn't achieve their dream.

"We will not talk of failure whilst there is breath in either of our bodies, Father Russo. We will succeed. We will bring peace and honour to this pocket of iniquity."

"It'll be difficult to influence anything in Girgenti if we no longer have a presence here."

"We have a presence here, Father. You christened him today."

Russo smiled for the first time since entering the vault. "And they even named him Lucio."

"Yes, after his grandfather," said Lucio di Bova.

Grendel's Mother
The Saga of the Wyrd-Wife

Susan Signe Morrison
Grendel's Mother, a queen from Beowulf, threatens the fragile political stability on this windswept land.
Paperback: 978-1-78535-009-2 ebook: 978-1-78535-010-8

Queen of Sparta
A Novel of Ancient Greece

T.S. Chaudhry
History has relegated her to the role of bystander, what if Gorgo, Queen of Sparta, had played a central role in the Greek resistance to the Persian invasion?
Paperback: 978-1-78279-750-0 ebook: 978-1-78279-749-4

Mercenary

R.J. Connor
Richard Longsword is a Mercenary, but this time it's not for money, this time it's for revenge…
Paperback: 978-1-78279-236-9 ebook: 978-1-78279-198-0

Black Tom
Terror on the Hudson

Ron Semple
A tale of sabotage, subterfuge and political shenanigans in Jersey City in 1916; America is on the cusp of war and the fate of the nation hinges on the decision of one young policeman.
Paperback: 978-1-78535-110-5 ebook: 978-1-78535-111-2

Destiny Between Two Worlds

A Novel about Okinawa

Jacques L Fuqua, Jr

A fateful October 1944 morning offered no inkling that the lives of thousands of Okinawans would be profoundly changed—forever.

Paperback: 978-1-78279-892-7 ebook: 978-1-78279-893-4

Cowards

Trent Portigal

A family's life falls into turmoil when the parents' timid political dissidence is discovered by their far more enterprising children.

Paperback: 978-1-78535-070-2 ebook: 978-1-78535-071-9

Godwine Kingmaker

Part One of The Last Great Saxon Earls

Mercedes Rochelle

The life of Earl Godwine is one of the enduring enigmas of English history. Who was this Godwine, first Earl of Wessex; unscrupulous schemer or protector of the English? The answer depends on who you ask...

Paperback: 978-1-78279-801-9 ebook: 978-1-78279-800-2

The Last Stork Summer

Mary Brigid Surber

Eva, a young Polish child, battles to survive the designation of "racially worthless" under Hitler's Germanization Program.

Paperback: 978-1-78279-934-4 ebook: 978-1-78279-935-1 $4.99 £2.99

Messiah Love

Music and Malice at a Time of Handel

Sheena Vernon

The tale of Harry Walsh's faltering steps on his journey to success and happiness, performing in the playhouses of Georgian London.

Paperback: 978-1-78279-768-5 ebook: 978-1-78279-761-6

A Terrible Unrest

Philip Duke

A young immigrant family must confront the horrors of the Colorado Coalfield War to live the American Dream.

Paperback: 978-1-78279-437-0 ebook: 978-1-78279-436-3

Readers of ebooks can buy or view any of these bestsellers by clicking on the live link in the title. Most titles are published in paperback and as an ebook. Paperbacks are available in traditional bookshops. Both print and ebook formats are available online.

Find more titles and sign up to our readers' newsletter at http://www.johnhuntpublishing.com/fiction

Follow us on Facebook at https://www.facebook.com/JHPfiction and Twitter at https://twitter.com/JHPFiction